The Body in the Library

Agatha Christie is known throughout the world as the Queen of Crime. Her books have sold over a billion copies in English with another billion in 100 foreign languages. She is the most widely published author of all time and in any language, outsold only by the Bible and Shakespeare. She is the author of 80 crime novels and short story collections, 19 plays, and six novels written under the name of Mary Westmacott.

Agatha Christie's first novel, *The Mysterious Affair at Styles*, was written towards the end of the First World War, in which she served as a VAD. In it she created Hercule Poirot, the little Belgian detective who was destined to become the most popular detective in crime fiction since Sherlock Holmes. It was eventually published by The Bodley Head in 1920.

In 1926, after averaging a book a year, Agatha Christie wrote her masterpiece. *The Murder of Roger Ackroyd* was the first of her books to be published by Collins and marked the beginning of an author-publisher relationship which lasted for 50 years and well over 70 books. *The Murder of Roger Ackroyd* was also the first of Agatha Christie's books to be dramatised – under the name *Alibi* – and to have a successful run in London's West End. *The Mousetrap*, her most famous play of all, opened in 1952 and is the longest-running play in history.

Agatha Christie was made a Dame in 1971. She died in 1976, since when a number of books have been published posthumously: the bestselling novel *Sleeping Murder* appeared later that year, followed by her autobiography and the short story collections *Miss Marple's Final Cases*, *Problem at Pollensa Bay* and *While the Light Lasts*. In 1998 *Black Coffee* was the first of her plays to be novelised by another author, Charles Osborne.

The Agatha Christie Collection

The Man In The Brown Suit
The Secret of Chimneys
The Seven Dials Mystery
The Mysterious Mr Quin
The Sittaford Mystery
The Hound of Death
The Listerdale Mystery
Why Didn't They Ask Evans?
Parker Pyne Investigates
Murder Is Easy
And Then There Were None
Towards Zero
Death Comes as the End
Sparkling Cyanide
Crooked House
They Came to Baghdad
Destination Unknown
Spider's Web *
The Unexpected Guest *
Ordeal by Innocence
The Pale Horse
Endless Night
Passenger To Frankfurt
Problem at Pollensa Bay
While the Light Lasts

Poirot

The Mysterious Affair at Styles
The Murder on the Links
Poirot Investigates
The Murder of Roger Ackroyd
The Big Four
The Mystery of the Blue Train
Black Coffee *
Peril at End House
Lord Edgware Dies
Murder on the Orient Express
Three-Act Tragedy
Death in the Clouds
The ABC Murders
Murder in Mesopotamia
Cards on the Table
Murder in the Mews
Dumb Witness
Death on the Nile
Appointment With Death
Hercule Poirot's Christmas
Sad Cypress
One, Two, Buckle My Shoe
Evil Under the Sun
Five Little Pigs

* novelised by Charles Osborne

The Hollow
The Labours of Hercules
Taken at the Flood
Mrs McGinty's Dead
After the Funeral
Hickory Dickory Dock
Dead Man's Folly
Cat Among the Pigeons
The Adventure of the Christmas Pudding
The Clocks
Third Girl
Hallowe'en Party
Elephants Can Remember
Poirot's Early Cases
Curtain: Poirot's Last Case

Marple

The Murder at the Vicarage
The Thirteen Problems
The Body in the Library
The Moving Finger
A Murder is Announced
They Do It With Mirrors
A Pocket Full of Rye
The 4.50 from Paddington
The Mirror Crack'd from Side to Side
A Caribbean Mystery
At Bertram's Hotel
Nemesis
Sleeping Murder
Miss Marple's Final Cases

Tommy & Tuppence

The Secret Adversary
Partners in Crime
N or M?
By the Pricking of My Thumbs
Postern of Fate

Published as Mary Westmacott

Giant's Bread
Unfinished Portrait
Absent in the Spring
The Rose and the Yew Tree
A Daughter's a Daughter
The Burden

Memoirs

An Autobiography
Come, Tell Me How You Live

Play Collections

The Mousetrap and Selected Plays
Witness for the Prosecution and
 Selected Plays

Agatha Christie

The Body in
the Library

HARPER

HARPER

An imprint of HarperCollins*Publishers*
77–85 Fulham Palace Road,
Hammersmith, London W6 8JB
www.harpercollins.co.uk

This *Agatha Christie Signature Edition* published 2002
15

First published in Great Britain by
Collins 1942

ISBN 13: 978 0 00 712083 3

Typeset by Palimpsest Book Production Limited,
Grangemouth, Stirlingshire

Printed and bound in Great Britain by
Clays Ltd, St Ives plc

To My Friend Nan

Foreword

There are certain clichés belonging to certain types of fiction. The 'bold bad baronet' for melodrama, the 'body in the library' for the detective story. For several years I treasured up the possibility of a suitable 'Variation on a well-known Theme'. I laid down for myself certain conditions. The library in question must be a highly orthodox and conventional library. The body, on the other hand, must be a wildly improbable and highly sensational body. Such were the terms of the problem, but for some years they remained as such, represented only by a few lines of writing in an exercise book. Then, staying one summer for a few days at a fashionable hotel by the seaside I observed a family at one of the tables in the dining-room; an elderly man, a cripple, in a wheeled chair, and with him was a family party of a younger generation. Fortunately they left the next day, so that my imagination could get to work unhampered by any kind of knowledge. When people ask 'Do you put real people in your books?' the answer is that, for me, it is quite impossible to write about anyone I know, or have ever spoken to, or indeed have even heard about! For some reason, it kills them for me stone dead. But I can take a 'lay figure' and endow it with qualities and imaginings of my own.

So an elderly crippled man became the pivot of the story. Colonel and Mrs Bantry, those old cronies of my Miss Marple, had just the right kind of library. In the manner of a cookery recipe add the following ingredients: a tennis pro, a young dancer, an artist, a girl guide, a dance hostess, etc., and serve up *à la* Miss Marple!

Agatha Christie

Chapter 1

Mrs Bantry was dreaming. Her sweet peas had just taken a First at the flower show. The vicar, dressed in cassock and surplice, was giving out the prizes in church. His wife wandered past, dressed in a bathing-suit, but as is the blessed habit of dreams this fact did not arouse the disapproval of the parish in the way it would assuredly have done in real life . . .

Mrs Bantry was enjoying her dream a good deal. She usually did enjoy those early-morning dreams that were terminated by the arrival of early-morning tea. Somewhere in her inner consciousness was an awareness of the usual early-morning noises of the household. The rattle of the curtain-rings on the stairs as the housemaid drew them, the noises of the second housemaid's dustpan and brush in the passage outside. In the distance the heavy noise of the front-door bolt being drawn back.

Another day was beginning. In the meantime she must extract as much pleasure as possible from the flower show – for already its dream-like quality was becoming apparent . . .

Below her was the noise of the big wooden shutters in the drawing-room being opened. She heard it, yet did not hear it. For quite half an hour longer the usual household noises would go on, discreet, subdued, not disturbing because they were so familiar. They would culminate in a swift, controlled sound of footsteps along the passage, the rustle of a print dress, the subdued chink of tea-things as the tray was deposited on the table outside, then the soft knock and the entry of Mary to draw the curtains.

In her sleep Mrs Bantry frowned. Something disturbing was penetrating through to the dream state, something out of its time. Footsteps along the passage, footsteps that were too hurried and too soon. Her ears listened unconsciously for the chink of china, but there was no chink of china.

The knock came at the door. Automatically from the depths of her dreams Mrs Bantry said: 'Come in.' The door opened – now there would be the chink of curtain-rings as the curtains were drawn back.

But there was no chink of curtain-rings. Out of the dim green light Mary's voice came – breathless, hysterical: 'Oh, ma'am, oh, ma'am, *there's a body in the library.*'

And then with a hysterical burst of sobs she rushed out of the room again.

II

Mrs Bantry sat up in bed.

Either her dream had taken a very odd turn or else – or else Mary had really rushed into the room and had said (incredible! fantastic!) that there was a body in the library.

'Impossible,' said Mrs Bantry to herself. 'I must have been dreaming.'

But even as she said it, she felt more and more certain that she had not been dreaming, that Mary, her superior self-controlled Mary, had actually uttered those fantastic words.

Mrs Bantry reflected a minute and then applied an urgent conjugal elbow to her sleeping spouse.

'Arthur, Arthur, wake up.'

Colonel Bantry grunted, muttered, and rolled over on his side.

'Wake up, Arthur. Did you hear what she said?'

'Very likely,' said Colonel Bantry indistinctly. 'I quite agree with you, Dolly,' and promptly went to sleep again.

Mrs Bantry shook him.

'You've got to listen. Mary came in and said that there was a body in the library.'

'Eh, what?'

'A *body* in the *library*.'

'Who said so?'

'Mary.'

Colonel Bantry collected his scattered faculties and proceeded to deal with the situation. He said:

'Nonsense, old girl; you've been dreaming.'

'No, I haven't. I thought so, too, at first. But I haven't. She really came in and said so.'

'Mary came in and said there was a body in the library?'

'Yes.'

'But there couldn't be,' said Colonel Bantry.

'No, no, I suppose not,' said Mrs Bantry doubtfully.

Rallying, she went on:

'But then why did Mary say there was?'

'She can't have.'

'She did.'

'You must have imagined it.'

'I didn't imagine it.'

Colonel Bantry was by now thoroughly awake and prepared to deal with the situation on its merits. He said kindly:

'You've been dreaming, Dolly, that's what it is. It's

that detective story you were reading – *The Clue of the Broken Match*. You know – Lord Edgbaston finds a beautiful blonde dead on the library hearthrug. Bodies are always being found in libraries in books. I've never known a case in real life.'

'Perhaps you will now,' said Mrs Bantry. 'Anyway, Arthur, you've got to get up and see.'

'But really, Dolly, it *must* have been a dream. Dreams often do seem wonderfully vivid when you first wake up. You feel quite sure they're true.'

'I was having quite a different sort of dream – about a flower show and the vicar's wife in a bathing-dress – something like that.'

With a sudden burst of energy Mrs Bantry jumped out of bed and pulled back the curtains. The light of a fine autumn day flooded the room.

'I did *not* dream it,' said Mrs Bantry firmly. 'Get up at once, Arthur, and go downstairs and see about it.'

'You want me to go downstairs and ask if there's a body in the library? I shall look a damned fool.'

'You needn't ask anything,' said Mrs Bantry. 'If there *is* a body – and of course it's just possible that Mary's gone mad and thinks she sees things that aren't there – well, somebody will tell you soon enough. *You* won't have to say a word.'

Grumbling, Colonel Bantry wrapped himself in his dressing-gown and left the room. He went along the passage and down the staircase. At the foot of it was a little knot of huddled servants; some of them were sobbing. The butler stepped forward impressively.

'I'm glad you have come, sir. I have directed that nothing should be done until you came. Will it be in order for me to ring up the police, sir?'

'Ring 'em up about what?'

The butler cast a reproachful glance over his shoulder at the tall young woman who was weeping hysterically on the cook's shoulder.

'I understood, sir, that Mary had already informed you. She said she had done so.'

Mary gasped out:

'I was so upset I don't know what I said. It all came over me again and my legs gave way and my inside turned over. Finding it like that – oh, oh, oh!'

She subsided again on to Mrs Eccles, who said: 'There, there, my dear,' with some relish.

'Mary is naturally somewhat upset, sir, having been the one to make the gruesome discovery,' explained the butler. 'She went into the library as usual, to draw the curtains, and – almost stumbled over the body.'

'Do you mean to tell me,' demanded Colonel Bantry, 'that there's a dead body in my library – *my* library?'

The butler coughed.

'Perhaps, sir, you would like to see for yourself.'

III

'Hallo, 'allo, 'allo. Police station here. Yes, who's speaking?'

Police-Constable Palk was buttoning up his tunic with one hand while the other held the receiver.

'Yes, yes, Gossington Hall. Yes? Oh, good-morning, sir.' Police-Constable Palk's tone underwent a slight modification. It became less impatiently official, recognizing the generous patron of the police sports and the principal magistrate of the district.

'Yes, sir? What can I do for you? – I'm sorry, sir, I didn't quite catch – a *body*, did you say? – yes? – yes, if you please, sir – that's right, sir – young woman not known to you, you say? – quite, sir. Yes, you can leave it all to me.'

Police-Constable Palk replaced the receiver, uttered a long-drawn whistle and proceeded to dial his superior officer's number.

Mrs Palk looked in from the kitchen whence proceeded an appetizing smell of frying bacon.

'What is it?'

'Rummest thing you ever heard of,' replied her husband. 'Body of a young woman found up at the Hall. In the Colonel's library.'

'Murdered?'

'Strangled, so he says.'

'Who was she?'

'The Colonel says he doesn't know her from Adam.'

'Then what was she doing in 'is library?'

Police-Constable Palk silenced her with a reproach-ful glance and spoke officially into the telephone.

'Inspector Slack? Police-Constable Palk here. A report has just come in that the body of a young woman was discovered this morning at seven-fifteen –'

IV

Miss Marple's telephone rang when she was dressing. The sound of it flurried her a little. It was an unusual hour for her telephone to ring. So well ordered was her prim spinster's life that unforeseen telephone calls were a source of vivid conjecture.

'Dear me,' said Miss Marple, surveying the ring-ing instrument with perplexity. 'I wonder who that can be?'

Nine o'clock to nine-thirty was the recognized time for the village to make friendly calls to neighbours. Plans for the day, invitations and so on were always issued then. The butcher had been known to ring up just before nine if some crisis in the meat trade had occurred. At intervals during the day spasmodic calls might occur, though it was considered bad form to ring after nine-thirty at night. It was true that Miss Marple's nephew, a writer, and therefore erratic, had been known to ring up at the most peculiar times, once as late as ten minutes to midnight. But whatever Raymond West's eccentricities, early rising was not one of them. Neither he nor anyone of Miss Marple's acquaintance would be likely to ring up before eight in the morning. Actually a quarter to eight.

Too early even for a telegram, since the post office did not open until eight.

'It must be,' Miss Marple decided, 'a wrong number.'

Having decided this, she advanced to the impatient instrument and quelled its clamour by picking up the receiver. 'Yes?' she said.

'Is that you, Jane?'

Miss Marple was much surprised.

'Yes, it's Jane. You're up very early, Dolly.'

Mrs Bantry's voice came breathless and agitated over the wires.

'The most awful thing has happened.'

'Oh, my dear.'

'We've just found a body in the library.'

For a moment Miss Marple thought her friend had gone mad.

'You've found a *what*?'

17

'I know. One doesn't believe it, does one? I mean, I thought they only happened in books. I had to argue for hours with Arthur this morning before he'd even go down and see.'

Miss Marple tried to collect herself. She demanded breathlessly: 'But whose body is it?'

'It's a blonde.'

'A what?'

'A blonde. A beautiful blonde – like books again. None of us have ever seen her before. She's just lying there in the library, dead. That's why you've got to come up at once.'

'You want *me* to come up?'

'Yes, I'm sending the car down for you.'

Miss Marple said doubtfully:

'Of course, dear, if you think I can be of any comfort to you –'

'Oh, I don't want comfort. But you're so good at bodies.'

'Oh no, indeed. My little successes have been mostly theoretical.'

'But you're very good at murders. She's been murdered, you see, strangled. What I feel is that if one has got to have a murder actually happening in one's house, one might as well enjoy it, if you know what I mean. That's why I want you to come and help me find out who did it and unravel the mystery and all that. It really *is* rather thrilling, isn't it?'

'Well, of course, my dear, if I can be of any *help* to you.'

'Splendid! Arthur's being rather difficult. He seems to think I shouldn't enjoy myself about it at all. Of course, I do know it's very sad and all that, but then I don't know the girl – and when you've seen her you'll understand what I mean when I say she doesn't look *real* at all.'

V

A little breathless, Miss Marple alighted from the Bantry's car, the door of which was held open for her by the chauffeur.

Colonel Bantry came out on the steps, and looked a little surprised.

'Miss Marple? – er – very pleased to see you.'

'Your wife telephoned to me,' explained Miss Marple.

'Capital, capital. She ought to have someone with her. She'll crack up otherwise. She's putting a good face on things at the moment, but you know what it is –'

At this moment Mrs Bantry appeared, and exclaimed:

'Do go back into the dining-room and eat your breakfast, Arthur. Your bacon will get cold.'

'I thought it might be the Inspector arriving,' explained Colonel Bantry.

'He'll be here soon enough,' said Mrs Bantry. 'That's why it's important to get your breakfast first. You need it.'

'So do you. Much better come and eat something. Dolly –'

'I'll come in a minute,' said Mrs Bantry. 'Go on, Arthur.'

Colonel Bantry was shooed back into the dining-room like a recalcitrant hen.

'*Now!*' said Mrs Bantry with an intonation of triumph. 'Come on.'

She led the way rapidly along the long corridor to the east of the house. Outside the library door Constable Palk stood on guard. He intercepted Mrs Bantry with a show of authority.

'I'm afraid nobody is allowed in, madam. Inspector's orders.'

'Nonsense, Palk,' said Mrs Bantry. 'You know Miss Marple perfectly well.'

Constable Palk admitted to knowing Miss Marple.

'It's very important that she should see the body,' said Mrs Bantry. 'Don't be stupid, Palk. After all, it's *my* library, isn't it?'

Constable Palk gave way. His habit of giving in to the gentry was lifelong. The Inspector, he reflected, need never know about it.

'Nothing must be touched or handled in any way,' he warned the ladies.

'Of course not,' said Mrs Bantry impatiently. 'We know *that*. You can come in and watch, if you like.'

Constable Palk availed himself of this permission. It had been his intention, anyway.

Mrs Bantry bore her friend triumphantly across the library to the big old-fashioned fireplace. She said, with a dramatic sense of climax: 'There!'

Miss Marple understood then just what her friend had meant when she said the dead girl wasn't real. The library was a room very typical of its owners. It was large and shabby and untidy. It had big sagging arm-chairs, and pipes and books and estate papers laid out on the big table. There were one or two good old family portraits on the walls, and some bad Victorian water-colours, and some would-be-funny hunting scenes. There was a big vase of Michaelmas daisies in the corner. The whole room was dim and mellow and casual. It spoke of long occupation and familiar use and of links with tradition.

And across the old bearskin hearthrug there was sprawled something new and crude and melodramatic.

The flamboyant figure of a girl. A girl with unnaturally fair hair dressed up off her face in elaborate curls and rings. Her thin body was dressed in a backless evening-dress of white spangled satin. The face was heavily made-up, the powder standing out grotesquely on its blue swollen surface, the mascara of the lashes lying thickly on the distorted cheeks, the scarlet of the lips looking like a gash. The finger-nails were enamelled in a deep blood-red and so were the toenails in their cheap silver sandal shoes. It was a cheap, tawdry, flamboyant figure – most incongruous in the solid old-fashioned comfort of Colonel Bantry's library.

Mrs Bantry said in a low voice:

'You see what I mean? It just isn't *true!*'

The old lady by her side nodded her head. She looked down long and thoughtfully at the huddled figure.

She said at last in a gentle voice:

'She's very young.'

'Yes – yes – I suppose she is.' Mrs Bantry seemed almost surprised – like one making a discovery.

Miss Marple bent down. She did not touch the girl. She looked at the fingers that clutched frantically at the front of the girl's dress, as though she had clawed it in her last frantic struggle for breath.

There was the sound of a car scrunching on the gravel outside. Constable Palk said with urgency:

'That'll be the Inspector . . .'

True to his ingrained belief that the gentry didn't

let you down, Mrs Bantry immediately moved to the door. Miss Marple followed her. Mrs Bantry said:

'That'll be all right, Palk.'

Constable Palk was immensely relieved.

VI

Hastily downing the last fragments of toast and marmalade with a drink of coffee, Colonel Bantry hurried out into the hall and was relieved to see Colonel Melchett, the Chief Constable of the county, descending from a car with Inspector Slack in attendance. Melchett was a friend of the Colonel's. Slack he had never much taken to – an energetic man who belied his name and who accompanied his bustling manner with a good deal of disregard for the feelings of anyone he did not consider important.

'Morning, Bantry,' said the Chief Constable. 'Thought I'd better come along myself. This seems an extraordinary business.'

'It's – it's—' Colonel Bantry struggled to express himself. 'It's *incredible – fantastic!*'

'No idea who the woman is?'

'Not the slightest. Never set eyes on her in my life.'

'Butler know anything?' asked Inspector Slack.

'Lorrimer is just as taken aback as I am.'

'Ah,' said Inspector Slack. 'I wonder.'

Colonel Bantry said:

'There's breakfast in the dining-room, Melchett, if you'd like anything?'

'No, no – better get on with the job. Haydock ought to be here any minute now – ah, here he is.'

Another car drew up and big, broad-shouldered Doctor Haydock, who was also the police surgeon, got out. A second police car had disgorged two plain-clothes men, one with a camera.

'All set – eh?' said the Chief Constable. 'Right. We'll go along. In the library, Slack tells me.'

Colonel Bantry groaned.

'It's incredible! You know, when my wife insisted this morning that the housemaid had come in and said there was a body in the library, I just wouldn't believe her.'

'No, no, I can quite understand that. Hope your missus isn't too badly upset by it all?'

'She's been wonderful – really wonderful. She's got old Miss Marple up here with her – from the village, you know.'

'Miss Marple?' The Chief Constable stiffened. 'Why did she send for her?'

'Oh, a woman wants another woman – don't you think so?'

Colonel Melchett said with a slight chuckle:

'If you ask me, your wife's going to try her hand

at a little amateur detecting. Miss Marple's quite the local sleuth. Put it over us properly once, didn't she, Slack?'

Inspector Slack said: 'That was different.'

'Different from what?'

'That was a local case, that was, sir. The old lady knows everything that goes on in the village, that's true enough. But she'll be out of her depth here.'

Melchett said dryly: 'You don't know very much about it yourself yet, Slack.'

'Ah, you wait, sir. It won't take me long to get down to it.'

VII

In the dining-room Mrs Bantry and Miss Marple, in their turn, were partaking of breakfast.

After waiting on her guest, Mrs Bantry said urgently: 'Well, Jane?'

Miss Marple looked up at her, slightly bewildered.

Mrs Bantry said hopefully:

'Doesn't it *remind* you of anything?'

For Miss Marple had attained fame by her ability to link up trivial village happenings with graver problems in such a way as to throw light upon the latter.

'No,' said Miss Marple thoughtfully, 'I can't say that

it does – not at the moment. I was reminded a little of Mrs Chetty's youngest – Edie, you know – but I think that was just because this poor girl bit her nails and her front teeth stuck out a little. Nothing more than that. And, of course,' went on Miss Marple, pursuing the parallel further, 'Edie was fond of what I call cheap finery, too.'

'You mean her dress?' said Mrs Bantry.

'Yes, a very tawdry satin – poor quality.'

Mrs Bantry said:

'I know. One of those nasty little shops where everything is a guinea.' She went on hopefully:

'Let me see, what happened to Mrs Chetty's Edie?'

'She's just gone into her second place – and doing very well, I believe.'

Mrs Bantry felt slightly disappointed. The village parallel didn't seem to be exactly hopeful.

'What I can't make out,' said Mrs Bantry, 'is what she could possibly be doing in Arthur's study. The window was forced, Palk tells me. She might have come down here with a burglar and then they quarrelled – but that seems such nonsense, doesn't it?'

'She was hardly dressed for burglary,' said Miss Marple thoughtfully.

'No, she was dressed for dancing – or a party of some kind. But there's nothing of that kind down here – or anywhere near.'

'N-n-o,' said Miss Marple doubtfully.

Mrs Bantry pounced.

'Something's in your mind, Jane.'

'Well, I was just wondering –'

'Yes?'

'Basil Blake.'

Mrs Bantry cried impulsively: 'Oh, no!' and added as though in explanation, 'I know his mother.'

The two women looked at each other.

Miss Marple sighed and shook her head.

'I quite understand how you feel about it.'

'Selina Blake is the nicest woman imaginable. Her herbaceous borders are simply marvellous – they make me green with envy. And she's frightfully generous with cuttings.'

Miss Marple, passing over these claims to consideration on the part of Mrs Blake, said:

'All the same, you know, there has been a lot of *talk*.'

'Oh, I know – I know. And of course Arthur goes simply livid when he hears Basil Blake mentioned. He was really *very* rude to Arthur, and since then Arthur won't hear a good word for him. He's got that silly slighting way of talking that these boys have nowadays – sneering at people sticking up for their school or the Empire or that sort of thing. And then, of course, the *clothes* he wears!'

'People say,' continued Mrs Bantry, 'that it doesn't matter what you wear in the country. I never heard such nonsense. It's just in the country that everyone notices.' She paused, and added wistfully: 'He was an adorable baby in his bath.'

'There was a lovely picture of the Cheviot murderer as a baby in the paper last Sunday,' said Miss Marple.

'Oh, but Jane, you don't thing *he* –'

'No, no, dear. I didn't mean that at all. That would indeed be jumping to conclusions. I was just trying to account for the young woman's presence down here. St Mary Mead is such an unlikely place. And then it seemed to me that the only possible explanation was Basil Blake. He *does* have parties. People came down from London and from the studios – you remember last July? Shouting and singing – the most *terrible* noise – everyone very drunk, I'm afraid – and the mess and the broken glass next morning simply unbelievable – so old Mrs Berry told me – and a young woman asleep in the bath with practically *nothing on*!'

Mrs Bantry said indulgently:

'I suppose they were film people.'

'Very likely. And then – what I expect you've heard – several week-ends lately he's brought down a young woman with him – a platinum blonde.'

Mrs Bantry exclaimed:

'You don't think it's *this* one?'

'Well – I wondered. Of course, I've never seen her close to – only just getting in and out of the car – and once in the cottage garden when she was sunbathing with just some shorts and a brassière. I never really saw her *face*. And all these girls with their make-up and their hair and their nails look so alike.'

'Yes. Still, it *might* be. It's an idea, Jane.'

Chapter 2

It was an idea that was being at that moment discussed by Colonel Melchett and Colonel Bantry.

The Chief Constable, after viewing the body and seeing his subordinates set to work on their routine tasks, had adjourned with the master of the house to the study in the other wing of the house.

Colonel Melchett was an irascible-looking man with a habit of tugging at his short red moustache. He did so now, shooting a perplexed sideways glance at the other man. Finally, he rapped out:

'Look here, Bantry, got to get this off my chest. Is it a fact that you don't know from Adam who this girl is?'

The other's answer was explosive, but the Chief Constable interrupted him.

'Yes, yes, old man, but look at it like this. Might be deuced awkward for you. Married man – fond of your

31

missus and all that. But just between ourselves – if you *were* tied up with this girl in any way, better say so *now*. Quite natural to want to suppress the fact – should feel the same myself. But it won't do. Murder case. Facts bound to come out. Dash it all, I'm not suggesting *you* strangled the girl – not the sort of thing you'd do – *I* know that. But, after all, she came here – to this house. Put it she broke in and was waiting to see you, and some bloke or other followed her down and did her in. Possible, you know. See what I mean?'

'Damn it all, Melchett, I tell you I've never set eyes on that girl in my life! I'm not that sort of man.'

'That's all right, then. Shouldn't blame you, you know. Man of the world. Still, if you say so – Question is, what was she doing down here? She doesn't come from these parts – that's quite certain.'

'The whole thing's a nightmare,' fumed the angry master of the house.

'The point is, old man, what was she doing in your library?'

'How should I know? *I* didn't ask her here.'

'No, no. But she *came* here, all the same. Looks as though she wanted to see you. You haven't had any odd letters or anything?'

'No, I haven't.'

Colonel Melchett inquired delicately:

'What were you doing yourself last night?'

'I went to the meeting of the Conservative Associ-
ation. Nine o'clock, at Much Benham.'

'And you got home when?'

'I left Much Benham just after ten – had a bit of
trouble on the way home, had to change a wheel. I got
back at a quarter to twelve.'

'You didn't go into the library?'

'No.'

'Pity.'

'I was tired. I went straight up to bed.'

'Anyone waiting up for you?'

'No. I always take the latchkey. Lorrimer goes to bed
at eleven unless I give orders to the contrary.'

'Who shuts up the library?'

'Lorrimer. Usually about seven-thirty this time of
year.'

'Would he go in there again during the evening?'

'Not with my being out. He left the tray with whisky
and glasses in the hall.'

'I see. What about your wife?'

'I don't know. She was in bed when I got home and
fast asleep. She may have sat in the library yesterday
evening or in the drawing-room. I forgot to ask her.'

'Oh well, we shall soon know all the details. Of
course, it's possible one of the servants may be concerned, eh?'

Colonel Bantry shook his head.

'I don't believe it. They're all a most respectable lot. We've had 'em for years.'

Melchett agreed.

'Yes, it doesn't seem likely that they're mixed up in it. Looks more as though the girl came down from town – perhaps with some young fellow. Though why they wanted to break into this house –'

Bantry interrupted.

'London. That's more like it. We don't have goings on down here – at least –'

'Well, what is it?'

'Upon my word!' exploded Colonel Bantry. 'Basil Blake!'

'Who's he?'

'Young fellow connected with the film industry. Poisonous young brute. My wife sticks up for him because she was at school with his mother, but of all the decadent useless young jackanapes! Wants his behind kicked! He's taken that cottage on the Lansham Road – you know – ghastly modern bit of building. He has parties there, shrieking, noisy crowds, and he has girls down for the weekend.'

'Girls?'

'Yes, there was one last week – one of these platinum blondes –'

The Colonel's jaw dropped.

'A platinum blonde, eh?' said Melchett reflectively.

'Yes. I say, Melchett, you don't think –'

The Chief Constable said briskly:

'It's a possibility. It accounts for a girl of this type being in St Mary Mead. I think I'll run along and have a word with this young fellow – Braid – Blake – what did you say his name was?'

'Blake. Basil Blake.'

'Will he be at home, do you know?'

'Let me see. What's today – Saturday? Usually gets here sometime Saturday morning.'

Melchett said grimly:

'We'll see if we can find him.'

II

Basil Blake's cottage, which consisted of all modern conveniences enclosed in a hideous shell of half timbering and sham Tudor, was known to the postal authorities, and to William Booker, builder, as 'Chatsworth'; to Basil and his friends as 'The Period Piece', and to the village of St Mary Mead at large as 'Mr Booker's new house'.

It was little more than a quarter of a mile from the village proper, being situated on a new building estate that had been bought by the enterprising Mr Booker just beyond the Blue Boar, with frontage on what had been a particularly unspoilt country lane. Gossington Hall was about a mile farther on along the same road.

Lively interest had been aroused in St Mary Mead when news went round that 'Mr Booker's new house' had been bought by a film star. Eager watch was kept for the first appearance of the legendary creature in the village, and it may be said that as far as appearances went Basil Blake was all that could be asked for. Little by little, however, the real facts leaked out. Basil Blake was *not* a film star – not even a film actor. He was a very junior person, rejoicing in the title of about fifteenth in the list of those responsible for Set Decorations at Lemville Studios, headquarters of British New Era Films. The village maidens lost interest, and the ruling class of censorious spinsters took exception to Basil Blake's way of life. Only the landlord of the Blue Boar continued to be enthusiastic about Basil and Basil's friends. The revenues of the Blue Boar had increased since the young man's arrival in the place.

The police car stopped outside the distorted rustic gate of Mr Booker's fancy, and Colonel Melchett, with a glance of distaste at the excessive half timbering of Chatsworth, strode up to the front door and attacked it briskly with the knocker.

It was opened much more promptly than he had expected. A young man with straight, somewhat long, black hair, wearing orange corduroy trousers and a royal-blue shirt, snapped out: 'Well, what do you want?'

'Are you Mr Basil Blake?'

'Of course I am.'

'I should be glad to have a few words with you, if I may, Mr Blake?'

'Who are you?'

'I am Colonel Melchett, the Chief Constable of the County.'

Mr Blake said insolently:

'You don't say so; how amusing!'

And Colonel Melchett, following the other in, understood what Colonel Bantry's reactions had been. The toe of his own boot itched.

Containing himself, however, he said with an attempt to speak pleasantly:

'You're an early riser, Mr Blake.'

'Not at all. I haven't been to bed yet.'

'Indeed.'

'But I don't suppose you've come here to inquire into my hours of bedgoing – or if you have it's rather a waste of the county's time and money. What is it you want to speak to me about?'

Colonel Melchett cleared his throat.

'I understand, Mr Blake, that last week-end you had a visitor – a – er – fair-haired young lady.'

Basil Blake stared, threw back his head and roared with laughter.

'Have the old cats been on to you from the village? About my morals? Damn it all, morals aren't a police matter. *You* know that.'

'As you say,' said Melchett dryly, 'your morals are no concern of mine. I have come to you because the body of a fair-haired young woman of slightly – er – exotic appearance has been found – murdered.'

'Strewth!' Blake stared at him. 'Where?'

'In the library at Gossington Hall.'

'At Gossington? At old Bantry's? I say, that's pretty rich. Old Bantry! The dirty old man!'

Colonel Melchett went very red in the face. He said sharply through the renewed mirth of the young man opposite him: 'Kindly control your tongue, sir. I came to ask you if you can throw any light on this business.'

'You've come round to ask me if I've missed a blonde? Is that it? Why should – hallo, 'allo, 'allo, what's this?'

A car had drawn up outside with a scream of brakes. Out of it tumbled a young woman dressed in flapping black-and-white pyjamas. She had scarlet lips, blackened eyelashes, and a platinum-blonde head. She strode up to the door, flung it open, and exclaimed angrily:

'Why did you run out on me, you brute?'

Basil Blake had risen.

'So there you are! Why shouldn't I leave you? I told you to clear out and you wouldn't.'

'Why the hell should I because you told me to? I was enjoying myself.'

'Yes – with that filthy brute Rosenberg. You know what *he's* like.'

'You were jealous, that's all.'

'Don't flatter yourself. I hate to see a girl I like who can't hold her drink and lets a disgusting Central European paw her about.'

'That's a damned lie. You were drinking pretty hard yourself – and going on with the black-haired Spanish bitch.'

'If I take you to a party I expect you to be able to behave yourself.'

'And I refuse to be dictated to, and that's that. You said we'd go to the party and come on down here afterwards. I'm not going to leave a party before I'm ready to leave it.'

'No – and that's why I left you flat. I was ready to come down here and I came. I don't hang round waiting for any fool of a woman.'

'Sweet, polite person you are!'

'You seem to have followed me down all right!'

'I wanted to tell you what I thought of you!'

'If you think you can boss me, my girl, you're wrong!'

'And if you think you can order me about, you can think again!'

They glared at each other.

It was at this moment that Colonel Melchett seized his opportunity, and cleared his throat loudly.

Basil Blake swung round on him.

'Hallo, I forgot you were here. About time you took yourself off, isn't it? Let me introduce you – Dinah Lee – Colonel Blimp of the County Police. And now, Colonel, that you've seen my blonde is alive and in good condition, perhaps you'll get on with the good work concerning old Bantry's little bit of fluff. Good-morning!'

Colonel Melchett said:

'I advise you to keep a civil tongue in your head, young man, or you'll let yourself in for trouble,' and stumped out, his face red and wrathful.

Chapter 3

In his office at Much Benham, Colonel Melchett received and scrutinized the reports of his subordinates:

'. . . so it all seems clear enough, sir,' Inspector Slack was concluding: 'Mrs Bantry sat in the library after dinner and went to bed just before ten. She turned out the lights when she left the room and, presumably, no one entered the room afterwards. The servants went to bed at half-past ten and Lorrimer, after putting the drinks in the hall, went to bed at a quarter to eleven. Nobody heard anything out of the usual except the third housemaid, and she heard too much! Groans and a blood-curdling yell and sinister footsteps and I don't know what. The second housemaid who shares a room with her says the other girl slept all night through without a sound. It's those ones that make up things that cause us all the trouble.'

'What about the forced window?'

'Amateur job, Simmons says; done with a common chisel – ordinary pattern – wouldn't have made much noise. Ought to be a chisel about the house but nobody can find it. Still, that's common enough where tools are concerned.'

'Think any of the servants know anything?'

Rather unwillingly Inspector Slack replied:

'No, sir, I don't think they do. They all seemed very shocked and upset. I had my suspicions of Lorrimer – reticent, he was, if you know what I mean – but I don't think there's anything in it.'

Melchett nodded. He attached no importance to Lorrimer's reticence. The energetic Inspector Slack often produced that effect on people he interrogated.

The door opened and Dr Haydock came in.

'Thought I'd look in and give you the rough gist of things.'

'Yes, yes, glad to see you. Well?'

'Nothing much. Just what you'd think. Death was due to strangulation. Satin waistband of her own dress, which was passed round the neck and crossed at the back. Quite easy and simple to do. Wouldn't have needed great strength – that is, if the girl were taken by surprise. There are no signs of a struggle.'

'What about time of death?'

'Say, between ten o'clock and midnight.'

'You can't get nearer than that?'

Haydock shook his head with a slight grin.

'I won't risk my professional reputation. Not earlier than ten and not later than midnight.'

'And your own fancy inclines to which time?'

'Depends. There was a fire in the grate – the room was warm – all that would delay rigor and cadaveric stiffening.'

'Anything more you can say about her?'

'Nothing much. She was young – about seventeen or eighteen, I should say. Rather immature in some ways but well developed muscularly. Quite a healthy specimen. She was virgo intacta, by the way.'

And with a nod of his head the doctor left the room.

Melchett said to the Inspector:

'You're quite sure she'd never been seen before at Gossington?'

'The servants are positive of that. Quite indignant about it. They'd have remembered if they'd ever seen her about in the neighbourhood, they say.'

'I expect they would,' said Melchett. 'Anyone of that type sticks out a mile round here. Look at that young woman of Blake's.'

'Pity it wasn't her,' said Slack; 'then we should be able to get on a bit.'

'It seems to me this girl must have come down

from London,' said the Chief Constable thoughtfully. 'Don't believe there will be any local leads. In that case, I suppose, we should do well to call in the Yard. It's a case for them, not for us.'

'Something must have brought her down here, though,' said Slack. He added tentatively: 'Seems to me, Colonel and Mrs Bantry *must* know something – of course, I know they're friends of yours, sir –'

Colonel Melchett treated him to a cold stare. He said stiffly:

'You may rest assured that I'm taking every possibility into account. *Every* possibility.' He went on: 'You've looked through the list of persons reported missing, I suppose?'

Slack nodded. He produced a typed sheet.

'Got 'em here. Mrs Saunders, reported missing a week ago, dark-haired, blue-eyed, thirty-six. 'Tisn't her – and, anyway, everyone knows except her husband that she's gone off with a fellow from Leeds – commercial. Mrs Barnard – she's sixty-five. Pamela Reeves, sixteen, missing from her home last night, had attended Girl Guide rally, dark-brown hair in pigtail, five feet five –'

Melchett said irritably:

'Don't go on reading idiotic details, Slack. This wasn't a schoolgirl. In my opinion –'

He broke off as the telephone rang. 'Hallo – yes –

yes, Much Benham Police Headquarters – what? Just a minute –'

He listened, and wrote rapidly. Then he spoke again, a new tone in his voice:

'Ruby Keene, eighteen, occupation professional dancer, five feet four inches, slender, platinum-blonde hair, blue eyes, *retroussé* nose, believed to be wearing white diamanté evening-dress, silver sandal shoes. Is that right? What? Yes, not a doubt of it, I should say. I'll send Slack over at once.'

He rang off and looked at his subordinate with rising excitement. 'We've got it, I think. That was the Glenshire Police' (Glenshire was the adjoining county). 'Girl reported missing from the Majestic Hotel, Danemouth.'

'Danemouth,' said Inspector Slack. 'That's more like it.'

Danemouth was a large and fashionable watering-place on the coast not far away.

'It's only a matter of eighteen miles or so from here,' said the Chief Constable. 'The girl was a dance hostess or something at the Majestic. Didn't come on to do her turn last night and the management were very fed up about it. When she was still missing this morning one of the other girls got the wind up about her, or someone else did. It sounds a bit obscure. You'd better go over to Danemouth at once, Slack. Report

45

there to Superintendent Harper, and co-operate with him.'

II

Activity was always to Inspector Slack's taste. To rush off in a car, to silence rudely those people who were anxious to tell him things, to cut short conversations on the plea of urgent necessity. All this was the breath of life to Slack.

In an incredibly short time, therefore, he had arrived at Danemouth, reported at police headquarters, had a brief interview with a distracted and apprehensive hotel manager, and, leaving the latter with the doubtful comfort of – 'got to make sure it *is* the girl, first, before we start raising the wind' – was driving back to Much Benham in company with Ruby Keene's nearest relative.

He had put through a short call to Much Benham before leaving Danemouth, so the Chief Constable was prepared for his arrival, though not perhaps for the brief introduction of: 'This is Josie, sir.'

Colonel Melchett stared at his subordinate coldly. His feeling was that Slack had taken leave of his senses.

The young woman who had just got out of the car came to the rescue.

'That's what I'm known as professionally,' she explained with a momentary flash of large, handsome white teeth. 'Raymond and Josie, my partner and I call ourselves, and, of course, all the hotel know me as Josie. Josephine Turner's my real name.'

Colonel Melchett adjusted himself to the situation and invited Miss Turner to sit down, meanwhile casting a swift, professional glance over her.

She was a good-looking young woman of perhaps nearer thirty than twenty, her looks depending more on skilful grooming than actual features. She looked competent and good-tempered, with plenty of common sense. She was not the type that would ever be described as glamorous, but she had nevertheless plenty of attraction. She was discreetly made-up and wore a dark tailor-made suit. Though she looked anxious and upset she was not, the Colonel decided, particularly grief-stricken.

As she sat down she said: 'It seems too awful to be true. Do you really think it's Ruby?'

'That, I'm afraid, is what we've got to ask you to tell us. I'm afraid it may be rather unpleasant for you.'

Miss Turner said apprehensively:

'Does she – does she – look very terrible?'

'Well – I'm afraid it may be rather a shock to you.' He handed her his cigarette-case and she accepted one gratefully.

47

Agatha Christie

'Do – do you want me to look at her right away?'

'It would be best, I think, Miss Turner. You see, it's not much good asking you questions until we're sure. Best get it over, don't you think?'

'All right.'

They drove down to the mortuary.

When Josie came out after a brief visit, she looked rather sick.

'It's Ruby all right,' she said shakily. 'Poor kid! Goodness, I do feel queer. There isn't' – she looked round wistfully – 'any gin?'

Gin was not available, but brandy was, and after gupling a little down Miss Turner regained her composure. She said frankly:

'It gives you a turn, doesn't it, seeing anything like that? Poor little Rube! What swine men are, aren't they?'

'You believe it was a man?'

Josie looked slightly taken aback.

'Wasn't it? Well, I mean – I naturally thought –'

'Any special man you were thinking of?'

She shook her head vigorously.

'No – not me. I haven't the least idea. Naturally Ruby wouldn't have let on to me if –'

'If what?'

Josie hesitated.

'Well – if she'd been – going about with anyone.'

Melchett shot her a keen glance. He said no more until they were back at his office. Then he began:

'Now, Miss Turner, I want all the information you can give me.'

'Yes, of course. Where shall I begin?'

'I'd like the girl's full name and address, her relationship to you and all you know about her.'

Josephine Turner nodded. Melchett was confirmed in his opinion that she felt no particular grief. She was shocked and distressed but no more. She spoke readily enough.

'Her name was Ruby Keene – her professional name, that is. Her real name was Rosy Legge. Her mother was my mother's cousin. I've known her all my life, but not particularly well, if you know what I mean. I've got a lot of cousins – some in business, some on the stage. Ruby was more or less training for a dancer. She had some good engagements last year in panto and that sort of thing. Not really classy, but good provincial companies. Since then she's been engaged as one of the dancing partners at the Palais de Danse in Brixwell – South London. It's a nice respectable place and they look after the girls well, but there isn't much money in it.' She paused.

Colonel Melchett nodded.

'Now this is where I come in. I've been dance and bridge hostess at the Majestic in Danemouth for three years. It's a good job, well paid and pleasant to do. You look after people when they arrive – size them up, of course – some like to be left alone and others are lonely and want to get into the swing of things. You try to get the right people together for bridge and all that, and get the young people dancing with each other. It needs a bit of tact and experience.'

Again Melchett nodded. He thought that this girl would be good at her job; she had a pleasant, friendly way with her and was, he thought, shrewd without being in the least intellectual.

'Besides that,' continued Josie, 'I do a couple of exhibition dances every evening with Raymond. Raymond Starr – he's the tennis and dancing pro. Well, as it happens, this summer I slipped on the rocks bathing one day and gave my ankle a nasty turn.'

Melchett had noticed that she walked with a slight limp.

'Naturally that put the stop to dancing for a bit and it was rather awkward. I didn't want the hotel to get someone else in my place. That's always a danger – for a minute her good-natured blue eyes were hard and sharp; she was the female fighting for existence – 'that they may queer your pitch, you see. So I thought of Ruby and suggested to the manager that I should get her down. I'd carry on with the hostess business and the bridge and all that. Ruby would just take on the dancing. Keep it in the family, if you see what I mean?'

Melchett said he saw.

'Well, they agreed, and I wired to Ruby and she came down. Rather a chance for her. Much better class than anything she'd ever done before. That was about a month ago.'

Colonel Melchett said:

'I understand. And she was a success?'

'Oh, yes,' Josie said carelessly, 'she went down quite well. She doesn't dance as well as I do, but Raymond's clever and carried her through, and she was quite nice-looking, you know – slim and fair and baby-looking. Overdid the make-up a bit – I was always on at her about that. But you know what girls are. She was only eighteen, and at that age they always go and overdo it. It doesn't do for a good-class place like the Majestic. I was always ticking her off about it and getting her to tone it down.'

Melchett asked: 'People liked her?'

'Oh, yes. Mind you, Ruby hadn't got much come-back. She was a bit dumb. She went down better with the older men than with the young ones.'

'Had she got any special friend?'

The girl's eyes met his with complete understanding.

'Not in the way *you* mean. Or, at any rate, not that *I* knew about. But then, you see, she wouldn't tell me.'

Just for a moment Melchett wondered why not – Josie did not give the impression of being a strict disciplinarian. But he only said: 'Will you describe to me now when you last saw your cousin.'

'Last night. She and Raymond do two exhibition dances – one at 10.30 and the other at midnight. They finished the first one. After it, I noticed Ruby dancing with one of the young men staying in the hotel. I was playing bridge with some people in the lounge. There's a glass panel between the lounge and the ballroom. That's the last time I saw her. Just after midnight Raymond came up in a terrible taking, said where was Ruby, she hadn't turned up, and it was time to begin. I *was* vexed, I can tell you! That's the sort of silly thing girls do and get the management's backs up and then they get the sack! I went up with him to her room, but she wasn't there. I noticed that she'd changed. The dress she'd been dancing in – a sort of pink, foamy thing with full skirts – was lying over a chair. Usually she kept the same dress on unless it was the special dance night – Wednesdays, that is.

'I'd no idea where she'd got to. We got the band to play one more foxtrot – still no Ruby, so I said to Raymond *I*'d do the exhibition dance with him. We chose one that was easy on my ankle and made it short – but it played up my ankle pretty badly all the same. It's all swollen this morning. Still Ruby didn't show up. We sat about waiting up for her until two o'clock. Furious with her, I was.'

Her voice vibrated slightly. Melchett caught the note of real anger in it. Just for a moment he wondered. The reaction seemed a little more intense than was justified by the facts. He had a feeling of something deliberately left unsaid. He said:

'And this morning, when Ruby Keene had not returned and her bed had not been slept in, you went to the police?'

He knew from Slack's brief telephone message from Danemouth that that was not the case. But he wanted to hear what Josephine Turner would say.

She did not hesitate. She said: 'No, *I* didn't.'

'Why not, Miss Turner?'

Her eyes met his frankly. She said:

'*You* wouldn't – in my place!'

'You think not?'

Josie said:

'I've got my job to think about. The one thing a hotel doesn't want is scandal – especially anything that brings in the police. I didn't think anything had happened to Ruby. Not for a minute! I thought she'd just made a fool of herself about some young man. I thought she'd turn up all right – and I was going to give her a good dressing down when she did! Girls of eighteen are such fools.'

Melchett pretended to glance through his notes.

'Ah, yes, I see it was a Mr Jefferson who went to the police. One of the guests staying at the hotel?'

Josephine Turner said shortly:

'Yes.'

Colonel Melchett asked:

'What made this Mr Jefferson do that?'

Josie was stroking the cuff of her jacket. There was a constraint in her manner. Again Colonel Melchett had a feeling that something was being withheld. She said rather sullenly:

'He's an invalid. He – he gets all het up rather easily. Being an invalid, I mean.'

Melchett passed on from that. He asked:

'Who was the young man with whom you last saw your cousin dancing?'

'His name's Bartlett. He'd been there about ten days.'

'Were they on very friendly terms?'

'Not specially, I should say. Not that *I* knew, anyway.'

Again a curious note of anger in her voice.

'What does he have to say?'

'Said that after their dance Ruby went upstairs to powder her nose.'

'That was when she changed her dress?'

'I suppose so.'

'And that is the last thing you know? After that she just –'

'Vanished,' said Josie. 'That's right.'

'Did Miss Keene know anybody in St Mary Mead? Or in this neighbourhood?'

'I don't know. She may have done. You see, quite a lot of young men come into Danemouth to the Majestic from all round about. I wouldn't know where they lived unless they happened to mention it.'

'Did you ever hear your cousin mention Gossington?'

'Gossington?' Josie looked patently puzzled.

'Gossington Hall.'

She shook her head.

'Never heard of it.' Her tone carried conviction. There was curiosity in it too.

'Gossington Hall,' explained Colonel Melchett, 'is where her body was found.'

'Gossington Hall?' She stared. 'How extraordinary!'

Melchett thought to himself: 'Extraordinary's the word!' Aloud he said:

'Do you know a Colonel or Mrs Bantry?'

Again Josie shook her head.

'Or a Mr Basil Blake?'

She frowned slightly.

'I think I've heard that name. Yes, I'm sure I have – but I don't remember anything about him.'

The diligent Inspector Slack slid across to his superior

officer a page torn from his note-book. On it was pencilled:

'*Col. Bantry dined at Majestic last week.*'

Melchett looked up and met the Inspector's eye. The Chief Constable flushed. Slack was an industrious and zealous officer and Melchett disliked him a good deal. But he could not disregard the challenge. The Inspector was tacitly accusing him of favouring his own class – of shielding an 'old school tie.'

He turned to Josie.

'Miss Turner, I should like you, if you do not mind, to accompany me to Gossington Hall.'

Coldly, defiantly, almost ignoring Josie's murmur of assent, Melchett's eyes met Slack's.

Chapter 4

St Mary Mead was having the most exciting morning it had known for a long time.

Miss Wetherby, a long-nosed, acidulated spinster, was the first to spread the intoxicating information. She dropped in upon her friend and neighbour Miss Hartnell.

'Forgive me coming so early, dear, but I thought, perhaps, you mightn't have heard the *news*.'

'What news?' demanded Miss Hartnell. She had a deep bass voice and visited the poor indefatigably, however hard they tried to avoid her ministrations.

'About the body in Colonel Bantry's library – a *woman's* body –'

'In Colonel Bantry's *library*?'

'Yes. Isn't it *terrible*?'

'His *poor* wife.' Miss Hartnell tried to disguise her deep and ardent pleasure.

'Yes, indeed. I don't suppose she had any idea.'

Miss Hartnell observed censoriously:

'She thought too much about her garden and not enough about her husband. You've got to keep an eye on a man – all the time – all the time,' repeated Miss Hartnell fiercely.

'I know. I know. It's really too dreadful.'

'I wonder what Jane Marple will say. Do you think she knew anything about it? She's so sharp about these things.'

'Jane Marple has gone up to Gossington.'

'What? This morning?'

'Very early. Before breakfast.'

'But really! I do think! Well, I mean, I think that is carrying things *too* far. We all know Jane likes to poke her nose into things – but I call this indecent!'

'Oh, but Mrs Bantry sent for her.'

'Mrs Bantry *sent* for her?'

'Well, the car came – with Muswell driving it.'

'Dear me! How very peculiar . . .'

They were silent a minute or two digesting the news.

'Whose body?' demanded Miss Hartnell.

'You know that dreadful woman who comes down with Basil Blake?'

'That terrible peroxide blonde?' Miss Hartnell was slightly behind the times. She had not yet advanced from peroxide to platinum. 'The one who lies about in the garden with practically nothing on?'

'Yes, my dear. There she was – on the hearthrug – *strangled*!'

'But what do you mean – at *Gossington*?'

Miss Wetherby nodded with infinite meaning.

'Then – Colonel Bantry *too* –?'

Again Miss Wetherby nodded.

'Oh!'

There was a pause as the ladies savoured this new addition to village scandal.

'What a wicked woman!' trumpeted Miss Hartnell with righteous wrath.

'Quite, quite abandoned, I'm afraid!'

'And Colonel Bantry – such a nice quiet man –'

Miss Wetherby said zestfully:

'Those quiet ones are often the worst. Jane Marple always says so.'

II

Mrs Price Ridley was among the last to hear the news.

A rich and dictatorial widow, she lived in a large house next door to the vicarage. Her informant was her little maid Clara.

'A *woman*, you say, Clara? *Found dead on Colonel Bantry's hearthrug?*'

'Yes, mum. And they say, mum, as she hadn't anything on at all, mum, not a stitch!'

'That will do, Clara. It is not necessary to go into details.'

'No, mum, and they say, mum, that at first they thought it was Mr Blake's young lady – what comes down for the weekends with 'im to Mr Booker's new 'ouse. But now they say it's quite a different young lady. And the fishmonger's young man, he says he'd never have believed it of Colonel Bantry – not with him handing round the plate on Sundays and all.'

'There is a lot of wickedness in the world, Clara,' said Mrs Price Ridley. 'Let this be a warning to you.'

'Yes, mum. Mother, she never *will* let me take a place where there's a gentleman in the 'ouse.'

'That will *do*, Clara,' said Mrs Price Ridley.

III

It was only a step from Mrs Price Ridley's house to the vicarage.

Mrs Price Ridley was fortunate enough to find the vicar in his study.

The vicar, a gentle, middle-aged man, was always the last to hear anything.

'Such a *terrible* thing,' said Mrs Price Ridley, panting a little, because she had come rather fast. 'I felt I must have your advice, your counsel about it, dear vicar.'

Mr Clement looked mildly alarmed. He said:

'Has anything happened?'

'Has anything *happened*?' Mrs Price Ridley repeated the question dramatically. 'The most terrible scandal! None of us had any idea of it. An abandoned woman, completely unclothed, strangled on Colonel Bantry's hearthrug.'

The vicar stared. He said:

'You – you are feeling quite well?'

'No wonder you can't believe it! *I* couldn't at first. The hypocrisy of the man! All these years!'

'Please tell me exactly what all this is about.'

Mrs Price Ridley plunged into a full-swing narrative. When she had finished Mr Clement said mildly:

'But there is nothing, is there, to point to Colonel Bantry's being involved in this?'

'Oh, dear vicar, you are so unworldly! But I must tell you a little story. Last Thursday – or was it the Thursday before? well, it doesn't matter – I was going up to London by the cheap day train. Colonel Bantry was in the same carriage. He looked, I thought, very abstracted. And nearly the whole way he buried himself

61

behind *The Times*. As though, you know, he didn't want to *talk*.'

The vicar nodded with complete comprehension and possible sympathy.

'At Paddington I said good-bye. He had offered to get me a taxi, but I was taking the bus down to Oxford Street – but he got into one, and I distinctly heard him tell the driver to go to – *where do you think?*'

Mr Clement looked inquiring.

'An address in *St John's Wood*!'

Mrs Price Ridley paused triumphantly.

The vicar remained completely unenlightened.

'That, I consider, *proves* it,' said Mrs Price Ridley.

IV

At Gossington, Mrs Bantry and Miss Marple were sitting in the drawing-room.

'You know,' said Mrs Bantry, 'I can't help feeling glad they've taken the body away. It's not *nice* to have a body in one's house.'

Miss Marple nodded.

'I know, dear. I know just how you feel.'

'You can't,' said Mrs Bantry; 'not until you've had one. I know you had one next door once, but that's not the same thing. I only hope,' she went on, 'that

Arthur won't take a dislike to the library. We sit there so much. What are you doing, Jane?'

For Miss Marple, with a glance at her watch, was rising to her feet.

'Well, I was thinking I'd go home. If there's nothing more I can do for you?'

'Don't go yet,' said Mrs Bantry. 'The finger-print men and the photographers and most of the police have gone, I know, but I still feel something might happen. You don't want to miss anything.'

The telephone rang and she went off to answer. She returned with a beaming face.

'I told you more things would happen. That was Colonel Melchett. He's bringing the poor girl's cousin along.'

'I wonder why,' said Miss Marple.

'Oh, I suppose, to see where it happened and all that.'

'More than that, I expect,' said Miss Marple.

'What do you mean, Jane?'

'Well, I think – perhaps – he might want her to meet Colonel Bantry.'

Mrs Bantry said sharply:

'To see if she recognizes him? I suppose – oh, yes, I suppose they're bound to suspect Arthur.'

'I'm afraid so.'

'As though Arthur could have anything to do with it!'

Miss Marple was silent. Mrs Bantry turned on her accusingly.

'And don't quote old General Henderson – or some frightful old man who kept his housemaid – at me. Arthur isn't like that.'

'No, no, of course not.'

'No, but he *really* isn't. He's just – sometimes – a little silly about pretty girls who come to tennis. You know – rather fatuous and avuncular. There's no harm in it. And why shouldn't he? After all,' finished Mrs Bantry rather obscurely, 'I've got the garden.'

Miss Marple smiled.

'You must not worry, Dolly,' she said.

'No, I don't mean to. But all the same I do a little. So does Arthur. It's upset him. All these policemen prowling about. He's gone down to the farm. Looking at pigs and things always soothes him if he's been upset. Hallo, here they are.'

The Chief Constable's car drew up outside.

Colonel Melchett came in accompanied by a smartly dressed young woman.

'This is Miss Turner, Mrs Bantry. The cousin of the – er – victim.'

'How do you do,' said Mrs Bantry, advancing with outstretched hand. 'All this must be rather awful for you.'

Josephine Turner said frankly: 'Oh, it is. None of it seems *real*, somehow. It's like a bad dream.'

Mrs Bantry introduced Miss Marple.

Melchett said casually: 'Your good man about?'

'He had to go down to one of the farms. He'll be back soon.'

'Oh –' Melchett seemed rather at a loss.

Mrs Bantry said to Josie: 'Would you like to see where – where it happened? Or would you rather not?'

Josephine said after a moment's pause:

'I think I'd like to see.'

Mrs Bantry led her to her library with Miss Marple and Melchett following behind.

'She was there,' said Mrs Bantry, pointing dramatically; 'on the hearthrug.'

'Oh!' Josie shuddered. But she also looked perplexed. She said, her brow creased: 'I just *can't* understand it! I *can't*!'

'Well, *we* certainly can't,' said Mrs Bantry.

Josie said slowly:

'It isn't the sort of place—' and broke off.

Miss Marple nodded her head gently in agreement with the unfinished sentiment.

'That,' she murmured, 'is what makes it so very interesting.'

'Come now, Miss Marple,' said Colonel Melchett

good-humouredly, 'haven't you got an explanation?'

'Oh yes, I've got an *explanation*,' said Miss Marple. 'Quite a feasible one. But of course it's only my own *idea*. Tommy Bond,' she continued, 'and Mrs Martin, our new schoolmistress. She went to wind up the clock and a frog jumped out.'

Josephine Turner looked puzzled. As they all went out of the room she murmured to Mrs Bantry: 'Is the old lady a bit funny in the head?'

'Not at all,' said Mrs Bantry indignantly.

Josie said: 'Sorry; I thought perhaps she thought she *was* a frog or something.'

Colonel Bantry was just coming in through the side door. Melchett hailed him, and watched Josephine Turner as he introduced them to each other. But there was no sign of interest or recognition in her face. Melchett breathed a sigh of relief. Curse Slack and his insinuations!

In answer to Mrs Bantry's questions Josie was pouring out the story of Ruby Keene's disappearance.

'Frightfully worrying for you, my dear,' said Mrs Bantry.

'I was more angry than worried,' said Josie. 'You see, I didn't know then that anything had happened to her.'

'And yet,' said Miss Marple, 'you went to the police. Wasn't that – excuse me – rather *premature*?'

Josie said eagerly:

'Oh, but I didn't. That was Mr Jefferson –'

Mrs Bantry said: 'Jefferson?'

'Yes, he's an invalid.'

'Not *Conway* Jefferson? But I know him well. He's an old friend of ours. Arthur, listen – Conway Jefferson. He's staying at the Majestic, and it was he who went to the police! Isn't that a coincidence?'

Josephine Turner said:

'Mr Jefferson was here last summer too.'

'Fancy! And we never knew. I haven't seen him for a long time.' She turned to Josie. 'How – how is he, nowadays?'

Josie considered.

'I think he's wonderful, really – quite wonderful. Considering, I mean. He's always cheerful – always got a joke.'

'Are the family there with him?'

'Mr Gaskell, you mean? And young Mrs Jefferson? And Peter? Oh, yes.'

There was something inhibiting Josephine Turner's usual attractive frankness of manner. When she spoke of the Jeffersons there was something not quite natural in her voice.

Mrs Bantry said: 'They're both very nice, aren't they? The young ones, I mean.'

Josie said rather uncertainly:

67

Agatha Christie

'Oh yes – yes, they are. I – we – yes, they are, *really.*'

V

'And what,' demanded Mrs Bantry as she looked through the window at the retreating car of the Chief Constable, 'did she mean by that? "They are, *really.*" Don't you think, Jane, that there's something –'

Miss Marple fell upon the words eagerly.

'Oh, I do – indeed I do. It's quite *unmistakable!* Her manner changed *at once* when the Jeffersons were mentioned. She had seemed quite natural up to then.'

'But what do you think it *is*, Jane?'

'Well, my dear, *you* know them. All I feel is that there is *something*, as you say, about them which is worrying that young woman. Another thing, did you notice that when you asked her if she wasn't anxious about the girl being missing, she said that she was *angry*! And she *looked* angry – *really* angry! That strikes me as *interesting*, you know. I have a feeling – perhaps I'm wrong – that that's her main reaction to the fact of the girl's death. She didn't care for her, I'm sure. She's not grieving in any way. But I do think, very definitely, that the thought of that girl,

Ruby Keene, makes her *angry*. And the interesting point is – *why?*'

'We'll find out!' said Mrs Bantry. 'We'll go over to Danemouth and stay at the Majestic – yes, Jane, you too. I need a change for my nerves after what has happened here. A few days at the Majestic – that's what we need. And you'll meet Conway Jefferson. He's a dear – a perfect dear. It's the saddest story imaginable. Had a son and daughter, both of whom he loved dearly. They were both married, but they still spent a lot of time at home. His wife, too, was the sweetest woman, and he was devoted to her. They were flying home one year from France and there was an accident. They were all killed: the pilot, Mrs Jefferson, Rosamund, and Frank. Conway had both legs so badly injured they had to be amputated. And he's been wonderful – his courage, his pluck! He was a very active man and now he's a helpless cripple, but he never complains. His daughter-in-law lives with him – she was a widow when Frank Jefferson married her and she had a son by her first marriage – Peter Carmody. They both live with Conway. And Mark Gaskell, Rosamund's husband, is there too most of the time. The whole thing was the most awful tragedy.'

'And now,' said Miss Marple, 'there's another tragedy –'

Mrs Bantry said: 'Oh yes – yes – but it's nothing to do with the Jeffersons.'

'Isn't it?' said Miss Marple. 'It was Mr Jefferson who went to the police.'

'So he did . . . You know, Jane, that *is* curious . . .'

Chapter 5

Colonel Melchett was facing a much annoyed hotel manager. With him was Superintendent Harper of the Glenshire Police and the inevitable Inspector Slack – the latter rather disgruntled at the Chief Constable's wilful usurpation of the case.

Superintendent Harper was inclined to be soothing with the almost tearful Mr Prestcott – Colonel Melchett tended towards a blunt brutality.

'No good crying over spilt milk,' he said sharply. 'The girl's dead – strangled. You're lucky that she wasn't strangled in your hotel. This puts the inquiry in a different county and lets your establishment down extremely lightly. But certain inquiries have got to be made, and the sooner we get on with it the better. You can trust us to be discreet and tactful. So I suggest you cut the cackle and come to the horses. Just what exactly do you know about the girl?'

'I knew nothing of her – nothing at all. Josie brought her here.'

'Josie's been here some time?'

'Two years – no, three.'

'And you like her?'

'Yes, Josie's a good girl – a nice girl. Competent. She gets on with people, and smoothes over differences – bridge, you know, is a touchy sort of game –' Colonel Melchett nodded feelingly. His wife was a keen but an extremely bad bridge player. Mr Prestcott went on: 'Josie was very good at calming down unpleasantnesses. She could handle people well – sort of bright and firm, if you know what I mean.'

Again Melchett nodded. He knew now what it was Miss Josephine Turner had reminded him of. In spite of the make-up and the smart turnout there was a distinct touch of the nursery governess about her.

'I depend upon her,' went on Mr Prestcott. His manner became aggrieved. 'What does she want to go playing about on slippery rocks in that damn' fool way? We've got a nice beach here. Why couldn't she bathe from that? Slipping and falling and breaking her ankle. It wasn't fair on *me*! I pay her to dance and play bridge and keep people happy and amused – not to go bathing off rocks and breaking her ankle. Dancers ought to be careful of their ankles – not take risks. I was very annoyed about it. It wasn't fair to the hotel.'

Melchett cut the recital short.

'And then she suggested this girl – her cousin – coming down?'

Prestcott assented grudgingly.

'That's right. It sounded quite a good idea. Mind you, I wasn't going to pay anything extra. The girl could have her keep; but as for salary, that would have to be fixed up between her and Josie. That's the way it was arranged. *I* didn't know anything about the girl.'

'But she turned out all right?'

'Oh yes, there wasn't anything wrong with her – not to look at, anyway. She was very young, of course – rather cheap in style, perhaps, for a place of this kind, but nice manners – quiet and well-behaved. Danced well. People liked her.'

'Pretty?'

It had been a question hard to answer from a view of the blue swollen face.

Mr Prestcott considered.

'Fair to middling. Bit weaselly, if you know what I mean. Wouldn't have been much without make-up. As it was she managed to look quite attractive.'

'Many young men hanging about after her?'

'I know what you're trying to get at, sir.' Mr Prestcott became excited. '*I* never saw anything. Nothing special. One or two of the boys hung around a bit – but all in the day's work, so to speak. Nothing in the strangling

line, I'd say. She got on well with the older people, too
– had a kind of prattling way with her – seemed quite
a kid, if you know what I mean. It amused them.'

Superintendent Harper said in a deep melancholy
voice:

'Mr Jefferson, for instance?'

The manager agreed.

'Yes, Mr Jefferson was the one I had in mind. She
used to sit with him and his family a lot. He used to take
her out for drives sometimes. Mr Jefferson's very fond
of young people and very good to them. I don't want to
have any misunderstanding. Mr Jefferson's a cripple;
he can't get about much – only where his wheel-chair
will take him. But he's always keen on seeing young
people enjoy themselves – watches the tennis and the
bathing and all that – and gives parties for young people
here. He likes youth – and there's nothing bitter about
him as there well might be. A very popular gentleman
and, I'd say, a very fine character.'

Melchett asked:

'And he took an interest in Ruby Keene?'

'Her talk amused him, I think.'

'Did his family share his liking for her?'

'They were always very pleasant to her.'

Harper said:

'And it was he who reported the fact of her being
missing to the police?'

He contrived to put into the word a significance and a reproach to which the manager instantly responded.

'Put yourself in my place, Mr Harper. *I* didn't dream for a minute anything was wrong. Mr Jefferson came along to my office, storming, and all worked up. The girl hadn't slept in her room. She hadn't appeared in her dance last night. She must have gone for a drive and had an accident, perhaps. The police must be informed at once! Inquiries made! In a state, he was, and quite high-handed. He rang up the police station then and there.'

'Without consulting Miss Turner?'

'Josie didn't like it much. I could see that. She was very annoyed about the whole thing – annoyed with Ruby, I mean. But what could she say?'

'I think,' said Melchett, 'we'd better see Mr Jefferson. Eh, Harper?'

Superintendent Harper agreed.

II

Mr Prestcott went up with them to Conway Jefferson's suite. It was on the first floor, overlooking the sea. Melchett said carelessly:

'Does himself pretty well, eh? Rich man?'

'Very well off indeed, I believe. Nothing's ever

stinted when he comes here. Best rooms reserved – food usually *à la carte*, expensive wines – best of everything.'

Melchett nodded.

Mr Prestcott tapped on the outer door and a woman's voice said: 'Come in.'

The manager entered, the others behind him.

Mr Prestcott's manner was apologetic as he spoke to the woman who turned her head at their entrance from her seat by the window.

'I am so sorry to disturb you, Mrs Jefferson, but these gentlemen are – from the police. They are very anxious to have a word with Mr Jefferson. Er – Colonel Melchett – Superintendent Harper, Inspector – er – Slack – Mrs Jefferson.'

Mrs Jefferson acknowledged the introduction by bending her head.

A plain woman, was Melchett's first impression. Then, as a slight smile came to her lips and she spoke, he changed his opinion. She had a singularly charming and sympathetic voice and her eyes, clear hazel eyes, were beautiful. She was quietly but not unbecomingly dressed and was, he judged, about thirty-five years of age.

She said:

'My father-in-law is asleep. He is not strong at all, and this affair has been a terrible shock to him. We had to have the doctor, and the doctor gave him a sedative. As soon as he wakes he will, I know, want to see you. In the meantime, perhaps I can help you? Won't you sit down?'

Mr Prestcott, anxious to escape, said to Colonel Melchett: 'Well – er – if that's all I can do for you?' and thankfully received permission to depart.

With his closing of the door behind him, the atmosphere took on a mellow and more social quality. Adelaide Jefferson had the power of creating a restful atmosphere. She was a woman who never seemed to say anything remarkable but who succeeded in stimulating other people to talk and setting them at their ease. She struck now the right note when she said:

'This business has shocked us all very much. We saw quite a lot of the poor girl, you know. It seems quite unbelievable. My father-in-law is terribly upset. He was very fond of Ruby.'

Colonel Melchett said:

'It was Mr Jefferson, I understand, who reported her disappearance to the police?'

He wanted to see exactly how she would react to that. There was a flicker – just a flicker – of – annoyance? concern? – he could not say what exactly, but there was *something*, and it seemed to him she had definitely to brace herself, as though to an unpleasant task, before going on.

She said:

'Yes, that is so. Being an invalid, he gets easily upset and worried. We tried to persuade him that it was all right, that there was some natural explanation, and that the girl herself would not like the police being notified. He insisted. Well' – she made a slight gesture – 'he was right and we were wrong.'

Melchett asked: 'Exactly how well did you know Ruby Keene, Mrs Jefferson?'

She considered.

'It's difficult to say. My father-in-law is very fond of young people and likes to have them round him. Ruby was a new type to him – he was amused and interested by her chatter. She sat with us a good deal in the hotel and my father-in-law took her out for drives in the car.'

Her voice was quite non-committal. Melchett thought to himself: 'She could say more if she chose.'

He said: 'Will you tell me what you can of the course of events last night?'

'Certainly, but there is very little that will be useful, I'm afraid. After dinner Ruby came and sat with us in the lounge. She remained even after the dancing had started. We had arranged to play bridge later, but we were waiting for Mark, that is Mark Gaskell, my brother-in-law – he married Mr Jefferson's daughter, you know – who had some important letters to write, and also for Josie. She was going to make a fourth with us.'

'Did that often happen?'

'Quite frequently. She's a first-class player, of course, and very nice. My father-in-law is a keen bridge player and whenever possible liked to get hold of Josie to make the fourth instead of an outsider. Naturally, as she has to arrange the fours, she can't always play with us, but she does whenever she can, and as' – her eyes smiled a little – 'my father-in-law spends a lot of money in the hotel, the management are quite pleased for Josie to favour us.'

Melchett asked:

'You like Josie?'

'Yes, I do. She's always good-humoured and cheerful, works hard and seems to enjoy her job. She's shrewd, though not well educated, and – well – never pretends about anything. She's natural and unaffected.'

'Please go on, Mrs Jefferson.'

'As I say, Josie had to get her bridge fours arranged and Mark was writing, so Ruby sat and talked with us a little longer than usual. Then Josie came along, and Ruby went off to do her first solo dance with Raymond – he's the dance and tennis professional. She came back to us afterwards just as Mark joined us. Then she went off to dance with a young man and we four started our bridge.'

She stopped, and made a slight insignificant gesture of helplessness.

'And that's all I know! I just caught a glimpse of her once dancing, but bridge is an absorbing game and I hardly glanced through the glass partition at the ballroom. Then, at midnight, Raymond came along to Josie very upset and asked where Ruby was. Josie, naturally, tried to shut him up but –'

Superintendent Harper interrupted. He said in his quiet voice: 'Why "*naturally*," Mrs Jefferson?'

'Well' – she hesitated, looked, Melchett thought, a little put out – 'Josie didn't want the girl's absence made too much of. She considered herself responsible for her in a way. She said Ruby was probably up in her bedroom, said the girl had talked about having a headache earlier – I don't think that was true, by the way; Josie just said it by way of excuse. Raymond went off and telephoned up to Ruby's room, but apparently there was no answer, and he came back in rather a state – temperamental, you know. Josie went off with him and tried to soothe him down, and in the end she danced with him instead of Ruby. Rather plucky of her, because you could see afterwards it had hurt her ankle. She came back to us when the dance was over and tried to calm down Mr Jefferson. He had got worked up by then. We persuaded him in the end to go to bed, told him Ruby had probably gone for a spin in a car and that they'd had a puncture. He went to bed worried, and this morning he began to agitate at once.' She paused. 'The rest you know.'

'Thank you, Mrs Jefferson. Now I'm going to ask you if you've any idea who could have done this thing.'

She said immediately: 'No idea whatever. I'm afraid I can't help you in the slightest.'

He pressed her. 'The girl never said anything? Nothing about jealousy? About some man she was afraid of? Or intimate with?'

Adelaide Jefferson shook her head to each query.

There seemed nothing more that she could tell them.

The Superintendent suggested that they should interview young George Bartlett and return to see Mr Jefferson later. Colonel Melchett agreed, and the three men went out, Mrs Jefferson promising to send word as soon as Mr Jefferson was awake.

'Nice woman,' said the Colonel, as they closed the door behind them.

'A very nice lady indeed,' said Superintendent Harper.

III

George Bartlett was a thin, lanky youth with a prominent Adam's apple and an immense difficulty in saying what he meant. He was in such a state of dither that it was hard to get a calm statement from him.

'I say, it is awful, isn't it? Sort of thing one reads about in the Sunday papers – but one doesn't feel it really happens, don't you know?'

'Unfortunately there is no doubt about it, Mr Bartlett,' said the Superintendent.

'No, no, of course not. But it seems so rum somehow. And miles from here and everything – in some country house, wasn't it? Awfully county and all that. Created a bit of a stir in the neighbourhood – what?'

Colonel Melchett took charge.

'How well did you know the dead girl, Mr Bartlett?'

George Bartlett looked alarmed.

'Oh, n-n-n-ot well at all, s-s-sir. No, hardly at all – if you know what I mean. Danced with her once or twice – passed the time of day – bit of tennis – *you* know.'

'You were, I think, the last person to see her alive last night?'

'I suppose I was – doesn't it sound awful? I mean, she was perfectly all right when I saw her – absolutely.'

'What time was that, Mr Bartlett?'

'Well, you know, I never know about time – wasn't very late, if you know what I mean.'

'You danced with her?'

'Yes – as a matter of fact – well, yes, I did. Early on in the evening, though. Tell you what, it was just after her exhibition dance with the pro. fellow. Must have been ten, half-past, eleven, I don't know.'

'Never mind the time. We can fix that. Please tell us exactly what happened.'

'Well, we danced, don't you know. Not that *I'm* much of a dancer.'

'How you dance is not really relevant, Mr Bartlett.'

George Bartlett cast an alarmed eye on the Colonel and stammered:

'No – er – n-n-n-o, I suppose it isn't. Well, as I say, we danced, round and round, and I talked, but Ruby didn't say very much and she yawned a bit. As I say, I don't dance awfully well, and so girls – well – inclined to give it a miss, if you know what I mean. She said she had a headache – I know where I get off, so I said righty ho, and that was that.'

'What was the last you saw of her?'

'She went off upstairs.'

'She said nothing about meeting anyone? Or going for a drive? Or – or – having a date?' The Colonel used the colloquial expression with a slight effort.

Bartlett shook his head.

'Not to me.' He looked rather mournful. 'Just gave me the push.'

'What was her manner? Did she seem anxious, abstracted, anything on her mind?'

George Bartlett considered. Then he shook his head.

'Seemed a bit bored. Yawned, as I said. Nothing more.'

Colonel Melchett said:

'And what did you do, Mr Bartlett?'

'Eh?'

'What did you do when Ruby Keene left you?'

George Bartlett gaped at him.

'Let's see now – what *did* I do?'

'We're waiting for you to tell us.'

'Yes, yes – of course. Jolly difficult, remembering things, what? Let me see. Shouldn't be surprised if I went into the bar and had a drink.'

'*Did* you go into the bar and have a drink?'

'That's just it. I *did* have a drink. Don't think it was just then. Have an idea I wandered out, don't you know? Bit of air. Rather stuffy for September. Very nice outside. Yes, that's it. I strolled around a bit, then I came in and had a drink and then I strolled back to the ballroom. Wasn't much doing. Noticed what's-her-name – Josie – was dancing again. With the tennis fellow. She'd been on the sick list – twisted ankle or something.'

'That fixes the time of your return at midnight. Do you intend us to understand that you spent over an hour walking about outside?'

'Well, I had a drink, you know. I was – well, I was thinking of things.'

This statement received more credulity than any other.

Colonel Melchett said sharply:

'What were you thinking about?'

'Oh, I don't know. Things,' said Mr Bartlett vaguely.

'You have a car, Mr Bartlett?'

'Oh, yes, I've got a car.'

'Where was it, in the hotel garage?'

'No, it was in the courtyard, as a matter of fact. Thought I might go for a spin, you see.'

'Perhaps you did go for a spin?'

'No – no, I didn't. Swear I didn't.'

'You didn't, for instance, take Miss Keene for a spin?'

'Oh, I say. Look here, what are you getting at? I didn't – I swear I didn't. Really, now.'

'Thank you, Mr Bartlett, I don't think there is anything more at present. *At present*,' repeated Colonel Melchett with a good deal of emphasis on the words.

They left Mr Bartlett looking after them with a ludicrous expression of alarm on his unintellectual face.

'Brainless young ass,' said Colonel Melchett. 'Or isn't he?'

Superintendent Harper shook his head.

'We've got a long way to go,' he said.

Chapter 6

Neither the night porter nor the barman proved help-ful. The night porter remembered ringing up to Miss Keene's room just after midnight and getting no reply. He had not noticed Mr Bartlett leaving or entering the hotel. A lot of gentlemen and ladies were strolling in and out, the night being fine. And there were side doors off the corridor as well as the one in the main hall. He was fairly certain Miss Keene had not gone out by the main door, but if she had come down from her room, which was on the first floor, there was a staircase next to it and a door out at the end of the corridor, leading on to the side terrace. She could have gone out of that unseen easily enough. It was not locked until the dancing was over at two o'clock.

The barman remembered Mr Bartlett being in the bar the preceding evening but could not say when. Somewhere about the middle of the evening, he thought.

Agatha Christie

Mr Bartlett had sat against the wall and was looking rather melancholy. He did not know how long he was there. There were a lot of outside guests coming and going in the bar. He had noticed Mr Bartlett but he couldn't fix the time in any way.

II

As they left the bar, they were accosted by a small boy of about nine years old. He burst immediately into excited speech.

'I say, are you the detectives? I'm Peter Carmody. It was my grandfather, Mr Jefferson, who rang up the police about Ruby. Are you from Scotland Yard? You don't mind my speaking to you, do you?'

Colonel Melchett looked as though he were about to return a short answer, but Superintendent Harper intervened. He spoke benignly and heartily.

'That's all right, my son. Naturally interests you, I expect?'

'You bet it does. Do you like detective stories? I do. I read them all, and I've got autographs from Dorothy Sayers and Agatha Christie and Dickson Carr and H. C. Bailey. Will the murder be in the papers?'

'It'll be in the papers all right,' said Superintendent Harper grimly.

'You see, I'm going back to school next week and I shall tell them all that I knew her – really knew her *well*.'

'What did you think of her, eh?'

Peter considered.

'Well, I didn't like her much. I think she was rather a stupid sort of girl. Mum and Uncle Mark didn't like her much either. Only Grandfather. Grandfather wants to see you, by the way. Edwards is looking for you.'

Superintendent Harper murmured encouragingly:

'So your mother and your Uncle Mark didn't like Ruby Keene much? Why was that?'

'Oh, I don't know. She was always butting in. And they didn't like Grandfather making such a fuss of her. I expect,' said Peter cheerfully, 'that they're glad she's dead.'

Superintendent Harper looked at him thoughtfully. He said: 'Did you hear them – er – say so?'

'Well, not exactly. Uncle Mark said: 'Well, it's one way out, anyway,' and Mums said: 'Yes, but such a horrible one,' and Uncle Mark said it was no good being hypocritical.'

The men exchanged glances. At that moment a respectable, clean-shaven man, neatly dressed in blue serge, came up to them.

'Excuse me, gentlemen. I am Mr Jefferson's valet.

He is awake now and sent me to find you, as he is very anxious to see you.'

Once more they went up to Conway Jefferson's suite. In the sitting-room Adelaide Jefferson was talking to a tall, restless man who was prowling nervously about the room. He swung round sharply to view the new-comers.

'Oh, yes. Glad you've come. My father-in-law's been asking for you. He's awake now. Keep him as calm as you can, won't you? His health's not too good. It's a wonder, really, that this shock didn't do for him.'

Harper said:

'I'd no idea his health was as bad as that.'

'He doesn't know it himself,' said Mark Gaskell. 'It's his heart, you see. The doctor warned Addie that he mustn't be over-excited or startled. He more or less hinted that the end might come any time, didn't he, Addie?'

Mrs Jefferson nodded. She said:

'It's incredible that he's rallied the way he has.'

Melchett said dryly:

'Murder isn't exactly a soothing incident. We'll be as careful as we can.'

He was sizing up Mark Gaskell as he spoke. He didn't much care for the fellow. A bold, unscrupulous, hawk-like face. One of those men who usually get their own way and whom women frequently admire.

'But not the sort of fellow I'd trust,' the Colonel thought to himself.

Unscrupulous – that was the word for him.

The sort of fellow who wouldn't stick at anything . . .

III

In the big bedroom overlooking the sea, Conway Jefferson was sitting in his wheeled chair by the window.

No sooner were you in the room with him than you felt the power and magnetism of the man. It was as though the injuries which had left him a cripple had resulted in concentrating the vitality of his shattered body into a narrower and more intense focus.

He had a fine head, the red of the hair slightly grizzled. The face was rugged and powerful, deeply sun-tanned, and the eyes were a startling blue. There was no sign of illness or feebleness about him. The deep lines on his face were the lines of suffering, not the lines of weakness. Here was a man who would never rail against fate but accept it and pass on to victory.

He said: 'I'm glad you've come.' His quick eyes took them in. He said to Melchett: 'You're the Chief Constable of Radfordshire? Right. And you're

Superintendent Harper? Sit down. Cigarettes on the table beside you.'

They thanked him and sat down. Melchett said:

'I understand, Mr Jefferson, that you were interested in the dead girl?'

A quick, twisted smile flashed across the lined face.

'Yes – they'll all have told you that! Well, it's no secret. How much has my family said to you?'

He looked quickly from one to the other as he asked the question.

It was Melchett who answered.

'Mrs Jefferson told us very little beyond the fact that the girl's chatter amused you and that she was by way of being a protégée. We have only exchanged half a dozen words with Mr Gaskell.'

Conway Jefferson smiled.

'Addie's a discreet creature, bless her. Mark would probably have been more outspoken. I think, Melchett, that I'd better tell you some facts rather fully. It's important, in order that you should understand my attitude. And, to begin with, it's necessary that I go back to the big tragedy of my life. Eight years ago I lost my wife, my son, and my daughter in an aeroplane accident. Since then I've been like a man who's lost half himself – and I'm not speaking of my physical plight! I was a family man. My daughter-in-law and my son-in-law have been very good to me. They've done all they can to take the place of my flesh and blood. But I've realized – especially of late, that they have, after all, their own lives to live.

'So you must understand that, essentially, I'm a lonely man. I like young people. I enjoy them. Once or twice I've played with the idea of adopting some girl or boy. During this last month I got very friendly with the child who's been killed. She was absolutely natural – completely naïve. She chattered on about her life and her experiences – in pantomime, with touring companies, with Mum and Dad as a child in cheap lodgings. Such a different life from any I've known! Never complaining, never seeing it as sordid. Just a natural, uncomplaining, hard-working child, unspoilt and charming. Not a lady, perhaps, but, thank God, neither vulgar nor – abominable word – "lady-like".

'I got more and more fond of Ruby. I decided, gentlemen, to adopt her legally. She would become – by law – my daughter. That, I hope, explains my concern for her and the steps I took when I heard of her unaccountable disappearance.'

There was a pause. Then Superintendent Harper, his unemotional voice robbing the question of any offence, asked: 'May I ask what your son-in-law and daughter-in-law said to that?'

Jefferson's answer came back quickly:

'What could they say? They didn't, perhaps, like it

very much. It's the sort of thing that arouses prejudice. But they behaved very well – yes, very well. It's not as though, you see, they were dependent on me. When my son Frank married I turned over half my worldly goods to him then and there. I believe in that. Don't let your children wait until you're dead. They want the money when they're young, not when they're middle-aged. In the same way when my daughter Rosamund insisted on marrying a poor man, I settled a big sum of money on her. That sum passed to him at her death. So, you see, that simplified the matter from the financial angle.'

'I see, Mr Jefferson,' said Superintendent Harper.

But there was a certain reserve in his tone. Conway Jefferson pounced upon it.

'But you don't agree, eh?'

'It's not for me to say, sir, but families, in my experience, don't always act reasonably.'

'I dare say you're right, Superintendent, but you must remember that Mr Gaskell and Mrs Jefferson aren't, strictly speaking, my *family*. They're not blood relations.'

'That, of course, makes a difference,' admitted the Superintendent.

For a moment Conway Jefferson's eyes twinkled. He said: 'That's not to say that they didn't think me an old fool! That *would* be the average person's reaction. But I wasn't being a fool. I know character. With education and polishing, Ruby Keene could have taken her place anywhere.'

Melchett said:

'I'm afraid we're being rather impertinent and inquisitive, but it's important that we should get at all the facts. You proposed to make full provision for the girl – that is, settle money upon her, but you hadn't already done so?'

Jefferson said:

'I understand what you're driving at – the possibility of someone's benefiting by the girl's death? But nobody could. The necessary formalities for legal adoption were under way, but they hadn't yet been completed.'

Melchett said slowly:

'Then, if anything happened to you –?'

He left the sentence unfinished, as a query. Conway Jefferson was quick to respond.

'Nothing's likely to happen to me! I'm a cripple, but I'm not an invalid. Although doctors *do* like to pull long faces and give advice about not overdoing things. Not overdoing things! I'm as strong as a horse! Still, I'm quite aware of the fatalities of life – my God, I've good reason to be! Sudden death comes to the strongest man – especially in these days of road casualties. But I'd provided for that. I made a new will about ten days ago.'

'Yes?' Superintendent Harper leaned forward.

'I left the sum of fifty thousand pounds to be held in trust for Ruby Keene until she was twenty-five, when she would come into the principal.'

Superintendent Harper's eyes opened. So did Colonel Melchett's. Harper said in an almost awed voice:

'That's a very large sum of money, Mr Jefferson.'

'In these days, yes, it is.'

'And you were leaving it to a girl you had only known a few weeks?'

Anger flashed into the vivid blue eyes.

'Must I go on repeating the same thing over and over again? I've no flesh and blood of my own – no nieces or nephews or distant cousins, even! I might have left it to charity. I prefer to leave it to an individual.' He laughed. 'Cinderella turned into a princess overnight! A fairy-godfather instead of a fairy-godmother. Why not? It's *my* money. *I* made it.'

Colonel Melchett asked: 'Any other bequests?'

'A small legacy to Edwards, my valet – and the remainder to Mark and Addie in equal shares.'

'Would – excuse me – the residue amount to a large sum?'

'Probably not. It's difficult to say exactly, investments fluctuate all the time. The sum involved, after death duties and expenses had been paid, would probably have come to something between five and ten thousand pounds net.'

'I see.'

'And you needn't think I was treating them shabbily. As I said, I divided up my estate at the time my children married. I left myself, actually, a very small sum. But after – after the tragedy – I wanted something to occupy my mind. I flung myself into business. At my house in London I had a private line put in connecting my bedroom with my office. I worked hard – it helped me not to think, and it made me feel that my – my mutilation had not vanquished me. I threw myself into work' – his voice took on a deeper note, he spoke more to himself than to his audience – 'and, by some subtle irony, everything I did prospered! My wildest speculations succeeded. If I gambled, I won. Everything I touched turned to gold. Fate's ironic way of righting the balance, I suppose.'

The lines of suffering stood out on his face again.

Recollecting himself, he smiled wryly at them.

'So you see, the sum of money I left Ruby was indisputably mine to do with as my fancy dictated.'

Melchett said quickly:

'Undoubtedly, my dear fellow, we are not questioning that for a moment.'

Conway Jefferson said: 'Good. Now I want to ask some questions in my turn, if I may. I want to hear – more about this terrible business. All I know is that she

– that little Ruby was found strangled in a house some twenty miles from here.'

'That is correct. At Gossington Hall.'

Jefferson frowned.

'Gossington? But that's –'

'Colonel Bantry's house.'

'Bantry! *Arthur Bantry*? But I know him. Know him and his wife! Met them abroad some years ago. I didn't realize they lived in this part of the world. Why, it's –'

He broke off. Superintendent Harper slipped in smoothly:

'Colonel Bantry was dining in the hotel here Tuesday of last week. You didn't see him?'

'Tuesday? Tuesday? No, we were back late. Went over to Harden Head and had dinner on the way back.'

Melchett said:

'Ruby Keene never mentioned the Bantrys to you?'

Jefferson shook his head.

'Never. Don't believe she knew them. Sure she didn't. She didn't know anybody but theatrical folk and that sort of thing.' He paused and then asked abruptly:

'What's Bantry got to say about it?'

'He can't account for it in the least. He was out at a Conservative meeting last night. The body was discovered this morning. He says he's never seen the girl in his life.'

Jefferson nodded. He said:

'It certainly seems fantastic.'

Superintendent Harper cleared his throat. He said:

'Have you any idea at all, sir, who can have done this?'

'Good God, I wish I had!' The veins stood out on his forehead. 'It's incredible, unimaginable! I'd say it couldn't have happened, if it hadn't happened!'

'There's no friend of hers – from her past life – no man hanging about – or threatening her?'

'I'm sure there isn't. She'd have told me if so. She's never had a regular "boyfriend." She told me so herself.'

Superintendent Harper thought:

'Yes, I dare say that's what *she* told you! But that's as may be!'

Conway Jefferson went on:

'Josie would know better than anyone if there had been some man hanging about Ruby or pestering her. Can't she help?'

'She says not.'

Jefferson said, frowning:

'I can't help feeling it must be the work of some maniac – the brutality of the method – breaking into a country house – the whole thing so unconnected and senseless. There are men of that type, men outwardly sane, but who decoy girls – sometimes children – away and kill them. Sexual crimes really, I suppose.'

Harper said:

'Oh, yes, there are such cases, but we've no knowledge of anyone of that kind operating in this neighbourhood.'

Jefferson went on:

'I've thought over all the various men I've seen with Ruby. Guests here and outsiders – men she'd danced with. They all seem harmless enough – the usual type. She had no special friend of any kind.'

Superintendent Harper's face remained quite impassive, but unseen by Conway Jefferson there was still a speculative glint in his eye.

It was quite possible, he thought, that Ruby Keene might have had a special friend even though Conway Jefferson did not know about it.

He said nothing, however. The Chief Constable gave him a glance of inquiry and then rose to his feet. He said:

'Thank you, Mr Jefferson. That's all we need for the present.'

Jefferson said:

'You'll keep me informed of your progress?'

'Yes, yes, we'll keep in touch with you.'

The two men went out.

Conway Jefferson leaned back in his chair.

His eyelids came down and veiled the fierce blue of his eyes. He looked suddenly a very tired man.

Then, after a minute or two, the lids flickered. He called: 'Edwards!'

From the next room the valet appeared promptly. Edwards knew his master as no one else did. Others, even his nearest, knew only his strength. Edwards knew his weakness. He had seen Conway Jefferson tired, discouraged, weary of life, momentarily defeated by infirmity and loneliness.

'Yes, sir?'

Jefferson said:

'Get on to Sir Henry Clithering. He's at Melborne Abbas. Ask him, from me, to get here today if he can, instead of tomorrow. Tell him it's urgent.'

Chapter 7

When they were outside Jefferson's door, Superintendent Harper said:

'Well, for what it's worth, we've got a motive, sir.'

'H'm,' said Melchett. 'Fifty thousand pounds, eh?'

'Yes, sir. Murder's been done for a good deal less
than that.'

'Yes, but –'

Colonel Melchett left the sentence unfinished. Harper,
however, understood him.

'You don't think it's likely in this case? Well, I don't
either, as far as that goes. But it's got to be gone into
all the same.'

'Oh, of course.'

Harper went on:

'If, as Mr Jefferson says, Mr Gaskell and Mrs
Jefferson are already well provided for and in receipt

of a comfortable income, well, it's not likely they'd set out to do a brutal murder.'

'Quite so. Their financial standing will have to be investigated, of course. Can't say I like the appearance of Gaskell much – looks a sharp, unscrupulous sort of fellow – but that's a long way from making him out a murderer.'

'Oh, yes, sir, as I say, I don't think it's *likely* to be either of them, and from what Josie said I don't see how it would have been humanly possible. They were both playing bridge from twenty minutes to eleven until midnight. No, to my mind there's another possibility much more likely.'

Melchett said: 'Boy friend of Ruby Keene's?'

'That's it, sir. Some disgruntled young fellow – not too strong in the head, perhaps. Someone, I'd say, she knew before she came here. This adoption scheme, if he got wise to it, may just have put the lid on things. He saw himself losing her, saw her being removed to a different sphere of life altogether, and he went mad and blind with rage. He got her to come out and meet him last night, had a row with her over it, lost his head completely and did her in.'

'And how did she come to be in Bantry's library?'

'I think that's feasible. They were out, say, in his car at the time. He came to himself, realized what he'd done, and his first thought was how to get rid of the body. Say they were near the gates of a big house at the time. The idea comes to him that if she's found there the hue and cry will centre round the house and its occupants and will leave him comfortably out of it. She's a little bit of a thing. He could easily carry her. He's got a chisel in the car. He forces a window and plops her down on the hearthrug. Being a strangling case, there's no blood or mess to give him away in the car. See what I mean, sir?'

'Oh, yes, Harper, it's all perfectly possible. But there's still one thing to be done. *Cherchez l'homme.*'

'What? Oh, very good, sir.'

Superintendent Harper tactfully applauded his superior's joke, although, owing to the excellence of Colonel Melchett's French accent he almost missed the sense of the words.

II

'Oh – er – I say – er – c-could I speak to you a minute?' It was George Bartlett who thus waylaid the two men. Colonel Melchett, who was not attracted to Mr Bartlett and who was anxious to see how Slack had got on with the investigation of the girl's room and the questioning of the chambermaids, barked sharply:

'Well, what is it – what is it?'

Young Mr Bartlett retreated a step or two, opening and shutting his mouth and giving an unconscious imitation of a fish in a tank.

'Well – er – probably isn't important, don't you know – thought I ought to tell you. Matter of fact, can't find my car.'

'What do you mean, can't find your car?'

Stammering a good deal, Mr Bartlett explained that what he meant was that he couldn't find his car.

Superintendent Harper said:

'Do you mean it's been stolen?'

George Bartlett turned gratefully to the more placid voice.

'Well, that's just it, you know. I mean, one can't tell, can one? I mean someone may just have buzzed off in it, not meaning any harm, if you know what I mean.'

'When did you last see it, Mr Bartlett?'

'Well, I was tryin' to remember. Funny how difficult it is to remember anything, isn't it?'

Colonel Melchett said coldly:

'Not, I should think, to a normal intelligence. I understood you to say just now that it was in the courtyard of the hotel last night –'

Mr Bartlett was bold enough to interrupt. He said:

'That's just it – was it?'

'What do you mean by "was it"? You said it *was*.'

'Well – I mean I *thought* it was. I mean – well, I didn't go out and look, don't you see?'

Colonel Melchett sighed. He summoned all his patience. He said:

'Let's get this quite clear. When was the last time you saw – actually *saw* your car? What make is it, by the way?'

'Minoan 14.'

'And you last saw it – when?'

George Bartlett's Adam's apple jerked convulsively up and down.

'Been trying to think. Had it before lunch yesterday. Was going for a spin in the afternoon. But somehow, you know how it is, went to sleep instead. Then, after tea, had a game of squash and all that, and a bathe afterwards.'

'And the car was then in the courtyard of the hotel?'

'Suppose so. I mean, that's where I'd put it. Thought, you see, I'd take someone for a spin. After dinner, I mean. But it wasn't my lucky evening. Nothing doing. Never took the old bus out after all.'

Harper said:

'But, as far as you knew, the car was still in the courtyard?'

'Well, naturally. I mean, I'd put it there – what?'

'Would you have noticed if it had *not* been there?'

Mr Bartlett shook his head.

'Don't think so, you know. Lots of cars going and coming and all that. Plenty of Minoans.'

Superintendent Harper nodded. He had just cast a casual glance out of the window. There were at that moment no less than eight Minoan 14s in the courtyard – it was the popular cheap car of the year.

'Aren't you in the habit of putting your car away at night?' asked Colonel Melchett.

'Don't usually bother,' said Mr Bartlett. 'Fine weather and all that, you know. Such a fag putting a car away in a garage.'

Glancing at Colonel Melchett, Superintendent Harper said: 'I'll join you upstairs, sir. I'll just get hold of Sergeant Higgins and he can take down particulars from Mr Bartlett.'

'Right, Harper.'

Mr Bartlett murmured wistfully:

'Thought I ought to let you know, you know. Might be important, what?'

III

Mr Prestcott had supplied his additional dancer with board and lodging. Whatever the board, the lodging was the poorest the hotel possessed.

Josephine Turner and Ruby Keene had occupied

rooms at the extreme end of a mean and dingy little corridor. The rooms were small, faced north on to a portion of the cliff that backed the hotel, and were furnished with the odds and ends of suites that had once, some thirty years ago, represented luxury and magnificence in the best suites. Now, when the hotel had been modernized and the bedrooms supplied with built-in receptacles for clothes, these large Victorian oak and mahogany wardrobes were relegated to those rooms occupied by the hotel's resident staff, or given to guests in the height of the season when all the rest of the hotel was full.

As Melchett saw at once, the position of Ruby Keene's room was ideal for the purpose of leaving the hotel without being observed, and was particularly unfortunate from the point of view of throwing light on the circumstances of that departure.

At the end of the corridor was a small staircase which led down to an equally obscure corridor on the ground floor. Here there was a glass door which led out on to the side terrace of the hotel, an unfrequented terrace with no view. You could go from it to the main terrace in front, or you could go down a winding path and come out in a lane that eventually rejoined the cliff road farther along. Its surface being bad, it was seldom used.

Inspector Slack had been busy harrying chambermaids and examining Ruby's room for clues. He had been lucky enough to find the room exactly as it had been left the night before.

Ruby Keene had not been in the habit of rising early. Her usual procedure, Slack discovered, was to sleep until about ten or half-past and then ring for breakfast. Consequently, since Conway Jefferson had begun his representations to the manager very early, the police had taken charge of things before the chambermaids had touched the room. They had actually not been down that corridor at all. The other rooms there, at this season of the year, were only opened and dusted once a week.

'That's all to the good as far as it goes,' Slack explained gloomily. 'It means that if there *were* anything to find we'd find it, but there isn't anything.'

The Glenshire police had already been over the room for fingerprints, but there were none unaccounted for. Ruby's own, Josie's, and the two chambermaids – one on the morning and one on the evening shift. There were also a couple of prints made by Raymond Starr, but these were accounted for by his story that he had come up with Josie to look for Ruby when she did not appear for the midnight exhibition dance.

There had been a heap of letters and general rubbish in the pigeon-holes of the massive mahogany desk in the corner. Slack had just been carefully sorting through them. But he had found nothing of a suggestive nature. Bills, receipts, theatre programmes, cinema stubs, newspaper cuttings, beauty hints torn from magazines. Of the letters there were some from 'Lil,' apparently a friend from the Palais de Danse, recounting various affairs and gossip, saying they 'missed Rube a lot. Mr Findeison asked after you ever so often! Quite put out, he is! Young Reg has taken up with May now you've gone. Barny asks after you now and then. Things going much as usual. Old Grouser still as mean as ever with us girls. He ticked off Ada for going about with a fellow.'

Slack had carefully noted all the names mentioned. Inquiries would be made – and it was possible some useful information might come to light. To this Colonel Melchett agreed; so did Superintendent Harper, who had joined them. Otherwise the room had little to yield in the way of information.

Across a chair in the middle of the room was the foamy pink dance frock Ruby had worn early in the evening with a pair of pink satin high-heeled shoes kicked off carelessly on the floor. Two sheer silk stockings were rolled into a ball and flung down. One had a ladder in it. Melchett recalled that the dead girl had had bare feet and legs. This, Slack learned, was her custom. She used make-up on her legs instead of stockings and only sometimes wore stockings for dancing, by this means saving expense. The wardrobe door was open and showed a variety of rather flashy evening dresses and a row of shoes below. There was some soiled underwear in the clothes-basket, some nail parings, soiled face-cleaning tissue and bits of cotton wool stained with rouge and nail-polish in the wastepaper basket – in fact, nothing out of the ordinary! The facts seemed plain to read. Ruby Keene had hurried upstairs, changed her clothes and hurried off again – *where*?

Josephine Turner, who might be supposed to know most of Ruby's life and friends, had proved unable to help. But this, as Inspector Slack pointed out, might be natural.

'If what you tell me is true, sir – about this adoption business, I mean – well, Josie would be all for Ruby breaking with any old friends she might have and who might queer the pitch, so to speak. As I see it, this invalid gentleman gets all worked up about Ruby Keene being such a sweet, innocent, childish little piece of goods. Now, supposing Ruby's got a tough boy friend – that won't go down so well with the old boy. So it's Ruby's business to keep that dark. Josie doesn't know much about the girl anyway – not about her friends and all that. But one thing she wouldn't stand for – Ruby's messing up things by carrying on with some undesirable fellow. So it stands to reason that Ruby (who, as I see it, was a sly little piece!) would keep very dark about seeing any old friend. She wouldn't let on to Josie anything about it – otherwise Josie would say: "No, you don't, my girl." But you know what girls are – especially young ones – always ready to make a fool of themselves over a tough guy. Ruby wants to see him. He comes down here, cuts up rough about the whole business, and wrings the girl's neck.'

'I expect you're right, Slack,' said Colonel Melchett, disguising his usual repugnance for the unpleasant way Slack had of putting things. 'If so, we ought to be able to discover this tough friend's identity fairly easily.'

'You leave it to me, sir,' said Slack with his usual confidence. 'I'll get hold of this "Lil" girl at that Palais de Danse place and turn her right inside out. We'll soon get at the truth.'

Colonel Melchett wondered if they would. Slack's energy and activity always made him feel tired.

'There's one other person you might be able to get a tip from, sir,' went on Slack, 'and that's the dance and tennis pro. fellow. He must have seen a lot of her and he'd know more than Josie would. Likely enough she'd loosen her tongue a bit to him.'

'I have already discussed that point with Superintendent Harper.'

'Good, sir. *I've* done the chambermaids pretty thoroughly! They don't know a thing. Looked down on these two, as far as I can make out. Scamped the service as much as they dared. Chambermaid was in here last at seven o'clock last night, when she turned down the bed and drew the curtains and cleared up a bit. There's a bathroom next door, if you'd like to see it?'

The bathroom was situated between Ruby's room and the slightly larger room occupied by Josie. It was illuminating. Colonel Melchett silently marvelled at the amount of aids to beauty that women could use. Rows of jars of face cream, cleansing cream, vanishing cream, skin-feeding cream! Boxes of different shades of powder. An untidy heap of every variety of lipstick. Hair lotions and 'brightening' applications. Eyelash black, mascara, blue stain for under the eyes, at least twelve different shades of nail varnish, face tissues, bits of cotton wool, dirty powder-puffs. Bottles of lotions – astringent, tonic, soothing, etc.

'Do you mean to say,' he murmured feebly, 'that women use all these things?'

Inspector Slack, who always knew everything, kindly enlightened him.

'In private life, sir, so to speak, a lady keeps to one or two distinct shades, one for evening, one for day. They know what suits them and they keep to it. But these professional girls, they have to ring a change, so to speak. They do exhibition dances, and one night it's a tango and the next a crinoline Victorian dance and then a kind of Apache dance and then just ordinary ball-room, and, of course, the make-up varies a good bit.'

'Good lord!' said the Colonel. 'No wonder the people who turn out these creams and messes make a fortune.'

'Easy money, that's what it is,' said Slack. 'Easy money. Got to spend a bit in advertisement, of course.'

Colonel Melchett jerked his mind away from the fascinating and age-long problem of woman's adornments. He said to Harper, who had just joined them:

'There's still this dancing fellow. Your pigeon, Superintendent?'

'I suppose so, sir.'

As they went downstairs Harper asked:

'What did you think of Mr Bartlett's story, sir?'

'About his car? I think, Harper, that that young man wants watching. It's a fishy story. Supposing that he did take Ruby Keene out in that car last night, after all?'

IV

Superintendent Harper's manner was slow and pleasant and absolutely non-committal. These cases where the police of two counties had to collaborate were always difficult. He liked Colonel Melchett and considered him an able Chief Constable, but he was nevertheless glad to be tackling the present interview

by himself. Never do too much at once, was Superintendent Harper's rule. Bare routine inquiry for the
first time. That left the persons you were interviewing
relieved and predisposed them to be more unguarded
in the next interview you had with them.

Harper already knew Raymond Starr by sight. A
fine-looking specimen, tall, lithe, and good-looking,
with very white teeth in a deeply-bronzed face. He was
dark and graceful. He had a pleasant, friendly manner
and was very popular in the hotel.

'I'm afraid I can't help you much, Superintendent. I
knew Ruby quite well, of course. She'd been here over
a month and we had practised our dances together and
all that. But there's really very little to say. She was
quite a pleasant and rather stupid girl.'

'It's her friendships we're particularly anxious to
know about. Her friendships with men.'

'So I suppose. Well, *I* don't know anything! She'd
got a few young men in tow in the hotel, but nothing
special. You see, she was nearly always monopolized
by the Jefferson family.'

'Yes, the Jefferson family.' Harper paused meditatively. He shot a shrewd glance at the young man.
'What did you think of that business, Mr Starr?'

Raymond Starr said coolly: 'What business?'

Harper said: 'Did you know that Mr Jefferson was
proposing to adopt Ruby Keene legally?'

This appeared to be news to Starr. He pursed up his lips and whistled. He said:

'The clever little devil! Oh, well, there's no fool like an old fool.'

'That's how it strikes you, is it?'

'Well – what else can one say? If the old boy wanted to adopt someone, why didn't he pick upon a girl of his own class?'

'Ruby Keene never mentioned the matter to you?'

'No, she didn't. I knew she was elated about something, but I didn't know what it was.'

'And Josie?'

'Oh, I think Josie must have known what was in the wind. Probably she was the one who planned the whole thing. Josie's no fool. She's got a head on her, that girl.'

Harper nodded. It was Josie who had sent for Ruby Keene. Josie, no doubt, who had encouraged the intimacy. No wonder she had been upset when Ruby had failed to show up for her dance that night and Conway Jefferson had begun to panic. She was envisaging her plans going awry.

He asked:

'Could Ruby keep a secret, do you think?'

'As well as most. She didn't talk about her own affairs much.'

'Did she ever say anything – anything at all – about

some friend of hers – someone from her former life who was coming to see her here, or whom she had had difficulty with – you know the sort of thing I mean, no doubt.'

'I know perfectly. Well, as far as I'm aware, there was no one of the kind. Not by anything she ever said.'

'Thank you, Mr Starr. Now will you just tell me in your own words exactly what happened last night?'

'Certainly. Ruby and I did our ten-thirty dance together –'

'No signs of anything unusual about her then?'

Raymond considered.

'I don't think so. I didn't notice what happened afterwards. I had my own partners to look after. I do remember noticing she wasn't in the ballroom. At midnight she hadn't turned up. I was very annoyed and went to Josie about it. Josie was playing bridge with the Jeffersons. She hadn't any idea where Ruby was, and I think she got a bit of a jolt. I noticed her shoot a quick, anxious glance at Mr Jefferson. I persuaded the band to play another dance and I went to the office and got them to ring up to Ruby's room. There wasn't any answer. I went back to Josie. She suggested that Ruby was perhaps asleep in her room. Idiotic suggestion really, but it was meant for the Jeffersons, of course! She came away with me and said we'd go up together.'

'Yes, Mr Starr. And what did she say when she was alone with you?'

'As far as I can remember, she looked very angry and said: "Damned little fool. She can't do this sort of thing. It will ruin all her chances. Who's she with, do you know?"

'I said that I hadn't the least idea. The last I'd seen of her was dancing with young Bartlett. Josie said: "She wouldn't be with *him*. What *can* she be up to? She isn't with that film man, is she?"'

Harper said sharply; '*Film man?* Who was he?'

Raymond said: 'I don't know his name. He's never stayed here. Rather an unusual-looking chap – black hair and theatrical-looking. He has something to do with the film industry, I believe – or so he told Ruby. He came over to dine here once or twice and danced with Ruby afterwards, but I don't think she knew him at all well. That's why I was surprised when Josie mentioned him. I said I didn't think he'd been here tonight. Josie said: "Well, she must be out with *someone*. What on earth am I going to say to the Jeffersons?" I said what did it matter to the Jeffersons? And Josie said it *did* matter. And she said, too, that she'd never forgive Ruby if she went and messed things up.

'We'd got to Ruby's room by then. She wasn't there, of course, but she'd been there, because the dress she had been wearing was lying across a chair. Josie looked in the wardrobe and said she thought she'd put on her old white dress. Normally she'd have changed into a black velvet dress for our Spanish dance. I was pretty angry by this time at the way Ruby had let me down. Josie did her best to soothe me and said she'd dance herself so that old Prestcott shouldn't get after us all. She went away and changed her dress and we went down and did a tango – exaggerated style and quite showy but not really too exhausting upon the ankles. Josie was very plucky about it – for it hurt her, I could see. After that she asked me to help her soothe the Jeffersons down. She said it was important. So, of course, I did what I could.'

Superintendent Harper nodded. He said:

'Thank you, Mr Starr.'

To himself he thought: 'It was important, all right! Fifty thousand pounds!'

He watched Raymond Starr as the latter moved gracefully away. He went down the steps of the terrace, picking up a bag of tennis balls and a racquet on the way. Mrs Jefferson, also carrying a racquet, joined him and they went towards the tennis courts.

'Excuse me, sir.'

Sergeant Higgins, rather breathless, stood at Harper's side.

The Superintendent, jerked from the train of thought he was following, looked startled.

'Message just come through for you from head-quarters, sir. Labourer reported this morning saw glare as of fire. Half an hour ago they found a burnt-out car in a quarry. Venn's Quarry – about two miles from here. Traces of a charred body inside.'

A flush came over Harper's heavy features. He said:

'What's come to Glenshire? An epidemic of violence? Don't tell me we're going to have a Rouse case now!'

He asked: 'Could they get the number of the car?'

'No, sir. But we'll be able to identify it, of course, by the engine number. A Minoan 14, they think it is.'

Chapter 8

Sir Henry Clithering, as he passed through the lounge of the Majestic, hardly glanced at its occupants. His mind was preoccupied. Nevertheless, as is the way of life, something registered in his subconscious. It waited its time patiently.

Sir Henry was wondering as he went upstairs just what had induced the sudden urgency of his friend's message. Conway Jefferson was not the type of man who sent urgent summonses to anyone. Something quite out of the usual must have occurred, decided Sir Henry.

Jefferson wasted no time in beating about the bush. He said:

'Glad you've come. Edwards, get Sir Henry a drink. Sit down, man. You've not heard anything, I suppose? Nothing in the papers yet?'

Sir Henry shook his head, his curiosity aroused.

'What's the matter?'

'Murder's the matter. I'm concerned in it and so are your friends the Bantrys.'

'Arthur and Dolly Bantry?' Clithering sounded incredulous.

'Yes, you see, the body was found in their house.'

Clearly and succinctly, Conway Jefferson ran through the facts. Sir Henry listened without interrupting. Both men were accustomed to grasping the gist of a matter. Sir Henry, during his term as Commissioner of the Metropolitan Police, had been renowned for his quick grip on essentials.

'It's an extraordinary business,' he commented when the other had finished. 'How do the Bantrys come into it, do you think?'

'That's what worries me. You see, Henry, it looks to me as though possibly the fact that I know them might have a bearing on the case. That's the only connection I can find. Neither of them, I gather, ever saw the girl before. That's what they say, and there's no reason to disbelieve them. It's most unlikely they *should* know her. Then isn't it possible that she was decoyed away and her body deliberately left in the house of friends of mine?'

Clithering said:

'I think that's far-fetched.'

'It's possible, though,' persisted the other.

'Yes, but unlikely. What do you want *me* to do?'

Conway Jefferson said bitterly:

'I'm an invalid. I disguise the fact – refuse to face it – but now it comes home to me. I can't go about as I'd like to, asking questions, looking into things. I've got to stay here meekly grateful for such scraps of information as the police are kind enough to dole out to me. Do you happen to know Melchett, by the way, the Chief Constable of Radfordshire?'

'Yes, I've met him.'

Something stirred in Sir Henry's brain. A face and figure noted unseeingly as he passed through the lounge. A straight-backed old lady whose face was familiar. It linked up with the last time he had seen Melchett.

He said:

'Do you mean you want me to be a kind of amateur sleuth? That's not my line.'

Jefferson said:

'You're *not* an amateur, that's just it.'

'I'm not a professional any more. I'm on the retired list now.'

Jefferson said: 'That simplifies matters.'

'You mean that if I were still at Scotland Yard I couldn't butt in? That's perfectly true.'

'As it is,' said Jefferson, 'your experience qualifies you to take an interest in the case, and any co-operation you offer will be welcomed.'

Clithering said slowly:

'Etiquette permits, I agree. But what do you really want, Conway? To find out who killed this girl?'

'Just that.'

'You've no idea yourself?'

'None whatever.'

Sir Henry said slowly:

'You probably won't believe me, but you've got an expert at solving mysteries sitting downstairs in the lounge at this minute. Someone who's better than I am at it, and who in all probability *may* have some local dope.'

'What are you talking about?'

'Downstairs in the lounge, by the third pillar from the left, there sits an old lady with a sweet, placid spinsterish face, and a mind that has plumbed the depths of human iniquity and taken it as all in the day's work. Her name's Miss Marple. She comes from the village of St Mary Mead, which is a mile and a half from Gossington, she's a friend of the Bantrys – and where crime is concerned she's the goods, Conway.'

Jefferson stared at him with thick, puckered brows. He said heavily:

'You're joking.'

'No, I'm not. You spoke of Melchett just now. The last time I saw Melchett there was a village tragedy. Girl supposed to have drowned herself. Police quite rightly suspected that it wasn't suicide, but murder. They thought they knew who did it. Along to me comes old Miss Marple, fluttering and dithering. She's afraid, she says, they'll hang the wrong person. She's got no evidence, but she knows who did do it. Hands me a piece of paper with a name written on it. And, by God, Jefferson, she was right!'

Conway Jefferson's brows came down lower than ever. He grunted disbelievingly:

'Woman's intuition, I suppose,' he said sceptically.

'No, she doesn't call it that. Specialized knowledge is her claim.'

'And what does that mean?'

'Well, you know, Jefferson, *we* use it in police work. We get a burglary and we usually know pretty well who did it – of the regular crowd, that is. We know the sort of burglar who acts in a particular sort of way. Miss Marple has an interesting, though occasionally trivial, series of parallels from village life.'

Jefferson said sceptically:

'What is she likely to know about a girl who's been brought up in a theatrical milieu and probably never been in a village in her life?'

'I think,' said Sir Henry Clithering firmly, 'that she might have ideas.'

II

Miss Marple flushed with pleasure as Sir Henry bore down upon her.

'Oh, Sir Henry, this is indeed a great piece of luck meeting you here.'

Sir Henry was gallant. He said:

'To me it is a great pleasure.'

Miss Marple murmured, flushing: 'So kind of you.'

'Are you staying here?'

'Well, as a matter of fact, we are.'

'*We?*'

'Mrs Bantry's here too.' She looked at him sharply. 'Have you heard yet? Yes, I can see you have. It is terrible, is it not?'

'What's Dolly Bantry doing here? Is her husband here too?'

'No. Naturally, they both reacted quite differently. Colonel Bantry, poor man, just shuts himself up in his study, or goes down to one of the farms, when anything like this happens. Like tortoises, you know, they draw their heads in and hope nobody will notice them. Dolly, of course, is *quite* different.'

'Dolly, in fact,' said Sir Henry, who knew his old friend fairly well, 'is almost enjoying herself, eh?'

'Well – er – yes. Poor dear.'

'And she's brought you along to produce the rabbits out of the hat for her?'

Miss Marple said composedly:

'Dolly thought that a change of scene would be a good thing and she didn't want to come alone.' She met his eye and her own gently twinkled. 'But, of course, your way of describing it is quite true. It's rather embarrassing for me, because, of course, I am no use at all.'

'No ideas? No village parallels?'

'I don't know very much about it all yet.'

'I can remedy that, I think. I'm going to call you into consultation, Miss Marple.'

He gave a brief recital of the course of events. Miss Marple listened with keen interest.

'Poor Mr Jefferson,' she said. 'What a very sad story. These terrible accidents. To leave him alive, crippled, seems more cruel than if he had been killed too.'

'Yes, indeed. That's why all his friends admire him so much for the resolute way he's gone on, conquering pain and grief and physical disabilities.'

'Yes, it is splendid.'

'The only thing I can't understand is this sudden outpouring of affection for this girl. She may, of course, have had some remarkable qualities.'

'Probably not,' said Miss Marple placidly.

'You don't think so?'

'I don't think her qualities entered into it.'

Sir Henry said:

'He isn't just a nasty old man, you know.'

'Oh, no, no!' Miss Marple got quite pink. 'I wasn't implying that for a minute. What I was trying to say was – very badly, I know – that he was just looking for a nice bright girl to take his dead daughter's place – and then this girl saw her opportunity and played it for all she was worth! That sounds rather uncharitable, I know, but I have seen so many cases of the kind. The young maid-servant at Mr Harbottle's, for instance. A *very* ordinary girl, but quiet with nice manners. His sister was called away to nurse a dying relative and when she got back she found the girl completely above herself, sitting down in the drawing-room laughing and talking and not wearing her cap or apron. Miss Harbottle spoke to her very sharply and the girl was impertinent, and then old Mr Harbottle left her quite dumbfounded by saying that he thought she had kept house for him long enough and that he was making other arrangements.

'Such a scandal as it created in the village, but poor Miss Harbottle had to go and live *most* uncomfortably in rooms in Eastbourne. People *said* things, of course, but I believe there was no familiarity of any kind – it was simply that the old man found it much pleasanter to have a young, cheerful girl telling him how clever and amusing he was than to have his sister continually pointing out his faults to him, even if she *was* a good economical manager.'

There was a moment's pause, and then Miss Marple resumed.

'And there was Mr Badger who had the chemist's shop. Made a lot of fuss over the young lady who worked in his toilet section. Told his wife they must look on her as a daughter and have her to live in the house. Mrs Badger didn't see it that way at all.'

Sir Henry said: 'If she'd only been a girl in his own rank of life – a friend's child –'

Miss Marple interrupted him.

'Oh! but that wouldn't have been nearly as satisfactory from his point of view. It's like King Cophetua and the beggar maid. If you're really rather a lonely, tired old man, and if, perhaps, your own family have been neglecting you' – she paused for a second – 'well, to befriend someone who will be overwhelmed with your magnificence – (to put it rather melodramatically, but I hope you see what I mean) – well, that's much more interesting. It makes you feel a much greater person – a beneficent monarch! The recipient is more likely to be dazzled, and that, of course, is a pleasant feeling for you.' She paused and said: 'Mr Badger, you know, bought the girl in his shop some really fantastic presents, a diamond bracelet and a most expensive radio-gramophone. Took out a lot of his savings to do so. However, Mrs Badger, who was a much more astute woman than poor Miss Harbottle (marriage, of course, *helps*), took the trouble to find out a few things. And when Mr Badger discovered that the girl was carrying on with a *very* undesirable young man connected with the racecourses, and had actually pawned the bracelet to give him the money – well, he was completely disgusted and the affair passed over quite safely. And he gave Mrs Badger a diamond ring the following Christmas.'

Her pleasant, shrewd eyes met Sir Henry's. He wondered if what she had been saying was intended as a hint. He said:

'Are you suggesting that if there had been a young man in Ruby Keene's life, my friend's attitude towards her might have altered?'

'It probably would, you know. I dare say, in a year or two, he might have liked to arrange for her marriage himself – though more likely he wouldn't – gentlemen are usually rather selfish. But I certainly think that if Ruby Keene had had a young man she'd have been careful to keep very quiet about it.'

'And the young man might have resented that?'

'I suppose that *is* the most plausible solution. It struck me, you know, that her cousin, the young woman who was at Gossington this morning, looked definitely *angry* with the dead girl. What you've told me explains *why*. No doubt she was looking forward to doing very well out of the business.'

'Rather a cold-blooded character, in fact?'

'That's too harsh a judgment, perhaps. The poor thing has had to earn her living, and you can't expect her to sentimentalize because a well-to-do man and woman – as you have described Mr Gaskell and Mrs Jefferson – are going to be done out of a further large sum of money to which they have really no particular moral right. I should say Miss Turner was a hard-headed, ambitious young woman, with a good temper and considerable *joie de vivre*. A little,' added Miss Marple, 'like Jessie Golden, the baker's daughter.'

'What happened to her?' asked Sir Henry.

'She trained as a nursery governess and married the son of the house, who was home on leave from India. Made him a very good wife, I believe.'

Sir Henry pulled himself clear of these fascinating side issues. He said:

'Is there any reason, do you think, why my friend Conway Jefferson should suddenly have developed this "Cophetua complex," if you like to call it that?'

'There might have been.'

'In what way?'

Miss Marple said, hesitating a little:

'I should think – it's only a suggestion, of course –

133

that perhaps his son-in-law and daughter-in-law *might* have wanted to get married again.'

'Surely he couldn't have objected to that?'

'Oh, no, not *objected*. But, you see, you must look at it from *his* point of view. He had a terrible shock and loss – so had they. The three bereaved people live together and the *link* between them is the loss they have all sustained. But Time, as my dear mother used to say, is a great healer. Mr Gaskell and Mrs Jefferson are young. Without knowing it themselves, they may have begun to feel restless, to resent the bonds that tied them to their past sorrow. And so, feeling like that, old Mr Jefferson would have become conscious of a sudden lack of sympathy without knowing its cause. It's usually that. Gentlemen so *easily* feel neglected. With Mr Harbottle it was Miss Harbottle going away. And with the Badgers it was Mrs Badger taking such an interest in Spiritualism and always going out to séances.'

'I must say,' said Sir Henry ruefully, 'that I dislike the way you reduce us all to a General Common Denominator.'

Miss Marple shook her head sadly.

'Human nature is very much the same anywhere, Sir Henry.'

Sir Henry said distastefully:

'Mr Harbottle! Mr Badger! And poor Conway! I hate

to intrude the personal note, but have you any parallel for *my* humble self in your village?'

'Well, of course, there is Briggs.'

'Who's Briggs?'

'He was the head gardener up at Old Hall. *Quite* the best man they ever had. Knew *exactly* when the under-gardeners were slacking off – quite uncanny it was! He managed with only three men and a boy and the place was kept better than it had been with six. And took several firsts with his sweet peas. He's retired now.'

'Like me,' said Sir Henry.

'But he still does a little jobbing – if he likes the people.'

'Ah,' said Sir Henry. 'Again like me. That's what I'm doing now – jobbing – to help an old friend.'

'Two old friends.'

'Two?' Sir Henry looked a little puzzled.

Miss Marple said:

'I suppose you meant Mr Jefferson. But I wasn't thinking of him. I was thinking of Colonel and Mrs Bantry.'

'Yes – yes – I see –' He asked sharply: 'Was that why you alluded to Dolly Bantry as "poor dear" at the beginning of our conversation?'

'Yes. She hasn't begun to realize things yet. *I* know because I've had more experience. You see, Sir Henry, it seems to me that there's a great possibility of this crime being the kind of crime that never *does* get solved. Like the Brighton trunk murders. But if that happens it will be absolutely disastrous for the Bantrys. Colonel Bantry, like nearly all retired military men, is really *abnormally* sensitive. He reacts very quickly to public opinion. He won't notice it for some time, and then it will begin to go home to him. A slight here, and a snub there, and invitations that are refused, and excuses that are made – and then, little by little, it will dawn upon him and he'll retire into his shell and get terribly morbid and miserable.'

'Let me be sure I understand you rightly, Miss Marple. You mean that, because the body was found in his house, people will think that *he* had something to do with it?'

'Of course they will! I've no doubt they're saying so already. They'll say so more and more. And people will cold shoulder the Bantrys and avoid them. That's why the truth has got to be found out and why I was willing to come here with Mrs Bantry. An open accusation is one thing – and quite easy for a soldier to meet. He's indignant and he has a chance of fighting. But this other *whispering* business will break him – will break them both. So you see, Sir Henry, we've *got* to find out the truth.'

Sir Henry said:

'Any ideas as to why the body should have been found in his house? There must be an explanation of that. Some connection.'

'Oh, of course.'

'The girl was last seen here about twenty minutes to eleven. By midnight, according to the medical evidence, she was dead. Gossington's about eighteen miles from here. Good road for sixteen of those miles until one turns off the main road. A powerful car could do it in well under half an hour. Practically *any* car could average thirty-five. But why anyone should either kill her here and take her body out to Gossington or should take her out to Gossington and strangle her there, I don't know.'

'Of course you don't, because it didn't happen.'

'Do you mean that she was strangled by some fellow who took her out in a car and he then decided to push her into the first likely house in the neighbourhood?'

'I don't think anything of the kind. I think there was a very careful plan made. What happened was that the plan went wrong.'

Sir Henry stared at her.

'Why did the plan go wrong?'

Miss Marple said rather apologetically:

'Such curious things happen, don't they? If I were to say that this particular plan went wrong because human beings are so much more vulnerable and sensitive than anyone thinks, it wouldn't sound sensible, would it? But that's what I believe – and –'

She broke off. 'Here's Mrs Bantry now.'

Chapter 9

Mrs Bantry was with Adelaide Jefferson. The former came up to Sir Henry and exclaimed: '*You?*'

'I, myself.' He took both her hands and pressed them warmly. 'I can't tell you how distressed I am at all this, Mrs B.'

Mrs Bantry said mechanically:

'*Don't call me Mrs B.!*' and went on: 'Arthur isn't here. He's taking it all rather seriously. Miss Marple and I have come here to sleuth. Do you know Mrs Jefferson?'

'Yes, of course.'

He shook hands. Adelaide Jefferson said:

'Have you seen my father-in-law?'

'Yes, I have.'

'I'm glad. We're anxious about him. It was a terrible shock.'

Mrs Bantry said:

'Let's come out on the terrace and have drinks and talk about it all.'

The four of them went out and joined Mark Gaskell, who was sitting at the extreme end of the terrace by himself.

After a few desultory remarks and the arrival of the drinks Mrs Bantry plunged straight into the subject with her usual zest for direct action.

'We can talk about it, can't we?' she said. 'I mean, we're all old friends – except Miss Marple, and she knows all about crime. And she wants to help.'

Mark Gaskell looked at Miss Marple in a somewhat puzzled fashion. He said doubtfully:

'Do you – er – write detective stories?'

The most unlikely people, he knew, wrote detective stories. And Miss Marple, in her old-fashioned spinster's clothes, looked a singularly unlikely person.

'Oh no, I'm not clever enough for *that*.'

'She's wonderful,' said Mrs Bantry impatiently. 'I can't explain now, but she is. Now, Addie, I want to know all about things. What was she really like, this girl?'

'Well –' Adelaide Jefferson paused, glanced across at Mark, and half laughed. She said: 'You're so direct.'

'Did you like her?'

'No, of course I didn't.'

'What was she really like?' Mrs Bantry shifted her inquiry to Mark Gaskell. Mark said deliberately:

'Common or garden gold-digger. And she knew her stuff. She'd got her hooks into Jeff all right.'

Both of them called their father-in-law Jeff.

Sir Henry thought, looking disapprovingly at Mark: 'Indiscreet fellow. Shouldn't be so outspoken.'

He had always disapproved a little of Mark Gaskell. The man had charm but he was unreliable – talked too much, was occasionally boastful – not quite to be trusted, Sir Henry thought. He had sometimes wondered if Conway Jefferson thought so too.

'But couldn't you *do* something about it?' demanded Mrs Bantry.

Mark said dryly:

'We might have – if we'd realized it in time.'

He shot a glance at Adelaide and she coloured faintly. There had been reproach in that glance.

She said:

'Mark thinks I ought to have seen what was coming.'

'You left the old boy alone too much, Addie. Tennis lessons and all the rest of it.'

'Well, I had to have some exercise.' She spoke apologetically. 'Anyway, I never dreamed –'

'No,' said Mark, 'neither of us ever dreamed. Jeff has always been such a sensible, level-headed old boy.'

Miss Marple made a contribution to the conversation.

'Gentlemen,' she said with her old-maid's way of

referring to the opposite sex as though it were a species of wild animal, 'are frequently not as level-headed as they seem.'

'I'll say you're right,' said Mark. 'Unfortunately, Miss Marple, we didn't realize that. We wondered what the old boy saw in that rather insipid and meretricious little bag of tricks. But we were pleased for him to be kept happy and amused. We thought there was no harm in her. No harm in her! I wish I'd wrung her neck!'

'Mark,' said Addie, 'you really *must* be careful what you say.'

He grinned at her engagingly.

'I suppose I must. Otherwise people will think I actually *did* wring her neck. Oh well, I suppose I'm under suspicion, anyway. If anyone had an interest in seeing that girl dead it was Addie and myself.'

'Mark,' cried Mrs Jefferson, half laughing and half angry, 'you really *mustn't*!'

'All right, all right,' said Mark Gaskell pacifically. 'But I do like speaking my mind. Fifty thousand pounds our esteemed father-in-law was proposing to settle upon that half-baked nitwitted little slypuss.'

'Mark, you mustn't – she's dead.'

'Yes, she's dead, poor little devil. And after all, why shouldn't she use the weapons that Nature gave her? Who am I to judge? Done plenty of rotten things myself in my life. No, let's say Ruby was entitled to plot and scheme and we were mugs not to have tumbled to her game sooner.'

Sir Henry said:

'What did you say when Conway told you he proposed to adopt the girl?'

Mark thrust out his hands.

'What could we say? Addie, always the little lady, retained her self-control admirably. Put a brave face upon it. I endeavoured to follow her example.'

'*I* should have made a fuss!' said Mrs Bantry.

'Well, frankly speaking, we weren't entitled to make a fuss. It was Jeff's money. We weren't his flesh and blood. He'd always been damned good to us. There was nothing for it but to bite on the bullet.' He added reflectively: 'But we didn't love little Ruby.'

Adelaide Jefferson said:

'If only it had been some other kind of girl. Jeff had two godchildren, you know. If it had been one of them – well, one would have *understood* it.' She added, with a shade of resentment: 'And Jeff's always seemed so fond of Peter.'

'Of course,' said Mrs Bantry. 'I always have known Peter was your first husband's child – but I'd quite forgotten it. I've always thought of him as Mr Jefferson's grandson.'

'So have I,' said Adelaide. Her voice held a note

that made Miss Marple turn in her chair and look at her.

'It was Josie's fault,' said Mark. 'Josie brought her here.'

Adelaide said:

'Oh, but surely you don't think it was deliberate, do you? Why, you've always liked Josie so much.'

'Yes, I did like her. I thought she was a good sport.'

'It was sheer accident her bringing the girl down.'

'Josie's got a good head on her shoulders, my girl.'

'Yes, but she couldn't foresee –'

Mark said:

'No, she couldn't. I admit it. I'm not really accusing her of planning the whole thing. But I've no doubt she saw which way the wind was blowing long before we did and kept very quiet about it.'

Adelaide said with a sigh:

'I suppose one can't blame her for that.'

Mark said:

'Oh, we can't blame anyone for anything!'

Mrs Bantry asked:

'Was Ruby Keene very pretty?'

Mark stared at her. 'I thought you'd seen –'

Mrs Bantry said hastily:

'Oh yes, I saw her – her body. But she'd been strangled, you know, and one couldn't tell –' She shivered.

Mark said, thoughtfully:

'I don't think she was really pretty at all. She certainly wouldn't have been without any make-up. A thin fer-rety little face, not much chin, teeth running down her throat, nondescript sort of nose –'

'It sounds revolting,' said Mrs Bantry.

'Oh no, she wasn't. As I say, with make-up she managed to give quite an effect of good looks, don't you think so, Addie?'

'Yes, rather chocolate-box, pink and white business. She had nice blue eyes.'

'Yes, innocent baby stare, and the heavily-blacked lashes brought out the blueness. Her hair was bleached, of course. It's true, when I come to think of it, that in colouring – artificial colouring, anyway – she had a kind of spurious resemblance to Rosamund – my wife, you know. I dare say that's what attracted the old man's attention to her.'

He sighed.

'Well, it's a bad business. The awful thing is that Addie and I can't help being glad, really, that she's dead –'

He quelled a protest from his sister-in-law.

'It's no good, Addie; I know what you feel. I feel the same. And I'm not going to pretend! But, at the same time, if you know what I mean, I really am most awfully concerned for Jeff about the whole business. It's hit him very hard. I –'

He stopped, and stared towards the doors leading out of the lounge on to the terrace.

'Well, well – see who's here. What an unscrupulous woman you are, Addie.'

Mrs Jefferson looked over her shoulder, uttered an exclamation and got up, a slight colour rising in her face. She walked quickly along the terrace and went up to a tall middle-aged man with a thin brown face, who was looking uncertainly about him.

Mrs Bantry said: 'Isn't that Hugo McLean?'

Mark Gaskell said:

'Hugo McLean it is. Alias William Dobbin.'

Mrs Bantry murmured:

'He's very faithful, isn't he?'

'Dog-like devotion,' said Mark. 'Addie's only got to whistle and Hugo comes trotting from any odd corner of the globe. Always hopes that some day she'll marry him. I dare say she will.'

Miss Marple looked beamingly after them. She said:

'I see. A romance?'

'One of the good old-fashioned kind,' Mark assured her. 'It's been going on for years. Addie's that kind of woman.'

He added meditatively: 'I suppose Addie telephoned him this morning. She didn't tell me she had.'

Edwards came discreetly along the terrace and paused at Mark's elbow.

'Excuse me, sir. Mr Jefferson would like you to come up.'

'I'll come at once.' Mark sprang up.

He nodded to them, said: 'See you later,' and went off.

Sir Henry leant forward to Miss Marple. He said:

'Well, what do you think of the principal beneficiaries of the crime?'

Miss Marple said thoughtfully, looking at Adelaide Jefferson as she stood talking to her old friend:

'I should think, you know, that she was a very devoted mother.'

'Oh, she is,' said Mrs Bantry. 'She's simply devoted to Peter.'

'She's the kind of woman,' said Miss Marple, 'that everyone likes. The kind of woman that could go on getting married again and again. I don't mean a *man's* woman – that's quite different.'

'I know what you mean,' said Sir Henry.

'What you both mean,' said Mrs Bantry, 'is that she's a good listener.'

Sir Henry laughed. He said:

'And Mark Gaskell?'

'Ah,' said Miss Marple, 'he's a downy fellow.'

'Village parallel, please?'

'Mr Cargill, the builder. He bluffed a lot of people into having things done to their houses they never

147

meant to do. And how he charged them for it! But he could always explain his bills away plausibly. A downy fellow. He married money. So did Mr Gaskell, I understand.'

'You don't like him.'

'Yes, I do. Most women would. But he can't take me in. He's a very attractive person, I think. But a little unwise, perhaps, to *talk* as much as he does.'

'Unwise is the word,' said Sir Henry. 'Mark will get himself into trouble if he doesn't look out.'

A tall dark young man in white flannels came up the steps to the terrace and paused just for a minute, watching Adelaide Jefferson and Hugo McLean.

'And that,' said Sir Henry obligingly, 'is X, whom we might describe as an interested party. He is the tennis and dancing pro. – Raymond Starr, Ruby Keene's partner.'

Miss Marple looked at him with interest. She said:

'He's very nice-looking, isn't he?'

'I suppose so.'

'Don't be absurd, Sir Henry,' said Mrs Bantry; 'there's no supposing about it. He *is* good-looking.'

Miss Marple murmured:

'Mrs Jefferson has been taking tennis lessons, I think she said.'

'Do you mean anything by that, Jane, or don't you?'

Miss Marple had no chance of replying to this down-right question. Young Peter Carmody came across the terrace and joined them. He addressed himself to Sir Henry:

'I say, are you a detective, too? I saw you talking to the Superintendent – the fat one is a superintendent, isn't he?'

'Quite right, my son.'

'And somebody told me you were a frightfully important detective from London. The head of Scotland Yard or something like that.'

'The head of Scotland Yard is usually a complete dud in books, isn't he?'

'Oh no, not nowadays. Making fun of the police is very old-fashioned. Do you know who did the murder yet?'

'Not yet, I'm afraid.'

'Are you enjoying this very much, Peter?' asked Mrs Bantry.

'Well, I am, rather. It makes a change, doesn't it? I've been hunting round to see if I could find any clues, but I haven't been lucky. I've got a souvenir, though. Would you like to see it? Fancy, Mother wanted me to throw it away. I do think one's parents are rather trying sometimes.'

He produced from his pocket a small matchbox. Pushing it open, he disclosed the precious contents.

'See, *it's a finger-nail. Her finger-nail!* I'm going to label it *Finger-nail of the Murdered Woman* and take it back to school. It's a good souvenir, don't you think?'

'Where did you get it?' asked Miss Marple.

'Well, it was a bit of luck, really. Because, of course, I didn't know she was going to be murdered *then*. It was before dinner last night. Ruby caught her nail in Josie's shawl and it tore it. Mums cut it off for her and gave it to me and said put it in the wastepaper basket, and I meant to, but I put it in my pocket instead, and this morning I remembered and looked to see if it was still there and it was, so now I've got it as a souvenir.'

'Disgusting,' said Mrs Bantry.

Peter said politely: 'Oh, do you think so?'

'Got any other souvenirs?' asked Sir Henry.

'Well, I don't know. I've got something that might be.'

'Explain yourself, young man.'

Peter looked at him thoughtfully. Then he pulled out an envelope. From the inside of it he extracted a piece of browny tapey substance.

'It's a bit of that chap George Bartlett's shoe-lace,' he explained. 'I saw his shoes outside the door this morning and I bagged a bit just in case.'

'In case what?'

'In case he should be the murderer, of course. He was the last person to see her and that's always frightfully suspicious, you know. Is it nearly dinner-time, do you think? I'm frightfully hungry. It always seems such a long time between tea and dinner. Hallo, there's Uncle Hugo. I didn't know Mums had asked *him* to come down. I suppose she sent for him. She always does if she's in a jam. Here's Josie coming. Hi, Josie!'

Josephine Turner, coming along the terrace, stopped and looked rather startled to see Mrs Bantry and Miss Marple.

Mrs Bantry said pleasantly:

'How d'you do, Miss Turner. We've come to do a bit of sleuthing!'

Josie cast a guilty glance round. She said, lowering her voice:

'It's awful. Nobody knows yet. I mean, it isn't in the papers yet. I suppose everyone will be asking me questions and it's so awkward. I don't know what I ought to say.'

Her glance went rather wistfully towards Miss Marple, who said: 'Yes, it will be a very difficult situation for you, I'm afraid.'

Josie warmed to this sympathy.

'You see, Mr Prestcott said to me: "Don't talk about it." And that's all very well, but everyone is sure to ask me, and you can't offend people, can you? Mr Prestcott said he hoped I'd feel able to carry on as usual – and he wasn't very nice about it, so of course I want to do my best. And I really don't see why it should all be blamed on me.'

Sir Henry said:

'Do you mind me asking you a frank question, Miss Turner?'

'Oh, do ask me anything you like,' said Josie, a little insincerely.

'Has there been any unpleasantness between you and Mrs Jefferson and Mr Gaskell over all this?'

'Over the murder, do you mean?'

'No, I don't mean the murder.'

Josie stood twisting her fingers together. She said rather sullenly:

'Well, there has and there hasn't, if you know what I mean. Neither of them have *said* anything. But I think they blamed it on me – Mr Jefferson taking such a fancy to Ruby, I mean. It wasn't my fault, though, was it? These things happen, and I never dreamt of such a thing happening beforehand, not for a moment. I – I was quite dumbfounded.'

Her words rang out with what seemed undeniable sincerity.

Sir Henry said kindly:

'I'm quite sure you were. But once it *had* happened?'

Josie's chin went up.

'Well, it was a piece of luck, wasn't it? Everyone's got the right to have a piece of luck sometimes.'

She looked from one to the other of them in a slightly defiant questioning manner and then went on across the terrace and into the hotel.

Peter said judicially:

'I don't think *she* did it.'

Miss Marple murmured:

'It's interesting, that piece of finger-nail. It had been worrying me, you know – how to account for her nails.'

'Nails?' asked Sir Henry.

'The dead girl's nails,' explained Mrs Bantry. 'They were quite *short*, and now that Jane says so, of course it *was* a little unlikely. A girl like that usually has absolute talons.'

Miss Marple said:

'But of course if she tore one off, then she might clip the others close, so as to match. Did they find nail parings in her room, I wonder?'

Sir Henry looked at her curiously. He said:

'I'll ask Superintendent Harper when he gets back.'

'Back from where?' asked Mrs Bantry. 'He hasn't gone over to Gossington, has he?'

Sir Henry said gravely:

'No. There's been another tragedy. Blazing car in a quarry –'

Miss Marple caught her breath.

'Was there someone in the car?'

'I'm afraid so – yes.'

Miss Marple said thoughtfully:

'I expect that will be the Girl Guide who's missing – Patience – no, Pamela Reeves.'

Sir Henry stared at her.

'Now why on earth do you think that, Miss Marple?'

Miss Marple got rather pink.

'Well, it was given out on the wireless that she was missing from her home – since last night. And her home was Daneleigh Vale; that's not very far from here. And she was last seen at the Girl-Guide Rally up on Danebury Downs. That's very close indeed. In fact, she'd have to pass through Danemouth to get home. So it does rather fit in, doesn't it? I mean, it looks as though she might have seen – or perhaps heard – something that no one was supposed to see and hear. If so, of course, she'd be a source of danger to the murderer and she'd have to be – removed. Two things like that *must* be connected, don't you think?'

Sir Henry said, his voice dropping a little:

'You think – a second murder?'

'Why not?' Her quiet placid gaze met his. 'When anyone has committed one murder, they don't shrink from another, do they? Nor even from a third.'

'A third? You don't think there will be a *third* murder?'

'I think it's just possible . . . Yes, I think it's highly possible.'

'Miss Marple,' said Sir Henry, 'you frighten me. Do you know who is going to be murdered?'

Miss Marple said: 'I've a very good idea.'

Chapter 10

Superintendent Harper stood looking at the charred and twisted heap of metal. A burnt-up car was always a revolting object, even without the additional gruesome burden of a charred and blackened corpse.

Venn's Quarry was a remote spot, far from any human habitation. Though actually only two miles as the crow flies from Danemouth, the approach to it was by one of those narrow, twisted, rutted roads, little more than a cart track, which led nowhere except to the quarry itself. It was a long time now since the quarry had been worked, and the only people who came along the lane were the casual visitors in search of blackberries. As a spot to dispose of a car it was ideal. The car need not have been found for weeks but for the accident of the glow in the sky having been seen by Albert Biggs, a labourer, on his way to work.

Albert Biggs was still on the scene, though all he had

to tell had been heard some time ago, but he continued to repeat the thrilling story with such embellishments as occurred to him.

'Why, dang my eyes, I said, whatever be that? Proper glow it was, up in the sky. Might be a bonfire, I says, but who'd be having bonfire over to Venn's Quarry? No, I says, 'tis some mighty big fire, to be sure. But whatever would it be, I says? There's no house or farm to that direction. 'Tis over by Venn's, I says, that's where it is, to be sure. Didn't rightly know what I ought to do about it, but seeing as Constable Gregg comes along just then on his bicycle, I tells him about it. 'Twas all died down by then, but I tells him just where 'twere. 'Tis over that direction, I says. Big glare in the sky, I says. Mayhap as it's a rick, I says. One of them tramps, as likely as not, set alight of it. But I did never think as how it might be a car – far less as someone was being burnt up alive in it. 'Tis a terrible tragedy, to be sure.'

The Glenshire police had been busy. Cameras had clicked and the position of the charred body had been carefully noted before the police surgeon had started his own investigation.

The latter came over now to Harper, dusting black ash off his hands, his lips set grimly together.

'A pretty thorough job,' he said. 'Part of one foot and shoe are about all that has escaped. Personally I myself couldn't say if the body was a man's or a woman's at the moment, though we'll get some indication from the bones, I expect. But the shoe is one of the black strapped affairs – the kind schoolgirls wear.'

'There's a schoolgirl missing from the next county,' said Harper; 'quite close to here. Girl of sixteen or so.'

'Then it's probably her,' said the doctor. 'Poor kid.'

Harper said uneasily: 'She wasn't alive when –?'

'No, no, I don't think so. No signs of her having tried to get out. Body was just slumped down on the seat – with the foot sticking out. She was dead when she was put there, I should say. Then the car was set fire to in order to try and get rid of the evidence.'

He paused, and asked:

'Want me any longer?'

'I don't think so, thank you.'

'Right. I'll be off.'

He strode away to his car. Harper went over to where one of his sergeants, a man who specialized in car cases, was busy.

The latter looked up.

'Quite a clear case, sir. Petrol poured over the car and the whole thing deliberately set light to. There are three empty cans in the hedge over there.'

A little farther away another man was carefully arranging small objects picked out of the wreckage. There was a scorched black leather shoe and with it

159

some scraps of scorched and blackened material. As Harper approached, his subordinate looked up and exclaimed:

'Look at this, sir. This seems to clinch it.'

Harper took the small object in his hand. He said:

'Button from a Girl Guide's uniform?'

'Yes, sir.'

'Yes,' said Harper, 'that does seem to settle it.'

A decent, kindly man, he felt slightly sick. First Ruby Keene and now this child, Pamela Reeves.

He said to himself, as he had said before:

'What's come to Glenshire?'

His next move was first to ring up his own Chief Constable, and afterwards to get in touch with Colonel Melchett. The disappearance of Pamela Reeves had taken place in Radfordshire though her body had been found in Glenshire.

The next task set him was not a pleasant one. He had to break the news to Pamela Reeve's father and mother . . .

II

Superintendent Harper looked up consideringly at the façade of Braeside as he rang the front door bell.

Neat little villa, nice garden of about an acre and

a half. The sort of place that had been built fairly freely all over the countryside in the last twenty years. Retired Army men, retired Civil Servants – that type. Nice decent folk; the worst you could say of them was that they might be a bit dull. Spent as much money as they could afford on their children's education. Not the kind of people you associated with tragedy. And now tragedy had come to them. He sighed.

He was shown at once into a lounge where a stiff man with a grey moustache and a woman whose eyes were red with weeping both sprang up. Mrs Reeves cried out eagerly:

'You have some news of Pamela?'

Then she shrank back, as though the Superintendent's commiserating glance had been a blow.

Harper said:

'I'm afraid you must prepare yourself for bad news.'

'Pamela –' faltered the woman.

Major Reeves said sharply:

'Something's happened – to the child?'

'Yes, sir.'

'Do you mean she's dead?'

Mrs Reeves burst out:

'Oh no, no,' and broke into a storm of weeping. Major Reeves put his arm round his wife and drew her to him. His lips trembled but he looked inquiringly at Harper, who bent his head.

'An accident?'

'Not exactly, Major Reeves. She was found in a burnt-out car which had been abandoned in a quarry.'

'In a car? In a quarry?'

His astonishment was evident.

Mrs Reeves broke down altogether and sank down on the sofa, sobbing violently.

Superintendent Harper said:

'If you'd like me to wait a few minutes?'

Major Reeves said sharply:

'What does this mean? Foul play?'

'That's what it looks like, sir. That's why I'd like to ask you some questions if it isn't too trying for you.'

'No, no, you're quite right. No time must be lost if what you suggest is true. But I can't believe it. Who would want to harm a child like Pamela?'

Harper said stolidly:

'You've already reported to your local police the circumstances of your daughter's disappearance. She left here to attend a Guides rally and you expected her home for supper. That is right?'

'Yes.'

'She was to return by bus?'

'Yes.'

'I understand that, according to the story of her fellow Guides, when the rally was over Pamela said she was going into Danemouth to Woolworth's, and would catch a later bus home. That strikes you as quite a normal proceeding?'

'Oh yes, Pamela was very fond of going to Woolworth's. She often went into Danemouth to shop. The bus goes from the main road, only about a quarter of a mile from here.'

'And she had no other plans, so far as you know?'

'None.'

'She was not meeting anybody in Danemouth?'

'No, I'm sure she wasn't. She would have mentioned it if so. We expected her back for supper. That's why, when it got so late and she hadn't turned up, we rang up the police. It wasn't like her not to come home.'

'Your daughter had no undesirable friends – that is, friends that you didn't approve of?'

'No, there was never any trouble of that kind.'

Mrs Reeves said tearfully:

'Pam was just a child. She was very young for her age. She liked games and all that. She wasn't precocious in any way.'

'Do you know a Mr George Bartlett who is staying at the Majestic Hotel in Danemouth?'

Major Reeves stared.

'Never heard of him.'

'You don't think your daughter knew him?'

'I'm quite sure she didn't.'

He added sharply: 'How does he come into it?'

'He's the owner of the Minoan 14 car in which your daughter's body was found.'

Mrs Reeves cried: 'But then he must –'

Harper said quickly:

'He reported his car missing early today. It was in the courtyard of the Majestic Hotel at lunch time yesterday. Anybody might have taken the car.'

'But didn't someone see who took it?'

The Superintendent shook his head.

'Dozens of cars going in and out all day. And a Minoan 14 is one of the commonest makes.'

Mrs Reeves cried:

'But aren't you doing something? Aren't you trying to find the – the devil who did this? My little girl – oh, my little girl! She wasn't burnt alive, was she? Oh, Pam, Pam . . . !'

'She didn't suffer, Mrs Reeves. I assure you she was already dead when the car was set alight.'

Reeves asked stiffly:

'How was she killed?'

Harper gave him a significant glance.

'We don't know. The fire had destroyed all evidence of that kind.'

He turned to the distraught woman on the sofa.

'Believe me, Mrs Reeves, we're doing everything we can. It's a matter of checking up. Sooner or later we shall find someone who saw your daughter in

Danemouth yesterday, and saw whom she was with. It all takes time, you know. We shall have dozens, hundreds of reports coming in about a Girl Guide who was seen here, there, and everywhere. It's a matter of selection and of patience – but we shall find out the truth in the end, never you fear.'

Mrs Reeves asked:

'Where – where is she? Can I go to her?'

Again Superintendent Harper caught the husband's eye. He said:

'The medical officer is attending to all that. I'd suggest that your husband comes with me now and attends to all the formalities. In the meantime, try and recollect anything Pamela may have said – something, perhaps, that you didn't pay attention to at the time but which might throw some light upon things. You know what I mean – just some chance word or phrase. That's the best way you can help us.'

As the two men went towards the door, Reeves said, pointing to a photograph:

'There she is.'

Harper looked at it attentively. It was a hockey group. Reeves pointed out Pamela in the centre of the team.

'A nice kid,' Harper thought, as he looked at the earnest face of the pigtailed girl.

His mouth set in a grim line as he thought of the charred body in the car.

He vowed to himself that the murder of Pamela Reeves should not remain one of Glenshire's unsolved mysteries.

Ruby Keene, so he admitted privately, might have asked for what was coming to her, but Pamela Reeves was quite another story. A nice kid, if he ever saw one. He'd not rest until he'd hunted down the man or woman who'd killed her.

Chapter 11

A day or two later Colonel Melchett and Superintendent Harper looked at each other across the former's big desk. Harper had come over to Much Benham for a consultation.

Melchett said gloomily:

'Well, we know where we are – or rather where we aren't!'

'Where we aren't expresses it better, sir.'

'We've got two deaths to take into account,' said Melchett. 'Two murders. Ruby Keene and the child Pamela Reeves. Not much to identify her by, poor kid, but enough. That shoe that escaped burning has been identified positively as hers by her father, and there's this button from her Girl Guide uniform. A fiendish business, Superintendent.'

Superintendent Harper said very quietly:

'I'll say you're right, sir.'

'I'm glad it's quite certain she was dead before the car was set on fire. The way she was lying, thrown across the seat, shows that. Probably knocked on the head, poor kid.'

'Or strangled, perhaps,' said Harper.

Melchett looked at him sharply.

'You think so?'

'Well, sir, there are murderers like that.'

'I know. I've seen the parents – the poor girl's mother's beside herself. Damned painful, the whole thing. The point for us to settle is – are the two murders connected?'

'I'd say definitely yes.'

'So would I.'

The Superintendent ticked off the points on his fingers.

'Pamela Reeves attended rally of Girl Guides on Danebury Downs. Stated by companions to be normal and cheerful. Did not return with three companions by the bus to Medchester. Said to them that she was going into Danemouth to Woolworth's and would take the bus home from there. The main road into Danemouth from the downs does a big round inland. Pamela Reeves took a short-cut over two fields and a footpath and lane which would bring her into Danemouth near the Majestic Hotel. The lane, in fact, actually passes the hotel on the west side. It's possible, therefore, that she

168

overheard or saw something – something concerning Ruby Keene – which would have proved dangerous to the murderer – say, for instance, that she heard him arranging to meet Ruby Keene at eleven that evening. He realizes that this schoolgirl has overheard, and he has to silence her.'

Colonel Melchett said:

'That's presuming, Harper, that the Ruby Keene crime was premeditated – not spontaneous.'

Superintendent Harper agreed.

'I believe it was, sir. It looks as though it would be the other way – sudden violence, a fit of passion or jealousy – but I'm beginning to think that that's not so. I don't see otherwise how you can account for the death of the Reeves child. If she was a witness of the actual crime, it would be late at night, round about eleven p.m., and what would she be doing round about the Majestic at that time? Why, at nine o'clock her parents were getting anxious because she hadn't returned.'

'The alternative is that she went to meet someone in Danemouth unknown to her family and friends, and that her death is quite unconnected with the other death.'

'Yes, sir, and I don't believe that's so. Look how even the old lady, old Miss Marple, tumbled to it at once that there was a connection. She asked at once if

169

the body in the burnt car was the body of the missing Girl Guide. Very smart old lady, that. These old ladies are sometimes. Shrewd, you know. Put their fingers on the vital spot.'

'Miss Marple has done that more than once,' said Colonel Melchett dryly.

'And besides, sir, there's the car. That seems to me to link up her death definitely with the Majestic Hotel. It was Mr George Bartlett's car.'

Again the eyes of the two men met. Melchett said:

'George Bartlett? Could be! What do you think?'

Again Harper methodically recited various points.

'Ruby Keene was last seen with George Bartlett. He says she went to her room (borne out by the dress she was wearing being found there), but did she go to her room and change *in order to go out with him*? Had they made a date to go out together earlier – discussed it, say, before dinner, and did Pamela Reeves happen to overhear?'

Melchett said: 'He didn't report the loss of his car until the following morning, and he was extremely vague about it then, pretended he couldn't remember exactly when he had last noticed it.'

'That might be cleverness, sir. As I see it, he's either a very clever gentleman pretending to be a silly ass, or else – well, he is a silly ass.'

'What we want,' said Melchett, 'is motive. As it

stands, he had no motive whatever for killing Ruby Keene.'

'Yes – that's where we're stuck every time. Motive. All the reports from the Palais de Danse at Brixwell are negative, I understand?'

'Absolutely! Ruby Keene had no special boy friend. Slack's been into the matter thoroughly – give Slack his due, he *is* thorough.'

'That's right, sir. Thorough's the word.'

'If there was anything to ferret out, he'd have ferreted it out. But there's nothing there. He got a list of her most frequent dancing partners – all vetted and found correct. Harmless fellows, and all able to produce alibis for that night.'

'Ah,' said Superintendent Harper. 'Alibis. That's what we're up against.'

Melchett looked at him sharply. 'Think so? I've left that side of the investigation to you.'

'Yes, sir. It's been gone into – very thoroughly. We applied to London for help over it.'

'Well?'

'Mr Conway Jefferson may think that Mr Gaskell and young Mrs Jefferson are comfortably off, but that is not the case. They're both extremely hard up.'

'Is that true?'

'Quite true, sir. It's as Mr Conway Jefferson said,

he made over considerable sums of money to his son and daughter when they married. That was over ten years ago, though. Mr Jefferson fancied himself as knowing good investments. He didn't invest in anything absolutely wild cat, but he was unlucky and showed poor judgment more than once. His holdings have gone steadily down. I should say the widow found it difficult to make both ends meet and send her son to a good school.'

'But she hasn't applied to her father-in-law for help?'

'No, sir. As far as I can make out she lives with him, and consequently has no household expenses.'

'And his health is such that he wasn't expected to live long?'

'That's right, sir. Now for Mr Mark Gaskell. He's a gambler, pure and simple. Got through his wife's money very soon. Has got himself tangled up rather critically just at present. He needs money badly – and a good deal of it.'

'Can't say I liked the looks of him much,' said Colonel Melchett. 'Wild-looking sort of fellow – what? And he's got a motive all right. Twenty-five thousand pounds it meant to him getting that girl out of the way. Yes, it's a motive all right.'

'They both had a motive.'

'I'm not considering Mrs Jefferson.'

'No, sir, I know you're not. And, anyway, the alibi

holds for both of them. They *couldn't* have done it. Just that.'

'You've got a detailed statement of their movements that evening?'

'Yes, I have. Take Mr Gaskell first. He dined with his father-in-law and Mrs Jefferson, had coffee with them afterwards when Ruby Keene joined them. Then he said he had to write letters and left them. Actually he took his car and went for a spin down to the front. He told me quite frankly he couldn't stick playing bridge for a whole evening. The old boy's mad on it. So he made letters an excuse. Ruby Keene remained with the others. Mark Gaskell returned when she was dancing with Raymond. After the dance Ruby came and had a drink with them, then she went off with young Bartlett, and Gaskell and the others cut for partners and started their bridge. That was at twenty minutes to eleven – and he didn't leave the table until after midnight. That's quite certain, sir. Everyone says so. The family, the waiters, everyone. Therefore *he* couldn't have done it. And Mrs Jefferson's alibi is the same. She, too, didn't leave the table. They're out, both of them – out.'

Colonel Melchett leaned back, tapping the table with a paper cutter.

Superintendent Harper said:

'That is, assuming the girl was killed before midnight.'

'Haydock said she was. He's a very sound fellow in police work. If he says a thing, it's so.'

'There might be reasons – health, physical idiosyncrasy, or something.'

'I'll put it to him.' Melchett glanced at his watch, picked up the telephone receiver and asked for a number. He said: 'Haydock ought to be at home at this time. Now, assuming that she was killed *after* midnight?'

Harper said:

'Then there might be a chance. There was some coming and going afterwards. Let's assume that Gaskell had asked the girl to meet him outside somewhere – say at twenty past twelve. He slips away for a minute or two, strangles her, comes back and disposes of the body later – in the early hours of the morning.'

Melchett said:

'Takes her by car thirty-odd miles to put her in Bantry's library? Dash it all, it's not a likely story.'

'No, it isn't,' the Superintendent admitted at once.

The telephone rang. Melchett picked up the receiver.

'Hallo, Haydock, is that you? Ruby Keene. Would it be possible for her to have been killed *after* midnight?'

'I told you she was killed between ten and midnight.'

'Yes, I know, but one could stretch it a bit – what?'

'No, you couldn't stretch it. When I say she was killed before midnight I mean before midnight, and don't try to tamper with the medical evidence.'

'Yes, but couldn't there be some physiological what-not? You know what I mean.'

'I know that you don't know what you're talking about. The girl was perfectly healthy and not abnormal in any way – and I'm not going to say she was just to help you fit a rope round the neck of some wretched fellow whom you police wallahs have got your knife into. Now don't protest. I know your ways. And, by the way, the girl wasn't strangled willingly – that is to say, she was drugged first. Powerful narcotic. She died of strangulation but she was drugged first.' Haydock rang off.

Melchett said gloomily: 'Well, that's that.'

Harper said:

'Thought I'd found another likely starter – but it petered out.'

'What's that? Who?'

'Strictly speaking, he's your pigeon, sir. Name of Basil Blake. Lives near Gossington Hall.'

'Impudent young jackanapes!' The Colonel's brow darkened as he remembered Basil Blake's outrageous rudeness. 'How's he mixed up in it?'

'Seems he knew Ruby Keene. Dined over at the Majestic quite often – danced with the girl. Do you remember what Josie said to Raymond when Ruby was discovered to be missing? "She's not with that film fellow, is she?" I've found out it was Blake, she meant. He's employed with the Lemville Studios, you know. Josie has nothing to go upon except a belief that Ruby was rather keen on him.'

'Very promising, Harper, very promising.'

'Not so good as it sounds, sir. Basil Blake was at a party at the studios that night. You know the sort of thing. Starts at eight with cocktails and goes on and on until the air's too thick to see through and everyone passes out. According to Inspector Slack, who's questioned him, he left the show round about midnight. At midnight Ruby Keene was dead.'

'Anyone bear out his statement?'

'Most of them, I gather, sir, were rather – er – far gone. The – er – young woman now at the bungalow – Miss Dinah Lee – says his statement is correct.'

'Doesn't mean a thing!'

'No, sir, probably not. Statements taken from other members of the party bear Mr Blake's statement out on the whole, though ideas as to time are somewhat vague.'

'Where are these studios?'

'Lemville, sir, thirty miles south-west of London.'

'H'm – about the same distance from here?'

'Yes, sir.'

Colonel Melchett rubbed his nose. He said in a rather dissatisfied tone:

'Well, it looks as though we could wash him out.'

'I think so, sir. There is no evidence that he was seriously attracted by Ruby Keene. In fact' – Superintendent Harper coughed primly – 'he seems fully occupied with his own young lady.'

Melchett said:

'Well, we are left with "X," an unknown murderer – so unknown Slack can't find a trace of him! Or Jefferson's son-in-law, who might have wanted to kill the girl – but didn't have a chance to do so. Daughter-in-law ditto. Or George Bartlett, who has no alibi – but unfortunately no motive either. Or with young Blake, who has an alibi and no motive. And that's the lot! No, stop, I suppose we ought to consider the dancing fellow – Raymond Starr. After all, he saw a lot of the girl.'

Harper said slowly:

'Can't believe he took much interest in her – or else he's a thundering good actor. And, for all practical purposes, he's got an alibi too. He was more or less in view from twenty minutes to eleven until midnight, dancing with various partners. I don't see that we can make a case against him.'

'In fact,' said Colonel Melchett, 'we can't make a case against anybody.'

177

'George Bartlett's our best hope. If we could only hit on a motive.'

'You've had him looked up?'

'Yes, sir. Only child. Coddled by his mother. Came into a good deal of money on her death a year ago. Getting through it fast. Weak rather than vicious.'

'May be mental,' said Melchett hopefully.

Superintendent Harper nodded. He said:

'Has it struck you, sir – that that may be the explanation of the whole case?'

'Criminal lunatic, you mean?'

'Yes, sir. One of those fellows who go about strangling young girls. Doctors have a long name for it.'

'That would solve all our difficulties,' said Melchett.

'There's only one thing I don't like about it,' said Superintendent Harper.

'What?'

'It's too easy.'

'H'm – yes – perhaps. So, as I said at the beginning where are we?'

'Nowhere, sir,' said Superintendent Harper.

Chapter 12

Conway Jefferson stirred in his sleep and stretched. His arms were flung out, long, powerful arms into which all the strength of his body seemed to be concentrated since his accident.

Through the curtains the morning light glowed softly.

Conway Jefferson smiled to himself. Always, after a night of rest, he woke like this, happy, refreshed, his deep vitality renewed. Another day!

So for a minute he lay. Then he pressed the special bell by his hand. And suddenly a wave of remembrance swept over him.

Even as Edwards, deft and quiet-footed, entered the room, a groan was wrung from his master.

Edwards paused with his hand on the curtains. He said: 'You're not in pain, sir?'

Conway Jefferson said harshly:

'No. Go on, pull 'em.'

The clear light flooded the room. Edwards, understanding, did not glance at his master.

His face grim, Conway Jefferson lay remembering and thinking. Before his eyes he saw again the pretty, vapid face of Ruby. Only in his mind he did not use the adjective vapid. Last night he would have said innocent. A naïve, innocent child! And now?

A great weariness came over Conway Jefferson. He closed his eyes. He murmured below his breath:

'Margaret . . .'

It was the name of his dead wife . . .

II

'I like your friend,' said Adelaide Jefferson to Mrs Bantry.

The two women were sitting on the terrace.

'Jane Marple's a very remarkable woman,' said Mrs Bantry.

'She's nice too,' said Addie, smiling.

'People call her a scandalmonger,' said Mrs Bantry, 'but she isn't really.'

'Just a low opinion of human nature?'

'You could call it that.'

'It's rather refreshing,' said Adelaide Jefferson, 'after having had too much of the other thing.'

Mrs Bantry looked at her sharply.

Addie explained herself.

'So much high-thinking – idealization of an unworthy object!'

'You mean Ruby Keene?'

Addie nodded.

'I don't want to be horrid about her. There wasn't any harm in her. Poor little rat, she had to fight for what she wanted. She wasn't bad. Common and rather silly and quite good-natured, but a decided little gold-digger. I don't think she schemed or planned. It was just that she was quick to take advantage of a possibility. And she knew just how to appeal to an elderly man who was – lonely.'

'I suppose,' said Mrs Bantry thoughtfully, 'that Conway *was* lonely?'

Addie moved restlessly. She said:

'He was – this summer.' She paused and then burst out: 'Mark will have it that it was all my fault. Perhaps it was, I don't know.'

She was silent for a minute, then, impelled by some need to talk, she went on speaking in a difficult, almost reluctant way.

'I – I've had such an odd sort of life. Mike Carmody, my first husband, died so soon after we were married – it – it knocked me out. Peter, as you know, was born after his death. Frank Jefferson was Mike's great friend.

181

So I came to see a lot of him. He was Peter's godfather – Mike had wanted that. I got very fond of him – and – oh! sorry for him too.'

'Sorry?' queried Mrs Bantry with interest.

'Yes, just that. It sounds odd. Frank had always had everything he wanted. His father and his mother couldn't have been nicer to him. And yet – how can I say it? – you see, old Mr Jefferson's personality is so strong. If you live with it, you can't somehow have a personality of your own. Frank felt that.

'When we were married he was very happy – wonderfully so. Mr Jefferson was very generous. He settled a large sum of money on Frank – said he wanted his children to be independent and not have to wait for his death. It was so nice of him – so generous. But it was much too sudden. He ought really to have accustomed Frank to independence little by little.

'It went to Frank's head. He wanted to be as good a man as his father, as clever about money and business, as far-seeing and successful. And, of course, he wasn't. He didn't exactly speculate with the money, but he invested in the wrong things at the wrong time. It's frightening, you know, how soon money goes if you're not clever about it. The more Frank dropped, the more eager he was to get it back by some clever deal. So things went from bad to worse.'

'But, my dear,' said Mrs Bantry, 'couldn't Conway have advised him?'

'He didn't want to be advised. The one thing he wanted was to do well on his own. That's why we never let Mr Jefferson know. When Frank died there was very little left – only a tiny income for me. And I – I didn't let his father know either. You see –'

She turned abruptly.

'It would have felt like betraying Frank to him. Frank would have hated it so. Mr Jefferson was ill for a long time. When he got well he assumed that I was a very-well-off widow. I've never undeceived him. It's been a point of honour. He knows I'm very careful about money – but he approves of that, thinks I'm a thrifty sort of woman. And, of course, Peter and I have lived with him practically ever since, and he's paid for all our living expenses. So I've never had to worry.'

She said slowly:

'We've been like a family all these years – only – only – you see (or don't you see?) I've never been Frank's *widow* to him – I've been Frank's *wife*.'

Mrs Bantry grasped the implication.

'You mean he's never accepted their deaths?'

'No. He's been wonderful. But he's conquered his own terrible tragedy by refusing to recognize death. Mark is Rosamund's husband and I'm Frank's wife –

and though Frank and Rosamund aren't exactly here with us – they are still existent.'

Mrs Bantry said softly:

'It's a wonderful triumph of faith.'

'I know. We've gone on, year after year. But suddenly – this summer – something went wrong in me. I felt – I felt rebellious. It's an awful thing to say, but I didn't want to think of Frank any more! All that was over – my love and companionship with him, and my grief when he died. It was something that had been and wasn't any longer.

'It's awfully hard to describe. It's like wanting to wipe the slate clean and start again. I wanted to be me – Addie, still reasonably young and strong and able to play games and swim and dance – just a *person*. Even Hugo – (you know Hugo McLean?) he's a dear and wants to marry me, but, of course, I've never really thought of it – but this summer I *did* begin to think of it – not seriously – only vaguely . . .'

She stopped and shook her head.

'And so I suppose it's true. *I neglected Jeff.* I don't mean *really* neglected him, but my mind and thoughts weren't with him. When Ruby, as I saw, amused him, I was rather glad. It left me freer to go and do my own things. I never dreamed – of course I never dreamed – that he would be so – so – *infatuated* by her!'

Mrs Bantry asked:

'And when you did find out?'

'I was dumbfounded – absolutely dumbfounded! And, I'm afraid, angry too.'

'*I*'d have been angry,' said Mrs Bantry.

'There was Peter, you see. Peter's whole future depends on Jeff. Jeff practically looked on him as a grandson, or so I thought, but, of course, he wasn't a grandson. He was no relation at all. And to think that he was going to be – disinherited!' Her firm, well-shaped hands shook a little where they lay in her lap. 'For that's what it felt like – and for a vulgar, gold-digging little simpleton – Oh! I could have killed her!'

She stopped, stricken. Her beautiful hazel eyes met Mrs Bantry's in a pleading horror. She said:

'*What an awful thing to say!*'

Hugo McLean, coming quietly up behind them, asked:

'What's an awful thing to say?'

'Sit down, Hugo. You know Mrs Bantry, don't you?'

McLean had already greeted the older lady. He said now in a low, persevering way:

'What was an awful thing to say?'

Addie Jefferson said:

'That I'd like to have killed Ruby Keene.'

Hugo McLean reflected a minute or two. Then he said:

'No, I wouldn't say that if I were you. Might be misunderstood.'

His eyes – steady, reflective, grey eyes – looked at her meaningly.

He said:

'*You've got to watch your step, Addie.*'

There was a warning in his voice.

III

When Miss Marple came out of the hotel and joined Mrs Bantry a few minutes later, Hugo McLean and Adelaide Jefferson were walking down the path to the sea together.

Seating herself, Miss Marple remarked:

'He seems very devoted.'

'He's been devoted for years! One of those men.'

'I know. Like Major Bury. He hung round an Anglo-Indian widow for quite ten years. A joke among her friends! In the end she gave in – but unfortunately ten days before they were to have been married she ran away with the chauffeur! Such a nice woman, too, and usually so well balanced.'

'People do do very odd things,' agreed Mrs Bantry. 'I wish you'd been here just now, Jane. Addie Jefferson was telling me all about herself – how her husband went through all his money but they never let Mr Jefferson know. And then, this summer, things felt different to her –'

Miss Marple nodded.

'Yes. She rebelled, I suppose, against being made to live in the past? After all, there's a time for everything. You can't sit in the house with the blinds down for ever. I suppose Mrs Jefferson just pulled them up and took off her widow's weeds, and her father-in-law, of course, didn't like it. Felt left out in the cold, though I don't suppose for a minute he realized who put her up to it. Still, he certainly wouldn't like it. And so, of course, like old Mr Badger when his wife took up Spiritualism, he was just ripe for what happened. Any fairly nice-looking young girl who listened prettily would have done.'

'Do you think,' said Mrs Bantry, 'that that cousin, Josie, got her down here deliberately – that it was a family plot?'

Miss Marple shook her head.

'No, I don't think so at all. I don't think Josie has the kind of mind that could foresee people's reactions. She's rather dense in that way. She's got one of those shrewd, limited, practical minds that never do foresee the future and are usually astonished by it.'

'It seems to have taken everyone by surprise,' said

Mrs Bantry. 'Addie – and Mark Gaskell too, apparently.'

Miss Marple smiled.

'I dare say he had his own fish to fry. A bold fellow with a roving eye! Not the man to go on being a sorrowing widower for years, no matter how fond he may have been of his wife. I should think they were both restless under old Mr Jefferson's yoke of perpetual remembrance.

'Only,' added Miss Marple cynically, 'it's easier for gentlemen, of course.'

IV

At that very moment Mark was confirming this judgment on himself in a talk with Sir Henry Clithering.

With characteristic candour Mark had gone straight to the heart of things.

'It's just dawned on me,' he said, 'that I'm Favourite Suspect No. 1 to the police! They've been delving into my financial troubles. I'm broke, you know, or very nearly. If dear old Jeff dies according to schedule in a month or two, and Addie and I divide the dibs also according to schedule, all will be well. Matter of fact, I owe rather a lot ... If the crash comes it will be a big one! If I can stave it off, it will be the other way round – I shall come out on top and be a very rich man.'

Sir Henry Clithering said:

'You're a gambler, Mark.'

'Always have been. Risk everything – that's my motto! Yes, it's a lucky thing for me that somebody strangled that poor kid. I didn't do it. I'm not a strangler. I don't really think I could ever murder anybody. I'm too easy-going. But I don't suppose I can ask the police to believe *that*! I must look to them like the answer to the criminal investigator's prayer! I had a motive, was on the spot, I am not burdened with high moral scruples! I can't imagine why I'm not in the jug already! That Superintendent's got a very nasty eye.'

'You've got that useful thing, an alibi.'

'An alibi is the fishiest thing on God's earth! No innocent person ever has an alibi! Besides, it all depends on the time of death, or something like that, and you may be sure if three doctors say the girl was killed at midnight, at least six will be found who will swear positively that she was killed at five in the morning – and where's my alibi then?'

'At any rate, you are able to joke about it.'

'Damned bad taste, isn't it?' said Mark cheerfully. 'Actually, I'm rather scared. One is – with murder! And don't think I'm not sorry for old Jeff. I am. But it's better this way – bad as the shock was – than if he'd found her out.'

'What do you mean, found her out?'

Mark winked.

'Where did she go off to last night? I'll lay you any odds you like she went to meet a man. Jeff wouldn't have liked that. He wouldn't have liked it at all. If he'd found she was deceiving him – that she wasn't the prattling little innocent she seemed – well – my father-in-law is an odd man. He's a man of great self-control, but that self-control can snap. And then – look out!'

Sir Henry glanced at him curiously.

'Are you fond of him or not?'

'I'm very fond of him – and at the same time I resent him. I'll try and explain. Conway Jefferson is a man who likes to control his surroundings. He's a benevolent despot, kind, generous, and affectionate – but his is the tune, and the others dance to his piping.'

Mark Gaskell paused.

'I loved my wife. I shall never feel the same for anyone else. Rosamund was sunshine and laughter and flowers, and when she was killed I felt just like a man in the ring who's had a knock-out blow. But the referee's been counting a good long time now. I'm a man, after all. I like women. I don't want to marry again – not in the least. Well, that's all right. I've had to be discreet – but I've had my good times all right. Poor Addie hasn't. Addie's a really nice woman. She's the kind of woman men want to marry, not to sleep with. Give her half a chance and she would marry again – and be very happy and make the chap happy too. But old Jeff saw her always as Frank's wife – and hypnotized her into seeing herself like that. He doesn't know it, but we've been in prison. I broke out, on the quiet, a long time ago. Addie broke out this summer – and it gave him a shock. It split up his world. Result – Ruby Keene.'

Irrepressibly he sang:

> 'But she is in her grave, and, oh,
> The difference to me!

'Come and have a drink, Clithering.'

It was hardly surprising, Sir Henry reflected, that Mark Gaskell should be an object of suspicion to the police.

Chapter 13

Dr Metcalf was one of the best-known physicians in Danemouth. He had no aggressive bedside manner, but his presence in the sick room had an invariably cheering effect. He was middle-aged, with a quiet pleasant voice.

He listened carefully to Superintendent Harper and replied to his questions with gentle precision.

Harper said:

'Then I can take it, Doctor Metcalf, that what I was told by Mrs Jefferson was substantially correct?'

'Yes, Mr Jefferson's health is in a precarious state. For several years now the man has been driving himself ruthlessly. In his determination to live like other men, he has lived at a far greater pace than the normal man of his age. He has refused to rest, to take things easy, to go slow – or any of the other phrases with which I and his other medical advisers have tendered our opinion. The result is that the man is an over-worked engine. Heart, lungs, blood pressure – they're all overstrained.'

'You say Mr Jefferson has absolutely refused to listen?'

'Yes. I don't know that I blame him. It's not what I say to my patients, Superintendent, but a man may as well wear out as rust out. A lot of my colleagues do that, and take it from me it's not a bad way. In a place like Danemouth one sees most of the other thing: invalids clinging to live, terrified of over-exerting themselves, terrified of a breath of draughty air, of a stray germ, of an injudicious meal!'

'I expect that's true enough,' said Superintendent Harper. 'What it amounts to, then, is this: Conway Jefferson is strong enough, physically speaking – or, I suppose I mean, muscularly speaking. Just what can he do in the active line, by the way?'

'He has immense strength in his arms and shoulders. He was a powerful man before his accident. He is extremely dexterous in his handling of his wheeled chair, and with the aid of crutches he can move himself about a room – from his bed to the chair, for instance.'

'Isn't it possible for a man injured as Mr Jefferson was to have artificial legs?'

'Not in his case. There was a spine injury.'

'I see. Let me sum up again. Jefferson is strong and fit in the muscular sense. He feels well and all that?'

Metcalf nodded.

'But his heart is in a bad condition. Any overstrain or exertion, or a shock or a sudden fright, and he might pop off. Is that it?'

'More or less. Over-exertion is killing him slowly, because he won't give in when he feels tired. That aggravates the cardiac condition. It is unlikely that exertion would kill him suddenly. But a sudden shock or fright might easily do so. That is why I expressly warned his family.'

Superintendent Harper said slowly:

'But in actual fact a shock *didn't* kill him. I mean, doctor, that there couldn't have been a much worse shock than this business, and he's still alive?'

Dr Metcalf shrugged his shoulders.

'I know. But if you'd had my experience, Superintendent, you'd know that case history shows the impossibility of prognosticating accurately. People who *ought* to die of shock and exposure *don't* die of shock and exposure, etc., etc. The human frame is tougher than one can imagine possible. Moreover, in my experience, a *physical* shock is more often fatal than a *mental* shock. In plain language, a door banging suddenly would be more likely to kill Mr Jefferson than the discovery that a girl he was fond of had died in a particularly horrible manner.'

'Why is that, I wonder?'

'The breaking of a piece of bad news nearly always sets up a defence reaction. It numbs the recipient. They are unable – at first – to take it in. Full realization takes a little time. But the banged door, someone jumping out of a cupboard, the sudden onslaught of a motor as you cross a road – all those things are immediate in their action. The heart gives a terrified leap – to put it in layman's language.'

Superintendent Harper said slowly:

'But as far as anyone would know, Mr Jefferson's death might easily have been caused by the shock of the girl's death?'

'Oh, easily.' The doctor looked curiously at the other. 'You don't think –'

'I don't know what I think,' said Superintendent Harper vexedly.

II

'But you'll admit, sir, that the two things would fit in very prettily together,' he said a little later to Sir Henry Clithering. 'Kill two birds with one stone. First the girl – and the fact of her death takes off Mr Jefferson too – before he's had any opportunity of altering his will.'

'Do you think he will alter it?'

'You'd be more likely to know that, sir, than I would. What do you say?'

'I don't know. Before Ruby Keene came on the scene I happen to know that he had left his money between Mark Gaskell and Mrs Jefferson. I don't see why he should now change his mind about that. But of course he might do so. Might leave it to a Cats' Home, or to subsidize young professional dancers.'

Superintendent Harper agreed.

'You never know what bee a man is going to get in his bonnet – especially when he doesn't feel there's any moral obligation in the disposal of his fortune. No blood relations in this case.'

Sir Henry said:

'He is fond of the boy – of young Peter.'

'D'you think he regards him as a grandson? You'd know that better than I would, sir.'

Sir Henry said slowly:

'No, I don't think so.'

'There's another thing I'd like to ask you, sir. It's a thing I can't judge for myself. But they're friends of yours and so you'd know. I'd like very much to know just how fond Mr Jefferson is of Mr Gaskell and young Mrs Jefferson.'

Sir Henry frowned.

'I'm not sure if I understand you, Superintendent?'

'Well, it's this way, sir. How fond is he of them as *persons* – apart from his relationship to them?'

'Ah, I see what you mean.'

'Yes, sir. Nobody doubts that he was very attached to them both – but he was attached to them, as I see it, because they were, respectively, the husband and the wife of his daughter and his son. But supposing, for instance, one of them had married again?'

Sir Henry reflected. He said:

'It's an interesting point you raise there. I don't know. I'm inclined to suspect – this is a mere opinion – that it would have altered his attitude a good deal. He would have wished them well, borne no rancour, but I think, yes, I rather think that he would have taken very little more interest in them.'

'In both cases, sir?'

'I think so, yes. In Mr Gaskell's, almost certainly, and I rather think in Mrs Jefferson's also, but that's not nearly so certain. I think he *was* fond of her for her own sake.'

'Sex would have something to do with that,' said Superintendent Harper sapiently. 'Easier for him to look on her as a daughter than to look on Mr Gaskell as a son. It works both ways. Women accept a son-in-law as one of the family easily enough, but there aren't many times when a woman looks on her son's wife as a daughter.'

Superintendent Harper went on:

'Mind if we walk along this path, sir, to the tennis court? I see Miss Marple's sitting there. I want to ask her to do something for me. As a matter of fact I want to rope you both in.'

'In what way, Superintendent?'

'To get at stuff that I can't get at myself. I want you to tackle Edwards for me, sir.'

'Edwards? What do you want from him?'

'Everything you can think of! Everything he knows and what he thinks! About the relations between the various members of the family, his angle on the Ruby Keene business. Inside stuff. He knows better than anyone the state of affairs – you bet he does! And he wouldn't tell *me*. But he'll tell *you*. And something *might* turn up from it. That is, of course, if you don't object?'

Sir Henry said grimly:

'I don't object. I've been sent for, urgently, to get at the truth. I mean to do my utmost.'

He added:

'How do you want Miss Marple to help you?'

'With some girls. Some of those Girl Guides. We've rounded up half a dozen or so, the ones who were most friendly with Pamela Reeves. It's possible that they may know something. You see, I've been thinking. It seems to me that if that girl was really going to Woolworth's she would have tried to persuade one of the other girls to go with her. Girls usually like to shop with someone.'

'Yes, I think that's true.'

'So I think it's possible that Woolworth's was only an excuse. I want to know where the girl was really going. She may have let slip something. If so, I feel Miss Marple's the person to get it out of these girls. I'd say she knows a thing or two about girls – more than I do. And, anyway, they'd be scared of the police.'

'It sounds to me the kind of village domestic problem that is right up Miss Marple's street. She's very sharp, you know.'

The Superintendent smiled. He said:

'I'll say you're right. Nothing much gets past her.'

Miss Marple looked up at their approach and welcomed them eagerly. She listened to the Superintendent's request and at once acquiesced.

'I should like to help you very much, Superintendent, and I think that perhaps I *could* be of some use. What with the Sunday School, you know, and the Brownies, and our Guides, and the Orphanage quite near – I'm on the committee, you know, and often run in to have a little talk with Matron – and then *servants* – I usually have very young maids. Oh, yes, I've quite a lot of experience in when a girl is speaking the truth and when she is holding something back.'

'In fact, you're an expert,' said Sir Henry.

Miss Marple flashed him a reproachful glance and said:

'Oh, *please* don't laugh at me, Sir Henry.'

'I shouldn't dream of laughing at you. You've had the laugh of me too many times.'

'One does see so much evil in a village,' murmured Miss Marple in an explanatory voice.

'By the way,' said Sir Henry, 'I've cleared up one point you asked me about. The Superintendent tells me that there were nail clippings in Ruby's wastepaper basket.'

Miss Marple said thoughtfully:

'There were? Then that's that . . .'

'Why did you want to know, Miss Marple?' asked the Superintendent.

Miss Marple said:

'It was one of the things that – well, that seemed *wrong* when I looked at the body. The hands were wrong, somehow, and I couldn't at first think *why*. Then I realized that girls who are very much made-up, and all that, usually have very long finger-nails. Of course, I know that girls everywhere do bite their nails – it's one of those habits that are very hard to break oneself of. But vanity often does a lot to help. Still, I presumed that this girl *hadn't* cured herself. And then the little boy – Peter, you know – he said something which showed that her nails *had* been long, only she caught one and broke it. So then, of course, she might have trimmed off the rest to make an even appearance, and I asked about clippings and Sir Henry said he'd find out.'

Sir Henry remarked:

'You said just now, "*one* of the things that seemed wrong when you looked at the body." Was there something else?'

Miss Marple nodded vigorously.

'Oh yes!' she said. 'There was the dress. The dress was *all* wrong.'

Both men looked at her curiously.

'Now why?' said Sir Henry.

'Well, you see, it was an old dress. Josie said so, definitely, and I could see for myself that it was shabby and rather worn. Now that's all wrong.'

'I don't see why.'

Miss Marple got a little pink.

'Well, the idea is, isn't it, that Ruby Keene changed her dress and went off to meet someone on whom she presumably had what my young nephews call a "crush"?'

The Superintendent's eyes twinkled a little.

'That's the theory. She'd got a date with someone – a boy friend, as the saying goes.'

'Then why,' demanded Miss Marple, 'was she wearing an old dress?'

The Superintendent scratched his head thoughtfully. He said:

'I see your point. You think she'd wear a new one?'

'I think she'd wear her best dress. Girls do.'

Sir Henry interposed.

'Yes, but look here, Miss Marple. Suppose she was going outside to this *rendezvous*. Going in an open car, perhaps, or walking in some rough going. Then she'd not want to risk messing a new frock and she'd put on an old one.'

'That would be the sensible thing to do,' agreed the Superintendent.

Miss Marple turned on him. She spoke with animation.

'The sensible thing to do would be to change into trousers and a pullover, or into tweeds. That, of course (I don't want to be snobbish, but I'm afraid it's unavoidable), that's what a girl of – of our class would do.

'A well-bred girl,' continued Miss Marple, warming to her subject, 'is always very particular to wear the right clothes for the right occasion. I mean, however hot the day was, a well-bred girl would never turn up at a point-to-point in a silk flowered frock.'

203

'And the correct wear to meet a lover?' demanded Sir Henry.

'If she were meeting him inside the hotel or some-where where evening dress was worn, she'd wear her best evening frock, of course – but *outside* she'd feel she'd look ridiculous in evening dress and she'd wear her most attractive sportswear.'

'Granted, Fashion Queen, but the girl Ruby –'

Miss Marple said:

'Ruby, of course, wasn't – well, to put it bluntly – Ruby *wasn't* a lady. She belonged to the class that wear their best clothes however unsuitable to the occasion. Last year, you know, we had a picnic outing at Scrantor Rocks. You'd be surprised at the unsuitable clothes the girls wore. Foulard dresses and patent shoes and quite elaborate hats, some of them. For climbing about over rocks and in gorse and heather. And the young men in their best suits. Of course, hiking's different again. That's practically a uniform – and girls don't seem to realize that shorts are very unbecoming unless they are very slender.'

The Superintendent said slowly:

'And you think that Ruby Keene –?'

'I think that she'd have kept on the frock she was wearing – her best pink one. She'd only have changed it if she'd had something newer still.'

Superintendent Harper said:

'And what's your explanation, Miss Marple?'

Miss Marple said:

'I haven't got one – yet. But I can't help feeling that it's important . . .'

III

Inside the wire cage, the tennis lesson that Raymond Starr was giving had come to an end.

A stout middle-aged woman uttered a few appreciative squeaks, picked up a sky-blue cardigan and went off towards the hotel.

Raymond called out a few gay words after her.

Then he turned towards the bench where the three onlookers were sitting. The balls dangled in a net in his hand, his racquet was under one arm. The gay, laughing expression on his face was wiped off as though by a sponge from a slate. He looked tired and worried.

Coming towards them, he said: '*That's* over.'

Then the smile broke out again, that charming, boyish, expressive smile that went so harmoniously with his suntanned face and dark lithe grace.

Sir Henry found himself wondering how old the man was. Twenty-five, thirty, thirty-five? It was impossible to say.

Raymond said, shaking his head a little:

'*She*'ll never be able to play, you know.'

'All this must be very boring for you,' said Miss Marple.

Raymond said simply:

'It is, sometimes. Especially at the end of the summer. For a time the thought of the pay buoys you up, but even that fails to stimulate imagination in the end!'

Superintendent Harper got up. He said abruptly:

'I'll call for you in half an hour's time, Miss Marple, if that will be all right?'

'Perfectly, thank you. I shall be ready.'

Harper went off. Raymond stood looking after him. Then he said: 'Mind if I sit here for a bit?'

'Do,' said Sir Henry. 'Have a cigarette?' He offered his case, wondering as he did so why he had a slight feeling of prejudice against Raymond Starr. Was it simply because he was a professional tennis coach and dancer? If so, it wasn't the tennis – it was the dancing. The English, Sir Henry decided, had a distrust for any man who danced too well! This fellow moved with too much grace! Ramon – Raymond – which was his name? Abruptly, he asked the question.

The other seemed amused.

'Ramon was my original professional name. Ramon and Josie – Spanish effect, you know. Then there was rather a prejudice against foreigners – so I became Raymond – very British –'

Miss Marple said:

'And is your real name something quite different?'

He smiled at her.

'Actually my real name is Ramon. I had an Argentine grandmother, you see –' (And that accounts for that swing from the hips, thought Sir Henry parenthetically.) 'But my first name is Thomas. Painfully prosaic.'

He turned to Sir Henry.

'You come from Devonshire, don't you, sir? From Stane? My people lived down that way. At Alsmonston.'

Sir Henry's face lit up.

'Are you one of the Alsmonston Starrs? I didn't realize that.'

'No – I don't suppose you would.'

There was a slight bitterness in his voice.

Sir Henry said awkwardly:

'Bad luck – er – all that.'

'The place being sold up after it had been in the family for three hundred years? Yes, it was rather. Still, our kind have to go, I suppose. We've outlived our usefulness. My elder brother went to New York. He's in publishing – doing well. The rest of us are scattered up and down the earth. I'll say it's hard to get a job nowadays when you've nothing to say for yourself except that you've had a public-school education! Sometimes, if you're lucky, you get taken on as a reception clerk at an hotel. The tie and the manner are an asset there. The only job I could get was showman in a plumbing establishment. Selling superb peach and lemon-coloured porcelain baths. Enormous showrooms, but as I never knew the price of the damned things or how soon we could deliver them – I got fired.

'The only things I *could* do were dance and play tennis. I got taken on at an hotel on the Riviera. Good pickings there. I suppose I was doing well. Then I overheard an old Colonel, real old Colonel, incredibly ancient, British to the backbone and always talking about Poona. He went up to the manager and said at the top of his voice:

'"Where's the *gigolo*? I want to get hold of the *gigolo*. My wife and daughter want to dance, yer know. Where is the feller? What does he sting yer for? It's the *gigolo* I want."'

Raymond went on:

'Silly to mind – but I did. I chucked it. Came here. Less pay but pleasanter work. Mostly teaching tennis to rotund women who will never, never, never be able to play. That and dancing with the neglected wallflower daughters of rich clients. Oh well, it's life, I suppose. Excuse today's hard-luck story!'

He laughed. His teeth flashed out white, his eyes crinkled up at the corners. He looked suddenly healthy and happy and very much alive.

Sir Henry said:

'I'm glad to have a chat with you. I've been wanting to talk with you.'

'About Ruby Keene? I can't help you, you know. I don't know who killed her. I knew very little about her. She didn't confide in me.'

Miss Marple said: 'Did you like her?'

'Not particularly. I didn't dislike her.'

His voice was careless, uninterested.

Sir Henry said:

'So you've no suggestions to offer?'

'I'm afraid not . . . I'd have told Harper if I had. It just seems to me one of those things! Petty, sordid little crime – no clues, no motive.'

'Two people had a motive,' said Miss Marple.

Sir Henry looked at her sharply.

'Really?' Raymond looked surprised.

'Miss Marple looked insistently at Sir Henry and he said rather unwillingly:

'Her death probably benefits Mrs Jefferson and Mr Gaskell to the amount of fifty thousand pounds.'

'What?' Raymond looked really startled – more than startled – upset. 'Oh, but that's absurd – absolutely absurd – Mrs Jefferson – neither of them – could have had anything to do with it. It would be incredible to think of such a thing.'

Miss Marple coughed. She said gently:

'I'm afraid, you know, you're rather an idealist.'

'I?' he laughed. 'Not me! I'm a hard-boiled cynic.'

'Money,' said Miss Marple, 'is a very powerful motive.'

'Perhaps,' Raymond said hotly. 'But that either of those two would strangle a girl in cold blood –' He shook his head.

Then he got up.

'Here's Mrs Jefferson now. Come for her lesson. She's late.' His voice sounded amused. 'Ten minutes late!'

Adelaide Jefferson and Hugo McLean were walking rapidly down the path towards them.

With a smiling apology for her lateness, Addie Jefferson went on to the court. McLean sat down on the bench. After a polite inquiry whether Miss Marple minded a pipe, he lit it and puffed for some minutes in silence, watching critically the two white figures about the tennis court.

He said at last:

'Can't see what Addie wants to have lessons for. Have a game, yes. No one enjoys it better than I do. But why *lessons*?'

'Wants to improve her game,' said Sir Henry.

'She's not a bad player,' said Hugo. 'Good enough, at all events. Dash it all, she isn't aiming to play at Wimbledon.'

He was silent for a minute or two. Then he said:

'Who *is* this Raymond fellow? Where do they come from, these pros? Fellow looks like a dago to me.'

'He's one of the Devonshire Starrs,' said Sir Henry.

'What? Not really?'

Sir Henry nodded. It was clear that this news was unpleasing to Hugo McLean. He scowled more than ever.

He said: 'Don't know why Addie sent for *me*. She seems not to have turned a hair over this business! Never looked better. Why send for me?'

Sir Henry asked with some curiosity:

'When did she send for you?'

'Oh – er – when all this happened.'

'How did you hear? Telephone or telegram?'

'Telegram.'

'As a matter of curiosity, when was it sent off?'

'Well – I don't know exactly.'

'What time did you receive it?'

'I didn't exactly receive it. It was telephoned on to me – as a matter of fact.'

'Why, where were you?'

'Fact is, I'd left London the afternoon before. I was staying at Danebury Head.'

'What – quite near here?'

'Yes, rather funny, wasn't it? Got the message when I got in from a round of golf and came over here at once.'

Miss Marple gazed at him thoughtfully. He looked hot and uncomfortable. She said: 'I've heard it's very pleasant at Danebury Head, and not very expensive.'

'No, it's not expensive. I couldn't afford it if it was. It's a nice little place.'

'We must drive over there one day,' said Miss Marple.

'Eh? What? Oh – er – yes, I should.' He got up. 'Better take some exercise – get an appetite.'

He walked away stiffly.

'Women,' said Sir Henry, 'treat their devoted admirers very badly.'

Miss Marple smiled but made no answer.

'Does he strike you as rather a dull dog?' asked Sir Henry. 'I'd be interested to know.'

'A little limited in his ideas, perhaps,' said Miss Marple. 'But with possibilities, I think – oh, definitely possibilities.'

Sir Henry in his turn got up.

'It's time for me to go and do my stuff. I see Mrs Bantry is on her way to keep you company.'

IV

Mrs Bantry arrived breathless and sat down with a gasp.

She said:

'I've been talking to chambermaids. But it isn't any good. I haven't found out a thing more! Do you think that girl can really have been carrying on with someone without everybody in the hotel knowing all about it?'

'That's a very interesting point, dear. I should say, definitely *not*. *Somebody* knows, depend upon it, if it's true! But she must have been very clever about it.'

Mrs Bantry's attention had strayed to the tennis court. She said approvingly:

'Addie's tennis is coming on a lot. Attractive young man, that tennis pro. Addie's looking quite nice-looking. She's still an attractive woman – I shouldn't be at all surprised if she married again.'

'She'll be a rich woman, too, when Mr Jefferson dies,' said Miss Marple.

'Oh, don't always have such a nasty mind, Jane! Why haven't you solved this mystery yet? We don't seem to be getting on at all. I thought you'd know *at once*.' Mrs Bantry's tone held reproach.

'No, no, dear. I didn't know at once – not for some time.'

Mrs Bantry turned startled and incredulous eyes on her.

'You mean you know *now* who killed Ruby Keene?'

'Oh yes,' said Miss Marple, 'I know *that*!'

'But Jane, who is it? Tell me at once.'

Miss Marple shook her head very firmly and pursed up her lips.

'I'm sorry, Dolly, but that wouldn't do at all.'

'Why wouldn't it do?'

'Because you're so indiscreet. You would go round telling everyone – or, if you didn't tell, you'd *hint*.'

'No, I wouldn't. I wouldn't tell a soul.'

'People who use that phrase are always the last to live up to it. It's no good, dear. There's a long way to go yet. A great many things that are quite obscure. You remember when I was so against letting Mrs Partridge collect for the Red Cross, and I couldn't say *why*. The reason was that her nose had twitched in just the same way that that maid of mine, Alice, twitched *her* nose when I sent her out to pay the books. Always paid them a shilling or so short, and said "it could go on to the next week's account," which, of course, was *exactly* what Mrs Partridge did, only on a much larger scale. Seventy-five pounds it was *she* embezzled.'

'Never mind Mrs Partridge,' said Mrs Bantry.

'But I had to explain to you. And if you care I'll

give you a *hint*. The trouble in this case is that everybody has been much too *credulous* and *believing*. You simply cannot *afford* to believe everything that people tell you. When there's anything fishy about, I never believe anyone at all! You see, I know human nature so well.'

Mrs Bantry was silent for a minute or two. Then she said in a different tone of voice:

'I told you, didn't I, that I didn't see why I shouldn't enjoy myself over this case. A real murder in my own house! The sort of thing that will never happen again.'

'I hope not,' said Miss Marple.

'Well, so do I, really. Once is enough. But it's *my* murder, Jane; I want to enjoy myself over it.'

Miss Marple shot a glance at her.

Mrs Bantry said belligerently:

'Don't you believe that?'

Miss Marple said sweetly:

'Of course, Dolly, if you tell me so.'

'Yes, but you never believe what people tell you, do you? You've just said so. Well, you're quite right.' Mrs Bantry's voice took on a sudden bitter note. She said: 'I'm not altogether a fool. You may think, Jane, that I don't know what they're saying all over St Mary Mead – all over the county! They're saying, one and all, that there's no smoke without fire, that if the girl was found in Arthur's library, then Arthur must know something about it. They're saying that the girl was Arthur's mistress – that she was his illegitimate daughter – that she was blackmailing him. They're saying anything that comes into their damned heads! And it will go on like that! Arthur won't realize it at first – he won't know what's wrong. He's such a dear old stupid that he'd never believe people would think things like that about him. He'll be cold-shouldered and looked at askance (whatever *that* means!) and it will dawn on him little by little and suddenly he'll be horrified and cut to the soul, and he'll fasten up like a clam and just *endure*, day after day, in misery.

'It's because of all that's going to happen to him that I've come here to ferret out every single thing about it that I can! This murder's *got* to be solved! If it isn't, then Arthur's whole life will be wrecked – and I won't have that happen. I won't! I won't! I won't!'

She paused for a minute and said:

'I *won't* have the dear old boy go through hell for something he didn't do. That's the only reason I came to Danemouth and left him alone at home – to find out the truth.'

'I know, dear,' said Miss Marple. 'That's why I'm here too.'

Chapter 14

In a quiet hotel room Edwards was listening deferentially to Sir Henry Clithering.

'There are certain questions I would like to ask you, Edwards, but I want you first to understand quite clearly my position here. I was at one time Commissioner of Police at Scotland Yard. I am now retired into private life. Your master sent for me when this tragedy occurred. He begged me to use my skill and experience in order to find out the truth.'

Sir Henry paused.

Edwards, his pale intelligent eyes on the other's face, inclined his head. He said: 'Quite so, Sir Henry.'

Clithering went on slowly and deliberately:

'In all police cases there is necessarily a lot of information that is held back. It is held back for various reasons – because it touches on a family skeleton, because it is considered to have no bearing on the case, because it would entail awkwardness and embarrassment to the parties concerned.'

Again Edwards said:

'Quite so, Sir Henry.'

'I expect, Edwards, that by now you appreciate quite clearly the main points of this business. The dead girl was on the point of becoming Mr Jefferson's adopted daughter. Two people had a motive in seeing that this should not happen. Those two people are Mr Gaskell and Mrs Jefferson.'

The valet's eyes displayed a momentary gleam. He said: 'May I ask if they are under suspicion, sir?'

'They are in no danger of arrest, if that is what you mean. But the police are bound to be suspicious of them and will continue to be so *until the matter is cleared up.*'

'An unpleasant position for them, sir.'

'Very unpleasant. Now to get at the truth one must have *all* the facts of the case. A lot depends, *must* depend, on the reactions, the words and gestures, of Mr Jefferson and his family. How did they feel, what did they show, what things were said? I am asking you, Edwards, for inside information – the kind of inside information that only you are likely to have. You know your master's moods. From observation of them you probably know what caused them. I am asking this, not as a policeman, but as a friend of Mr Jefferson's.

That is to say, if anything you tell me is not, in my opinion, relevant to the case, I shall not pass it on to the police.'

He paused. Edwards said quietly:

'I understand you, sir. You want me to speak quite frankly – to say things that in the ordinary course of events I should not say – and that, excuse me, sir, *you* wouldn't dream of listening to.'

Sir Henry said:

'You're a very intelligent fellow, Edwards. That's exactly what I *do* mean.'

Edwards was silent for a minute or two, then he began to speak.

'Of course I know Mr Jefferson fairly well by now. I've been with him quite a number of years. And I see him in his "off" moments, not only in his "on" ones. Sometimes, sir, I've questioned in my own mind whether it's good for anyone to fight fate in the way Mr Jefferson has fought. It's taken a terrible toll of him, sir. If, sometimes, he could have given way, been an unhappy, lonely, broken old man – well, it might have been better for him in the end. But he's too proud for that! He'll go down fighting – that's his motto.

'But that sort of thing leads, Sir Henry, to a lot of nervous reaction. He looks a good-tempered gentleman. I've seen him in violent rages when he could hardly speak for passion. And the one thing that roused him, sir, was deceit . . .'

'Are you saying that for any particular reason, Edwards?'

'Yes, sir, I am. You asked me, sir, to speak quite frankly?'

'That is the idea.'

'Well, then, Sir Henry, in my opinion the young woman that Mr Jefferson was so taken up with wasn't worth it. She was, to put it bluntly, a common little piece. And she didn't care tuppence for Mr Jefferson. All that play of affection and gratitude was so much poppycock. I don't say there was any harm in her – but she wasn't, by a long way, what Mr Jefferson thought her. It was funny, that, sir, for Mr Jefferson was a shrewd gentleman; he wasn't often deceived over people. But there, a gentleman isn't himself in his judgment when it comes to a young woman being in question. Young Mrs Jefferson, you see, whom he'd always depended upon a lot for sympathy, had changed a good deal this summer. He noticed it and he felt it badly. He was fond of her, you see. Mr Mark he never liked much.'

Sir Henry interjected:

'And yet he had him with him constantly?'

'Yes, but that was for Miss Rosamund's sake. Mrs Gaskell that was. She was the apple of his eye. He adored her. Mr Mark was Miss Rosamund's husband. He always thought of him like that.'

'Supposing Mr Mark had married someone else?'

'Mr Jefferson, sir, would have been furious.'

Sir Henry raised his eyebrows. 'As much as that?'

'He wouldn't have shown it, but that's what it would have been.'

'And if Mrs Jefferson had married again?'

'Mr Jefferson wouldn't have liked that either, sir.'

'Please go on, Edwards.'

'I was saying, sir, that Mr Jefferson fell for this young woman. I've often seen it happen with the gentlemen I've been with. Comes over them like a kind of disease. They want to protect the girl, and shield her, and shower benefits upon her – and nine times out of ten the girl is very well able to look after herself and has a good eye to the main chance.'

'So you think Ruby Keene was a schemer?'

'Well, Sir Henry, she was quite inexperienced, being so young, but she had the makings of a very fine schemer indeed when she'd once got well into her swing, so to speak! In another five years she'd have been an expert at the game!'

Sir Henry said:

'I'm glad to have your opinion of her. It's valuable. Now do you recall any incident in which this matter was discussed between Mr Jefferson and his family?'

'There was very little discussion, sir. Mr Jefferson announced what he had in mind and stifled any protests. That is, he shut up Mr Mark, who was a bit outspoken. Mrs Jefferson didn't say much – she's a quiet lady – only urged him not to do anything in a great hurry.'

Sir Henry nodded.

'Anything else? What was the girl's attitude?'

With marked distaste the valet said:

'I should describe it, sir, as jubilant.'

'Ah – jubilant, you say? You had no reason to believe, Edwards, that' – he sought about for a phrase suitable to Edwards – 'that – er – her affections were engaged elsewhere?'

'Mr Jefferson was not proposing marriage, sir. He was going to adopt her.'

'Cut out the "elsewhere" and let the question stand.'

The valet said slowly: 'There *was* one incident, sir. I happened to be a witness of it.'

'That is gratifying. Tell me.'

'There is probably nothing in it, sir. It was just that one day the young woman, chancing to open her handbag, a small snapshot fell out. Mr Jefferson pounced on it and said: "Hallo, Kitten, who's this, eh?"

'It was a snapshot, sir, of a young man, a dark young man with rather untidy hair and his tie very badly arranged.

'Miss Keene pretended that she didn't know anything about it. She said: "I've no idea, Jeffie. No idea at all. I don't know how it could have got into my bag. *I* didn't put it there!"

'Now, Mr Jefferson, sir, wasn't quite a fool. That story wasn't good enough. He looked angry, his brows came down heavy, and his voice was gruff when he said:

'"Now then, Kitten, now then. *You* know who it is right enough."

'She changed her tactics quick, sir. Looked frightened. She said: "I do recognize him now. He comes here sometimes and I've danced with him. I don't know his name. The silly idiot must have stuffed his photo into my bag one day. These boys are too silly for anything!" She tossed her head and giggled and passed it off. But it wasn't a likely story, was it? And I don't think Mr Jefferson quite believed it. He looked at her once or twice after that in a sharp way, and sometimes, if she'd been out, he asked her where she'd been.'

Sir Henry said: 'Have you ever seen the original of the photo about the hotel?'

'Not to my knowledge, sir. Of course, I am not much downstairs in the public departments.'

Sir Henry nodded. He asked a few more questions, but Edwards could tell him nothing more.

Agatha Christie

II

In the police station at Danemouth, Superintendent Harper was interviewing Jessie Davis, Florence Small, Beatrice Henniker, Mary Price, and Lilian Ridgeway.

They were girls much of an age, differing slightly in mentality. They ranged from 'county' to farmers' and shopkeepers' daughters. One and all they told the same story – Pamela Reeves had been just the same as usual, she had said nothing to any of them except that she was going to Woolworth's and would go home by a later bus.

In the corner of Superintendent Harper's office sat an elderly lady. The girls hardly noticed her. If they did, they may have wondered who she was. She was certainly no police matron. Possibly they assumed that she, like themselves, was a witness to be questioned.

The last girl was shown out. Superintendent Harper wiped his forehead and turned round to look at Miss Marple. His glance was inquiring, but not hopeful.

Miss Marple, however, spoke crisply.

'I'd like to speak to Florence Small.'

The Superintendent's eyebrows rose, but he nodded and touched a bell. A constable appeared.

Harper said: 'Florence Small.'

The girl reappeared, ushered in by the constable.

She was the daughter of a well-to-do farmer – a tall girl with fair hair, a rather foolish mouth, and frightened brown eyes. She was twisting her hands and looked nervous.

Superintendent Harper looked at Miss Marple, who nodded.

The Superintendent got up. He said:

'This lady will ask you some questions.'

He went out, closing the door behind him.

Florence shot an uneasy glance at Miss Marple. Her eyes looked rather like one of her father's calves.

Miss Marple said: 'Sit down, Florence.'

Florence Small sat down obediently. Unrecognized by herself, she felt suddenly more at home, less uneasy. The unfamiliar and terrorizing atmosphere of a police station was replaced by something more familiar, the accustomed tone of command of somebody whose business it was to give orders. Miss Marple said:

'You understand, Florence, that it's of the utmost importance that everything about poor Pamela's doings on the day of her death should be known?'

Florence murmured that she quite understood.

'And I'm sure you want to do your best to help?'

Florence's eyes were wary as she said, of course she did.

'To keep back any piece of information is a very serious offence,' said Miss Marple.

The girl's fingers twisted nervously in her lap. She swallowed once or twice.

'I can make allowances,' went on Miss Marple, 'for the fact that you are naturally alarmed at being brought into contact with the police. You are afraid, too, that you may be blamed for not having spoken sooner. Possibly you are afraid that you may also be blamed for not stopping Pamela at the time. But you've got to be a brave girl and make a clean breast of things. If you refuse to tell what you know now, it will be a very serious matter indeed – *very* serious – practically *perjury*, and for that, as you know, you can be sent to prison.'

'I – I don't –'

Miss Marple said sharply:

'Now don't prevaricate, Florence! Tell me all about it at once! Pamela wasn't going to Woolworth's, was she?'

Florence licked her lips with a dry tongue and gazed imploringly at Miss Marple like a beast about to be slaughtered.

'Something to do with the films, wasn't it?' asked Miss Marple.

A look of intense relief mingled with awe passed over Florence's face. Her inhibitions left her. She gasped:

'Oh, *yes!*'

'I thought so,' said Miss Marple. 'Now I want all the details, please.'

Words poured from Florence in a gush.

'Oh! I've been ever so worried. I promised Pam, you see, I'd never say a word to a soul. And then when she was found all burnt up in that car – oh! it was horrible and I thought I should *die* – I felt it was all my fault. I ought to have stopped her. Only I never thought, not for a minute, that it wasn't all right. And then I was asked if she'd been quite as usual that day and I said "Yes" before I'd had time to think. And not having said anything then I didn't see how I could say anything later. And, after all, I didn't know anything – not really – only what Pam told me.'

'What did Pam tell you?'

'It was as we were walking up the lane to the bus – on the way to the rally. She asked me if I could keep a secret, and I said "Yes," and she made me swear not to tell. She was going into Danemouth for a film test after the rally! She'd met a film producer – just back from Hollywood, he was. He wanted a certain type, and he told Pam she was just what he was looking for. He warned her, though, not to build on it. You couldn't tell, he said, not until you saw a person photographed. It might be no good at all. It was a kind of Bergner part, he said. You had to have someone quite young for it. A schoolgirl, it was, who changes places with

Agatha Christie

a revue artist and has a wonderful career. Pam's acted in plays at school and she's awfully good. He said he could see she could act, but she'd have to have some intensive training. It wouldn't be all beer and skittles, he told her, it would be damned hard work. Did she think she could stick it?'

Florence Small stopped for breath. Miss Marple felt rather sick as she listened to the glib rehash of countless novels and screen stories. Pamela Reeves, like most other girls, would have been warned against talking to strangers – but the glamour of the films would obliterate all that.

'He was absolutely businesslike about it all,' continued Florence. 'Said if the test was successful she'd have a contract, and he said that as she was young and inexperienced she ought to let a lawyer look at it before she signed it. But she wasn't to pass on that *he'd* said that. He asked her if she'd have trouble with her parents, and Pam said she probably would, and he said: "Well, of course, that's always a difficulty with anyone as young as you are, but I think if it was put to them that this was a wonderful chance that wouldn't happen once in a million times, they'd see reason." But, anyway, he said, it wasn't any good going into that until they knew the result of the test. She mustn't be disappointed if it failed. He told her about Hollywood and about Vivien Leigh – how she'd suddenly taken London by storm – and how these sensational leaps into fame did happen. He himself had come back from America to work with the Lemville Studios and put some pep into the English film companies.'

Miss Marple nodded.

Florence went on:

'So it was all arranged. Pam was to go into Danemouth after the rally and meet him at his hotel and he'd take her along to the studios (they'd got a small testing studio in Danemouth, he told her). She'd have her test and she could catch the bus home afterwards. She could say she'd been shopping, and he'd let her know the result of the test in a few days, and if it was favourable Mr Harmsteiter, the boss, would come along and talk to her parents.

'Well, of course, it sounded too wonderful! I was green with envy! Pam got through the rally without turning a hair – we always call her a regular poker face. Then, when she said she was going into Danemouth to Woolworth's she just winked at me.

'I saw her start off down the footpath.' Florence began to cry. 'I ought to have stopped her. I ought to have stopped her. I ought to have known a thing like that couldn't be true. I ought to have told someone. Oh dear, I wish I was *dead*!'

'There, there.' Miss Marple patted her on the shoulder.

'It's quite all right. No one will blame you. You've done the right thing in telling me.'

She devoted some minutes to cheering the child up.

Five minutes later she was telling the story to Superintendent Harper. The latter looked very grim.

'The clever devil!' he said. 'By God, I'll cook his goose for him. This puts rather a different aspect on things.'

'Yes, it does.'

Harper looked at her sideways.

'It doesn't surprise you?'

'I expected something of the kind.'

Superintendent Harper said curiously:

'What put you on to this particular girl? They all looked scared to death and there wasn't a pin to choose between them as far as I could see.'

Miss Marple said gently:

'You haven't had as much experience with girls telling lies as I have. Florence looked at you very straight, if you remember, and stood very rigid and just fidgeted with her feet like the others. But you didn't watch her as she went out of the door. I knew at once then that she'd got something to hide. They nearly always relax too soon. My little maid Janet always did. She'd explain quite convincingly that the mice had eaten the end of a cake and give herself away by smirking as she left the room.'

'I'm very grateful to you,' said Harper.

He added thoughtfully: 'Lemville Studios, eh?'

Miss Marple said nothing. She rose to her feet.

'I'm afraid,' she said, 'I must hurry away. So glad to have been able to help you.'

'Are you going back to the hotel?'

'Yes – to pack up. I must go back to St Mary Mead as soon as possible. There's a lot for me to do there.'

Chapter 15

Miss Marple passed out through the french windows of her drawing-room, tripped down her neat garden path, through a garden gate, in through the vicarage garden gate, across the vicarage garden, and up to the drawing-room window, where she tapped gently on the pane.

The vicar was busy in his study composing his Sunday sermon, but the vicar's wife, who was young and pretty, was admiring the progress of her offspring across the hearthrug.

'Can I come in, Griselda?'

'Oh, do, Miss Marple. Just *look* at David! He gets so angry because he can only crawl in reverse. He wants to get to something and the more he tries the more he goes backwards into the coal-box!'

'He's looking very bonny, Griselda.'

'He's not bad, is he?' said the young mother, endeavouring to assume an indifferent manner. 'Of course I don't *bother* with him much. All the books say a child should be left alone as much as possible.'

'Very wise, dear,' said Miss Marple. 'Ahem, I came to ask if there was anything special you are collecting for at the moment.'

The vicar's wife turned somewhat astonished eyes upon her.

'Oh, heaps of things,' she said cheerfully. 'There always are.'

She ticked them off on her fingers.

'There's the Nave Restoration Fund, and St Giles's Mission, and our Sale of Work next Wednesday, and the Unmarried Mothers, and a Boy Scouts' Outing, and the Needlework Guild, and the Bishop's Appeal for Deep Sea Fishermen.'

'Any of them will do,' said Miss Marple. 'I thought I might make a little round – with a book, you know – if you would authorize me to do so.'

'Are you up to something? I believe you are. Of course I authorize you. Make it the Sale of Work; it would be lovely to get some real money instead of those awful sachets and comic pen-wipers and depressing children's frocks and dusters all done up to look like dolls.

'I suppose,' continued Griselda, accompanying her guest to the window, 'you wouldn't like to tell me what it's all about?'

'Later, my dear,' said Miss Marple, hurrying off.

With a sigh the young mother returned to the hearthrug and, by way of carrying out her principles of stern neglect, butted her son three times in the stomach so that he caught hold of her hair and pulled it with gleeful yells. Then they rolled over and over in a grand rough-and-tumble until the door opened and the vicarage maid announced to the most influential parishioner (who didn't like children):

'Missus is in here.'

Whereupon Griselda sat up and tried to look dignified and more what a vicar's wife should be.

II

Miss Marple, clasping a small black book with pencilled entries in it, walked briskly along the village street until she came to the crossroads. Here she turned to the left and walked past the *Blue Boar* until she came to Chatsworth, alias 'Mr Booker's new house.'

She turned in at the gate, walked up to the front door and knocked briskly.

The door was opened by the blonde young woman named Dinah Lee. She was less carefully made-up than usual, and in fact looked slightly dirty. She was wearing grey slacks and an emerald jumper.

Agatha Christie

'Good morning,' said Miss Marple briskly and cheerfully. 'May I just come in for a minute?'

She pressed forward as she spoke, so that Dinah Lee, who was somewhat taken aback at the call, had no time to make up her mind.

'Thank you so much,' said Miss Marple, beaming amiably at her and sitting down rather gingerly on a 'period' bamboo chair.

'Quite warm for the time of year, is it not?' went on Miss Marple, still exuding geniality.

'Yes, rather. Oh, quite,' said Miss Lee.

At a loss how to deal with the situation, she opened a box and offered it to her guest. 'Er – have a cigarette?'

'Thank you so much, but I don't smoke. I just called, you know, to see if I could enlist your help for our Sale of Work next week.'

'Sale of Work?' said Dinah Lee, as one who repeats a phrase in a foreign language.

'At the vicarage,' said Miss Marple. 'Next Wednesday.'

'Oh!' Miss Lee's mouth fell open. 'I'm afraid I couldn't –'

'Not even a small subscription – half a crown perhaps?'

Miss Marple exhibited her little book.

'Oh – er – well, yes, I dare say I could manage that.'

The girl looked relieved and turned to hunt in her handbag.

Miss Marple's sharp eyes were looking round the room.

She said:

'I see you've no hearthrug in front of the fire.'

Dinah Lee turned round and stared at her. She could not but be aware of the very keen scrutiny the old lady was giving her, but it aroused in her no other emotion than slight annoyance. Miss Marple recognized that. She said:

'It's rather dangerous, you know. Sparks fly out and mark the carpet.'

'Funny old Tabby,' thought Dinah, but she said quite amiably if somewhat vaguely:

'There used to be one. I don't know where it's got to.'

'I suppose,' said Miss Marple, 'it was the fluffy, woolly kind?'

'Sheep,' said Dinah. 'That's what it looked like.'

She was amused now. An eccentric old bean, this.

She held out a half-crown. 'Here you are,' she said.

'Oh, thank you, my dear.'

Miss Marple took it and opened the little book.

'Er – what name shall I write down?'

Dinah's eyes grew suddenly hard and contemptuous.

'Nosey old cat,' she thought, 'that's all she came for – prying around for scandal!'

She said clearly and with malicious pleasure:

'Miss Dinah Lee.'

Miss Marple looked at her steadily.

She said:

'This is Mr Basil Blake's cottage, isn't it?'

'Yes, and *I*'m Miss Dinah Lee!'

Her voice rang out challengingly, her head went back, her blue eyes flashed.

Very steadily Miss Marple looked at her. She said:

'Will you allow me to give you some advice, even though you may consider it impertinent?'

'I *shall* consider it impertinent. You had better say nothing.'

'Nevertheless,' said Miss Marple, 'I am going to speak. I want to advise you, very strongly, not to continue using your maiden name in the village.'

Dinah stared at her. She said:

'What – what do you mean?'

Miss Marple said earnestly:

'In a very short time you may need all the sympathy and goodwill you can find. It will be important to your husband, too, that he shall be thought well of. There is a prejudice in old-fashioned country districts against people living together who are not married. It has amused you both, I dare say, to pretend that

that is what you are doing. It kept people away, so that you weren't bothered with what I expect you would call "old frumps." Nevertheless, old frumps have their uses.'

Dinah demanded:

'How did you know we are married?'

Miss Marple smiled a deprecating smile.

'Oh, my dear,' she said.

Dinah persisted.

'No, but how *did* you know? You didn't – you didn't go to Somerset House?'

A momentary flicker showed in Miss Marple's eyes.

'Somerset House? Oh, no. But it was quite easy to *guess*. Everything, you know, gets round in a village. The – er – the kind of quarrels you have – typical of early days of marriage. Quite – *quite* unlike an illicit relationship. It has been said, you know (and, I think, quite truly), that you can only really get under anybody's skin if you are married to them. When there is no – no *legal* bond, people are much more careful, they have to keep assuring themselves how happy and halcyon everything is. They have, you see, to *justify* themselves. They dare not quarrel! Married people, I have noticed, quite enjoy their battles and the – er – appropriate reconciliations.'

She paused, twinkling benignly.

'Well, I –' Dinah stopped and laughed. She sat

down and lit a cigarette. 'You're absolutely marvellous!' she said.

Then she went on:

'But why do you want us to own up and admit to respectability?'

Miss Marple's face was grave. She said:

'Because, any minute now, *your husband may be arrested for murder*.'

III

For several moments Dinah stared at her. Then she said incredulously:

'Basil? Murder? Are you joking?'

'No, indeed. Haven't you seen the papers?'

Dinah caught her breath.

'You mean – that girl at the Majestic Hotel. Do you mean they suspect Basil of killing her?'

'Yes.'

'But it's nonsense!'

There was the whir of a car outside, the bang of a gate. Basil Blake flung open the door and came in, carrying some bottles. He said:

'Got the gin and the vermouth. Did you –?'

He stopped and turned incredulous eyes on the prim, erect visitor.

Dinah burst out breathlessly:

'Is she mad? She says you're going to be arrested for the murder of that girl Ruby Keene.'

'Oh, God!' said Basil Blake. The bottles dropped from his arms on to the sofa. He reeled to a chair and dropped down in it and buried his face in his hands. He repeated: 'Oh, my God! Oh, my God!'

Dinah darted over to him. She caught his shoulders.

'Basil, look at me! It isn't true! I know it isn't true! I don't believe it for a moment!'

His hand went up and gripped hers.

'Bless you, darling.'

'But why should they think – You didn't even *know* her, did you?'

'Oh, yes, he knew her,' said Miss Marple.

Basil said fiercely:

'Be quiet, you old hag. Listen, Dinah darling, I hardly knew her at all. Just ran across her once or twice at the Majestic. That's all, I swear that's all.'

Dinah said, bewildered:

'I don't understand. Why should anyone suspect you, then?'

Basil groaned. He put his hands over his eyes and rocked to and fro.

Miss Marple said:

'What did you do with the hearthrug?'

His reply came mechanically:

'I put it in the dustbin.'

Miss Marple clucked her tongue vexedly.

'That was stupid – very stupid. People don't put good hearthrugs in dustbins. It had spangles in it from her dress, I suppose?'

'Yes, I couldn't get them out.'

Dinah cried: 'But what are you both talking about?'

Basil said sullenly:

'Ask her. She seems to know all about it.'

'I'll tell you what I think happened, if you like,' said Miss Marple. 'You can correct me, Mr Blake, if I go wrong. I think that after having had a violent quarrel with your wife at a party and after having had, perhaps, rather too much – er – to drink, you drove down here. I don't know what time you arrived –'

Basil Blake said sullenly:

'About two in the morning. I meant to go up to town first, then when I got to the suburbs I changed my mind. I thought Dinah might come down here after me. So I drove down here. The place was all dark. I opened the door and turned on the light and I saw – and I saw –'

He gulped and stopped. Miss Marple went on:

'You saw a girl lying on the hearthrug – a girl in a white evening dress – strangled. I don't know whether you recognized her then –'

Basil Blake shook his head violently.

'I couldn't look at her after the first glance – her face was all blue – swollen. She'd been dead some time and she was *there* – in *my* room!'

He shuddered.

Miss Marple said gently:

'You weren't, of course, quite yourself. You were in a fuddled state and your nerves are not good. You were, I think, panic-stricken. You didn't know what to do –'

'I thought Dinah might turn up any minute. And she'd find me there with a dead body – a girl's dead body – and she'd think I'd killed her. Then I got an idea – it seemed, I don't know why, a good idea at the time – I thought: I'll put her in old Bantry's library. Damned pompous old stick, always looking down his nose, sneering at me as artistic and effeminate. Serve the pompous old brute right, I thought. He'll look a fool when a dead lovely is found on his hearthrug.' He added, with a pathetic eagerness to explain: 'I was a bit drunk, you know, at the time. It really seemed positively *amusing* to me. Old Bantry with a dead blonde.'

'Yes, yes,' said Miss Marple. 'Little Tommy Bond had very much the same idea. Rather a sensitive boy with an inferiority complex, he said teacher was always picking on him. He put a frog in the clock and it jumped out at her.

'You were just the same,' went on Miss Marple, 'only of course, bodies are more serious matters than frogs.'

Basil groaned again.

'By the morning I'd sobered up. I realized what I'd done. I was scared stiff. And then the police came here – another damned pompous ass of a Chief Constable. I was scared of him – and the only way I could hide it was by being abominably rude. In the middle of it all Dinah drove up.'

Dinah looked out of the window.

She said:

'There's a car driving up now . . . there are men in it.'

'The police, I think,' said Miss Marple.

Basil Blake got up. Suddenly he became quite calm and resolute. He even smiled. He said:

'So I'm for it, am I? All right, Dinah sweet, keep your head. Get on to old Sims – he's the family lawyer – and go to Mother and tell her everything about our marriage. She won't bite. And don't worry. *I didn't do it.* So it's bound to be all right, see, sweetheart?'

There was a tap on the cottage door. Basil called 'Come in.' Inspector Slack entered with another man. He said:

'Mr Basil Blake?'

'Yes.'

'I have a warrant here for your arrest on the charge of murdering Ruby Keene on the night of September 21st last. I warn you that anything you say may be used at your trial. You will please accompany me now. Full facilities will be given you for communicating with your solicitor.'

Basil nodded.

He looked at Dinah, but did not touch her. He said:

'So long, Dinah.'

'Cool customer,' thought Inspector Slack.

He acknowledged the presence of Miss Marple with a half bow and a 'Good morning,' and thought to himself:

'Smart old Pussy, *she's* on to it! Good job we've got that hearthrug. That and finding out from the car-park man at the studio that he left that party at *eleven* instead of midnight. Don't think those friends of his meant to commit perjury. They were bottled and Blake told 'em firmly the next day it was twelve o'clock when he left and they believed him. Well, *his* goose is cooked good and proper! Mental, I expect! Broadmoor, not hanging. First the Reeves kid, probably strangled her, drove her out to the quarry, walked back into Danemouth, picked up his own car in some side lane, drove to this party, then back to Danemouth, brought Ruby Keene out here, strangled her, put her in old Bantry's library, then probably got the wind up about the car in the quarry, drove there, set it on fire, and got back here. Mad – sex and blood lust – lucky *this* girl's escaped. What they call recurring mania, I expect.'

Alone with Miss Marple, Dinah Blake turned to her. She said:

'I don't know who you are, but you've got to understand this – *Basil didn't do it.*'

Miss Marple said:

'I know he didn't. I know who *did* do it. But it's not going to be easy to prove. I've an idea that something you said – just now – may help. It gave me an idea – the *connection* I'd been trying to find – now what *was* it?'

Chapter 16

'I'm home, Arthur!' declared Mrs Bantry, announcing the fact like a Royal Proclamation as she flung open the study door.

Colonel Bantry immediately jumped up, kissed his wife, and declared heartily: 'Well, well, that's splendid!'

The words were unimpeachable, the manner very well done, but an affectionate wife of as many years' standing as Mrs Bantry was not deceived. She said immediately:

'Is anything the matter?'

'No, of course not, Dolly. What should be the matter?'

'Oh, I don't know,' said Mrs Bantry vaguely. 'Things are so queer, aren't they?'

She threw off her coat as she spoke and Colonel Bantry picked it up as carefully and laid it across the back of the sofa.

All exactly as usual – yet not as usual. Her husband, Mrs Bantry thought, seemed to have shrunk. He looked thinner, stooped more; they were pouches under his eyes and those eyes were not ready to meet hers.

He went on to say, still with that affectation of cheerfulness:

'Well, how did you enjoy your time at Danemouth?'

'Oh! it was great fun. You ought to have come, Arthur.'

'Couldn't get away, my dear. Lot of things to attend to here.'

'Still, I think the change would have done you good. And you like the Jeffersons?'

'Yes, yes, poor fellow. Nice chap. All very sad.'

'What have you been doing with yourself since I've been away?'

'Oh, nothing much. Been over the farms, you know. Agreed that Anderson shall have a new roof – can't patch it up any longer.'

'How did the Radfordshire Council meeting go?'

'I – well – as a matter of fact I didn't go.'

'Didn't *go*? But you were taking the chair?'

''Well, as a matter of fact, Dolly – seems there was some mistake about that. Asked me if I'd mind if Thompson took it instead.'

'I *see*,' said Mrs Bantry.

She peeled off a glove and threw it deliberately into

the wastepaper basket. Her husband went to retrieve it, and she stopped him, saying sharply:

'Leave it. I hate gloves.'

Colonel Bantry glanced at her uneasily.

Mrs Bantry said sternly:

'Did you go to dinner with the Duffs on Thursday?'

'Oh, that! It was put off. Their cook was ill.'

'Stupid people,' said Mrs Bantry. She went on: 'Did you go to the Naylors' yesterday?'

'I rang up and said I didn't feel up to it, hoped they'd excuse me. They quite understood.'

'They did, did they?' said Mrs Bantry grimly.

She sat down by the desk and absent-mindedly picked up a pair of gardening scissors. With them she cut off the fingers, one by one, of her second glove.

'What *are* you doing, Dolly?'

'Feeling destructive,' said Mrs Bantry.

She got up. 'Where shall we sit after dinner, Arthur? In the library?'

'Well – er – I don't think so – eh? Very nice in here – or the drawing-room.'

'I think,' said Mrs Bantry, 'that we'll sit in the library!'

Her steady eye met his. Colonel Bantry drew himself up to his full height. A sparkle came into his eye.

He said:

Agatha Christie

'You're right, my dear. We'll sit in the library!'

II

Mrs Bantry put down the telephone receiver with a sigh of annoyance. She had rung up twice, and each time the answer had been the same: Miss Marple was out.

Of a naturally impatient nature, Mrs Bantry was never one to acquiesce in defeat. She rang up in rapid succession the vicarage, Mrs Price Ridley, Miss Hartnell, Miss Wetherby, and, as a last resource, the fishmonger who, by reason of his advantageous geographical position, usually knew where everybody was in the village.

The fishmonger was sorry, but he had not seen Miss Marple at all in the village that morning. She had not been her usual round.

'Where *can* the woman be?' demanded Mrs Bantry impatiently aloud.

There was a deferential cough behind her. The discreet Lorrimer murmured:

'You were requiring Miss Marple, madam? I have just observed her approaching the house.'

Mrs Bantry rushed to the front door, flung it open, and greeted Miss Marple breathlessly:

'I've been trying to get you *everywhere*. Where have

you been?' She glanced over her shoulder. Lorrimer had discreetly vanished. 'Everything's *too* awful! People are beginning to cold-shoulder Arthur. He looks *years* older. We *must* do something, Jane. *You* must do something!'

Miss Marple said:

'You needn't worry, Dolly,' in a rather peculiar voice.

Colonel Bantry appeared from the study door.

'Ah, Miss Marple. Good morning. Glad you've come. My wife's been ringing you up like a lunatic.'

'I thought I'd better bring you the news,' said Miss Marple, as she followed Mrs Bantry into the study.

'News?'

'Basil Blake has just been arrested for the murder of Ruby Keene.'

'Basil Blake?' cried the Colonel.

'But he didn't do it,' said Miss Marple.

Colonel Bantry took no notice of this statement. It is doubtful if he even heard it.

'Do you mean to say he strangled that girl and then brought her along and put her in *my* library?'

'He put her in your library,' said Miss Marple. 'But he didn't kill her.'

'Nonsense! If he put her in my library, of course he killed her! The two things go together.'

'Not necessarily. He found her dead in his own cottage.'

'A likely story,' said the Colonel derisively. 'If you find a body, why, you ring up the police – naturally – if you're an honest man.'

'Ah,' said Miss Marple, 'but we haven't all got such iron nerves as you have, Colonel Bantry. You belong to the old school. This younger generation is different.'

'Got no stamina,' said the Colonel, repeating a well-worn opinion of his.

'Some of them,' said Miss Marple, 'have been through a bad time. I've heard a good deal about Basil. He did A.R.P. work, you know, when he was only eighteen. He went into a burning house and brought out four children, one after another. He went back for a dog, although they told him it wasn't safe. The building fell in on him. They got him out, but his chest was badly crushed and he had to lie in plaster for nearly a year and was ill for a long time after that. That's when he got interested in designing.'

'Oh!' The Colonel coughed and blew his nose. 'I – er – never knew that.'

'He doesn't talk about it,' said Miss Marple.

'Er – quite right. Proper spirit. Must be more in the young chap than I thought. Always thought he'd shirked the war, you know. Shows you ought to be careful in jumping to conclusions.'

Colonel Bantry looked ashamed.

'But, all the same' – his indignation revived – 'what did he mean trying to fasten a murder on *me*?'

'I don't think he saw it like that,' said Miss Marple. 'He thought of it more as a – as a joke. You see, he was rather under the influence of alcohol at the time.'

'Bottled, was he?' said Colonel Bantry, with an Englishman's sympathy for alcoholic excess. 'Oh, well, can't judge a fellow by what he does when he's drunk. When I was at Cambridge, I remember I put a certain utensil – well, well, never mind. Deuce of a row there was about it.'

He chuckled, then checked himself sternly. He looked piercingly at Miss Marple with eyes that were shrewd and appraising. He said: '*You* don't think he did the murder, eh?'

'I'm sure he didn't.'

'And you think you know who did?'

Miss Marple nodded.

Mrs Bantry, like an ecstatic Greek chorus, said: 'Isn't she wonderful?' to an unhearing world.

'Well, who was it?'

Miss Marple said:

'I was going to ask you to help me. I think, if we went up to Somerset House we should have a very good idea.'

Chapter 17

Sir Henry's face was very grave.

He said:

'I don't like it.'

'I am aware,' said Miss Marple, 'that it isn't what you call orthodox. But it *is* so important, isn't it, to be quite *sure* – "to make assurance doubly sure," as Shakespeare has it. I think, if Mr Jefferson would agree –?'

'What about Harper? Is he to be in on this?'

'It might be awkward for him to know too much. But there might be a hint from you. To watch certain persons – have them trailed, you know.'

Sir Henry said slowly:

'Yes, that would meet the case . . .'

Agatha Christie

II

Superintendent Harper looked piercingly at Sir Henry Clithering.

'Let's get this quite clear, sir. You're giving me a hint?'

Sir Henry said:

'I'm informing you of what my friend has just informed me – he didn't tell me in confidence – that he proposes to visit a solicitor in Danemouth tomorrow for the purpose of making a new will.'

The Superintendent's bushy eyebrows drew downwards over his steady eyes. He said:

'Does Mr Conway Jefferson propose to inform his son-in-law and daughter-in-law of that fact?'

'He intends to tell them about it this evening.'

'I see.'

The Superintendent tapped his desk with a penholder. He repeated again: 'I see . . .'

Then the piercing eyes bored once more into the eyes of the other man. Harper said:

'So you're not satisfied with the case against Basil Blake?'

'Are you?'

The Superintendent's moustaches quivered. He said:

'Is Miss Marple?'

The two men looked at each other.

Then Harper said:

'You can leave it to me. I'll have men detailed. There will be no funny business, I can promise you that.'

Sir Henry said:

'There is one more thing. You'd better see this.'

He unfolded a slip of paper and pushed it across the table.

This time the Superintendent's calm deserted him. He whistled:

'So that's it, is it? That puts an entirely different complexion on the matter. How did you come to dig up this?'

'Women,' said Sir Henry, 'are eternally interested in marriages.'

'Especially,' said the Superintendent, 'elderly single women.'

III

Conway Jefferson looked up as his friend entered.

His grim face relaxed into a smile.

He said:

'Well, I told 'em. They took it very well.'

'What did you say?'

'Told 'em that, as Ruby was dead, I felt that the fifty

thousand I'd originally left her should go to something that I could associate with her memory. It was to endow a hostel for young girls working as professional dancers in London. Damned silly way to leave your money – surprised they swallowed it. As though *I*'d do a thing like that!'

He added meditatively:

'You know, I made a fool of myself over that girl. Must be turning into a silly old man. I can see it now. She was a pretty kid – but most of what I saw in her I put there myself. I pretended she was another Rosamund. Same colouring, you know. But not the same heart or mind. Hand me that paper – rather an interesting bridge problem.'

IV

Sir Henry went downstairs. He asked a question of the porter.

'Mr Gaskell, sir? He's just gone off in his car. Had to go to London.'

'Oh! I see. Is Mrs Jefferson about?'

'Mrs Jefferson, sir, has just gone up to bed.'

Sir Henry looked into the lounge and through to the ballroom. In the lounge Hugo McLean was doing a crossword puzzle and frowning a good deal over it. In the ballroom Josie was smiling valiantly into the face of a stout, perspiring man as her nimble feet avoided his destructive tread. The stout man was clearly enjoying his dance. Raymond, graceful and weary, was dancing with an anaemic-looking girl with adenoids, dull brown hair, and an expensive and exceedingly unbecoming dress.

Sir Henry said under his breath:

'*And so to bed,*' and went upstairs.

V

It was three o'clock. The wind had fallen, the moon was shining over the quiet sea.

In Conway Jefferson's room there was no sound except his own heavy breathing as he lay, half propped up on pillows.

There was no breeze to stir the curtains at the window, but they stirred ... For a moment they parted, and a figure was silhouetted against the moonlight. Then they fell back into place. Everything was quiet again, but there was someone else inside the room.

Nearer and nearer to the bed the intruder stole. The deep breathing on the pillow did not relax.

There was no sound, or hardly any sound. A finger

and thumb were ready to pick up a fold of skin, in the other hand the hypodermic was ready.

And then, suddenly, out of the shadows a hand came and closed over the hand that held the needle, the other arm held the figure in an iron grasp.

An unemotional voice, the voice of the law, said:

'No, you don't. I want that needle!'

The light switched on and from his pillows Conway Jefferson looked grimly at the murderer of Ruby Keene.

Chapter 18

Sir Henry Clithering said:

'Speaking as Watson, I want to know your methods, Miss Marple.'

Superintendent Harper said:

'*I*'d like to know what put you on to it first.'

Colonel Melchett said:

'You've done it again, by Jove! I want to hear all about it from the beginning.'

Miss Marple smoothed the puce silk of her best evening gown. She flushed and smiled and looked very self-conscious.

She said: 'I'm afraid you'll think my "methods", as Sir Henry calls them, are terribly amateurish. The truth is, you see, that most people – and I don't exclude policemen – are far too trusting for this wicked world. They believe what is told them. I never do. I'm afraid I always like to prove a thing for myself.'

Agatha Christie

'That is the scientific attitude,' said Sir Henry.

'In this case,' continued Miss Marple, 'certain things were taken for granted from the first – instead of just confining oneself to the facts. The facts, as I noted them, were that the victim was quite young and that she bit her nails and that her teeth stuck out a little – as young girls' so often do if not corrected in time with a plate – (and children are very naughty about their plates and taking them out when their elders aren't looking).

'But that is wandering from the point. Where was I? Oh, yes, looking down at the dead girl and feeling sorry, because it is always sad to see a young life cut short, and thinking that whoever had done it was a very wicked person. Of course it was all very confusing her being found in Colonel Bantry's library, altogether too like a book to be *true*. In fact, it made the wrong pattern. It wasn't, you see, *meant*, which confused us a lot. The *real* idea had been to plant the body on poor young Basil Blake (a *much* more likely person), and his action in putting it in the Colonel's library delayed things considerably, and must have been a source of great annoyance to the *real* murderer.

'Originally, you see, Mr Blake would have been the first object of suspicion. They'd have made inquiries at Danemouth, found he knew the girl, then found he had tied himself up with another girl, and they'd have assumed that Ruby came to blackmail him, or something like that, and that he'd strangled her in a fit of rage. Just an ordinary, sordid, what I call *night-club* type of crime!

'But that, of course, *all went wrong*, and interest became focused much too soon on the Jefferson family – to the great annoyance of a *certain person*.

'As I've told you, I've got a very suspicious mind. My nephew Raymond tells me (in fun, of course, and quite affectionately) that I have a mind like a *sink*. He says that most Victorians have. All I can say is that the Victorians knew a good deal about human nature.

'As I say, having this rather insanitary – or surely *sanitary*? – mind, I looked at once at the *money* angle of it. Two people stood to benefit by this girl's death – you couldn't get away from that. Fifty thousand pounds is a lot of money – especially when you are in financial difficulties, as both these people were. Of course they both seemed very nice, agreeable people – they didn't seem *likely* people – but one never can tell, can one?

'Mrs Jefferson, for instance – everyone liked her. But it did seem clear that she had become very restless that summer, and that she was tired of the life she led, completely dependent on her father-in-law. She knew, because the doctor had told her, that he couldn't live long – so *that* was all right – to put it callously – or it *would* have been all right if Ruby Keene hadn't come along. Mrs Jefferson was passionately devoted to her son, and some women have a curious idea that crimes committed for the sake of their offspring are almost morally justified. I have come across that attitude once or twice in the village. "Well, 'twas all for Daisy, you see, miss," they say, and seem to think that that makes doubtful conduct quite all right. Very *lax* thinking.

'Mr Mark Gaskell, of course, was a much more likely starter, if I may use such a sporting expression. He was a gambler and had not, I fancied, a very high moral code. But, for certain reasons, I was of the opinion that a *woman* was concerned in this crime.

'As I say, with my eye on motive, the money angle seemed *very* suggestive. It was annoying, therefore, to find that both these people had alibis for the time when Ruby Keene, according to the medical evidence, had met her death.

'But soon afterwards there came the discovery of the burnt-out car with Pamela Reeves's body in it, and then the whole thing leaped to the eye. The alibis, of course, were worthless.

'I now had two *halves* of the case, and both quite convincing, but they did not fit. There must *be* a connection, but I could not find it. The one person whom I *knew* to be concerned in the crime hadn't got a motive.

'It was stupid of me,' said Miss Marple meditatively.

'If it hadn't been for Dinah Lee I shouldn't have thought of it – the most obvious thing in the world. Somerset House! Marriage! It wasn't a question of only Mr Gaskell or Mrs Jefferson – there were the further possibilities of *marriage*. If either of those two was married, or even was *likely* to marry, *then the other party to the marriage contract was involved too.* Raymond, for instance, might think he had a pretty good chance of marrying a rich wife. He had been very assiduous to Mrs Jefferson, and it was his charm, I think, that awoke her from her long widowhood. She had been quite content just being a daughter to Mr Jefferson – like Ruth and Naomi – only Naomi, if you remember, took a lot of trouble to arrange a suitable marriage for Ruth.

'Besides Raymond there was Mr McLean. She liked him very much and it seemed highly possible that she would marry him in the end. *He* wasn't well off – and he was not far from Danemouth on the night in question. So it seemed, didn't it,' said Miss Marple, 'as though *anyone* might have done it?'

'But, of course, really, in my mind, I *knew*. You couldn't get away, could you, from those bitten nails?'

'Nails?' said Sir Henry. 'But she tore her nail and cut the others.'

'Nonsense,' said Miss Marple. '*Bitten* nails and close *cut* nails are quite different! Nobody could mistake them who knew anything about girl's nails – very ugly, bitten nails, as I always tell the girls in my class. Those nails, you see, were a *fact*. And they could only mean one thing. *The body in Colonel Bantry's library wasn't Ruby Keene at all.*

'And that brings you straight to the one person who must be concerned. *Josie!* Josie identified the body. She knew, she *must* have known, that it wasn't Ruby Keene's body. She said it was. She was puzzled, completely puzzled, at finding that body where it was. She practically betrayed that fact. Why? Because *she* knew, none better, where it ought to have been found! In Basil Blake's cottage. Who directed our attention to Basil? Josie, by saying to Raymond that Ruby might have been with the film man. And before that, by slipping a snapshot of him into Ruby's handbag. Who cherished such bitter anger against the dead girl that she couldn't hide it even when she looked down at her dead? Josie! Josie, who was shrewd, practical, hard as nails, and *all out for money*.

'That is what I meant about believing too readily. Nobody thought of disbelieving Josie's statement that the body was Ruby Keene's. Simply because it didn't seem at the time that she could have any motive for lying. Motive was always the difficulty – Josie was clearly involved, but Ruby's death seemed, if anything, contrary to her interests. It was not till Dinah Lee mentioned Somerset House that I got the connection.

'Marriage! If Josie and Mark Gaskell were actually married – then the whole thing was clear. As we know now, Mark and Josie were married a year ago. They were keeping it dark until Mr Jefferson died.

'It was really quite interesting, you know, tracing out the course of events – seeing exactly how the plan had worked out. Complicated and yet simple. First of all the selection of the poor child, Pamela, the approach to her from the film angle. A screen test – of course the poor child couldn't resist it. Not when it was put up to her as plausibly as Mark Gaskell put it. She comes to the hotel, he is waiting for her, he takes her in by the side door and introduces her to Josie – one of their make-up experts! That poor child, it makes me quite sick to think of it! Sitting in Josie's bathroom while Josie bleaches her hair and makes up her face and varnishes her finger-nails and toenails. During all this, the drug was given. In an icecream soda, very likely. She goes off into a coma. I imagine that they put her into one of the empty rooms opposite – they were only cleaned once a week, remember.

'After dinner Mark Gaskell went out in his car – to the sea-front, *he* said. That is when he took Pamela's body to the cottage dressed in one of Ruby's old dresses and arranged it on the hearthrug. She was still unconscious, but not dead, when he strangled her with the belt of the frock . . . Not nice, no – but I hope and pray she knew nothing about it. Really, I feel quite pleased to think of him being hanged . . . That must have been just after ten o'clock. The he drove back at top speed and found the others in the lounge where Ruby Keene, *still alive*, was dancing her exhibition dance with Raymond.

'I should imagine that Josie had given Ruby instructions beforehand. Ruby was accustomed to doing what Josie told her. She was to change, go into Josie's room and wait. She, too, was drugged, probably in after-dinner coffee. She was yawning, remember, when she talked to young Bartlett.

'Josie came up later to "look for her" – *but nobody but Josie went into Josie's room*. She probably finished the girl off then – with an injection, perhaps, or a blow on the back of the head. She went down, danced with Raymond, debated with the Jeffersons where Ruby could be, and finally went to bed. In the early hours of the morning she dressed the girl in Pamela's clothes, carried the body down the side stairs – she was a strong muscular young woman – fetched George Bartlett's car, drove two miles to the quarry, poured petrol over the car and set it alight. Then she walked back to the hotel, probably timing her arrival there for eight or nine o'clock – up early in her anxiety about Ruby!'

'An intricate plot,' said Colonel Melchett.

'Not more intricate than the steps of a dance,' said Miss Marple.

'I suppose not.'

'She was very thorough,' said Miss Marple. 'She even foresaw the discrepancy of the nails. That's why she managed to break one of Ruby's nails on her shawl. It made an excuse for pretending that Ruby had clipped her nails close.'

Harper said: 'Yes, she thought of everything. And the only real proof you had, Miss Marple, was a schoolgirl's bitten nails.'

'More than that,' said Miss Marple. 'People *will* talk too much. Mark Gaskell talked too much. He was speaking of Ruby and he said "her teeth ran down her throat." But the dead girl in Colonel Bantry's library had teeth that stuck *out*.'

Conway Jefferson said rather grimly:

'And was the last dramatic *finale* your idea, Miss Marple?'

Miss Marple confessed. 'Well, it *was*, as a matter of fact. It's so nice to be *sure*, isn't it?'

'Sure is the word,' said Conway Jefferson grimly.

'You see,' said Miss Marple, 'once Mark and Josie knew that you were going to make a new will, they'd *have* to do something. They'd already committed *two* murders on account of the money. So they might as

269

well commit a third. Mark, of course, must be absolutely clear, so he went off to London and established an alibi by dining at a restaurant with friends and going on to a night club. Josie was to do the work. They still wanted Ruby's death to be put down to Basil's account, so Mr Jefferson's death must be thought due to his heart failing. There was digitalin, so the Superintendent tells me, in the syringe. Any doctor would think death from heart trouble quite natural in the circumstances. Josie had loosened one of the stone balls on the balcony and she was going to let it crash down afterwards. His death would be put down to the shock of the noise.'

Melchett said: 'Ingenious devil.'

Sir Henry said: 'So the third death you spoke of was to be Conway Jefferson?'

Miss Marple shook her head.

'Oh no – I meant Basil Blake. They'd have got him hanged if they could.'

'Or shut up in Broadmoor,' said Sir Henry.

Conway Jefferson grunted. He said:

'Always knew Rosamund had married a rotter. Tried not to admit it to myself. She was damned fond of him. Fond of a murderer! Well, he'll hang as well as the woman. I'm glad he went to pieces and gave the show away.'

Miss Marple said:

'She was always the strong character. It was her plan throughout. The irony of it is that she got the girl down here herself, never dreaming that she would take Mr Jefferson's fancy and ruin all her own prospects.'

Jefferson said:

'Poor lass. Poor little Ruby . . .'

Adelaide Jefferson and Hugo McLean came in. Adelaide looked almost beautiful tonight. She came up to Conway Jefferson and laid a hand on his shoulder. She said, with a little catch in her breath:

'I want to tell you something, Jeff. At once. I'm going to marry Hugo.'

Conway Jefferson looked up at her for a moment. He said gruffly:

'About time you married again. Congratulations to you both. By the way, Addie, I'm making a new will tomorrow.'

She nodded. 'Oh yes, I know.'

Jefferson said:

'No, you don't. I'm settling ten thousand pounds on you. Everything else I have goes to Peter when I die. How does that suit you, my girl?'

'Oh, *Jeff*!' Her voice broke. 'You're *wonderful*!'

'He's a nice lad. I'd like to see a good deal of him – in the time I've got left.'

'Oh, you shall!'

'Got a great feeling for crime, Peter has,' said

Conway Jefferson meditatively. 'Not only has he got the fingernail of the murdered girl – one of the murdered girls, anyway – but he was lucky enough to have a bit of Josie's shawl caught in with the nail. So he's got a souvenir of the murderess too! That makes him *very* happy!'

II

Hugo and Adelaide passed by the ballroom. Raymond came up to them.

Adelaide said, rather quickly:

'I must tell you my news. We're going to be married.'

The smile on Raymond's face was perfect – a brave, pensive smile.

'I hope,' he said, ignoring Hugo and gazing into her eyes, 'that you will be very, very happy . . .'

They passed on and Raymond stood looking after them.

'A nice woman,' he said to himself. 'A very nice woman. And she would have had money too. The trouble I took to mug up that bit about the Devonshire Starrs . . . Oh well, my luck's out. Dance, dance, little gentleman!'

And Raymond returned to the ballroom.

THE MAGNATE'S MISTRESS

BY
MIRANDA LEE

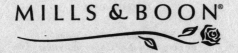

MILLS & BOON®

*First published in Great Britain 2004
Harlequin Mills & Boon Limited,
Eton House, 18-24 Paradise Road, Richmond, Surrey TW9 1SR*

© Miranda Lee 2004

ISBN 0 263 83767 X

Set in Times Roman 10½ on 12 pt.
01-0904-40858

*Printed and bound in Spain
by Litografia Rosés, S.A., Barcelona*

CHAPTER ONE

THE beep-beep which signalled an incoming text message had Tara dropping her book and diving for her cellphone.

Max! It had to be Max. He was the only person who text-messaged her these days.

Arriving Mascot at 1530, she read with her heart already thudding. *QF310. Can you pick me up? Let me know.*

A glance at her bedside clock said five to twelve. If his plane was to arrive at three-thirty this afternoon, Max had to be already in the air.

She immediately texted him back.

Will be there.

She smiled wryly at the brevity and lack of sentiment in both their messages. There was no *I can't wait to see you, darling.* No *I've missed you terribly.* All very matter-of-fact.

Max was a matter-of-fact kind of man. Mostly.

Not quite so matter-of-fact in bed. A quiver rippled down Tara's spine at the image of Max in the throes of making love to her.

No. Not at all matter-of-fact on those occasions.

Tara glanced at the clock again. Nearly noon.

Not a lot of time for her to get ready, catch a train

into town, collect Max's car and drive out to the airport. She would have to hurry.

Jumping up from the bed reminded Tara of why she'd been lying back down at this late hour on a Saturday morning. A new wave of nausea rolled through her and she just made it to the bathroom in time before retching.

Darn. Why did she have to have a tummy bug today of all days? It had been almost a month since she'd seen Max, the current crisis in the travel industry having kept him on the hop overseas for ages. Hong Kong had been one of the cities worst affected. When she'd complained during his last phone call two nights ago that she'd forget what he looked like soon, Max had promised to see what he could do this weekend. He was flying to Auckland on the Friday for an important business meeting and might have time to duck over to Sydney on the weekend before returning to Hong Kong.

But Tara hadn't seriously expected anything. She never liked to get her hopes up too much. It was too depressing when she was disappointed. Still, maybe Max was finally missing her as much as she was missing him.

Which was why the last thing she needed today was to feel sick. She might only have the one night with him this time and she wanted to make the most of it. But it would be hard to enjoy his company if she felt like chucking up all the time.

A sigh reverberated through her as she flushed the toilet.

'Are you all right in there?' her mother called through the bathroom door.

'I'm fine,' Tara lied, experience warning her not to say anything. Her mother would fuss. Tara disliked being fussed over. No doubt she was only suffering from the same twenty-four-hour gastric bug which was going through Sydney's western suburbs like wildfire. Her sister's family had had it this past week, and she'd been over there last weekend for a family barbeque.

Actually, now that she'd been sick, Tara felt considerably better. A shower would make her feel even better, she reasoned, and turned on the spray.

Her arrival in the kitchen an hour later with freshly blow-dried hair, a perfectly made-up face and a new outfit on had her mother giving her a narrow-eyed once-over.

'I see his lord and master must be arriving for one of his increasingly fleeting visits,' Joyce said tartly, then went back to whatever cake she was making.

Saturday was Joyce Bond's baking day; had been for as long as Tara could remember. Such rigid routines grated on Tara's more spontaneous nature. She often wished that her mother would surprise her by doing something different on a Saturday for once. She also wished she would surprise her with a different attitude towards Max.

'Mum, please don't,' Tara said wearily, and popped

a slice of bread into the toaster. Her stomach had settled enough for her to handle some Vegemite toast, but she still wasn't feeling wonderful.

Joyce spun round from the kitchen counter to glower at her daughter. Her impossibly beautiful daughter.

Tara had inherited the best of each of her parents. She had her father's height, his lovely blond hair, clear skin, good teeth and striking green eyes. Joyce had contributed a cute nose, full lips and an even fuller bust, which looked infinitely better on Tara than it ever had on her own less tall, short-waisted body.

Joyce hadn't been surprised when one of the wealthy men who patronised the exclusive jewellery boutique where Tara worked had made a beeline for her. She wasn't surprised—or even too worried—when Tara confessed that she was no longer a virgin. Joyce had always thought it a minor miracle that a girl with Tara's looks had reached twenty-four without having slept with a man. After all, her daughter's many boyfriends must have tried to get the girl into bed.

Tara had always claimed she was waiting for Prince Charming to come along. Joyce's younger daughter was somewhat of an idealist, a full-on romantic. An avid reader, she was addicted to novels which featured wonderful heroes and happy-ever-after endings.

In the beginning, Joyce had hoped that Max Richmond *was* her daughter's Prince Charming. He had most of the attributes. Wealth. Good looks. Youth. *Relative* youth, anyway. He'd been thirty-five when they'd begun seeing each other.

But in the last twelve months Joyce had come to feel differently about her daughter's relationship with the handsome hotel magnate. It had finally become clear that Max Richmond was never going to marry his lovely young mistress.

For that was what Tara had swiftly become. Not a proper girlfriend, or a partner, as people sometimes called their loved ones these days. A *mistress*, expected to be there when he called and be silent when he left. Expected to give everything and receive nothing in return, except for the corrupting gifts rich men invariably gave to their mistresses.

Designer clothes. Jewellery. Perfume. Flowers.

A fresh bouquet of red roses was delivered every week when Max was away. But who ordered them? Joyce often wondered. The man himself, or his secretary?

If Tara had been the kind of good-time girl who could handle such a relationship, Joyce would have held her tongue. But Tara was nothing of the kind. Underneath her sophisticated and sexy-looking exterior lay a soft, sensitive soul. A good girl. When Max Richmond eventually dumped her, she was going to be shattered.

Joyce's thoughts had fired a slow-burning fury, along with her tongue.

'Don't what?' she snapped. 'Don't tell it like it is?

I'm not going to sit by silently and say nothing, Tara. I love you too much for that. You're wasting your life on that man. He will never give you what you really want. He's just using you.'

Tara refrained from reminding her mother how often she'd been told in this house that she didn't know *what* she wanted in life. Joyce had frowned over her daughter not using her arts degree to get a job in Sydney. Instead, a restless Tara had gone tripping off to Japan to teach English for two years, at the same time using the opportunity to see as much of Asia as she could. When she'd returned to Sydney eighteen months ago her mother had expected her to look for a teaching position here. Instead, she'd taken a job as a shop assistant at Whitmore Opals, till she decided what she wanted to do next. Her announcement recently that she was going back to university next year to study psychology had been met with rolling eyes, as if to say, there she goes again.

In a way, her mother was right. She didn't know what she wanted to be, career-wise, the way some people did. But she knew what she *didn't* want. She didn't want to be tied down at home with children the way Jen was. And she didn't want to bake cakes every single Saturday.

'So what *is* it that you think I really want, Mum?' she asked, rather curious to find out what secret observation her mother had made.

'Why, what most women want deep down. A home, and a family. And a husband, of course.'

Tara shook her head. Given that her mother was rising sixty, she supposed there were excuses for holding such an old-fashioned viewpoint.

But the bit about a husband was rather ironic, considering her mother's personal background. Joyce had been widowed for over twenty years, Tara's electrician father having been killed in a work accident when Tara was just three. Her mother had raised her two daughters virtually single-handed. She'd worked hard to provide for them. She'd scrimped and saved and even bought her own house. Admittedly, it was not a flash house. But it was a house. *And,* she'd never married again. In fact, there'd never been another man in her life after Tara's father.

'It may come as a surprise to you, Mum,' Tara said as she removed the popped-up toast, 'but I don't want any of that. Not yet, anyway. I'm only twenty-four. There are plenty of years ahead for me to settle down to marriage and motherhood. I like my life the way it is. I'm looking forward to going back to uni next year. Meanwhile, I have an interesting job, some good friends and a fabulous lover.'

'Whom you rarely see. As for your supposed good friends, name one you've been out with in the last six months!'

Tara couldn't.

'See what I mean?' her mother went on accusingly. 'You never go out with your old friends any more because you're compelled to keep your weekends free, in case his lord and master deigns to drop in on your life. For pity's sake, Tara, do you honestly think your jet-setting lover is spending every weekend of his alone when he doesn't come home?'

Joyce regretted the harsh words the moment she saw her daughter's face go a sickly shade of grey.

Tara gripped the kitchen counter and willed the bile in her throat to go back down. 'You don't know what you're talking about, Mum. Max would never do that.'

'Are you sure of that?' Joyce said, but more softly this time. 'He doesn't love you, Tara. Not the way you love him.'

'Yes, he does. And even if he didn't, I'd still want him.'

Oh, yes, that was one thing she *was* sure about.

'I won't give him up for anything, or anyone,' she announced fiercely, and took a savage bite of toast.

'He's going to break your heart.'

Tara's heart contracted. Would he? She couldn't imagine it. Not her Max. Not deliberately. He wasn't like that. Her mother didn't understand. Max just didn't want marriage at this time in his life. Or kids. He'd explained all that to her right from the beginning. He'd told her up front that his life was too busy for a wife and a family. Since his father had been incapacitated by a stroke, the full responsibility of running the family firm had fallen on him. Looking after a huge chain of international hotels was a massive job, especially with the present precarious state of tourism and travel. Max spent more than half his life on a plane. All he could promise her for now was the occasional weekend.

He'd given her the opportunity to tell him to get lost, *before* she got in any deeper. But of course that had been *after* he'd taken her to bed and shown her a world she'd never envisaged, a world of incredible pleasure.

How could you give up perfection, just because everything wasn't perfect?

Tara threw the rest of her toast in the bin under the sink, then straightened with a sigh. 'If you disapprove of my relationship with Max this much, Mum,' she said unhappily, 'perhaps it's time I moved out of home.'

She could well afford to rent a place of her own on her salary. Her pay as a shop assistant at Whitmore Opals was boosted by generous commission each month. She was their top salesgirl, due to her natural affinity for people and her ability to speak fluent Japanese. A lot of the shop's customers were wealthy Japanese visitors and businessmen who appreciated being served by a pretty Australian girl who spoke their language like a native.

'And go where?' her mother threw back at her. 'To your lover's penthouse? He won't like that. You're only welcome there when *he's* there.'

'You don't know that. There again, you don't know Max. How could you? You never say more than two words to him on the phone and you've never invited him here.'

'He wouldn't want to come here,' she grumbled. 'This house isn't fancy enough for a man who lives on the top floor of Sydney's plushest hotel, and whose family owns a waterfront mansion on Point Piper. *Which*, might I point out, he's not taken you to, not even over Christmas? Have you noticed that, Tara? You're not good enough to be taken home to meet his parents. You're to be kept a dirty little secret. That's what you are, Tara. A *kept* woman.'

Tara had had enough of this. 'Firstly, there is nothing dirty about my relationship with Max. We love each other and he treats me like a princess. Secondly, Max does not keep me a dirty little secret. We often go out together in public, as you very well know. You used to show your friends the photographs in the paper. Quite proudly, if I recall.'

'That was when I thought something would come of your relationship. When I thought he would marry you. But there have been no photographs in the paper lately, I've noticed. Maybe because he doesn't have time to take you out any more. But I'll bet he still has time to take you to bed!'

Tara clenched her jaw hard lest she say something she would later regret. She loved her mother dearly. And she supposed she could understand why the woman worried about her and Max. But modern life was very complicated when it came to personal relationships. Things weren't as cut and dried as they had been in Joyce's day.

Still, it was definitely time to find somewhere else

to live. Tara could not bear to have to defend herself and Max all the time. It would sour her relationship with her mother.

She could see now that she should not have come back home to live after her return from Tokyo. Her two years away had cut the apron strings and she should have left them cut. But when her mother had met her at the airport on her return, Tara didn't have the heart to dash Joyce's presumption that her daughter was back to stay with her. And frankly, it had been rather nice to come home to her old bedroom and her old things. *And* to her mother's cooking.

But that had been several months before she'd met Max and fallen head over heels in love.

Things were different now.

Still, if she moved out of home, her mother was going to be very lonely. She often said how much she enjoyed Tara's company. Tara's board money helped make life easier for Joyce as well. Her widow's pension didn't stretch all that far.

Guilt screamed in to add to Tara's distress.

Oh, dear. What was a daughter to do?

She would talk to Max about the situation, and see what he said. Max had a wonderful way of making things seem clear and straightforward. Solutions to problems were Max's stock-in-trade. As were decisions. He spent most of his life solving problems and making decisions.

Max was a very decisive man. A little inflexible,

however, Tara conceded. And opinionated. And un-forgiving.

Very unforgiving, actually.

'Look, Mum, there are reasons why Max hasn't taken me home to meet his parents,' she started ex-plaining to her mother. 'It has nothing to do with our working class background. His own father was born working-class, but he…' Tara broke off abruptly be-fore she revealed things told to her in strict confi-dence. Max would not appreciate her blurting out the skeletons in his family's closet, even to her mother. 'Let's leave all this for now,' she said with a sigh. 'I don't feel up to arguing with you over Max today.'

The moment she added those last words, Tara re-gretted them, for her mother's eyes instantly turned from angry to worried. Her mother was a chronic worrier when it came to matters of health.

'I *thought* I heard you being sick earlier,' Joyce said.

'It's nothing. Just a tummy bug. Probably the same thing Jen and her kids had. I'm feeling better now.'

'Are you sure that's what it is?' her mother asked, still looking concerned.

'Well, I don't think I'm dying of some dreaded disease,' Tara said. 'Truly, Mum, you have to stop looking up those health websites on the internet. You're becoming a hypochondriac.'

'I meant,' her mother bit out, 'do you think you could be pregnant?'

'Pregnant!' Tara was totally taken aback. Dear

heaven. Mothers! *Truly.* 'No, Mum, I am definitely *not* pregnant.' She'd had a period during the weeks Max had been away, which meant if she was pregnant, it had been because of an immaculate conception!

Besides, if there was one thing Tara was fanatical about, it was birth control. The last thing *she* wanted at this time in her life was a baby. Max wasn't the only one.

When they'd first become lovers, Max had said he'd use condoms. But after one broke one night last year and they'd spent an anxious two weeks, Tara had taken over the job of preventing a pregnancy. She even had her cellphone programmed so that it beeped at the same time every day, a reminder to take her pill. Six pm on the dot. She also kept a spare box of pills in Max's bathroom, in case she accidentally left hers at home.

Her mother's tendency to always expect the worst to happen in life had trained Tara to be an expert in preventative action.

'There is no sure form of contraception,' Joyce pointed out firmly. 'Except saying no.'

Tara refrained from telling her mother that saying no to Max would never be on her agenda.

'I have to get going,' she said. 'The next train for the city is due in ten minutes.'

'When will you be back?' her mother called after her as she hurried from the kitchen. 'Or don't you know?'

It hit home. That last remark. Because Tara *didn't* know. She never seemed to know these days. In that, her mother was right. Max came and went like a whirlwind, often without much information or explanation. He expected her to understand how busy he was at the moment. Which she did on the whole. *Didn't* she?

'I'll let you know, Mum,' Tara called back as she scooped up her carry-all and swept out the door. 'Bye.'

CHAPTER TWO

HER wrist-watch said three-forty as Tara slid Max's silver Mercedes into an empty parking space, then yanked the car keys out of the ignition. Ten seconds later she was hurrying across the sun-drenched car park, wishing she was wearing her joggers, instead of high-heeled slip-on white sandals. They were sexy shoes but impossible to run in. She'd found that out on the way to the station back at home.

Missing the train had put her in a right quandary.

Did she wait for the next train or catch a taxi?

A taxi from Quakers Hill to the city would cost a bomb.

Unfortunately, Joyce had instilled some of her frugal ways in both her daughters, so whilst Tara could probably have afforded the fare, she couldn't bring herself to do it. Aside from the sheer extravagance, she was saving this year to pay for next year's uni fees.

She'd momentarily contemplated using the credit card Max had given her, and which she occasionally used for clothes. But only when he was with her, and only when it was for something he insisted she buy, and which she wouldn't wear during her day-to-day life. Things like evening gowns and outrageously expensive lingerie. Things she kept in Max's penthouse for her life there.

Till now, she'd never used the card for everyday expenses. When she considered it this time, her mother's earlier words about her being a kept woman made up her mind for her. Maybe if she'd been still feeling sick, she'd have surrendered to temptation and taken a taxi, but the nausea which had been plaguing her all morning had finally disappeared. So she'd bought herself some food and sat and waited for the next train, and now she was running late.

Tara increased the speed of her stride, her stiletto heels click-clacking faster on the cement path. Her heart started to beat faster as well, a mixture of agitation and anticipation. With a bit of luck, Max's plane might not have arrived yet. She'd hate him to think she didn't care enough to be on time. Still, planes rarely seemed to land on schedule. Except when you didn't want them to, of course.

The contrariness of life.

Once inside the arrivals terminal, Tara swiftly checked the overhead information screens, groaning when she saw that Max's plane *had* landed, although only ten minutes earlier. The exit gate assigned was gate B.

Surely he could not be through Customs yet, she told herself as she hurried once more, her progress slightly hampered by having to dodge groups of people. Gate B, typically, was down the other end of the building.

Most of the men she swept past turned for a second glance, but Tara was used to that. Blondes surely did get more than their fair share of male attention, especially tall, pretty ones with long, flowing hair and even longer legs.

Tara also conceded that her new white hipsters were on the eye-poppingly tight side today. She'd been doing some comfort eating lately and had put on a couple of pounds since she'd bought them at a summer sale a fortnight ago. It was as well they were made of stretch material. Still, lord knew what the view of her was like from behind. Pretty in-your-face, no·doubt.

Her braless state might have stopped traffic as well, *if* she'd been wearing a T-shirt or a singlet top.

Thankfully, she wasn't wearing either. The pink shirt she'd chosen that day did a fair job of hiding her unfettered breasts.

In her everyday life, Tara always wore a bra. But Max liked her braless. Or so he'd said one night, soon after they'd starting seeing each other. And, being anxious to please him, she'd started leaving off her bra whenever she was with him.

But as time had gone by, she'd become aware of the type of stares she'd received from other men when Max had taken her out in public.

And she hadn't liked it.

Nowadays, when she was with Max, she still left her bra off, but compromised by never wearing anything too revealing. She chose evening gowns with heavily beaded bodices, or solid linings. For dressy day wear, she stuck to dresses and covering jackets. For casual wear, she wore shirts and blouses rather than tight or clingy tops. Tara liked the idea of keeping her bared breasts for her lover only.

Her nipples tightened further at the mere thought of Max touching them.

She would have to wait for that pleasure, however, till they were alone in Max's hotel suite. Although Max seemed to like her displaying her feminine curves in public, he was not a man to make love anywhere but in total privacy. And that included kissing.

The first time he'd come home after being away, she'd thrown her arms around him in public and given him a big kiss. His expression when she finally let him come up for air had been one of agitation, and distaste. He'd explained to her later that he found it embarrassing, and could she please refrain from turning him on to that degree when he could not do anything about it?

He *had* added later that he was more than happy for her to be as provocative and as assertive as she liked in private. But once stung by what she'd seen as a rejection of her overtures—and affection—Tara now never made the first move where lovemaking was concerned. She always left it up to Max.

Not that she ever had to wait long. Behind closed doors, Max's coolly controlled façade soon dropped away to reveal a hot-blooded and often insatiable lover. His visits home might have become shorter and less frequent over the last few months—as Tara's mother had observed—but whilst he was here in Sydney, he was all Tara's. They spent most of Max's visits in bed.

Her mother would see this as conclusive evidence that she was just a sex object to Max. A kept woman. In other words, a mistress.

But her mother was not there when Max took her in his arms. She didn't see the look in his eyes; didn't feel the tenderness in his touch; or the uncontrollable trembling which racked his body whenever he made love to her.

Max *loved* her. Tara was sure of it.

His not wanting to marry her at this time in his life was a matter of timing, not lack of love. Max had never said that marriage was *never* on his agenda.

And as she'd told her mother, *she* was in no hurry to get married, anyway. What she was in a hurry for was to get to gate B, collect Max and take him back to the Regency Royale Hotel, post-haste.

Fate must have been on her side, for no sooner had she ground to a breathless halt not far from gate B than Max emerged through the customs exit, striding purposefully down the ramp, carrying his laptop in one hand and wheeling a black carry-on suitcase in the other.

Tara supposed he didn't look all that much different from dozens of other well-dressed businessmen there at the airport that day. Perhaps taller than most. More broad-shouldered. And more handsome.

But just the sight of him did things to her that she could never explain to her mother. She came alive as she was never alive when she wasn't with him. Her brain bubbled with joy and the blood fizzed in her veins.

Tara conceded not every twenty-four-year-old girl's heart would flutter madly at Max's more conservative brand of handsome, or his very conservative mode of dressing. Tara rarely saw him in anything but a suit. Today's was charcoal-grey. Single-breasted, combined with a crisp white shirt and a striped blue tie.

All very understated.

But Tara liked the air of stability and security which Max's untrendy image projected. She liked the fact that he always looked a man of substance. And she very much liked his looks.

Yet till now, she'd never really analysed him feature by feature. It had been his overall appearance, and his overall aura which had initially taken her breath away. And which had kept her captivated ever since.

But as Max made his way through gate B, his eyes having not yet connected with hers, Tara found herself studying Max's looks more objectively than usual.

Now, that was one classically handsome guy, she decided. Not a pretty boy, but not a rough diamond, either.

A masculine-looking man, Max had a large but

well-balanced face, surrounded by a thick head of dark brown hair, always cut with short back and sides, and always combed from a side-parting. His ears were nicely flat against his well-shaped head. His intelligent blue eyes were deeply set, bisected by a long, straight nose and accentuated with thick, dark brown brows. His mouth, despite its full bottom lip, had not a hint of femininity about it and invariably held an uncompromising expression.

Max was not a man who smiled a lot. Mostly, his lips remained firmly shut, his penetrating blue eyes glittering with a hardness which Tara found sexy, but which she imagined could be forbidding, especially when he was annoyed, or angry. Tara suspected he could be a formidable boss, if crossed. She'd heard him a few times over the phone when he'd been laying down the law to various employees.

But with her, he was never really annoyed, or angry. He *had* been frustrated that time when she'd kissed him in public. And exasperated when she refused to let him buy her a car. But that was it.

Tara knew that when he finally caught sight of her standing there, waiting for him, he *would* smile.

And suddenly, it was there, that slow curve to his lips, that softer gleam in his eyes, and it was all she could do not to run to him and throw herself into his arms. Instead, she stayed right where she was, smiling her joy back at him whilst he walked slowly towards her.

'For a few seconds, I thought you weren't here,' he said once they were standing face to face.

'I almost wasn't,' she confessed. 'I was running horribly late. You should have seen me a minute ago, trying to bolt across the car park in these shoes.'

He glanced down at the offending shoes, then slowly let his eyes run up her body. By the time his gaze reached her mouth, her lips had gone bone-dry.

'Are you sure it was the shoes, or those wicked white trousers? How on earth did you get them on? You must have had them sewn on.'

'They're stretchy.'

His eyes glittered in that sexy way she adored. 'Thank the lord for that. I had visions of spending half the night getting them off you. You know, you really shouldn't wear gear like that to greet me when we've been apart for nearly a month. It does terrible things to me.'

'I thought you liked me to dress sexily,' she said, piqued that he hadn't bothered to ask her why she was late. It occurred to her with a degree of shock that maybe he didn't care.

'That depends on how long I've been away. Thank goodness you're wearing a bra.'

'But I'm not.'

He stared at her chest, then up at her mouth. 'I wish you hadn't told me that,' he muttered.

'For pity's sake, Max, is there no pleasing you to-day?'

'You please me all the time,' he returned thickly,

and putting his laptop down, he actually reached out to stroke a tender hand down her cheek. If that didn't stun her, his next action did.

He kissed her, his hand sliding down and around under her hair, cupping the back of her neck whilst his mouth branded hers with purpose and passion.

The kiss must have lasted a full minute, leaving Tara weak-kneed with desire and flushed with embarrassment. For people were definitely staring at them.

'Max!' she protested huskily when his hand then slid down her shirt over her right breast.

'That's what you get for meeting me in those screw-me shoes,' he whispered.

When Tara gaped at him, Max laughed.

'You little hypocrite. You deliberately dressed to tease me today, and then you pretend to be shocked when you get the reaction you wanted. Here. Give me my car keys and take this,' he ordered and handed her the laptop. 'I want one hand free to keep you in line, you bad girl.'

Tara's cheeks continued to burn as she was ushered from the terminal with Max's hand firmly clamped to her bejeaned backside. Her head was fairly whirling with mixed messages and emotions.

In all the times she had picked Max up at the airport, he had never made her feel like this. As if sex was the *only* thing on his mind, and on hers. And whilst she was flustered by this change in behaviour—could her mother have been right about Max just using her for sex?—she was also undeniably turned on.

Neither of them said a single word till they were standing by the Mercedes and Max had put his things into the boot.

'Fifteen minutes,' Max said as he slammed the boot shut and turned to her.

'What?'

By then she was hot all over, not just her cheeks.

'Fifteen minutes,' Max repeated. 'That's how long till we're alone. I suspect it's going to be the longest fifteen minutes of my life.' His eyes ran all over her again, finally lingering on her mouth. 'If I kiss you again, I won't be able to wait. I'll ravage you in the back seat of this car and to hell with everything.'

Tara wasn't sure if she liked this beastlike Max as much as the civilised one she was used to. But she suspected that if he kissed her again, she wouldn't *care* if he ravaged her on the back seat.

In fact, she was already imagining him doing just that, and it sent her head spinning.

Just then, a couple of young fellows walked by and one of them ogled her before pursing his lips in a mock kiss. When he turned to his mate and said something, they both laughed.

Tara cringed.

'Then please don't kiss me,' she choked out.

Max, who hadn't seen this exchange, shook his head at her. 'Still playing the tease? That's a new one for you, Tara. What's happened to the sweet, naive, extremely innocent virgin I met a year ago?'

'She's been sleeping with you for a year,' she countered, stung by his inference that this change to-day was all hers.

His eyes darkened. 'Do I detect a degree of dissat-isfaction in those words? Is that why you were late today? Because you were thinking of not coming to pick me up at all?'

'So glad that you finally cared enough to ask why I was late!' she snapped. 'For your information, I had words with my mother and then I missed my train.'

Did he look relieved? She couldn't be sure. Max was not an easy man to read.

'What was the argument about?'

'You.'

That surprised him. 'What about me?'

'Mum thinks you're just using me.'

'And what do you think?'

'I told her you loved me.'

'I do.'

Tara's heart lurched at his words. *Do you, Max? Do you, really?*

'If you truly loved me,' she pointed out agitatedly, 'then you wouldn't talk about ravaging me in the back seat of a car in a public car park.'

He seemed startled, before a thoughtful frown gath-ered on his high forehead. 'I see the way your mind is working, but you're wrong. And so was I. You're not a tease, or a hypocrite. You're still the incurable romantic you always were. But that's all right. That's what I love about you. Come along, then, princess. Let's get you home, where we can dive into our lovely four-poster bed and make beautiful romantic love all weekend long.'

'Do we have a whole weekend this time, Max?' Tara asked eagerly, relieved that the threat of being publicly ravaged in the back seat of Max's car had been averted.

'Unfortunately, no. I have to catch a plane back to Hong Kong around one tomorrow afternoon.

'Sorry,' he added when her face fell. 'But things there are going from bad to worse. Who knows where it will all end? Still, that's not your concern.'

'But I like to hear about your work problems,' she said truthfully, and touched his arm.

He stiffened for a second before picking up her hand and kissing her fingertips. The entire surface of Tara's skin broke out into goose-pimples.

'I haven't come home to talk about work, Tara,' he murmured. 'I've come home to relax for a night. With my beautiful girlfriend.'

Tara beamed at him. 'You called me your girl-friend.'

Max looked perplexed. 'Well, that's what you are, isn't it?'

'Yes. Yes, that's what I am. I hope,' she muttered under her breath as she turned away from him and hurried round to the passenger side.

She could feel his eyes on her as she climbed into

the car. But she didn't want to see what was in them. It was enough for now that he'd called her his girl-friend. Enough that he'd declared his love. She didn't want to see the heat in his gaze and misinterpret it. Of course he desired her, as she desired him. Of course!

But he won't ever give you what you want, Tara.

Yes, he would, she reassured herself as the car sped towards the city. Till he left for the airport tomorrow, he would give her his company, and his love, and his body. Which was all that she wanted right at this moment. His body possibly most of all.

Even now, she was thinking of the hours she would spend in bed with him, of the way she felt when he caressed and kissed her all over, when he made her melt with just a touch of his finger or a stab of his tongue. She especially liked it when he played with her endlessly, bringing her again and again to the brink of ecstasy, only to draw back at the last moment, making her wait in a state of exquisite tension till he was inside her.

Those were the best times, when they reached satisfaction together, when she held him close and she felt their hearts beating as one.

The car zoomed down into the tunnel which would take them swiftly to the city, the enveloping darkness making Tara even more aware of the man beside her. She glanced over at his strong profile, then at his hands on the wheel.

Her thighs suddenly pressed together at the thought of him taking her, her insides tightening.

When Tara sucked in sharply Max's head turned and his eyes glittered over at her. 'What are you thinking about?'

She blushed and he laughed, breaking her tension.

'Same here. But we're almost there now. It won't be long to wait.'

CHAPTER THREE

THE Regency Hotel—recently renamed the Regency Royale by Max—was situated towards the northern end of the city centre, not far from Circular Quay. Touted as one of Sydney's plushest hotels, it had a décor to suit its name. Guests could be forgiven for thinking they'd stepped back in time once they entered the reception area of the Regency, with its wood-panelled walls, velvet-covered couches and huge crystal chandeliers.

The arcade which connected the entrance of the hotel to the lobby proper was just as lavish, also resonant of England in past times, with its intricately tiled floor and stained-glass ceiling. The boutiques and bars which lined the arcade reflected a similar sense of period style and grace.

Max had once told Tara that was why he'd bought the Regency. Because of its period look.

The Royale chain specialised in hotels which weren't modern-looking in design or décor. Because modern, Max told her, always eventually dated. History and grandeur were what he looked for in a hotel.

Tara had to agree that this made sound business sense. Of all the hotels in Sydney, the Regency

Royale stood out for its style and good, old-fashioned service. But it was the look of the place which captivated guests. The day she came here for her interview at Whitmore Opals eighteen months ago, she'd spent a good while walking around the place, both amazed and admiring.

Today, however, as Max ushered her along the arcade past her place of employment, her focus was on anything but the hotel. Her thoughts were entirely on the man whose hand was clamped firmly around her elbow, and on the state of almost desperate desire he'd reduced her to.

Never, in the twelve months they'd been seeing each other, had she experienced anything quite like this. She'd always been happy for Max to make love to her. But never had she wanted him this badly.

'Afternoon, Mr Richmond,' a security guard greeted as he walked towards them.

'Afternoon, Jack,' Max replied, and actually stopped to talk to the man whilst Tara clenched her teeth in her jaw.

It was probably only a minute before they moved on but it felt like an eternity.

'Glad to see you again, Mr Richmond,' another employee chirped after a few more metres.

'Same here, Warren.'

This time Max didn't stop, thank goodness. Tara smothered a sigh of relief, even happier when Max bypassed the reception desk and headed straight for the lifts. Not that he needed to book in, for heaven's sake. But Max was a hands-on hotel owner who liked to be kept informed over the ins and outs of everything. He usually stopped by Reception for a brief chat on arrival.

In the past, Tara hadn't minded his stopping to talk to his employees. She'd always admired the way Max knew every employee by their first name, from the valet-parking attendants to the managers.

Today, however, she was extremely irritated by the delays. Which wasn't like her at all.

The alcove which housed the lifts was not empty. A man in his forties, and presumably his wife, were standing there, waiting for a lift. They didn't look like tourists. Or members of Sydney's élite. Their clothes and faces betrayed them as working-class Australians, perhaps staying here in Sydney's flashest hotel for some special event, or occasion.

'I will never stay in this hotel again,' the man grumbled. 'I'd go somewhere right now if it didn't mean losing my deposit. I couldn't believe that girl, insisting that I hadn't booked a harbour-view room. As if I would bring you here for our silver anniversary and not get the very best room I could afford.'

'It doesn't matter, Tom,' the wife placated. 'I'm sure all the rooms here are lovely.'

'That's not the point. It's the principle of the thing. And that girl behind the desk was quite rude, I thought.'

'Not really,' the woman said with a nervous glance

towards Max and Tara. 'It was just a mix-up. These things happen. Let's try not to let it spoil our night.'

Tara smothered a groan when she felt Max's fingertips tighten around her elbow. She knew, as she glanced up at his tightly drawn face, that he was going to do something about this situation.

'Excuse me, sir,' he said, just as the lift doors opened. 'But I couldn't help overhearing. I'm Max Richmond, the owner of this hotel. If you'll allow me, I'd like to accompany you back to Reception, where I will sort this out to your satisfaction.'

'Max,' Tara whispered urgently.

'You go on, darling,' he said. 'I'll be up as quick as I can. Slip into something more comfortable,' he murmured as he pecked her on the cheek.

Tara stared after him as he led the awestruck couple away, struggling to contain her bitter disappointment and understand that of course, he couldn't have done anything else. Not her Max. Hadn't she tried to tell her mother what a good man he was?

But did he have to be good right at this moment? She would have much preferred him to be bad. *Very* bad.

Again, Tara was amazed by the intensity of her craving, her sudden wish for Max to make love to her not quite so tenderly as he usually did. Maybe Max had been right after all. Maybe she *had* dressed as she had today to tease and arouse him. Yet her clothes weren't all that different from what she usually wore. This change seemed to be coming from inside her.

Now that she came to think of it, she felt more aware of her body than usual today. Her breasts. Her nipples. Her belly. She craved to have them stroked, and licked, and kissed. She craved…oh, she wasn't sure what she craved. She just craved.

Agitated, Tara fished her keycard out of her bag and hurried into the lift before anyone else could come along. She wanted to be alone with her frustrations, and her bewilderment.

But she wasn't alone in the lift. She had company. Herself, in the reflection she made in the mirrored section of the walls. Was that her, the creature looking back at her with dilated green eyes and flushed cheeks?

Yes. That was her. Tara, the suddenly sex-mad tart.

Shaking her head at herself, Tara dropped her gaze to the floor for the ride up, determined not to look up into those knowing mirrors till the lift doors opened.

The mirrors were actually a new addition, Max having had the lifts recently renovated in keeping with the rest of the hotel. The floor she was staring down at was now covered in thick red carpet which ran up the walls to waist height, at which point the mirrors took over.

Tara knew without glancing up that the ceiling overhead shone like gold. Probably not in real gold but the effect was the same. Recessed lighting was the only visible concession to the twenty-first century, along with the tiny and very discreet cameras situated in the corners.

Tight security was a must in the Regency Royale, its guest list ranging from pop stars to presidents, with the occasional prince thrown in for good measure. There was even a heliport on top of the building so that these more esteemed guests could arrive and leave with less drama and more safety. Nevertheless, Max only allowed a few helicopter movements each week, partly because of local-authority restrictions but mostly because he couldn't stand the noise himself. His penthouse apartment occupied the floor just below the heliport.

Everything was deathly quiet, however, when Tara emerged from the lift into the spacious lobby which led to the penthouse door. She used another passkey to let herself inside, where it was almost as quiet, just a small humming sound from the air-conditioning which kept all the rooms at a steady twenty-four degrees Celsius, regardless of the temperature outside.

The perfect temperature for lovers and lovemaking, came the immediate thought. For being naked and walking around naked.

This last thought startled Tara. Because that was one thing she never did. Walked around naked. The idea was theoretically exciting, but the reality made her cringe. She would feel embarrassed, and awkward.

Or would she?

Tara knew she looked good in the buff. Certainly better than most girls, though she couldn't claim this was due to any hard work on her part. Mother nature had just been kind to her. Tara suspected Max wouldn't have minded if she'd been a little less shy. He was always asking her to join him in the shower and she always refused.

Maybe this weekend might be a good place to try to overcome that particular hang-up. She doubted she would ever feel as wicked, or as driven, as she did at this moment. She could not wait to get her hands on Max. The thought of washing him all over in the shower was not unattractive, just a bit daunting.

A shudder ran through her. She would think about that later. There were other things she had to do first, such as whip around and turn some lamps on.

Max loved lamp-light, and whilst it was still bright and sunny outside—the sun wouldn't set for hours— the inside of Max's penthouse always required some lighting. Mostly this was due to the wraparound terraces and the wide eaves. On top of that, the décor of the penthouse was very much in keeping with the décor of the hotel, which meant it wasn't madly modern like some penthouses, with great open-plan living areas and huge plate-glass windows.

The décor was still period, with wallpapered walls and rich carpets on the floors. French doors lead out onto the balconies and heavy silk curtains draped over the windows. The furniture was all antique. Warm woods covered in velvet or brocade in rich colours. It was like an Edwardian English mansion set up in the sky. As big as a mansion too, with formal lounge and dining rooms, four bedrooms, three bathrooms, a study, a library, a billiard room, along with a large kitchen, laundry and utility rooms.

Everything was exquisite and *very* expensive.

Tara hadn't realised the size or extravagance of the place on the first night she'd spent with Max. She'd been overwhelmed by the events and the experience, rather than her surroundings. But the following morning, she'd soon been confronted by the extreme wealth of the man who'd just become her first lover. Initially, she'd been dumbstruck, then totally convinced that he would only want a girl like her for a one-night stand.

But Max had reassured her for the rest of that incredible weekend that a casual encounter was not what he wanted from her at all. Tara recalled thinking at the time that she had found nothing casual in letting him take her virginity less than three hours after she'd first set eyes on him. If she hadn't known she'd fallen instantly and deeply in love with the man, she would have been disgusted with herself.

Naturally, she'd been thrilled that he found her as special as she found him, and here she was, one year later, with her own private key, getting things ready for her man in the way that women in love had done so for centuries. If it fleetingly crossed Tara's mind that her role in her lover's life *was* more like a mistress than a real girlfriend, she dismissed it with the added thought that it wouldn't always be like this. One day, things would change. Max would have more time for her. Till then, she aimed to enjoy the time with him she did have and that part of him which was solely hers.

At least, she *hoped* it was solely hers.

Yes, of course it was. Her mother was wrong about that, as she was wrong about Max all round. The man who was at this moment doing nice things for that couple downstairs was not the kind of man to be unfaithful, or a callous user. She really had to stop letting her mother undermine her faith in Max, or spoil what promised to be a very exciting night.

With a defiant toss of her head, Tara turned and hurried down the plushly carpeted corridor which led to Max's personal quarters, fiercely aware that the last few minutes away from Max's rousing presence hadn't dampened her desires in the slightest. In fact, having sex with Max was all she could think about at that moment, which was not her usual priority when Max came home these days. Mostly, she just wanted to spend time with the man she loved. His lovemaking, though wonderful, was more of a bonus than the be-all and end-all.

Today, it was not only top priority, but close to becoming an emergency!

It was Max's fault, she decided as she swept into the bedroom and starting fumbling with the tiny pearl buttons of her pink shirt. The way he'd looked at her at the airport. The things he'd said about her clothes. That kiss, and then his threat to ravage her on the back seat of the car.

Tara finally stripped off her blouse then kicked off her shoes.

'My screw-me shoes,' she said with a wicked little laugh as she bent to pick them up, carrying the shirt and the shoes into the adjoining dressing room, where she'd put her bag earlier on. There, she stripped off her jeans and undies, stuffing them into the bag's side-pocket for later washing. The shirt she hung up in her section of the walk-in wardrobe. The shoes she put into the special shoe rack before running her eyes along the clothes she kept at Max's place, looking for something more comfortable to slip into.

Her mother's *kept*-woman tag flashed into her mind at the sight of so many designer evening gowns, all paid for by Max, each worn to one of the many swanky dos Max had taken her to during the first few months of their relationship. Dinner parties at the homes of top politicians. Gala openings at the opera house. Art exhibitions. Balls. The races.

You name it, she'd been there on Max's arm.

Actually, she *had* objected the first time he'd suggested buying her a designer dress. But he'd swept aside her possibly feeble protest with what had seemed like acceptable reasoning.

He could well afford it, he'd pronounced. But possibly his most persuasive argument of all was that it gave him great pleasure to see his gorgeous girlfriend in clothes befitting her beauty.

How could she possibly say no?

The lingerie, Tara realised as her eyes shifted further along the rack, had been more recent gifts, brought home from Max's more frequent trips overseas. She had negligee sets from Paris, London, Rome, New York.

These were all she seemed to wear for him these days, now that she came to think of it. Max hadn't taken her outside the door of this penthouse for some time. No doubt he wouldn't this evening either.

'Good!' she pronounced aloud with a dizzying rush of excitement, and pulled out a green satin wrap which she knew complemented her fair colouring and green eyes. The matching nightgown she left on the hanger. No point in wearing *too* much.

Tossing the wrap over her arm, she headed for the bathroom and was about to have a quick shower before Max arrived when she remembered she hadn't put her pills and her mobile phone on the bedside chest as she usually did. Dashing back to the dressing room, she retrieved the items from her bag and bolted into the bedroom to do just that. Then she stopped to quickly turn the bedclothes back before glancing around to see that everything was ready for a romantic interlude.

Not that Max's bedroom needed anything to enhance its already romantic décor. Everything about it was rich and sensual. The soft gold carpet was extra thick and the gold-embossed cream wallpaper extra rich, both perfect foils for the dark mahogany wood used in all the elegant furniture. The four-poster bed. The bedside chests. The dressing table and matching stool. The cheval mirror that stood in one corner and the wingbacked chairs that occupied the other corners.

The soft furnishings were rich and sensual-looking as well, all made in a satin-backed brocade which carried a gold fleur-de-lis design over an olive-green background. A huge crystal and brass chandelier hung from the centre of the ceiling, but there were also several dainty crystal wall lights dotted around the room.

Tara loved it when it was dark and all the lights were turned off except those. The room took on a magical glow which was so romantic. Much better than the bedside lamps which she thought threw too much light onto the bed. And them.

Of course, the pièce de résistance in Max's bedroom was the four-poster bed. Huge, it was, with great carved posts and bedhead. The canopy above was made of the same material as all the other soft furnishings, draped around the edges and trimmed with a gold fringe. There were side-curtains, which theoretically could be drawn to surround the bed, but were always kept pulled back and secured to the bedposts with gold tasselled cords.

Tara ran her fingers idly through one of the tassels and wondered what it would be like to be in bed with Max with the curtains drawn.

'What are you thinking now?'

'Oh!' Tara gasped, whirling to find Max standing in the doorway of the bedroom, staring at her with coldly glittering eyes.

'I... I didn't hear you come in,' she babbled, her heart pounding madly as she tried to cover herself with her hands.

With a sigh Max stalked into the room, his face now showing exasperation. 'Don't you think we've gone past that, Tara? I mean, I do know what you look like naked. Surely you must know that I'd *like* it if you walked around in front of me nude,' he finished as he took off his jacket and threw it onto the nearest chair.

She just stared at him, her heartbeat almost in suspension. But her mind was racing. Yes, yes, it was saying. I'd like to do that, too. Truly. I just can't seem to find the courage.

'And there I was,' he muttered as he yanked his tie off, 'thinking today that you might have finally decided you wanted more than for me to make love to you under the covers with the lights turned down.

'It's all right,' he added a bit wearily when she remained frozen and tongue-tied. 'I understand. You're shy. Though heaven knows why. You have the most beautiful body God ever gave to a woman. And you're passionate enough, between the sheets.'

Turning away from her, he tossed the tie on top of the jacket then started undoing the buttons on his shirt.

'Go and put something on,' he bit out, not looking at her. 'If you must.'

Tara dashed into the bathroom and shakily pulled on the green wrap, hating herself for feeling relieved.

When she finally returned to the bedroom, Max was sitting on the foot of the bed, taking off his shoes and socks. His shirt was hanging open, but he hadn't taken it off.

Tara's heart sank. Did he think she was *that* modest? She *loved* his chest, with its broad shoulders, wonderfully toned muscles and smattering of curls.

'Did…did you fix up things for those people?' she asked somewhat sheepishly.

'Naturally,' he replied without looking up at her. 'I had them moved into one of the honeymoon suites, on the house. And I told them they could have a free harbour-view room for their anniversary next year.'

'Oh, Max, that was generous of you. And very smart. That man would have bad-mouthed the hotel for years, you know. To anyone who would listen. Now he'll say nothing but good things. People love getting something for free. I know I do. I can never resist those buy-one, get one-free promotions.'

'Really?' He finally looked up, but his clouded eyes indicated that he was suddenly off in another world. Max did that sometimes. Tara knew better than to ask him what he was thinking about. Whenever she did, he always said 'nothing important'.

'So which honeymoon suite are they in?' she asked instead. The hotel was famous for its four themed honeymoon suites, which Tara knew cost a bomb to stay in. Bookings showed that the Arabian Nights suite was the most popular, followed by the Naughty

Nautical suite, the French Bordello suite and, lastly, the Tropical Paradise suite.

'What? Oh, there was only the one available tonight. The French Bordello. Mr Travis seemed tickled pink. Can't say the same for Mrs Travis. She seemed a little nervous. Maybe she's on the shy side. Like you.'

'I'm not all that shy,' Tara dared to say at last.

Max darted her a dry look.

'All right, I am, a bit,' she went on, swallowing when he stood up and started undoing his trouser belt.

The prospect of watching him strip down to total nakedness before he'd even kissed her was definitely daunting. But at the same time she wanted him to, wanted him to do what she wasn't bold enough to do, wanted him to force her to stop being so silly.

'Don't panic,' he said drily and, whipping out his belt, deposited it with his other clothes. 'I won't take anything more off. I'm going to have a shower, and when I come out I'll be wearing my bathrobe. Meantime, why don't you order us something from Room Service? I don't know about you but I'm starving. I nodded off on the plane so I didn't get to eat anything. I've made us a booking for dinner at eight but that's hours away.'

'We're going out to dinner?' Tara said, taken aback.

'I've only booked the restaurant here in the hotel. Is that all right with you?'

'Oh, yes. I love going to dinner with you there. It's

just that…well, the last couple of times you've come home, we've eaten in.'

'Yes, I know. And I'm sorry. That was selfish of me. But, as I said earlier, you're a different girl between the sheets, so I try to keep you there as long as possible.'

She blushed. 'Don't make fun of me, Max.'

He groaned and walked round to draw her into his arms. 'I'm not making fun of you, princess. I would never do that. You're you and I love you just the way you are.'

'Kiss me, Max,' she said quite fiercely.

His eyes searched hers. 'I don't think that's a good idea. Not yet.'

'But I can't wait any longer!'

'*You* can't wait. Hell, Tara, what is it with you today? Are you punishing me for neglecting you lately?'

'I just want you to kiss me. No, I *need* you to kiss me.'

With a groan, he kissed her. Then he kissed her some more, till her knees went to water and she was clinging to him for dear life. When he swept her up and dropped her less than gently onto the bed, Tara made no protest. Neither did she turn her eyes away whilst he started ripping off the rest of his clothes.

She wanted to look. Wanted to see him wanting her.

Her breath caught at the extent of his desire.

He loomed over her, tugging the sash of her robe

undone, throwing the sides back to bare her body to his blazing eyes.

For what felt like an eternity, he drank her in, leaving her breathless and blushing. Then, with a few more savage yanks, the satin robe joined his clothes on the floor.

There was no tender foreplay. No gentle kisses all over. Just immediate sex. Rough and raw. Maybe not quite ravagement but close to.

And oh, how she thrilled to the primitive urgency of his passion. And to her own.

She splintered apart in no time, rocked by the force of her orgasm, overwhelmed by the experience, and by a degree of emotional confusion.

As the last spasm died away, a huge wave of exhaustion flooded Tara's body, her limbs growing as heavy as her eyelids. She could not keep them open. She could not stay awake. With a sigh, she sank into the abyss of sleep.

CHAPTER FOUR

MAX stared down at her with a stunned look on his face.

Asleep! She'd fallen asleep!

He shook his head in utter bewilderment. Tara never fell asleep afterwards.

On top of that, she'd actually *enjoyed* his making love to her like that! Hell, no, she'd *exulted* in it! She'd dragged him over the edge with her in record time. And now she was out like a light, more peaceful than he'd ever seen her.

Relief swamped him at the realisation he didn't have to feel *too* much remorse over losing control and being less than the careful, considerate, patient lover he'd come to believe Tara wanted, and needed. *Not* losing control when he was around her this past year had been a terrible battle between the lust she evoked in him, and the love.

Max thought he'd done pretty well…until today.

If only she hadn't met him looking delicious in those skin-tight jeans and those sexy shoes. If only she hadn't told him she wasn't wearing a bra. If only he hadn't kissed her then and there.

His relationship with Tara was full of 'if only's, the main one being if only he hadn't stopped to look in the window of Whitmore Opals that Friday night, and spotted her inside.

It had been lust at first sight. When she'd agreed to have drinks with him less than ten minutes after his going in and introducing himself, he'd been sure he was in for a wild night with a woman of the world. With his impossible workload and repeated overseas trips, Max's sex life had been reduced to the occasional one-nighter with women who knew the score, and Tara seemed just the ticket to ride.

But the reality had proven so different. Her telling him shakily that she was a virgin even before he'd got her bra off had certainly put the brakes on the type of activities he'd been planning. Max had been shocked, but also entranced. Who would have believed it?

Fortunately, finding out before he'd gone too far gave him the opportunity to slow things down and make sure her first experience was pleasurable and not painful. He'd taken her to bed and really taken his time with her.

Looking back, making love to her at all had probably been a mistake. He should have cut and run. But he hadn't; that very first time had made him swiftly decide that one night with Tara would not be enough. He'd kept her in his bed all weekend, making love to her as he hadn't made love to a female in years. Sweetly. Tenderly. And totally selflessly.

Unfortunately, this was what Tara came to expect from him every time. Max soon realised he was dealing with a girl whose appearance belied her real nature. Underneath the sexy-looking blonde surface, the long legs and fabulous boobs, lay a naively romantic girl.

In *some* ways, Tara could be surprisingly mature. She was well-educated, well-read and well-travelled. And she certainly had a way with people, exuding a charm and social grace far beyond her years.

But when it came to sex she was like a hothouse flower, gorgeous to look at but incredibly soft and fragile.

Or so he'd thought, up till now.

Max sat back on his haunches and stared down at her beautiful but unconscious body, lying in shameless abandonment in front of his eyes.

If only she would lie like that for him when she was awake…

Max almost laughed at this new 'if only'.

But maybe she would in the near future, came the exciting thought. She'd said she wasn't totally shy and maybe she wasn't. Maybe she just lacked the confidence to do what she really wanted to do. All she needed was some masterful persuasion at the right time, and a whole new world would open for her.

Up till this moment, Max had reluctantly accepted that Tara didn't seem the raunchy type of girl. He'd reasoned it was worth sacrificing some more exotic experiences to feel what Tara could make him feel, what she'd made him feel from their very first night together.

But tonight had shown him that maybe, they could share more erotic lovemaking together in future.

Max became aroused just thinking of the things he'd like to do with her, and her with him. Not a good idea when it looked as if she would be asleep for some time. A shower was definitely called for. A cold one.

Wincing at his discomfort, he climbed off the bed and carefully eased the bedclothes from underneath Tara's luscious derriere, rolling her gently onto the bottom sheet before pulling the other one up to her shoulders. She stirred but didn't wake, though the sheet did slip down to reveal one of her incredible breasts.

Max bent and pressed his lips softly to the exposed nipple before whirling away and heading straight for the bathroom.

CHAPTER FIVE

'WHAT?'

The startled word shot from Tara's lips as she sat bolt upright in bed. She blinked, then glanced somewhat glazedly around before realising what had woken her so abruptly.

It was the alarm on her mobile phone, telling her it was six o'clock, reminding her it was time to take her pill.

With a groan, she leant over and picked up the small pink handset, pressing the button which turned off the alarm. The sudden silence in the room highlighted Max's absence. She wondered where he was, then wished she hadn't. She didn't want to think about Max at that moment.

Tara retrieved her packet of pills from the bedside chest, popped today's pill through the foil then swallowed it promptly without bothering about getting any water. The doctor had warned her that you had to take the mini Pill around the same time every day or risk getting pregnant. Tara didn't take hers *around* the same time. She took it at *exactly* the same time every day.

That done, she threw back the sheet and—after checking that Max wasn't lurking in the doorway watching her—Tara rose to her feet. She winced at the wetness between her legs.

Impossible to pretend any longer that she didn't remember what had happened before she fell asleep.

Why she was even trying to forget suddenly annoyed her. She hadn't done anything to be ashamed of. Neither had Max, for that matter.

So he'd made love to her more forcefully than usual. So what? He'd delivered exactly what she'd been subconsciously wanting since he'd threatened to ravage her at the airport. And how she'd loved it!

Tara quivered all over at the memory. Had she ever experienced anything with Max quite so powerful before? She didn't think so.

The sight of her green wrap lying tidily across the foot of the bed brought a frown to her forehead. Max must have picked it up off the floor whilst she was asleep. His own clothes as well. They were now draped over one of the chairs.

He hadn't dressed again, she realised with a tightening of her stomach. He was somewhere in the penthouse, probably wearing nothing but his favourite bathrobe. Tara hurried into the bathroom to check, and yes, his bathrobe was missing from where it usually hung on the back of the bathroom door. And his towels were still damp. Obviously, he'd showered whilst she'd been asleep.

Swallowing, Tara hung her wrap up on the empty hook behind the door, wound her hair into a knot on top of her head, then stepped into the spacious, marble-lined shower cubicle.

She wasn't yet sure what she was going to do after she'd showered. All she knew was that her body was already rebuilding a head of steam far hotter than the water which was currently cascading over her body.

She didn't spend much time in the shower. Just long enough to ensure that she was freshly washed and nicely perfumed. She was careful not to wet her hair. She didn't want to present herself to Max like some bedraggled kitten come in from a storm. Her hair was not at its best when wet. And she wanted to look her *very* best.

No, Tara amended mentally as she towelled herself down then slipped her arms into the silky wrap. She didn't want to look her best, but her sexiest. She wanted to tempt Max into stopping doing whatever he was doing and take her back to bed. Right now.

For a second she almost left the wrap hanging open, but in the end decided that was tacky. So she tied it just as tightly as usual. Actually, even a bit tighter, so that her small waist was emphasised, as well as the rest of her curvy figure.

Swallowing, Tara took one final glance in the huge mirror which stretched along above the double vanity basins. On another day, at another time, she would have taken the time to make her face up all over again. There was little of her pink lipstick left, and her mascara had smudged all around her eyes. But she rather liked her slightly dishevelled look. She even liked the way her hair was up. Roughly, with some escaping strands hanging around her face. She looked like a woman who'd just come from her lover's bed. She looked…wanton.

Spinning on her bare heels, Tara headed for the bedroom door.

The hallway that led from the master bedroom to the main body of the penthouse seemed to go on forever. By the time she reached the main living room, she wasn't sure if she was terrified or over-excited. Her heart was going like a jack-hammer and her mouth was drier than the Simpson Desert.

But Max was not there.

Disappointment rather than relief showed her that nerves were not the most dominating force in her body at that moment. Desire was much stronger.

Whirling, she hurried down the hallway which led to Max's den, his favourite area of the penthouse when he was up and about. It was actually two rooms, connected by concertina doors which were always kept open. The first room you entered was a study-cum-library, a very masculine room with no windows, book-lined walls, a desk in one corner and several oversized, leather-studded chairs in which to sit and read. The next room was the billiard room, which had a huge, green-felted billiard table, a pub-like bar in one corner, complete with stools, and lots of French doors which opened onto the balcony.

Max was an excellent snooker player and had tried to teach Tara in their early days together, when they had time for more than bed. But she was never much good and they hadn't played in ages.

Tara wasn't about to suggest a game today. She had other games in mind, a thought which both shocked and stirred her. She'd never thought of making love as a game before.

Her hand shook as it reached for the brass door knob but no way was she going to back out now. But she didn't barge straight in. Tara had been brought up with better manners than that. She tapped on the door before she opened it, then popped her head inside.

Max, she swiftly saw, was sitting in his favourite chair, bathed in a circle of soft light from the lamp which stood behind the chair. Yes, he was wearing the white towelling bathrobe, she noted. And yes, nothing else, not even on his feet.

But he wasn't exactly sitting around, impatiently waiting for her to wake up so that he could make love to her again. He was working. *And* drinking. His laptop was open and balanced across his thighs, he was sipping a very large Scotch and chatting to someone on the phone at the same time.

Max was one of those rare men who could actually do more than one thing at a time.

'Ah, there you are,' she said, containing her irritation with difficulty.

Instead of asking him if it was all right if she interrupted him, as she usually would have, Tara walked straight in and shut the door behind her.

He was taken aback, she could see. But that was just too bad. This was *her* time with him, no one else's.

When he put up his hand towards her in a stopping gesture and kept on talking—something about a website—rebellion overcame Tara's usually automatic tendency to obey him. Slowly, she moved towards him across the expanse of dark green carpet, her hips swaying seductively, her breasts moving underneath the wrap. The act of walking parted the silky material around her knees, giving tantalising glimpses of her bare legs.

One of his brows arched as he eyed her up and down. 'I'll have to speak to you later, Pierce,' he said into the phone. 'Something's just come up.'

'*Much* later,' Tara said as he clicked off the call. Pierce was only Max's PA, after all. He could wait.

Max smiled an odd smile before dropping his eyes back to the laptop screen. 'I have something I have to finish up here first, Tara,' he said without looking up at her again. 'Why don't you toddle off back to bed and I'll join you there as soon as I can?'

Pique fired her tongue before she could think better of it. 'What if I don't want to go back to bed? What if I want to stay here? What if I want you to stop working right here and now?'

Slowly, his eyes rose. Hard and glittering, they were, just as she liked them. He sipped some more of his drink whilst he studied her over the rim of the glass.

His gaze was knowing. He was mentally stripping her, making her face flush and her nipples tighten.

'*Make* me,' he said at last, his voice soft and low and dark.

His challenging words sent a bolt of electricity zig-zagging through her, firing her blood *and* her resolve not to weaken. Because she knew what he wanted. He wanted to see her, *all* of her. Not lying in a bed, but standing upright, in front of him. Facing him.

Her heartbeat quickened whilst her hands went to the sash on her wrap. She might have fumbled if the knot had been difficult, but she only had to tug the ends of the ties to make the bow unravel. In a split-second, the sides of the wrap fell apart.

But he showed no reaction whatsoever, just went back to sipping his drink.

Shock at his low level of interest held her frozen, and finally, his eyes dropped back to the screen in his lap.

'Go back to bed, Tara,' he said. 'Clearly, you're not cut out for the role of seductress just yet.'

Stung, she stripped the robe off and dropped it to the floor. When he still didn't pay her any attention, she went right up to him and banged the lid of the laptop down.

'*Look* at me,' she hissed.

He looked at her, his narrow-eyed gaze now travelling with exquisitely exciting slowness over every inch of her nakedness.

'Very nice,' he murmured. 'But it's nothing I haven't seen before.'

'You might see something new,' she threw at him, 'if you put that drink down. And that infernal computer.'

He closed the laptop and placed it beside the chair, but kept the drink. He looked her over again as he leant back into the chair and took another mouthful of whisky.

Now fear did return. The fear of making a fool of herself.

'I'm waiting,' he said, and finally placed the near-empty glass on the small round side-table next to the chair.

Tara swallowed.

'Come, come, Tara. This is *your* show. I'm curious to see how far you'll go before you turn tail and run. I'm not going to help you one little bit.'

Tara gaped at him as the realisation struck that he didn't just want her to parade herself in front of him. He wanted *her* to make love to *him*.

If he'd issued this type of challenge on any other day before today, she probably *would* have turned tail and run. But today was a different day in more ways than one. Today, a new and exciting dimension had entered their relationship and she refused to retreat from it.

Don't think, she told herself as she stepped forward to stand between his stretched-out legs. Just do what he thinks you don't dare to do.

She heard his sharp intake of breath when she knelt down and reached for the sash on his robe.

Don't look up at his face, she warned herself shakily.

She didn't want to see any undermining shock, or surprise, in his eyes. He'd told her once he didn't mind how provocative or assertive she was in private. Well, he was just about to get a dose of provocative assertiveness, even if she was quaking inside.

The sash on his robe was as easy to undo as her own, being only looped over. Pushing the sides of the robe back was not so easy, because she knew what would confront her when she did so.

Her eyes widened at the sight of him.

So his apparent uninterest had all been a lie! He was already aroused. Fiercely so.

Tara resisted the urge to close her eyes and put her mind elsewhere. Her days of cowardice were over. She *would* look at him there, and touch him there, and kiss him there.

Yet oddly, once she started stroking the velvety length of him, once she felt Max quiver and grow even harder beneath her hands, any reluctance or revulsion melted away. Tara found herself consumed by the intense desire to make the beast emerge in him again, to drive him wild with pleasure and need, to love him as she had never loved him before.

Max could not believe it when she took him into her mouth, making the blood roar through his veins, his flesh expand even further, threatening to make him lose all control.

Surely she would not want that. Surely not!

Max groaned his worry that he might not be able to stop himself. Then groaned again when her head lifted, showing him that he had wanted her to continue more than anything he had wanted in a long time.

But any disappointment was swiftly allayed by her crawling up onto the chair onto his lap. She was even at that moment straddling his tautly held thighs, her knees fitting into the far corners of the chair.

He gasped when she took him in her hands again and directed him up into her body. Her hot, wet, delicious body. She sank downwards and suddenly he was there, totally inside her. Her face lifted and their eyes met, hers dilated, his stunned.

'Max,' was all she said before she bent down to kiss his mouth, her hands cupping his face, her tongue sliding deep into his mouth.

How often had he hoped for a Tara like this?

Then she began to ride him. Slowly at first, but then with more passion. The wilder rise and fall of her hips wrenched her mouth away from his. Her hands fell to his shoulders to steady herself, her fingernails biting into his flesh till suddenly her back arched, her flesh gripping his like a vice.

'Oooh,' she cried out.

The power of her climax was mind-blowing. He exploded in erotic response, the pleasure blinding as, all the while, she kept moving upon him, rocking back and forth, her eyes shut, her breathing ragged.

Afterwards, she sank down against his chest, her head nestling into the base of his throat. His arms encircled her back and he held her like that for quite a while, both of them silent and content.

But inevitably, the significance of what had just happened came home to him. His gorgeous Tara had finally abandoned her inhibitions.

Suddenly, he wanted her in every way a man and a woman could make love.

Tara sat up straight, her startled eyes searching his.

'Too soon?' he said, his hands sliding down her back to cup her bottom.

She shook her head.

He kept on caressing her bottom, and soon her lips fell apart on a sensual sigh of surrender. Max had never felt such love for her. Or such desire.

He was glad that their dinner reservation wasn't till eight o'clock. He had plans for the hour and a half till then, and none of them had anything to do with going back to bed.

CHAPTER SIX

'THAT gold colour looks fabulous on you,' Max said as they waited for the lift to take them down to the restaurant. 'So does the dress. I'm glad you took my suggestion to wear it tonight.'

Tara almost laughed. *Suggestion!* He hadn't suggested. He'd insisted.

The dress was a cheong-san, brought home by Max after an earlier trip to Hong Kong. Made in gold satin, it might have looked demure with its knee-length hem and high Chinese collar, except for the fact it was skin-tight, with slits up the sides which exposed a good deal of thigh. It was an extremely sensual garment.

Not that Tara needed help in feeling sensual at that moment. The last couple of hours had left all her senses heightened and her body humming. She'd certainly aroused the beast in Max with her provocative behaviour, along with another couple of Maxes. Max, the insatiable. And Max, the rather ruthless.

She shivered at the memory of the interlude on the billiard table.

Tara had briefly thought of sex as a game before going into Max's den. She hadn't realised at the time that Max was far ahead of her in the playing of erotic games, making her now wonder how many other women he'd entertained in the past in such a fashion.

At least, she *hoped* they'd been in the past.

A long and more objective look at Max—so resplendent tonight in black tie—confirmed what Tara had always subconsciously known. That women would throw themselves at him in droves. *She* had, hadn't she?

'Max,' she said with sudden worry in her voice and in her eyes.

'What, my darling?'

When he took her hand and raised it to his lips, she looked deep into *his* eyes.

'Have you ever been unfaithful to me?'

'Never,' he returned, so swiftly and so strongly that she had to believe him.

And yet…

'Why do you ask?' he went on, clearly perturbed by her question.

'I can see by tonight,' she said carefully, 'that I haven't exactly…satisfied you these past twelve months.'

'That's not true, Tara. I've been very happy with you,' he claimed.

A flicker in his eyes, however, showed otherwise.

'I don't believe you, Max. Tell me the truth.'

'Look, I admit there have been moments when I wished you were more comfortable with your body, and your sexuality. But I was not discontented. I love *you*, Tara, not just making love to you. Still, I'm glad you've finally realised that sex can be enjoyed in lots of different ways. It doesn't always have to be slow and serious. It can be fast and furious. Or it can just be fun. You had fun tonight, didn't you?'

Fun. Had it been fun? It had certainly been exciting, and compelling.

'I…I guess so.'

His smile was wry. 'Come, now, Tara. You loved it. All of it. Don't deny it.'

'I guess I'm just not used to being so wicked.'

'Wicked!' Max exclaimed, laughing. 'We weren't wicked. A little naughty perhaps. But not wicked. I could show you wicked later tonight, if you'd like.'

'What…what do you mean? Doing what?'

'I've always wanted to put those cords around my bed to far better use than tying back the curtains.'

Tara tried to feel scandalised. Instead, curiosity claimed her. What would it feel like for Max to tie her to the bed, to render her incapable of stopping him from looking at her all over, and touching her all over?

Just thinking about it gave her a hint as to what it would actually feel like. *Wicked.*

Heat filled her face. And the rest of her.

'I can see that's a bit of a leap for you,' Max said wryly. 'Forget I mentioned it.'

But how *could* she forget? He'd put the image into her mind. She would never be able to look at that bed now without thinking of herself bound to the bed-posts!

The lift doors opened. When she stood there, still in a daze, Max took her hand and pulled her into the lift.

'Come along, princess, stop the daydreaming. We have to go down and eat. We're already a quarter of an hour late, courtesy of your keeping me in the shower longer than I intended.'

'*Me* keeping *you* in the shower!' she gasped. 'You liar! It was *you*. You wouldn't let me get out till I…till I…'

'Till you'd finished what you started. Yes, I know. Sorry. You're right. I got a bit carried away. But I didn't hear you objecting.'

'I could hardly speak at the time,' she countered with a defiant glower.

He laughed. 'That's the girl. Give it back to me. That's what I want from you always, Tara. Lots of fire and spirit. I'm never at my best around yes people.'

'That's rubbish, Max, and you know it. You love yes people. I hear you on the phone all the time, giving orders and expecting to be instantly obeyed. You like being the boss, in the bedroom as well as every-where else! You expect all your lackeys to do exactly what they're told, when they're told.'

'Aah, yes, but you're not one of my lackeys.'

'I'm not so sure,' she snapped. 'Isn't a mistress another form of lackey?'

'Mistress! Good lord, what a delightfully old-fashioned word. But I like it. Mistress,' he repeated thoughtfully. 'Yes, you would make me a perfect mistress. *Now*.' And with a wicked gleam in his eye, he put her fingers to his lips once more.

Tara pulled her hand away. She might have hit him if the lift doors hadn't opened at that moment.

A brunette was standing there, waiting for the lift. A strikingly attractive brunette with big brown eyes, eyes which grew bigger when they saw Max, then narrowed as they shifted over to Tara.

Max's fingers tightened around Tara's.

'Hello, Max,' the brunette said first. 'Long time, no see.'

'Indeed,' Max replied, but said no more.

Tara could feel the tension gripping all of Max's body through his hand. No, not tension. Hostility. He hated this woman, for whatever reason. Why? Had he loved her once?

Tara stared at the brunette more closely, trying to guess her age for one thing. Impossible to tell accurately. Maybe mid-to late-twenties. She had the sleek look of the very rich, which meant she might be older. Weekly visits to beauty salons could hold back the hands of time. Her face was clear of wrinkles and superbly made up. But her shoulder-length, shiny dark-brown hair was her crowning glory, framing her face in a layered bob with not a single strand out of place.

She made Tara conscious of her own hair, which

was scraped back from her face and pulled up high on her head into a tight knot, the only style she could manage in the small amount of time Max had given her to get ready. Less than fifteen minutes earlier, her whole head had been sopping wet.

'You're looking well,' the brunette addressed to Max.

'If you'll excuse us, Alicia,' Max said. 'We are already late for our dinner reservation.' And he ushered Tara away, stunning Tara with his rudeness. Ever since she'd met Max, she'd never known him to act like that with anyone.

Tara did not glance back, or say a word during the short walk from the lift to the restaurant. She remained discretely silent whilst the *maître d'* greeted them, then instructed their personal waiter—a good-looking young guy named Jarod—to show them to their table.

It was a very special table, reserved for special occasions and people who wanted total privacy from the other diners. Set in a back corner of the restaurant, the candlelit table was housed in a tiny room, which was dimly lit and very atmospheric.

The first time Max had brought her here, she'd thought it was so romantic. Subsequent visits had been just as romantic. Tonight, however, the encounter with the brunette had turned Tara's mind away from romance. Unless one could consider jealousy an element of romance. Max could say what he liked but the way that woman had looked at him—just for a

moment—had been with the eyes of a woman who'd
been more than a passing acquaintance, or an employee.

As the minutes dragged on—Max was spending an
inordinate amount of time studying the drinks
menu—her agitation increased. By the time the waiter
departed and the opportunity presented itself to ask
him about the infernal woman, Tara feared she was
going to put her questions all wrong. She dithered
over what to actually say.

'There's no need to be jealous,' Max pronounced
abruptly. 'Alicia was Stevie's girlfriend, not mine.'

'I wasn't jealous,' Tara lied with a lift of her chin.
'Just bewildered by your rudeness. So what did this
Alicia do to Stevie to make you hate her so much?'

'The moment my brother was diagnosed with tes-
ticular cancer, Alicia dumped him like a shot. Said
she couldn't cope.'

Tara was stunned to see Max's hands tremble as
he raked them through his hair.

'My God, *she* couldn't cope,' he growled. 'How
did she think Stevie was going to cope when the girl
he loved—and who he *thought* loved him—didn't
stand by him through his illness? I blame her entirely
for his treatment being unsuccessful. When she left
him, he lost the will to live.'

'But I thought…'

'Yes, yes, I blame my father, too. But Alicia even
more so. At least Dad never pretended a devotion to
Stevie. When he didn't come home to be by his dying

son's bedside, it wasn't such a shock. Not to Stevie, anyway. He told me just days before he died that Dad didn't love him the way he loved me.' Max's deeply set blue eyes looked haunted. 'God, Tara, do you know how I felt when he said that? Stevie, who was such a good boy, who'd never hurt anyone in his life. How could any father not love him more than me? I wasn't a patch on my little brother.'

Tara frowned. Max had told her ages ago about the circumstances surrounding his younger brother's tragic death. Yet he'd never mentioned Stevie's girl-friend's part in it.

'Why didn't you tell me about Alicia, Max? You told me what your father did.'

'I don't like to talk about Stevie. I told you as much as I had to, to explain why I didn't invite you home to visit my parents, especially last Christmas. Alicia was irrelevant to that explanation,' he finished brusquely. 'Aah, here's the champagne.'

Tara wasn't totally satisfied with Max's explana-tion but stayed silent whilst the waiter opened the bottle, poured them both a glass then finally departed after Max told him to return in ten minutes for their meal order.

'It's not like you to order champagne,' she said as she took a sip. Max usually ordered red wine.

'I thought we would share a bottle. To celebrate the anniversary of our meeting. It was a year ago today that I walked into Whitmore's. Of course, it was a Friday not a Saturday, but the date's spot-on.'

'Oh, Max, how sweet of you to remember!'

'I'm a sweet guy.'

Tara smiled. 'You can be. Obviously. But I wouldn't say sweetness is one of your best-known attributes.'

'No?' He smiled across the table, reminding her for the second time that night how very handsome he was. 'So what *is* my best-known attribute?'

She couldn't help it. She blushed.

Max laughed. 'I will take that as a compliment. Although you've hardly been able to compare, since I'm your one and only lover. At least, I presume I am. Though maybe not for long, after today.'

'What on earth do you mean by that?'

'Maybe you'll want to fly to other places. Experience other men.'

Tara stared at him. 'You don't know me very well if you think that. What happened earlier, Max, is because I love you deeply and trust you totally. I could never be like that with some other man. I would just die of embarrassment and shame.'

His eyes softened on her. 'You really mean that, don't you?'

'Of course I do!'

He shook his head. 'You're one in a million, Tara. There truly aren't many women like you out there for men like me. True love is a luxury not often enjoyed by the rich and famous. Our attractiveness lies in our bank balances, not our selves.'

'I don't believe that. You're far too cynical, Max.'

'I've met far too many Alicias not to be cynical. Do you know that within six months of telling Stevie she loved him but couldn't cope, she'd married another heir to a fortune? Then, when she'd divorced that sucker twelve months later, she even had the temerity to make a line for me one night when our paths crossed.'

'And?'

'And what?'

'Don't take me for a total fool, Max. Something happened between you two. I felt it.'

He sighed. 'You feel too much sometimes. OK, so I was in a vengeful mood that night. When Alicia started coming on to me, I played along with it. When I suggested leaving the party we were attending she jumped at the chance, even though she'd come with someone else. I took her to a club, where we drank and danced.'

Danced! Tara's stomach crunched down hard at the mere thought of another woman in her Max's arms. She knew it was before they'd met, but still…

'I waited for her to make her excuses about Stevie,' Max continued as he twisted his champagne glass round and round. 'I knew she would. But what she said really floored me. She told me that she'd only dated Stevie to be near me. She told me that she'd never really loved my brother. It was me she'd loved all along. She claimed she only married that other man because she thought she had no chance with me.

I told her what I thought of her and her so-called love and walked out.'

Tara never said a word, because she suspected that what the woman had said might be true. She'd seen a photograph of Stevie and whilst he had been a nice-looking boy, his face had lacked Max's strength and charisma.

'Love is just a weapon to such women,' Max added testily. 'My own mother pretends she still loves my father, despite his having been a neglectful husband, as well as a neglectful father. Why? Because it would probably cost too much money to divorce him. I overheard her tell a lady friend once that she knew about Dad's womanising ways, but turned a blind eye. Even now that he's in a wheelchair, a wretched wreck of a man, she stays with him, catering to his every need. They're as bad as each other, bound together by their greed and their lack of moral fibre. That's why I have as little as possible to do with them these days. Both of them make me sick.'

Tara was stunned by his outburst, and the depth of his bitterness. Bitterness was never good for anyone's soul. Neither was revenge. It was very self-destructive.

'But you could be wrong, Max,' she ventured quietly. 'Your mother might very well love your father. There might be things you don't know. We rarely know what goes on inside a marriage. I found that out last weekend. I always thought my sister was unhappy in her marriage. She fell pregnant, you see, during her last year at school. Dale wasn't much older, and still doing his plumbing apprenticeship. They got married, with Jen thinking she could finish her schooling. But she was too sick during her pregnancy to study. Then, when her first baby was barely six months old, she fell pregnant again. She's always complaining about her life, and her husband. She says he spends too much time and money drinking with his mates. But when I asked her why she didn't leave him and get a divorce, she looked at me as though I was mad. Told me she was *very* happy with Dale and would never dream of getting a divorce. So maybe you're wrong, Max. It *is* possible, you know,' she added with a wry little smile.

He smiled back. 'Possible. But not probable. Look, let's not spoil tonight with such talk. Let's just eat some wonderful food together and drink this wonderful champagne. I want to get you delightfully tipsy so that I can take you back upstairs and have my truly wicked way with you.'

Although Tara's stomach flipped at the prospect, she stayed calm on the surface, suspecting that Max was watching her for her reaction. As much as she was curious, she wasn't sure if the reality would be as exciting as the fantasy. And even if it was, what about the consequences? Did she really want Max thinking she would do *anything* he asked? What next?

'You think that's the answer to my co-operation?' she asked coolly. 'Getting me drunk?'

'Is it?'

'I hope not.'

'Then how about this?' And he extracted a small gold velvet box from his pocket.

Tara stared at the ring-sized box.

An engagement ring. He'd bought her an engagement ring. He was going to ask her to marry him!

The shot of adrenalin which instantly charged through her bloodstream made a mockery of her denial to her mother that marriage to Max was not what she wanted at this moment in her life.

Clearly, her body knew things which her brain did not.

'Go on,' he said, and reached over to put the gold box on the white tablecloth in front of her. 'Open it.'

Something about the scenario suddenly didn't fit Tara's image of how a man like Max would ask her to marry him. It was all far too casual. *He* was far too casual.

She sucked in a deep breath, then let it out slowly, gathering herself before opening the box. When she did, and her eyes fell upon a huge topaz dress ring, she was ready to react as she was sure Max expected her to react, with seeming pleasure and gratitude.

'Oh, Max, it's lovely! Thank you so much.'

'I knew it would match that dress. That's why I wanted you to wear it tonight. Go on,' he said eagerly. 'Put it on. See if it fits.'

She slipped it on the middle finger of her right hand.

'Perfect,' she said, and held it out to show him.

The diamond-cut stone sparkled under the candle-light. 'But you really shouldn't have, Max. You make me feel guilty that I didn't buy you anything. I had no idea you were such a romantic.'

'I think I'm catching the disease from you.'

'I don't know why you keep calling me a roman-tic.'

'When a girl of your looks reaches twenty-four still a virgin then I know she's a romantic.'

'Maybe. Maybe not. I consider myself more of an idealist. I didn't want to have sex till I *really* wanted it. I wasn't waiting for love to strike so much as pas-sion. Which it did. With you. I didn't realise I was in love with you till the following morning. How long did it take till you realised you loved me?'

'The moment you smiled at me in that shop I was a goner.'

'Oh, Max, now who's being the romantic?'

He smiled. 'Aah, here comes Jarod to take our or-der. Let me order for you tonight, darling. Now that you're breaking out in other ways, I think it's time you tried some different foods.'

'If you insist.'

He grinned. 'I insist.'

Tara sat back and sipped her champagne whilst Max went to town with their meal order. He'd always liked ordering the rarest and most exotic foods on the menu for himself.

Clearly, Max was happier now with her than ever. Tara glanced down at the topaz ring and told herself it had been silly of her to want it to be an engagement ring.

Max was right. She *was* a romantic.

'You don't like it,' Max said.

Tara glanced up to see that Jarod had departed and Max was looking at her with a worried frown.

'Of course I do,' she said with a quick smile. 'It's gorgeous.'

'So what were you thinking about that made you look so wistful?'

She shrugged. 'I guess I'd like to spend more time with the wonderful man who gave it to me.'

'Your wish is my command, my darling. How would you like to quit that job of yours and come with me when I go overseas?'

Tara's mouth dropped open.

'I take it that stunned look on your face means a yes?'

'I... I... Yes. Yes, of course. But Max, are you sure?'

'I wouldn't have asked you if I wasn't sure.'

So why haven't you asked me this before now?

The question zoomed into her mind like an annoying bee, buzzing around in her brain, searching for the truth. What had changed in their relationship that he suddenly wanted her with him all the time?

Tara hated the answer that would not be denied.

The sex. The sex between them had changed.

'Why now, Max?' she couldn't stop herself asking whilst her stomach had tightened into a knot.

He shrugged. 'Do you want the truth? Or romantic bulldust?'

'Romantic bulldust, of course.'

He laughed. 'OK. I love you. I love you so much that I can no longer stand leaving you behind when I go away. I want you with me, every day. I want you in my bed, every night. How's that?'

'Pretty good. Now how about the truth?'

Max looked at her and knew he would never tell her the truth, which was that he was afraid of losing her if he left her behind. He suspected she had never felt anything like she'd felt with him today. How, now, could he expect her to patiently wait for him to come home? She might not actively look for other lovers, but men would always pursue Tara...

'The truth,' he repeated, doing his best to look in command of the situation. 'The truth is I love you, Tara. I love you so much I can't stand the thought of leaving you behind when I go away. I want you with me, every day. I want you in my bed, every night.'

And wasn't *that* the truth!

Tara tried not to burst into tears. She had a feeling that sobbing all over the place was not what Max wanted in a mistress. Because of course, if she did this, if she quit her job and let Max pay for everything whilst she travelled with him, that was what she would be. Possibly, that was all she would ever be. There was no guarantee their relationship would end in marriage, no matter how much Max said he loved her.

Still, there'd never been any guarantees of that. He'd never given her any. And he wasn't giving her any now.

Tara thought of what her mother had said about how he would *never* give her what she wanted. Once again, she tried to pin down in her mind what she actually wanted from Max at this stage in her life. That ring business had rocked her a bit. Suddenly, she wasn't at all sure. The only thing she *was* sure of was that she didn't want to lose Max. Now more than ever.

'I'll have to give Whitmore's two weeks' notice,' she said, her voice on the suddenly breathless side. Her heart was racing madly and her mouth had gone dry. 'I can't just leave them in the lurch. February is top tourist season for the Japanese.'

'Fine. But what about next weekend? I have to go back to Auckland, negotiate with some owners there about a hotel. If I arrange plane tickets for you, would you join me there?'

'I wouldn't be able to leave till the Saturday morning. We'd only have the one night together.'

'Better than nothing,' he said, blue eyes gleaming in the candlelight.

'Yes,' she agreed, a tremor ripping down her spine. By next Saturday, her body would be screaming for him.

She picked up her glass and took a decent swallow, aware that he was watching her closely.

'Are you all right, Tara?' he asked, softly but knowingly, she thought.

'No,' she returned sharply. 'No, I'm not. And it's all your fault. I feel like a cat on a hot tin roof.'

'Aaah.'

There was a wealth of satisfaction—and knowledge—in that aaah.

'Would you like me to have our meals sent up to the penthouse?'

Tara blinked, then stared at him. If she blindly said yes, it would be the end of her. She would be his in whatever way he wanted her. There would be no further questioning over what *she* wanted, because what she wanted would be what *he* wanted.

But how could she say no when she wanted it too? To be his. To let him take her back into that world he had shown her today, that dizzying, dazzling world where sensation was heaped upon sensation, where giving pleasure was as satisfying as receiving it, where the mind was set free of worry and all its focus was centred on the physical.

'Can we take the champagne too?' she heard herself saying, shocked to the core at how cool her voice sounded.

'Absolutely.' Max was already on his feet.

'Will you still respect me in the morning?' she said with a degree of self-mockery as he walked round the table towards her.

Placing one hand under her chin, he tipped up her face for a kiss which was cruel in its restraint.

He's teasing me, she realised. Giving me a taste of what's to come.

'Tell me you love me,' he murmured when his mouth lifted.

'I love you.'

'Let's go.'

CHAPTER SEVEN

'I'M BEING punished for last night,' Tara groaned.

'You've just got a hangover,' Max reassured her, sitting down on the side of the bed and stroking her hair back from her forehead. 'You must have had too much champagne.'

'I'll never touch the stuff again,' Tara said, not sure which was worse. Her headache or her swirling stomach.

'Pity,' Max said with a wry smile. 'You really were *very* cooperative.'

'Don't remind me.'

Max laughed. 'I'll get you a couple of painkillers and a glass of water.'

Max disappeared into the bathroom, leaving Tara with her misery and her memories of the night before. Impossible to forget what she had allowed. Ridiculous to pretend that she hadn't thrilled to it all.

Tara groaned, then groaned again. She was going to be sick.

Her dash to the bathroom was desperate, shoving Max out of the way. She just had time to hold her hair back and out of the way before everything came up that she'd eaten the night before. It came up and came up till she was left exhausted and shaken.

It's just a hangover, she told herself as Max helped her over to the basin, where she rinsed out her mouth and washed her face. Or the same virus I had yesterday morning. I couldn't possibly be pregnant. Mum put that silly thought into my head. And it *is* silly. I had a period, for pity's sake.

'Poor darling,' Max comforted as he carried her back to bed and placed her still naked body gently inside the sheets. When she started shivering he covered her up with a quilt and tucked it around her. 'No point taking any tablets if you're throwing up. I'll go get you that glass of water. And a cool washer to put on your forehead. That helps sometimes. Take it from one who knows. I've had a few dreadful hangovers in my time. Still, you must be extra-susceptible to champagne, because you didn't have *that* much. I think I had the major share. And we wasted a bit. On you.'

'Don't remind me about that, either,' she said wretchedly. 'Could you dispose of that disgusting champagne bottle? I don't want to look at it.'

'Come, now, Tara, you loved it last night. *All* of it,' he said as he swept the empty bottle off the bedside table and headed for the doorway. 'But I will tolerate your morning-after sensitivities,' he tossed over his shoulder, 'in view of your fragile condition.'

Her fragile condition...

Tara bit her bottom lip as the question over her being sick for a second morning in a row returned to haunt her. Max was right. She hadn't had that much champagne. Hard to pin her hopes on the gastric virus going around, either. With that, Jen and her kids had been running to use the loo all the time. Then there was her sudden recovery yesterday afternoon and evening, only for her to become nauseous again this morning.

If she hadn't had a period recently then she would have presumed she was pregnant, as her mother had. Was it possible to have a period and still be pregnant? Tara had read of a few such cases. They weren't proper periods, just breakthrough bleeding, mostly related to women who'd fallen pregnant whilst on the Pill. Nothing was a hundred per cent safe, except abstinence. Her mother had told her *that,* too.

'Oh, God,' she sobbed, and stuffed a hand into her mouth.

'That bad, huh?' Max said as he strode back into the bedroom, carrying a glass of water with some ice in it. 'Do you want me to ring the house medico? I have one on call here at the weekends.'

'No! No doctor.'

'OK, OK,' Max soothed, coming round to place the glass on the bedside table. 'No doctor. I'm just trying to help. I don't like seeing you this sick.'

'What you don't like is not having your new little sex slave on tap this morning!'

The horrible words were out of her mouth before she could stop them. She saw Max's head jerk back. Saw the shock in his eyes.

Tara was truly appalled at herself. 'I'm sorry,' she

cried. 'I didn't mean that. Truly. I'm not myself this morning. I'm a terrible person when I'm sick.' And when I'm petrified I might be pregnant.

The very thought sent her head whirling some more. She didn't want to be pregnant. Not now. Not when Max had just asked her to travel with him. Not when her life had just become so exciting.

'It's all right, Tara. I understand.'

'No, no, you don't.'

'I think I do. What happened yesterday. And last night. It was a case of too much too soon. I became greedy. I should have taken things more slowly with you. You might have enjoyed yourself at the time, but hindsight has a way of bringing doubts and worries. It's good, in a way, that this morning has given us both a breather. Even if it's not under pleasant circumstances for you.'

'You don't mind?'

His smile was wry. 'Mind? Of course I mind. I'd love to be making love to you right at this moment. But I'm a patient man. I can wait till next weekend. And next time, I promise I won't frighten you with my demands.'

'You…you didn't frighten me, Max.'

He stared into her eyes. 'No? Are you sure?'

'I'm sure. I liked everything we did together.'

He let out a sigh of relief. 'I'm so glad to hear that. I have to confess I was a bit worried that I might have gone too far last night. Not at the time. But when I woke, this morning.'

Not as worried as *she* was this morning.

Max sat down beside her on the bed and started stroking her head again. 'Still, I don't want you to ever think you have to do anything you don't want to do, Tara. I love *you,* not just having sex with you. All right?'

She nodded, but tears threatened. Max might say that now, but what if she *was* pregnant? Would he be so noble when faced with her having his baby? Or would he do and say things which might threaten their relationship for good?

Endless complications flooded into her mind, almost overwhelming her with fear, and feelings of impending doom.

But you don't *know* you're pregnant, she tried telling herself. You could very well be wrong.

Yes, yes, she would cling to that thought. At least till Max left. She couldn't continue thinking and acting this way or she would surely break down and blurt out what was bothering her. And she really didn't want to do that. Max had enough things on his mind these days without burdening him with premature news of an unconfirmed pregnancy.

No, she had to pull herself together and stop being such a panic artist. Max had a couple of hours yet before he left for the airport. Surely she could stay calm for that length of time. Why spoil the rest of his stay with negativity and pessimism? What would that achieve? He was being so sweet and understanding this morning. It wasn't fair to take her secret fears out on him, especially when it was only a guess, and based on nothing but her feeling nauseous two mornings in a row.

Hardly conclusive proof.

'Max…'

'Yes?'

'I'm feeling a bit better now. My stomach is much more settled. Do you think I should try something to eat? Maybe some toast?'

'I think that would be an excellent idea. Eating is another good cure for a hangover. I'll have Room Service send some up.' And he stood up to walk round to the extension that sat on his bedside chest. 'I'll order myself a decent breakfast at the same time. Just coffee won't cut it this morning. Not with airline food beckoning me later today. I need something far more substantial.'

Tara pulled herself up into a sitting position, dragging the sheet up with her over her breasts and tucking it modestly around her. As much as she might have discovered a new abandon when she was turned on, she was still not an exhibitionist.

'You know, Max,' she said when he'd finished ordering, 'you should keep some staple foods in your kitchen. Cereals last for weeks. So does long-life milk and juice. And bread freezes. It's rather extravagant to order everything you eat from Room Service.'

'Maybe, but I intend to keep on doing it. I work incredibly long hours and I have no intention of spending my precious leisure time in the kitchen. I have far more enjoyable things to do when I'm on R & R.' And he gave her a wickedly knowing smile.

Tara was taken aback. Maybe she was extra-sensitive this morning, but she didn't like Max describing the time he spent with her as R & R—rest and recreation.

She dropped her eyes to her lap to stop his noting her negative reaction and found herself staring at the huge topaz ring which was still on her finger. His gift was the only thing he hadn't removed from her last night.

Suddenly, she saw it not as an anniversary present, but the beginning of many such gifts, given to her for services rendered; rewards for travelling with him and filling his rest and recreation hours in the way he liked most.

She pictured their sex games being played out in lavish hotel rooms all over the world, Max's demands becoming more and more outrageous in line with the extravagance of his gifts. Soon, she'd be dripping in diamonds and designer clothes. But underneath, she wouldn't be wearing *any* underwear. In the end, she would become his sex slave for real, bought and paid for, fashioned to fulfil his every desire. She would cease to be her own person. She'd just be a possession. A toy, to be taken out and played with during Max's leisure time, and ignored when he went back to his real life. His work.

Of course, such a sex toy had to be perfect, physically. It could never be allowed to get fat. Or pregnant.

Pregnant sex slaves had two choices. They either got rid of their babies. Or they themselves were dispensed with.

Both scenarios horrified Tara.

'Max!' she exclaimed, her eyes flying upwards.

But Max was no longer in the bedroom. Tara had been so consumed with her thoughts—and her imaginary future—that she hadn't noticed his leaving.

'Max!' she called out and the door of his dressing room opened. He emerged, dressed in one of his conservative grey business suits, though not teamed with his usual white shirt today. His shirt was a blue, the same blue as his eyes. And his tie was a sleek, shiny silver, a change from his usual choice. His hair was still damp from a recent shower and slicked straight back from his head.

He looked dashing, she thought. And very sexy.

But then, Max *was* very sexy.

An image flashed into her mind of his tipping champagne from the bottle over her breasts, then bending to lick it off. Slowly. So very slowly. She'd pleaded with him to stop teasing her.

But he'd ignored her pleas.

That was part of the game, wasn't it?

The best part. The most exciting part.

'What?' he asked, frowning over at her.

'I… I didn't know where you were,' she said lamely, hating herself for her sudden weakness. She'd been going to tell him that she'd changed her mind about travelling with him; that she didn't really like the way things were heading.

But the words had died in her throat at the sight of him. It was so true what they said. The mind could be willing but the flesh was very weak.

'Thought I might as well get dressed before Room Service called,' he explained. 'I know how you don't like the butler coming in when you're in bed. Besides, no point in staying in my bathrobe with you feeling under the weather, is there?'

The front door bell rang right at that moment. Max hurried from the room, returning in no time, wheeling a traymobile. By then, Tara had decided she was being a drama queen. Max loved her and she loved him. It was only natural that he would ask her to travel with him. And it was only natural that she would go.

As for her pregnancy…

That was as far-fetched an idea as her becoming some kind of mindless sex slave. She had always had a strong sense of her own self. Her mother called her wilful and her sister said she was incredibly stubborn. If Max started crossing the line where she was concerned, she would simply tell him so and come home. Nothing could be simpler.

'Now, that's what I like to see,' Max said as he tossed her one of the Sunday papers. 'Almost a happy face.'

She smiled at him. 'Nothing like feeling better to make you feel better.'

He scowled. 'Now she tells me, *after* I'm dressed.'

'That was not an invitation for more sex, Max Richmond. I think we've indulged enough for one weekend. I would hate to think that all I'd be if and when I travel with you is a means of rest and relaxation.'

He frowned at her. 'If and when? Did I hear correctly? I thought you'd agreed to come with me. It was just a matter of giving your notice.'

'Yes, well, I've been having some second thoughts.'

Tara knew how to play that game. The hard-to-get game.

For years before she'd met Max, she'd played it to the hilt. Whilst she'd not been so successful with Max, she suspected that it would do him good to be a little less sure of her.

'Aah,' he said. 'I see. Hence, the sex-slave accusation.'

'Yes…'

Max sighed, then came over to sit on the bed once more.

'I don't know how many times I have to tell you this weekend, Tara, but I love you. Deeply. I want you with me for more than just sex. I enjoy just being with you, even when we're not making love. I enjoy your company and your conversation. I enjoy your wit and your charm with other people. Taking you out is a delight. *You* are a delight. When you're not sick, that is,' he added drily, dampening her pleasure in his compliments.

'Charming,' she said. 'So if I ever get sick, I will be tossed aside, like a toy whose batteries have run low?'

'No more of this nonsense!' he pronounced, and rose to his feet. 'You're coming with me and that's that. So what would you like on your toast? There is a choice of honey, Vegemite and jam. Strawberry jam, by the look of it.'

'Vegemite.'

'Vegemite toast coming up, then.'

Tara raised no further objections to travelling with him.

But she resolved not to ever let him take away her much valued sense of independence. She'd always been her own person and would hate to think that her love for Max would eventually turn her into some kind of puppet.

She munched away on her toast and watched him tuck into his huge breakfast, which he ate whilst sitting with her on the bed. He chatted away when he could, pleasing her with the news that the comment she'd made yesterday about never being able to resist a buy-one, get-one-free sale had inspired him to make such an offer with his hotel in Hong Kong.

Stay one week, get one free was now posted on its website and was already bringing in results with scads of bookings.

'We won't make a great profit on the accommodation,' he told her. 'But empty rooms don't return a cent. Hopefully, the type of guest this promotion attracts will spend all the money they think they've saved in other places in the hotel. Pierce thought I was crazy, but that was yesterday. This morning he's singing my praises. Says I'm a genius. Forgive me for not telling him that my little genius is my girl-friend. Male ego is a terrible thing.'

Tara suspected that it was.

But it was also an attractive thing. It gave Max his competitiveness, and his drive. It made him the man he was, the man she loved.

'Isn't it unusual to have a male PA?' she remarked, somewhat idly.

'Unusual maybe. But wise, given the amount of time we spend overseas together.'

Tara blinked as the meaning behind Max's words sank in. 'Did you hire Pierce *because* he's a man?'

'You mean because I didn't want to risk becoming involved with a female secretary?'

'Yes.'

'Absolutely. Been there, done that, and it was messy.'

'How long ago?'

'A good year or so before I met you.'

'Did you sleep with her?'

Max pulled a face. 'I wish you hadn't asked me that.'

'Did you sleep with her?'

'Once or twice.'

'Was it once, or twice?'

'More than that, actually. Look, it was messy, as I said.'

'Tell me about it.'

He sighed. 'I'd rather not.'

'I want to know. You know all about my past.'

'Tara, you don't *have* a past.'

'Yes, I do. I might not have slept with guys but I made out with quite a few. I told you all about them that first night. I want to know, Max. Tell me.'

'OK, but it isn't pretty.'

'Was *she* pretty?'

'Pretty? No, Grace was not pretty. Not plain, either. Very slim. Nicely groomed. With red hair. Out of a bottle. She was already my personal assistant when Dad had his stroke. Up till then I'd taken care of the money side of things in the firm, here at home in Sydney. Suddenly, I had to go overseas. A lot. I took her with me. The man she was living with at the time didn't like it and broke up with her. We'd never been involved before but all of a sudden, we were together every day of the week. We were both lonely, and stressed out. One night, over too many drinks, she made a pass at me and it just happened. It wasn't love on my part. And she said it wasn't on hers. It was more a matter of mutual convenience. I should have stopped it. I still feel guilty that I didn't. Finally, when I tried to, she told me she was pregnant.'

Tara sucked in sharply.

'She wasn't,' he went on. 'It was just a ploy to get

me to marry her. Frankly, I was suspicious right from the start. I'd always used condoms and there'd never been an accident, not like that one I had with you last year. When I insisted on accompanying her to a doctor to find out how far pregnant she was, she broke down and confessed she wasn't at all.'

'And if she had been, Max? What then? What would you have done?'

He shrugged. 'I honestly don't know. But she wasn't, so I didn't have to face that dilemma. Thank God. But it made me wary, I can tell you. Hence, Pierce.'

'I see. And what happened to her?'

'I'm pleased to say she went back home to the man she'd been living with before. I had a note from her some months later to say they were getting married, and this time she really was having a baby. I was happy for her because I suspect she thought she was past having a child. She wasn't all that young, you see. She was forty by then.'

'An older woman,' Tara said with an edge to her voice. 'And an experienced one, I'll bet. Did you learn some of those kinky games from her, Max? Was that why you couldn't stop? Because she never had to be persuaded to finish anything she started?'

'Stop it, Tara,' Max snapped. 'Stop it right now. You have no reason to be jealous of Grace. I'm sorry my past is not as pure as yours but I won't be cross-questioned on it. And I won't apologise for it. I'm a mortal man. I've made mistakes in my life, but hopefully I have learned from them.'

Putting aside his breakfast tray, he stood up. 'I think perhaps I should get going before you find something else to argue about. I can see you're out of sorts this morning in more ways than one. When you do feel well enough to go home, for pity's sake use the credit card I gave you to take a taxi this time. I noticed in the statements I receive that you never use the darned thing these days.'

'Fine,' she said, wanting him to just go so that she could cry.

His eyes narrowed on her. 'I wish I knew what was going on in that pretty head of yours.'

'Not much. Blonde-bimbo mistresses aren't known for their brains.'

'Tara…'

'I know. I'm acting like a fool. Forgive me.' Tears pricked at her eyes.

'Oh, Tara…' And he started walking towards her.

She knew, without his saying a word, that he was going to take her into his arms. If he did that, she was going to disintegrate and say even more stupid things.

'Please don't come near me,' she said sharply. 'I smell of sick.'

He stopped, his eyes tormented. 'I don't want to leave you on this note.'

'You can make it up to me next weekend in Auckland, when I feel better.'

'That's a week away.'

'Ring me from Hong Kong, then. But not tonight. Tonight I want to go to bed early and sleep. I'm wrecked.'

He smiled. 'Same here. I'll be sleeping on that plane. All right, I'll ring you tomorrow night. Can I peck you on the forehead?'

'If you must.'

'Oh, I must,' he said softly as his lips brushed over her forehead. 'I must…'

Tara waited till he was definitely gone before she dissolved into some very noisy weeping.

CHAPTER EIGHT

TARA stared at the blue line, all her fears crystallised.

She was pregnant.

Stumbling back from the vanity basin, she sank down onto the toilet seat, her head dropping into her hands.

But somehow, she was beyond tears. She'd cried for ages after Max left. Cried and cried.

It had been close to two o'clock by the time she'd pulled herself together enough to get dressed and go downstairs to buy a pregnancy-testing kit from the chemist shop in the foyer.

And now there was no longer any doubt. Or guessing. She was going to have Max's baby.

Tara shook her head from side to side. It wasn't fair. She'd taken every precaution. This shouldn't be happening to her. What on earth was she going to do?

Tara sucked in deeply as she lifted her head. What *could* she do?

Nothing. The same way Jen had done nothing when Dale had got her pregnant. The Bond sisters hadn't been brought up to have abortions.

Not that Tara wanted to get rid of Max's baby. If she could just get past her fear over what Max would say and do when he found out, she might even feel happy about it.

But that was her biggest problem, wasn't it?

Telling Max.

What if he accused her of deliberately getting pregnant? Even worse, what if he demanded she get a termination?

That would be the death knell of their relationship, she knew. Because it would prove to her once and for all that he didn't really love her.

A huge wave of depression washed through her, taking Tara lower than she'd ever been in her life before. If she discovered Max didn't really love her, how could she stand it? How would she cope?

You'll have to cope, girl, came back the stern answer. You're going to become a mother. You're going to be needed. Having some kind of breakdown is simply not on.

Tara squared her shoulders as her self-lecture had some effect. But when she thought of having to tell her own mother about the baby she wilted again.

Not yet, Tara decided with a shudder. She couldn't tell her yet. Maybe she wouldn't tell Max yet, either. First babies didn't show for quite a while. Maybe she could delay the confrontation with Max till she was over four months, past the safe time for a termination. As much as Tara was confident he couldn't succeed in talking her into an abortion, she didn't want him to even try.

Unfortunately, she had no idea just how far pregnant she actually was. That was her first job. To find out.

Jen, Tara thought with a lifting of spirit. Jen had a nice doctor that she'd gone to when she was having her babies. Tara had gone with her a couple of times and had really liked him. On top of that, Jen wouldn't be too shocked, or read her the Riot Act. How could she when she'd got pregnant herself when she'd only been seventeen?

Yes, she would tell Jen, then ask her to arrange an appointment with her doctor. Preferably for this week, *before* her supposed trip to New Zealand. Tara need to know where things stood. Though really, unless her morning sickness went away, she couldn't see herself going anywhere overseas for ages.

Tara stood up and returned to the bedroom, where she sat down on Max's side of the bed and picked up the phone. After pressing the number for an outside line, she was about to punch in Jen's number when she realised she hadn't called her mother at all this weekend. Yet she'd promised to let her know when she'd be back.

Tara sighed. Really, once Max was on the scene, she couldn't think about anything or anyone else. The man had obsessed her these last twelve months. He probably would have obsessed her more after this incredible weekend, if his baby hadn't come along to put a halt to the proceedings. As much as she had thrilled to his forceful lovemaking—and it didn't seem to have hurt the baby—she really couldn't let him continue to make love to her in such a wild fashion.

Which meant her idea of keeping the baby secret for weeks wouldn't work. Max wouldn't understand why she wanted him to go back to his former style of slow, gentle lovemaking all of a sudden.

No. She would have to tell him the truth. And soon.

Now Tara wasn't sure whether to view this pregnancy as a saviour, or one huge sacrifice all round. No travelling overseas. No adventurous sex. Possibly, no Max at all!

Her chin trembled at this last thought.

Oh, life was cruel. Too cruel.

Tara slumped down on the bed and burst into tears again, the phone clutched in her hands. This time, her crying jag was considerably shorter than the last. Only ten minutes or so.

I'm definitely getting it together, she told herself as she dabbed at her eyes with the sheet, then took several gathering breaths.

'Time to ring Mum,' she said aloud, proud of her firm voice, and her firm finger. The number entered, she waited for her mother to answer.

'Hi there.'

'Oh. Oh, Jen. It's *you*!'

'Hi, Tara. Yep. It's me. I came over to visit Mum. She seemed a bit down. Dale's minding the kids. We're playing Scrabble and eating far too much cake. I presume his lord and master is in town?'

'Er— *Was.* He's gone now.'

'Brother, he doesn't stay long these days, does he?'

'Jen, can we talk? I mean…can Mum hear what you're saying?'

'Hold it a sec. Mum, it's Tara… Tara, Mum wants to know when you're coming home.'

'Shortly.'

'Shortly, Mum,' Tara heard Jen say. 'Why don't you go make us a cuppa while I have a chat with my little sister? I haven't talked to Tara in ages. Great. I'm alone now, Tara,' she said more quietly. 'What's up?'

'I… I'm pregnant.'

Jen stayed silent for a second, then just said, 'Bummer.'

'Is that it? Just *bummer*? I was hoping for some words of sympathy and wisdom.'

'Sorry. It was the shock. So how did this happen? I mean, I know how it *happened*. You had sex. I meant…did you forget the Pill one day or something?'

'Nope. Took it right on the dot every day.'

'Now, that is a real bummer. I was at least stupid and careless when I fell pregnant. Oh, Tara, what are you going to do?'

'Have my baby. The same way you did.'

'Yeah. We're suckers for doing the right thing, aren't we? So does Max know yet? I presume not.'

'No. I only found out myself a few minutes ago. The test went bluer than blue.'

'What do you think he'll say?'

'My head goes round and round every time I think about that. He's not going to be happy.'

'Men are never happy over unexpected pregnancies. But if he loves you, he'll stick by you. Dale went ballistic at first but after a while he calmed down, and really he was like a rock after that. Much better than me, actually. I cried for weeks and weeks.'

'I remember.'

'Do you think Max might ask you to marry him?'

'He's made it clear that marriage and kids are definitely not on his agenda, so your guess is as good as mine.'

'No, it isn't, Tara. You know the man. I don't. Does he love you?'

'He says he does.'

'You don't sound convinced.'

Tara sighed. 'I'm a bit mixed up about Max at the moment.'

'Is the pregnancy causing that, or what's going on in your relationship right now? Mum told me he's hardly ever around any more.'

Tara resented having to defend Max but, in fairness to the man, she felt she should. 'He's been very busy with all the world crises in the tourist industry. On the plus side, he did ask me just this weekend to quit my job and travel with him in future.' Tara didn't add that she was more qualified for the role of travelling companion since finding her sexual wings.

'Wow! And what did you say to that? Silly question. Yes, of course. I know you're crazy about the man.'

'I can't see myself travelling at all in the near future. I'm sick as a dog every morning. I need to see a doctor, Jen. Do you think you could get an appointment with your doctor this week?'

'He might be able to fit you in. But he won't be able to cure you of morning sickness. You'll just have to ride that out. Have a packet of dry biscuits by your bed and eat a couple before you get up. That helps. So, how far gone are you?'

'That's another thing. I don't know. Before this weekend, I hadn't seen Max in almost a month. Yet I had a period whilst he was away. At least, I thought I did. There was some bleeding when my period was due.'

'Yeah, that can happen. You're probably about six weeks gone if you're chucking up. But you need to have it checked out. Don't worry. I'll explain to the receptionist that it's an emergency. Now, when are you going to tell lover-boy?'

'Max,' Tara corrected firmly. 'Call him Max.'

'I'd like to call him lots of things, actually. But Max isn't one of them. Look, once you've been to the doctor and had things properly confirmed, you *have* to tell him. Even if he doesn't want to marry you, he's legally required to support this baby. You have no idea how much having children costs these days. Do you have private health cover?'

'For pity's sake, Jen, do you have to be so...so... pragmatic? I've just found out I'm having a baby. It's a very emotional time for me.'

'You can be emotional later. First things first, which is your welfare and the welfare of your child. Trust me. I know better than you in this.'

'I wish I hadn't told you at all!'

'Don't be ridiculous. You need all the support you can get. Which reminds me. You really should tell Mum.'

'Are you kidding? I'm going to delay that disaster area for as long as possible. Promise me you won't tell her, Jen. Right now. *Promise.*'

'OK. I think you're wrong, but it's your call. Speaking of calls, I'll ring the surgery first thing tomorrow morning. Then I'll ring you at work to let you know. I'll come with you, of course.'

'Would you? Oh, Jen, that would be great. I...I feel kind of... Oh, I don't know. I just can't seem to get my head around all this. A baby, for heaven's sake. I'm going to have a baby!' Tears threatened again.

'A beautiful baby, I'll warrant. And you'll love it to pieces.'

Tara gulped down the lump in her throat. 'Will I? I've never thought of myself as good mother material. I'm too...restless.'

'You just didn't know what you wanted. Having a baby will bring your life into focus. Er—we'd better sign off now before Mum comes back.'

'Yes, I really couldn't cope with the third degree

she'd give me. You won't forget to call me tomorrow?'

'I won't forget.'

'OK. Bye for now.'

Jen hung up, then grimaced up at her mother, who was standing there, mugs in hand.

'You heard that last bit, didn't you?'

Joyce nodded.

'She…she's too scared to tell you,' Jen said quietly, knowing by the look on her mother's face that she was about to have a hissy fit.

'But why?' Joyce wailed, putting the mugs down on the coffee-table next to the Scrabble board and flopping down into her chair.

'You know why, Mum. It's the same reason I didn't want to tell you when *I* was pregnant. Daughters want their mothers to be proud of them, not ashamed.'

'But Jen, I was never ashamed of you. Just disappointed for you. And worried. You were so young. And neither of you had any money.'

'What's age or money got to do with it? Love's what matters, Mum, when it comes to kids and marriage. Dale loved me and I loved him. We've had some tough times but we're going to make it. Unfortunately, I'm not so sure Max Richmond loves our Tara. Certainly not enough to give up his jet-setting lifestyle. That's why she's in such a tizz, because she knows it too. She's going to need a lot of support through this, Mum.'

'But how can I support her when I'm not supposed to even know?'

'She'll tell you. Just give her a little time.'

'From the sounds of things, she hasn't told Max Richmond.'

'Not yet. She's just found out herself, I gather, and he's not there.'

'He's never going to be there for her.'

'Probably. But he can be forced to support her financially. At least she won't be poor.'

'Yes, that's true. But Tara never wanted his money. You know she's not that kind of girl. She just wanted him to love her.'

'Yeah, I do know. She's always been a real romantic. She's been living in a fantasy world with her fantasy lover and now the real world has come up and bitten her, big time.'

Joyce was shaking her head. 'I've been afraid of something like this for a long time. If that man lets her down, I'm not sure she'll be able to cope.'

'She'll be upset, but she'll cope, Mum. You brought us up to be survivors. We're a stubborn pair. Trust me on that.'

'You're both good girls.'

'More's the pity. If Tara wasn't so damned good, she wouldn't have a problem.'

'Jen, you don't think she'd ever...'

'No. Never in a million years. She's going to have this baby whether lover-boy wants her to or not.'

Joyce looked shocked. 'You mean he might try to persuade her to get rid of it?'

'It's highly likely, don't you think?'

'She does love him a lot, Jen. If he puts the pressure on, she might do what he wants. Women in love can sometimes do things they regret later.'

'If he does that, *he'll* be the one to regret it,' Jen said fiercely. 'Tara would never forgive him, *or* herself. Look, I'd better drink this tea and get on home, Mum. Don't worry too much about Tara. Max can't put any pressure on her yet, because she doesn't intend telling him yet. OK?'

Joyce nodded, but inside she was beside herself with worry. Yet she could do nothing to help, because she wasn't supposed to know!

She glanced over at Jen and tried to work out why it was that daughters always misunderstood their mothers. All she wanted was for them to be happy.

Fancy Jen thinking she'd been ashamed of her when she fell pregnant. How could she possibly be ashamed of her daughters for doing exactly what she had done herself? Fallen madly in love. Maybe she would tell them one day that she had been pregnant when she'd married her beloved Bill.

Tears filled Joyce's eyes as she thought of the handsome man who'd swept her off her feet and into his bed before she could blink. How she'd loved that man. When he'd died, she could not bear to ever have another man touch her, though there'd been plenty who'd tried. Her daughters might be surprised to know that. But she'd only ever wanted her Bill.

'Please don't cry, Mum,' Jen said, reaching over to touch her mother's hand. 'Tara will be fine. You'll see.'

Joyce found a watery smile from somewhere. 'I hope so, love.'

'She's strong, is our Tara. And stubborn. Max won't find it easy to make her do anything she doesn't want to do. And she doesn't want to get rid of her baby. Come on, give me a hug and dry those tears. If you're all puffy-eyed when Tara gets home, she'll think I told you and then there'll be hell to pay. Promise me now that you won't let on.'

Joyce gave her daughter a hug and a promise. But it was difficult not to worry once she was alone, so she did the one thing she always did when she started to stress over one of her daughters. She took out the photo albums which contained the visual memories of all the good times they'd had as a family before her Bill died.

It always soothed her fears, looking at the man she'd loved so much and whom she still loved. She liked to talk to him; ask his advice.

He told her to hang in there, the way he always did. And to be patient. Some things took time. Time. And work. And faith.

She frowned over this last piece of advice. She had faith in Tara. The trouble was she had no faith in Max Richmond.

CHAPTER NINE

MAX replaced the receiver, a deep frown drawing his
brows together. Something was wrong. He could feel
it. He'd been feeling it all week.

Tara was different. Each night she'd cut his calls
off after only a few minutes with some pitiful excuse.
Her hair was wet. She wanted to watch some TV
show. Tonight she'd said she had to go because she'd
forgotten to feed her mother's cat and her mother was
out playing bingo.

As if that couldn't have waited!

Then there was her definite lack of enthusiasm over
their meeting up in Auckland. Tonight she'd even
said she might not be able to make it. They were
short-handed at Whitmore's this weekend and she felt
obliged to help out. Would he mind terribly if she
didn't come?

When he'd said that he definitely would, she'd
sighed and said she would see what she could do, but
not to count on her coming. She hadn't said she loved
him before she ended the call, the way she usually
did. Just a rather strained goodbye.

Last weekend had been a mistake, Max realised.
He'd frightened her.

He shook his head. Hell, didn't she realise he didn't

really care about that kind of sex? All he wanted was to be with *her*.

He would ring her back, reassure her. It wasn't late. Only eight o'clock, her time.

When Mrs Bond answered the phone, he was startled. But not for long. Hadn't he subconsciously known Tara was lying to him?

'Max Richmond here, Mrs Bond. Can I speak to Tara, please?'

'No, you may not!' the woman snapped. 'I'm not going to let you upset her any more tonight. She's been through enough today.'

'What? But I didn't upset her tonight. And what do you mean she's been through enough today? What's going on that I don't know about?'

'Oh, Mum,' he heard Tara say in the background. 'How could you? You promised. I should never have told you.'

'He has to know, Tara. And the sooner the better. Why should you shoulder this burden all on your own?'

Max was taken aback. 'Burden? What burden? Speak to *me*, woman. Tell me what's going on.'

But she didn't answer him. All he heard was muffled sounds. His blood pressure soared as a most dreadful feeling of helplessness overwhelmed him. He wanted to be there, not here, hanging on the end of a phone thousands of miles away. If he was there, he'd make them both look at him and talk to him.

'Hey!' he shouted down the line. 'Is anyone there? Mrs Bond. Answer me, damn it!'

More sounds. A door slamming. A sigh.

'It's me,' Tara said with another sigh.

'Thank heaven. Tara, tell me what's going on.'

'I suppose there's no point in keeping it a secret any longer. I'm pregnant, Max.'

'Pregnant!' He was floored. 'But how c—?'

'Before you go off on one,' she swept on rather impatiently, '*no*, I didn't do this on purpose and *no*, I didn't even do it by accident. I took that darned Pill at the same time every day. I even had what I thought was a period a few weeks back. The doctor I saw today said that can happen. It's rare but not unheard-of. I'm about six or seven weeks gone, according to the ultrasound.'

A baby. Tara was going to have his baby. She wasn't tired of him, or frightened of him. She was just pregnant.

'Say something, for pity's sake!' she snapped.

'I was thinking.'

'I'll bet you were. Look, if you think I'm *happy* about this, then you're dead wrong. I'm not. The last thing I wanted at this time in my life was to have a baby. If being pregnant feels the way I've been feeling every morning then maybe I'll *never* want to have one.'

'So that's why you were sick the other morning!' Max exclaimed. 'It wasn't the champagne.'

'No, it wasn't the champagne,' she reiterated tetchily. 'It was *your* baby.'

'Yes, I understand, Tara. And your mother's right. This is my responsibility as much as it is yours. So how long have you known? You didn't know last weekend, did you?' Surely she wouldn't have encouraged him to act the way he had if she knew she was pregnant!

'No, of course I didn't. But when I woke up on the Sunday morning, chucking up two mornings in a row, I began to suspect.'

'Aah, so that's why you were so irritable with me that morning. I understand now. Poor baby.'

'Yes, it is a poor baby, to not be wanted by its parents.'

'You really *don't* want this baby?' His heart sank. When Grace had told him she was having a baby, he hadn't felt anything like what he was feeling now. He really wanted this child. It was his, and Tara's. A true love-child.

Tara's silence at the other end of the phone was more than telling. *He* might want their baby, but she didn't. She'd already raced off to a doctor to find out how far pregnant she was. Why? To see if it wasn't too late to have a termination?

Panic filled his heart.

'This is not the end of the world, Tara,' he said carefully. 'I don't want you making any hasty decisions. We should work this out together. Look, I won't go to New Zealand tomorrow. Pierce can han-

dle that. I'll catch an overnight flight to Sydney. I
should be able to get a seat. I'll catch a taxi straight
out to your place as soon as I land and we'll sit down
and work things out together. OK?'

Again, she didn't say a word.

'Tara…'

'What?'

The word was sharp. Sour, even. Max tried to understand how she felt, falling pregnant like that when
she'd taken every precaution against it. She was only
young, and just beginning to blossom, sexually speaking. She'd definitely been very excited about travelling with him. She probably felt her whole life was
ruined with her being condemned to domestic bore-
dom whilst he continued to jet-set around the world.

But having a termination was not the answer. Not
for Tara. It would haunt her forever.

'Promise me you'll be there when I arrive,' he said.
'Even if the plane is late, promise me you won't go
to work tomorrow.'

'Why should I make promises to you when you
haven't made any to me? Go to hell, Max.' And she
slammed the phone down in his ear.

Max gaped, then groaned once he saw what he'd
done wrong. He should have told her again that he
loved her. He should have reassured her straight away
that he would be there for her, physically, emotionally
and financially. Maybe he should have even asked her
to marry her as a demonstration of his commitment
to her and the child.

Of course, it wasn't an ideal situation, marrying because of a baby. He'd shunned marriage and children so far because he'd never wanted to neglect a family the way his father had. But the baby was a *fait accompli* and he truly loved Tara. Compromises could be made.

Yes, marriage was the answer. He would ring her back and ask her to marry him.

He swiftly pressed redial.

'Damn and blast!' he roared when the number was engaged.

Max tried her mobile but it was turned off. Clearly, she didn't want to speak to him. She was too angry. And she had every right to be. He was a complete idiot.

Max paced the hotel room for about thirty agitated seconds before returning to the phone and pressing redial once more. Again, nothing but the engaged tone. He immediately rang Pierce in the next room and asked him to get on to the airlines and find him a seat on an overnight flight to Sydney, money no object. He was to beg or bribe his way onto a plane.

'But what about New Zealand?' Pierce asked, obviously confused by these orders.

'You'll have to go there in my place,' Max said. 'Do you think you can handle that situation on your own?'

'Do I have complete authority? Or will I have to keep you in touch by phone during negotiations?'

'You have a free hand. You decide if the hotel is

a good buy, and if it is, buy it. At a bargain price, of course.'

'You kidding me?'

'No.'

'Wow. This is fantastic. To what do I owe this honour?'

'To my impending marriage.'

'Your what?'

'Tara's pregnant.'

'Good lord.'

Max could understand Pierce's surprise. Max was not the sort of man to make such mistakes. But he wasn't in the mood to explain the circumstances surrounding Tara's unexpected pregnancy.

'Just get on to the airlines, Pierce. Pronto. Then ring me back.'

'Will do. And boss?'

'Yes?'

'Thanks.'

'If you do a good job, there'll be a permanent promotion for you. And a lot more travelling. I'm planning on cutting down on my overseas trips in future. But first things first. Get me on a plane for Sydney. Tonight!'

Max didn't sleep much on the plane. Pierce had managed to get him a first-class seat on a QANTAS flight. He spent most of the time thinking, and planning. By the time the jumbo landed at Mascot soon after dawn, he had all his actions and arguments ready to convince Tara that marriage was the best and only option.

'A brief stop at the Regency Royale,' he told the taxi driver. 'Then I'm going on to Quakers Hill.'

The driver looked pleased. Quakers Hill was quite a considerable fare, being one of the outer western suburbs.

Max hadn't been out that way in ages, and what he saw amazed him. Where farms had once dotted the surrounding hillsides, there now sat rows and rows of new houses. Not small houses, either. Large, double-storeyed homes.

Tara's place, however, was not one of those. Her address was in the older section of Quakers Hill, near the railway station, a very modest fibro cottage with no garage and little garden to speak of. The small squares of lawn on either side of the front path were brown after the summer and what shrubs there were looked bedraggled and tired. In fact the whole house looked tired. It could surely do with a makeover. Or at least a lick of paint. But of course, Tara's mum was a widow, had been for a long time. She'd had no sons to physically help her maintain her home.

It suddenly struck Max as he opened the squeaky iron gate and walked up onto the small front porch that Tara's upbringing would not have been filled with luxuries. He recalled how awestruck she'd been the morning after the first night they'd spent together, when she'd walked through the penthouse and oohed and aahed at everything.

For the first time, a small doubt entered his mind about her falling pregnant. Could she be lying about it having been a rare accident? Could she have planned it? Was it a ploy to *get* him to marry her?

If it was, she would have to be the cleverest, most devious female he had ever known.

No, he decided as he rang the doorbell. The Tara he knew and loved was no gold-digger. She had a delightfully transparent character. She wasn't capable of that kind of manipulative behaviour. She was as different from the Alicias of this world as chalk was to cheese.

That was why he loved her so much.

The door opened and Max peered down into eyes which were nothing like Tara's. In fact, the short, plump, dark-haired woman glowering up at him was nothing like Tara at all, except perhaps for her nose. She had the same cute little upturned nose.

'You've wasted your time coming here, Mr Richmond,' she said sharply. 'You should have rung first.'

'I thought it best to speak to Tara in person. I did try to ring last night from the airport, but Tara must have taken the phone off the hook. She wasn't answering her mobile, either. Look, Mrs Bond, I can understand your feelings where I'm concerned. You think I'm one of those rich guys who prey on beautiful young girls, but you're wrong. I love your daughter and I would never do anything to hurt her. Now, could you tell her that I'm here, please?'

His words seemed to have taken some of the anger out of the woman's face. But she still looked concerned. 'That's what I'm trying to tell you. She's not here.'

'What? You mean she's gone to work, even after she knew I was coming?'

'No. She left here last night. Packed a bag and took a taxi to I don't know where.'

Max's astonishment was soon overtaken by frustration. The woman *had* to be lying. 'What do you mean you don't know where? That's crazy. You're her mother. She would have told you where she was going.'

A guilty colour zoomed into the woman's cheeks. 'We had an argument. She was angry with me for making her tell you about the baby. And I was angry with her for hanging up on you, then taking the phone off the hook. I thought she was being silly. And stubborn. I... I...'

Joyce bit her bottom lip to stop herself from crying. If only she could go back to yesterday. She'd handled the situation terribly from the moment Tara had told her about the baby. After the initial shock had worn off, she'd begun badgering the girl about telling Max and demanding that he marry her. When Tara threw back at her that men these days didn't marry girls just because they were pregnant, Joyce had been less than complimentary over the morals of men like Max Richmond, *and* the silly girls who became involved with them. By the time the man himself had rung last night, Joyce had been determined to somehow let him know that Tara was having his baby.

She'd thought she was doing the right thing. But she'd been wrong. It had not been her decision to make. Tara was a grown woman, even if Joyce had difficulty seeing her daughter as that. To her, she would always be *her* baby.

'I don't know where she's gone. Honestly, Mr Richmond,' she said, her head drooping as tears pricked at her eyes.

'Max,' he said gently, feeling genuinely sorry for the woman. 'I think it's about time you called me Max, don't you? Especially since I'm going to be your son-in-law.'

Joyce's moist eyes shot back up to his. 'You…you mean that? You're going to marry my Tara?'

'If she'll have me.'

'If she'll *have* you. The girl *adores* you.'

'Not enough to stay here when I asked her to.'

'I was partly to blame for that. I…I didn't handle the news of her pregnancy very well.'

'Don't worry, neither did I. Did she say something before she left?'

'She said to tell you she had to have some time by herself. Away from everyone telling her what to do. She said it was her body and her life and she needed some space to come to terms with the situation and work out what she was going to do. I spoke to Jen after she left. Jen's her older sister, by the way…'

'Yes, I know all about Jen.'

'You *do*?' Joyce was surprised.

Max's smile was wry. 'We do talk sometimes, Tara and I.'

The implication sent some pink into Joyce's cheeks. But truly, now that she'd met the man in the flesh, she couldn't blame Tara for losing her head over him. He was just so handsome. And impressive, with an aura of power and success about him. A wonderful dresser too. That black suit must have cost a small fortune.

'You were saying?' he prompted. 'Something about Tara's sister.'

'Oh, yes, well, I thought at first that Tara might have gone there, so I called Jen. I was probably on the phone when you rang from the airport. Tara had taken it off the hook but I put it back on later. Much later, I guess,' she added sheepishly. 'Anyway, she wasn't there and Jen didn't know where she might have gone. I was feeling awful because I thought I'd made her run away. But Jen said it was also because she was frightened you might try to talk her into getting rid of the baby when you got here.'

Max was appalled. But he could see that it wasn't an unreasonable assumption.

'And there I was,' he said wearily, 'worrying that *she* might do that.'

'Oh, no. Tara would never have an abortion. Never!'

'I'm glad to hear that. Because she'd never get over it, if she did. She's far too sweet and sensitive a soul.'

Joyce was touched that he knew Tara so well. This was not a man who wanted her daughter for her beauty alone. 'You…you really love Tara, don't you?'

'With all my heart. Clearly, however, she doesn't believe that. And I have only myself to blame. I've been thinking about our relationship all night on the plane and I can see I've been incredibly selfish and arrogant. People say actions speak louder than words, but not once did I stop to think what my actions were shouting to Tara. No wonder she had no faith in my committing to her and the baby. All I've ever given her were words. And words are so damned cheap. I have to show her now that I mean what I say. But first, I have to find her. Do you think you might invite me in for a cup of coffee, Mrs Bond, and we'll try to work out where she might have gone?'

'Joyce, Max,' she said with a smile which did remind him of Tara. 'If I'm going to be your mother-in-law, then I think you should call me Joyce.'

CHAPTER TEN

MAX waved Joyce goodbye through the taxi window, feeling pleased that he'd been able to make the woman believe that his intentions towards Tara were, at last, honourable. Not an easy task, given the way he'd treated her daughter this past year.

Joyce had not been backward in coming forward over his misdeeds. He was accused of having taken Tara for granted. Of neglecting her shamefully. But worst of all, of not caring enough to see how a girl like Tara would feel with his not making a definite commitment to her a lot sooner.

She'd poo-poohed Max's counter-arguments that Tara hadn't wanted marriage and children up till this point any more than he had.

'Tara needs security and commitment more than most girls,' she'd explained. 'She was more upset at losing her father than her older sister, yet Tara was only three at the time. She cried herself to sleep every night for months after the funeral. Having met you, I think, in a way, you are more than a lover to her. You are a father figure as well.'

Max hadn't been too pleased with this theory. It had made him feel old. He didn't entirely agree with it, either. Maybe Joyce didn't know her daughter as well as she thought she did. The grown-up Tara was a highly independent creature, not some cling-on. Yes, she was sensitive. And yes, she probably needed reassurance at this time in her life. But he didn't believe she thought of him as a father figure. Hell, she didn't even think of him as a father figure for their baby! If she had, she wouldn't have run away like this.

'Where in heaven's name *are* you, Tara?' he muttered under his breath.

'You say somethin', mate?' the taxi driver asked.

'Just having a grumble,' Max replied.

'Nothin' to grumble about, mate. The sun's out. We're winnin' the cricket. Life's good.'

Max thought about that simple philosophy and decided he could embrace it, if only he knew where Tara was.

He and Joyce decided she probably hadn't gone too far at night. Probably to a friend's house. The trouble was he'd discovered Tara had dropped all of her friends during the year she'd spent being his lady friend.

That was the term Joyce had tactfully used, although he had a feeling she was dying to use some other derogatory term, like mistress. Tara's mother hadn't missed an opportunity to put the knife in and twist it a little. Guilt gnawed away at him, alongside some growing frustration.

If Tara thought she could punish him this way indefinitely, then she was very much mistaken. He had ways and means at his disposal to find his missing girlfriend, especially one as good-looking and notice-able as Tara. In fact, he had one of two choices. He could hire a private investigator to find her, or he could spend a small fortune another way and hope-fully come up with a quicker solution.

Max decided on this latter way.

Leaning forward, he gave the taxi driver a different address from the Regency Royale, after which he set-tled back and started working out what he would say to Tara when they finally came face to face.

Two hours later—they'd hit plenty of traffic on the way back to the city—Max was in his penthouse at the hotel. Snatching up some casual clothes, he headed straight for the shower. Once refreshed and dressed in crisp cream trousers and a blue yachting top, he headed for the lift again. Thankfully, Joyce had fed him as they'd talked, so he didn't need to order any food from Room Service. It crossed his mind to make himself some coffee, but decided he didn't want to wait. Having made up his mind what other things he had to do that day, Max wasn't about to dilly-dally. If he had one virtue—Joyce didn't seem to think he had too many—it was decisiveness.

This time he called for his own car, and within minutes was driving east of the city. Thankfully, by then, the traffic was lighter. It was just after eleven-thirty, the sun was well up in the summer sky and Max would have rather gone anywhere than where he was going.

His stomach knotted as he approached his parents' home. He hadn't been to see them since Christmas, a token visit which he felt he couldn't avoid. Ever since Stevie's death, he'd kept his visits to a minimum. They were always a strain, even more so since his father's stroke. The accusing, angry words he might have once spoken—and which might have cleared the air between father and son—were always held back. He could hardly bear to watch his mother, either. He resented the way she tended to his father. So patiently, with never a cross word.

Maybe Tara was right. Maybe she really did love the man. She'd certainly been prepared to forgive him for lots of things.

Max wondered if he could ever really forgive his father. He doubted it. But he'd have to pretend to, if he was to have any chance of convincing Tara he was man enough to be a good father to their baby.

Max parked his car at the kerb outside his parents' Point Piper mansion and just sat there for a minute or two, looking at the place. It was certainly a far cry from Tara's house. Aside from the house, which ran over three levels, there were the perfectly manicured gardens at the front, a huge solar-heated pool out the back and magnificent harbour views from most of the rooms.

It was a home fit for a king. Or a prince.

He'd been brought up here, taking it all for granted. The perfect house. The private schools. Membership of the nearby yacht club.

And then there were the women. The ones who'd targeted him from the moment he'd been old enough to have sex. The ones who'd done anything and everything to get him to fall in love with them.

But he hadn't loved any of them.

The only woman he'd ever fallen for was Tara.

And she was in danger of slipping away from him, if he wasn't careful.

With his stomach still in knots, Max climbed out from behind the wheel and went inside. He still had keys. He hadn't moved out of home till after the episode with Stevie.

His mother was sitting out on the top terrace, reading the newspaper to his father, who was in his wheelchair beside her. Dressed in pale blue trousers and a pretty floral top, she was immaculately groomed as usual. Her streaked blonde hair was cut short in a modern style and she was wearing make-up and pearl earrings.

For as long as Max could remember, she'd looked much younger than her age, but today, in the harsh sunlight, she looked every one of her fifty-nine years. And then some.

Her father's appearance, however, shocked him more than his mother's. Before his stroke he'd been a vibrant, handsome man with a fit, powerful body and thick head of dark hair. Now his hair was white, his muscles withered, his skin deeply lined. He looked eighty, yet he was only sixty-two.

For the first time, some sympathy stirred in Max's

soul. Plus a measure of guilt. How come he hadn't noticed the extent of his father's deterioration at Christmas? It had only been a couple of months ago.

Maybe he hadn't noticed because he hadn't wanted to. It was easier to cling to old resentments rather than see that his father was going downhill at a rate of knots, or that his mother might need some hands-on help. Much easier to hate than to love.

Max realised in that defining moment that he didn't really hate his parents. He never had. He just didn't understand them. Tara was right when she'd said people never knew what went on in a marriage.

One thing Max did know, however, as he watched his mother reach out to tenderly touch his father's arm. She did love the man. And if the way his father looked back was any judge, then that love was returned.

Max's heart turned over as he hoped that Tara would always look at him like that.

Neither of them had seen him yet, standing there just inside the sliding glass doors which led out onto the terrace. When he slid one back, his mother's head jerked up and around, her blue eyes widening with surprise, and then pleasure.

'Max!' she exclaimed. 'Ronald, it's Max.'

'Max…' His father's hands fumbled as they reached to swivel his chair around. His eyes, too, mirrored surprise. But they were tired eyes, Max thought. Dead eyes.

All the life had gone out of him.

'Max,' the old man repeated as though he could still not believe his son had come to visit.

'Hi there, Mum. Dad,' he said as he came forward and bent to kiss his mother on the cheek. 'You're both looking well,' he added as he pulled up a chair.

His father croaked out a dry laugh. 'I look terrible and I know it.'

Max smiled a wry smile. The old man wasn't quite dead yet.

'You know, Dad, when I was a boy you told me that God helps those who help themselves. You obviously practised what you preached all your life. After all, you worked your way up from a valet-parking attendant to being one of Australia's most successful hotel owners.'

Max generously refrained from reminding his father that marrying the daughter of an established hotel baron had been a leg-up, especially when Max's maternal grandfather was already at death's door. Within weeks of Max's grandfather dying, Ronald Richmond had sold off the hotels that didn't live up to his ideals and started up the Royale chain. He hadn't looked back, till three years ago, when his stroke had forced his premature retirement.

'I have to say I'm a bit disappointed,' Max went on, 'that you seem to have thrown in the towel this time. Frankly, I expected more from you than this.'

Some more fire sparked in the old man's eyes, which was exactly what Max had intended.

'What would you know about it, boy? My whole right side is virtually useless.'

'Something which could be remedied with therapy. You should be thankful that your speech wasn't affected. Some people can't talk after a stroke.'

'My eyes are bad,' he grumbled. 'Your mother has to read to me.'

'But you're not blind. Look, how about I line up a top physiotherapist to come in every day and work with you? He'll have you up and out of that wheelchair in no time.'

'That would be wonderful, Max,' his mother said. 'Wouldn't it, Ronald?'

'It's too late,' his father muttered. 'I'm done for.'

'Rubbish!' Max countered. 'Never too late. That's another of your own philosophies, might I remind you? Besides, I need you up and about in time for my wedding.'

'Your wedding!' they chorused, their expressions shocked.

'Yep. I'm getting married.'

After that, Max was regaled with questions. He thought he lied very well, telling them all about Tara and the baby, but nothing about her disappearance. He made it sound like a done deal that he and Tara would walk down the aisle in the near future. He also promised to bring her over to meet them by the end of the weekend. He made some excuse that she was away visiting friends for the next couple of days.

Talk about optimism!

Over lunch he also told his father that he planned to stay in Australia more in future and delegate some of the overseas travelling to his assistant.

'Good idea,' his father said, nodding. 'When a man has a family, he should not be away from home too much. I was away from home too much. Far too much.'

When tears suddenly welled up in his father's eyes, his mother immediately jumped up. 'I think it's time for your afternoon nap, dear,' she said. 'He gets tired very easily these days,' she directed at a shocked Max as she wheeled his father off. 'I won't be long. Have another cup of coffee.'

Max did just that, sitting there, sipping some coffee and doing some serious thinking till his mother returned.

She threw Max an odd look as she sat down. 'I'm so glad you stayed. Usually, you bolt out the door as soon as you can. Your becoming a father yourself has changed you, Max. You're different today. Softer. And more compassionate. Perhaps the time is right for me to tell you the truth about Stevie.'

Max stiffened. 'What…what do you mean…the truth?'

His mother heaved a deep sigh, her eyes not quite meeting his. 'Stevie was not your father's child.'

Max gaped.

'I thought you might have guessed,' she went on when he said nothing. 'After all, Stevie was very different from you. And from your father. He also had brown eyes. Two blue-eyed parents can't have a brown-eyed child, you know.'

Max shook his head. 'I didn't know that. Did Stevie?'

'Thankfully, no. At least…he never said he did.'

'So that's why Dad didn't love him.'

'You're wrong, Max. Your father did love Stevie. The trouble was every time he looked at him, he was reminded of the fact that I had slept with another man.'

'But I thought Dad was the unfaithful one!'

His mother stared at him. 'Why do you say that?'

'Years ago, I overheard you telling a friend that you knew Dad had other women, but you just turned a blind eye.'

His mother looked so sad. 'I'm so sorry you heard that. You must have thought me very weak. Or very wicked.'

'I didn't know what to think. I've never known what to think about you two. At least I can now understand why Dad treated Stevie differently from me.'

'He did try, Max. But it was very hard on him. He never seemed to know what to say to Stevie. Or how to act with him. It was much easier with you, because you were like two peas in a pod. But that didn't mean he didn't care about Stevie. When he was diagnosed with cancer, your father was terribly upset. His way of coping with his grief was to work harder. He couldn't bear to see the boy in pain. He knows now that he should have come home to be with Stevie. He understands what it's like when the people you love aren't there for you when you're ill.'

She didn't look at him directly. Neither were her words said in an accusing tone. But Max felt guilty all the same. He hadn't been any better than his father, had he? He'd let both his parents down by not being here to help.

'Your father feels his stroke was a punishment for his letting Stevie down,' his mother choked out.

Max could not deny that he had entertained similar thoughts himself over the past three years. Suddenly, however, they seemed terribly mean-spirited, and very immature. But he could not find the right words to say and was sitting there in an awkward silence, when his mother spoke once more.

'Do you want to know about Stevie's real father, or not?'

'Yes,' Max said sincerely. 'Yes, I do.'

'I have to go back to the beginning of my relationship with your father so that you can get the full picture.'

'OK.'

She smiled a wry smile. 'I hope you won't be too shocked at me.'

Max could not imagine that anything more his mother could say today would shock him.

'I'm no saint myself, Mum,' he reassured, and so she began her story.

She'd first met his father when he parked her car for her one day at one of her own father's hotels.

She'd fallen in love with him at first sight, and had pursued him shamelessly as only a spoiled and beautiful rich woman could do. She confessed to seducing him with sex and playing to his ambitious nature with her money and her contacts. Not to mention her potential fortune. She was her wealthy father's only child.

The trouble was she'd never believed he truly loved her when he married her, and was always besieged by doubts. The arrival of their first-born son—Max himself—calmed her for a while. Her husband seemed besotted, if not with her then definitely with his child. She began to feel more secure in her marriage. But after her father died and her husband started travelling overseas more and more often, all her doubts over his love increased. There was a photograph in a newspaper of him with some gorgeous socialite in London. She flew into a jealous rage when her husband finally came home, accusing him of being unfaithful. He claimed he wasn't but she didn't believe him.

Their marriage entered one of those dangerous phases. Ronald started staying away even more and she started going out on her own. She met Stevie's father at an art exhibition. *His* art exhibition. He was an up-and-coming artist. She'd argued with her husband over the phone earlier in the evening over his delaying his return home yet again and was in a reckless mood. She drank too much and the rest, as they said, was history.

Perversely, Ronald arrived home the next night, and when she discovered she was pregnant a month later she didn't know whose baby she was having. When the baby was born with blue eyes, she thought Stevie was Max's full brother. But by six months his eyes had changed to brown and he looked nothing like Max's father.

When Ronald confronted her with his suspicions, she confessed her indiscretion and her husband went crazy, showing her at last that he did love her. But the marriage had been irreparably damaged. After that, she suspected her husband was no longer faithful to her when he went away. A few times, she found evidence of other women on his clothes. Lipstick and perfume. She turned a blind eye for fear that he might actually divorce her. She tried to make a life for herself with charity work and society functions but she was very unhappy.

She reiterated that when Stevie was diagnosed with cancer, Ronald *had* been genuinely upset. Unfortunately, his way of handling such an emotional crisis was to go into his cave, so to speak, and work harder than ever.

'Stevie might have survived his sickness,' his mother added, 'if it hadn't been for his girlfriend dumping him. That was what depressed him far more than his father not being around. Trust me on that. Stevie and I were very close and he told me everything he felt.'

Max nodded. 'I can imagine. I've never known a

boy like Stevie. The way he could express his feelings. I wish I could be like that sometimes.'

'His biological father was like that,' his mother
said. 'A real talker. And a deep thinker. A sweet, soft,
sensitive man whom you couldn't help liking. He
made me feel so special that night. He didn't know I
was married, of course. He was shocked when I told
him afterwards. Didn't want anything more to do with
me. As I said, a nice man.'

'I see. So he never knew about Stevie?'

'God, no. No, I never saw him again. Sadly, he
died a few years later. Cancer. And they say it's not
hereditary…'

Tears glistened in her eyes as she looked straight
at Max. 'Your father finally forgave me. But can
you?'

Not ever being at his best with words, Max stood
up and came round to bend and kiss his mother on
the cheek.

Her hands lifted to cover his, which had come to
rest on her shoulders. She patted them, then glanced
up at him. 'Thank you. You're a good boy, Max. But
a terrible liar. Now, why don't you sit back down and
tell *me* the total truth about this girl of yours? I'd
especially like to know how someone as clever as you
could have made the mistake of making her pregnant
in the first place. Or was that *her* idea? You are a
very rich man, after all.'

Max walked back to settle in his chair before answering.

'I have to confess that idea did briefly occur to me. But only briefly. You'll see when you meet Tara that she does not have a greedy, or a manipulative bone in her body.'

'Tara,' his mother said. 'Such a lovely name.'

'She's a lovely girl.'

'And was it her idea for you to come here today?'

'Not directly. But she would have approved. The fact is, Mum, I don't know where Tara is. She's run away.'

'Run away! Max, whatever did you do?'

'It's what I *didn't* do which caused the problem. When she told me she was having a baby, I didn't tell her I loved her. And I didn't ask her to marry me.'

'Oh, Max… No wonder she ran away. She must be heartbroken.'

'Don't say that, Mum,' he said with a tightening in his chest. 'I don't want to hear that. I'm just hanging in here as it is, waiting for tomorrow.'

'What's going to happen tomorrow?'

He told her.

CHAPTER ELEVEN

TARA lay in bed, slowly nibbling on one of the dry biscuits she'd put beside the bed the night before. Hopefully, they would make her feel well enough to rise shortly and go for a walk on the beach.

Yesterday, she'd stayed in bed most of the day before going for a walk. But then yesterday she'd been desperately tired.

Today she'd woken more refreshed, but still nauseous. Hence the biscuits.

It had been good of Kate to give her some, no questions asked. Although there'd been a slight speculative gleam in her eyes as she'd handed Tara the plate of biscuits after dinner last night.

But that was Kate all over. The woman was kind and accommodating without being a sticky-beak, all good qualities for anyone who ran a bed and breakfast establishment. Tara had met her a few years ago when she'd stayed here at Kate's Place with some of her uni friends. It was popular with students because it had been cheap and conveniently located, only a short stroll to Wamberal Beach.

When she'd been thinking of where she could go and be by herself for a while, Tara had immediately thought of Kate's Place. Wamberal was not far away from Sydney—an hour and a half's drive north—but far enough away that she would feel secure that she wouldn't run into Max, or anyone who knew Max.

So on Thursday night she'd taken a taxi to Hornsby railway station, then a train to Gosford, then another taxi to Wamberal Beach. Rather naively, in a way. What would she have done if Kate had sold the place in the years since she'd stayed there? Or if she didn't have any spare rooms to rent?

Fate had been on her side this time and whilst Kate had gone more upmarket—renaming her refurbished home Kate's Beachside B & B—she had still been in the room-renting business, although the number of rooms available had been reduced to three.

Fortunately, all of them were vacant. The end of February, whilst still summer, was not peak tourist season. On top of that she'd stopped advertising, not wanting to be full all of the time.

'I'm getting old,' she'd complained as she showed Tara upstairs. 'But I'd be bored if I stopped having people to stay altogether. And terribly lonely. Still, I might have to give it away when I turn seventy next year. Or give in and hire a cleaner.'

Tara had selected the bedroom at the front of the two-storeyed home, which had a lovely view of the beach as well as an *en suite* bathroom. No way did she want to have to race down hallways to a communal bathroom first thing in the morning.

True to form, Kate hadn't asked her any questions on her arrival, although Tara had spotted some concern in the elderly woman's eyes. She supposed it was rare for a guest to show up, unannounced and un-booked, at ten-thirty at night. Tara's excuse that it was a spur-of-the-moment impulse had probably not been believed.

But Kate at least appreciated that she was an adult with the right to come and go as she pleased, some-thing Tara wished other people recognised. She was not a child who had to be directed. She did have a mind of her own and she was quite capable of making decisions, provided she was given the time to work out what was best for herself, and the baby.

Impossible to even think at home at the moment with her mother criticising and nagging all the time. Jen wasn't much better. She seemed to have forgotten how emotional and irrational *she* was when she found out she was pregnant.

Of course, Tara would not have bolted quite so melodramatically if Max hadn't been on his way. Max of the 'we should work this out together' mode.

Huh! Tara knew what that meant. Max, taking total control and telling her what to do.

From what she'd seen, Max had no idea how to truly work together with anyone or anything. Max ordered and people obeyed.

She'd been obeying him for twelve months.

But not any more.

The time had come for mutiny.

Her first step had been to put herself beyond his reach. Which she had. And, to be honest, taking that action had felt darned good. Clearly, she'd been harbouring more resentment than she realised over Max's dominant role in their relationship.

Not so good was the niggling remorse she felt over her mother. By last night guilt had begun to override her desperate need for peace and privacy. She would have to ring her mother today. It wasn't fair to leave her worrying.

And she would be worrying. Tara had no doubt of that.

A firm tap-tap on her bedroom door had Tara calling out that she was coming before gingerly swinging her feet onto the floor and standing up. As she reached for the silky housecoat she'd brought with her, she was pleased to find her stomach hadn't heaved at all when she got to her feet. Those biscuits seemed to have done the trick.

But still, she didn't hurry, taking her time as she padded across the floral rug which covered most of the polished floorboards. Kate's décor leant towards old world, but Tara liked it.

She opened the door to find Kate standing there with a newspaper in her hands and a worried look on her face.

'Yes?' Tara asked.

Kate didn't say a word. She just handed the newspaper to Tara. It was opened and folded back at page three.

Tara went cold all over as she stared down at the full-page photograph of herself, an enlargement of the one she knew Max kept in his wallet. It had been taken on one of their first dinner dates, at a restaurant where a photographer went around and snapped photos of people who were likely to buy them as mementos. Targeted were groups partying there for special occasions, plus romantic couples possibly celebrating their engagements, or just their love for each other.

Tara could see the happiness shining out of her eyes in that photograph. She doubted her eyes would reflect the same emotion at that moment.

Her teeth clenched hard in her jaw as she glared down at the words written across the bottom of the photograph.

Tara, your loved ones are worried about you. Please call home. If anyone knows Tara's whereabouts, contact the following number for a substantial reward.

Tara's head shot up. 'Please don't tell me you rang it. That's not my home phone number. It belongs to my boyfriend.'

'Not me, love. But Milly Jenson did. My busybody neighbour. She must have had a good look at you when you went out walking yesterday afternoon. I think her conscience finally got the better of her and she came and told me what she'd done. Either that, or she was indulging in more mischief-making. Either way, I thought you'd want to know.'

'I certainly do. Thanks, Kate,' she said, her head whirling with the news Max was on his way up here.

'Boyfriend, eh? Not one you'll be wanting to see again, I'll warrant. Do you want me to drive you anywhere, love? I can get you away from here before he arrives. Milly gave him this address over an hour ago, so he could be arriving any time soon.'

Tara thought about running away again, then decided there was little point. Wherever she went, someone would spot her and call Max and that would be that. Her stand-out looks had always been a curse. Oh, how she would have preferred to be less striking. Less tall. Less blonde!

She shook her head as she stared down again at the photograph in the paper.

'Thank you, Kate, but no. I'll talk to him when he arrives. But not here. I have no intention of meekly staying here till he arrives. I'll get dressed right now and go for a walk on the beach. You can point him in that direction when he arrives. OK?'

'Only OK if he's no danger to you, love. He hasn't been beating you up, has he?'

'Good lord, no! Max would never do anything like that. But as you might have gathered he's very rich. And used to getting his own way. He's also the father of my baby. I'm pregnant, Kate.'

'Yes, so I gathered, love. That's a popular old remedy, eating dry biscuits when you're suffering from morning sickness. As soon as you asked me for them, I guessed.'

'You didn't say anything.'

'Not my place. I keep my nose out of other people's private business. Except when it comes to arrogant members of the opposite sex. One of the reasons I never married was because I couldn't stand it when men thought they could run my life. Oh, yes, I had quite a few suitors when I was younger. All wanting me to marry them, especially the ones I slept with. One became very insistent once he found out I was having his baby. More than insistent. Violent, actually. As if I would ever marry a man who hit me. Or inflict such a father on an innocent child.'

Tara's mouth had dropped open slightly at these astonishing revelations. But it seemed Kate was not yet finished baring her soul, or her rather adventurous past.

'If it had been more acceptable back in my day, I would have chosen to be a single mother. But I didn't. I did something else, love, something I've always bitterly regretted. Girls these days have so many options. So don't do what I did, love. You have your baby and to hell with what this man says or wants. He can't be much of a man if you ran away from him like that.'

'He's not a bad man,' Tara said. 'Or a violent one. He's just…domineering.'

'Does he want you to have an abortion?'

'I don't know.'

'Mmm… Does he love you?'

She frowned down at the photograph, then nodded.

'Yes. I think he does. As much as he is capable of loving.'

'He sounds a bit mixed up.'

'You know what, Kate, I think he is. Yet he's very successful. And filthy rich.'

'And wickedly handsome, no doubt,' Kate said drily.

'Oh, yes. That too.'

Kate pulled a face. 'They always are. I'll see what I think of him when he arrives, then I'll put him through the third degree before I tell him where you've gone. Would you mind if I did that?'

Tara had to laugh. 'Not at all. Do him good.'

'Right. You hurry and get yourself dressed now. And take one of the sunhats from off the pegs by the front door. Put your hair up under it. And pop some sunglasses on. Otherwise you'll have everyone on the beach who's seen this photograph in this morning's paper running home to call that number.'

'I'll do that. And Kate…'

'Yes?'

'Thank you. You've been very kind. And wonderfully understanding.'

Kate smiled a surprisingly mischievous smile. 'We girls have to stick together.'

Max stomped over the sand, disbelieving of what that woman had just put him through before telling him where Tara was. Anyone would think he was a murderer instead of a man in love, trying to do the right thing!

His gaze scanned the various semi-naked bodies sprawled over the warm sand. None of them was Tara. He would recognise her in a heartbeat. He headed for the water's edge and stood there, searching for her tell-tale head of fair hair amongst the swimmers. Not there, either.

A rogue wave suddenly washed further up the beach than the others, totally soaking his expensive Italian loafers.

Max swore.

Still, ruining a pair of shoes was the least of his worries at that moment. Where was Tara? Had that old tartar lied to him? Was Tara at this very moment on her way somewhere else?

Max's stomach began to churn. And then he saw her, further down the wide arch of beach, paddling along the water's edge, coming towards him.

It wasn't her hair which revealed her identity. Her long blonde mane was out of sight underneath a large straw hat. It was her legs which gave her away. Not many girls had legs like Tara's.

She was wearing shorts. Denim, with frayed edges. And a red singlet top. No bra, he noticed as she drew closer.

The automatic stirring of his body annoyed him. This was not why he had come. Tara already knew he wanted her sexually. He had to convince her that he wanted her for much more than that.

Willing his flesh back under control, he marched towards her, determined not to let desire distract him. For he suspected if it did, he was doomed to failure. And failure was not something Max could cope with today. His mission was to win Tara back, not lose her. Instinct warned him that making love to her in any way, shape or form would lose her for sure. His job was to convince her that he would make a good husband and father, not just a good lover.

Tara had spotted Max some time back, but she gave no signal to him, watching surreptitiously as he'd made his way with some difficulty across the soft sand. He was hardly dressed for the beach in grey dress trousers and a long-sleeved white silk shirt, even though the shirt *was* rolled up at the sleeves and left open at the neck.

It had amused her when the wave washed over his shoes. She wasn't so amused now as he hurried towards her. Most annoying was the way her body went into full foreplay mode at his approach. Her heartbeat quickened. Her nipples hardened. Her belly tightened. All in anticipation of his touch.

Disgusting, she thought. Deplorable!

Delicious, another darker, more devilish part of her brain whispered.

She sighed. Clearly, she still had to be careful with him. Her sexual vulnerability remained high.

Of course, if this was a romantic movie, both of them would suddenly break into a run and throw themselves into each other's arms. They would kiss, the music would soar and THE END would come up on the screen.

But this was not a movie. It was real life with real people and real issues. Serious relationship problems were never solved with one kiss. Making love was a masking agent, not a lasting solution.

No way was she going to let him touch her. Not today, anyway.

'Max,' she said drily when he was close enough.

Thankfully, he ground to a halt outside of grabbing and kissing distance. Though was it Max doing that which worried her the most? Or her own silly self?

'So you found me,' she added, and crossed her arms. Not only did the action demonstrate he wasn't all that welcome, but it also hid her infernal nipples.

'With some difficulty,' came his sharp return.

Clearly, he was not in a good mood. Kate must have given him heaps. But not as much as *she* was going to give him.

'I don't know how you can say that. One little—or should I say not so little?—photograph in the paper, with the added incentive of a reward, and Bob's your uncle, you had your man.'

His gaze ran down her body then up again. 'No one in their wildest dreams, Tara, would call you a man.'

Tara pulled a face at him. 'You know, it must be wonderful to have enough money to buy anything you want.'

His eyes searched hers, as though he was weighing up her attitude. Her sarcastic tone had to be telling him something.

'You're still angry with me,' he said. 'And you have every right to be. I didn't handle your news the other night at all well.'

'No. You certainly didn't.'

'There again, you didn't give me much opportunity to make things right by hanging up on me and then running away. That was hardly fair, Tara. Even you have to agree your news was a shock. I was not prepared for it.'

'Tough. I did what I had to do. For me.'

'And have you come to any decisions during your time alone?'

'Would you mind if we walk while we talk?'

Tara just started walking, forcing him to fall into step beside her.

'I'd prefer to go sit somewhere private together.'

I'll just bet you would, she thought ruefully. Before she knew it he would be kissing her and she'd either go to mush, or hit him. Neither prospect pleased her. This was her chance to show him that she would not live her life on *his* terms. Seeing him in the flesh again, however, had brought home to her that he still wielded great power over her. She had to be very careful. And very strong.

'I'm hardly dressed for the beach, Tara,' he pointed out. 'I'm ruining my shoes for starters.'

'You chose to come up here, Max. I didn't make

you. Take off your shoes, if you're worried about them. And roll up your trousers.'

To her astonishment, he did just that. Unfortunately, it made her even more physically aware of him. Being pregnant didn't seem to have dampened her desires one iota. If anything, she craved Max's lovemaking even more. How contrary could you get?

'I called your mother,' he said when they started walking again. 'Told her I'd found you. Joyce said to tell you to believe me when I say that I would never have tried to talk you into an abortion.'

Any relief Tara felt over this news was overshadowed by shock, and anger. She ground to a halt and spun in the sand to face him.

'*Joyce?* Since when did you call my mother *Joyce*? And since when has she started taking *your* side?'

'Since we had a good chat yesterday morning.'

Tara laughed. A dry, knowing laugh. 'I get it. You told Mum you were prepared to marry me and she melted. That's the be-all and end-all with Mum. Marriage.'

'You make it sound like a crime.'

'It is if you marry for all the wrong reasons.'

'You think my loving you is a wrong reason?'

Tara found it increasingly difficult to hold her temper. 'You've told me you love me. But not one mention of marriage. So why now? As if I don't know. You've decided you want your child. You're getting older and it's suddenly come home to you that maybe an heir in your image and likeness would be a very nice thing to have, along with a silly, besotted wife who thinks the sun shines out of your bum and who'll wait around for you for weeks at a time, no questions asked.'

'Now wait a minute!'

'No, *you* wait a minute. It's your turn to do the waiting, buster.'

An angry colour slanted across his cheekbones, and his hands tightened their grip on his shoes.

But he stayed tactfully silent, allowing her the opportunity to say what was on her mind. And there was plenty!

'You must have thought you were on to a good thing this past year. You never explained and I never complained. Of course, things weren't absolutely perfect for you. Whilst I'm sure it was exciting and ego-stroking at first to have a virgin in your bed—something tells me you hadn't had the pleasure of one of *those* before!—I didn't quite have the confidence you would have liked. Till last weekend. After which, suddenly, I was being invited to travel with you.'

'That's not true!' he protested.

'Of course it's true! I've finally grown up, Max. I don't see you through rose-coloured glasses any more. I can even appreciate your reasoning. Why go to the trouble of finding suitable one-night stands in whatever city you were in, when you could take the new me with you for the price of a plane ticket?'

She saw his eyes darken, but she hadn't finished.

'Even better was the fact that I had the makings of such a *cheap* mistress. A dress here and there. The odd outing. Some champagne and you'd be In Like Flynn.'

'Now, hold it right there!' he ground out. 'Firstly, I was never unfaithful to you. Not once. Secondly, I never thought of you as my mistress. I always meant to marry you, Tara. When the time was right.'

'Really? And when would that have been?'

'When I was less busy and you were older. My asking you to travel with me was a compromise. I was afraid of losing you. Just as I'm afraid of losing you now. Losing you and our baby.'

It shocked Tara, his admitting to such emotions. Max, the macho man, was not given to admitting that he was afraid of losing anything. But then she realised his confessing such fears was his way of *not* losing. His words were designed to weaken her resolve, to make her do what *he* wanted, as usual.

'I love you, Tara,' he went on. 'I've loved you from the beginning. I know I told you I didn't want marriage and children, and I meant it at the time. But things have changed. You're going to have my baby.'

'Yes, Max, I am. And yes, things have changed. But you haven't. You're still the same Max I met. The same exciting, successful, ambitious, ruthless man. Just look at what you did to find me. What kind of man does something like that?'

'The kind you fell in love with. But you're wrong, Tara. I *can* change. I've already started.'

'How? I see no evidence of it.'

'Come back to Sydney with me and I'll show you.'

'No.'

His head jerked back, blue eyes shocked. 'No?'

'No. That's part of your problem, Max. People jump to do your bidding far too much. I've been way too accommodating where you're concerned. I've always done what you wanted. Now you can do what *I* want for a change.'

'Tell me and I'll do it,' he stated boldly.

And rather recklessly, Tara thought. No way would he agree to what she was about to demand. But it would be interesting to see how he tried to wriggle out of it.

'All right. Go home, collect some beach clothes and come back up here. Kate will rent you a room. Stay here, with me, for a week. Separate rooms. No sex. We'll spend quality time together, but we'll just talk.'

Tara was quietly confident he would never just drop his business commitments like that.

'It's a deal,' he said.

Tara blinked in shock, but reserved her judgement till he actually followed through.

'What happens at the end of the week?' he asked.

'I'll let you know…at the end of the week.'

'That doesn't seem fair.'

'I'm not going to explain and you're not to complain. You are just to do what I want, when I want.'

'But no sex.'

'Absolutely no sex.'

'Mmm. Are you sure you can handle that?'

Her chin lifted. 'No trouble,' she lied.

'I will only agree to those conditions if, at the end of the week, I get to take you out to dinner, then back to bed for the night. The whole night. In the same bed.'

'Why does there have to be a catch?'

'Darling, there's always a catch. There's no such thing as a free lunch, or a free week of total slavery and submission. Which is what you're asking for. I know you want me to prove to you that I love you. That I don't want you just for sex. Fine. I'm happy to do that. But then I want the chance to show you that I do love you. *My* way.'

Tara's heart turned over. She knew, once she was in his arms again, that all her new resolves would weaken. She had one week to achieve all she wanted to achieve. One week to make Max see that the only way they could be truly happy was if he offered her a genuine partnership, not just a ring on her finger.

'You sure have developed a way with words all of a sudden,' she tossed back at him. 'We'll see if you can keep it up for a week.'

He laughed. 'I'll have no trouble keeping it up. Especially if you go round looking like that all the time.'

Tara flushed. 'If you try to seduce me, Max, you'll be sorry.'

'You don't know who you're talking to, honey.

This is the boy who went for three days without food. Going without sex couldn't be as hard as that. Oops. Scratch that word hard and replace it with difficult.'

Tara frowned at him. This was the first time he'd spoken of himself when he was a boy. That was something she would get him to do during the next week. Open up to her about his childhood. Intimacy was not just about sex, but also about knowing all there was to know about your partner.

'Why did you go without food?'

'Mum was raising funds for some charity. She spent half her life doing that. This time, she got us kids involved. Stevie found sponsors who paid various amounts for his reading books. I think he read eighty-five books. I chose to starve. Got paid a fortune for every day I went without food. Much easier than reading. I hate reading.'

'Nothing's changed in that regard,' Tara said drily. 'You don't have any decent books at the penthouse. Just boring stuff about business and sport. You don't know what you're missing, Max. Reading is a fabulous past-time. I'll read you some good books this week whilst we lie on the beach. Kate has a wonderful selection of best-sellers.'

Max winced.

'Having second thoughts already?' Tara said in a challenging tone.

'Definitely not,' he replied. And smiled.

Tara wasn't sure she liked that smile. There was something sneaky about it.

'I'd better get going if I'm to get back today,' he said.

'You only have to pack a few clothes.'

'And make a few phone calls. I have to let Pierce know where I'll be, for one thing.'

'If you take or make one business phone call during your week up here, Max, the deal's off.'

Max suspected she was bluffing, but he had to admire her stance. Tara didn't realise it but he would never marry a mealy-mouthed woman, or one who kow-towed to him all the time. Most of his life, he'd been pursued by women who indulged his every desire, in bed and out of it. He liked it that Tara was finally standing up to him; that she was so strong. She was going to make a wonderful wife and mother.

His eyes softened on her. 'Fair enough. I'll leave my mobile at home.' With his father. Do the old man good to have to make some business decisions. Probably perk him up no end. But not as much as that physio he'd hired yesterday to come in every day and work those atrophied muscles. Max had stayed with his parents all day Friday, inspiring both of them with their new role as grandparents-to-be, leaving them looking younger than when he arrived. 'I'll be back before you can say Jack Robinson.'

'Don't speed,' she warned him. 'I'd like our child to have a live father, not a memorial in some ceme-tery.'

'Right. No speeding. Any other instructions? Or rules?'

Her head tipped to one side and her lips pursed.

God, how he would love to just slide his hands around that lovely long neck of hers and kiss that luscious mouth till it was soft and malleable. Till *she* was soft and malleable.

Instead, he had to stand there and play at being a sensitive, new-age guy. Not a role Max aspired to. He had definite ideas about male roles in life, and wishy-washy wimp was not one of them. He could not wait for this week to be over. Already he was looking forward to the following Saturday night.

'None that I can think of at the moment,' she said. 'But I'll have a written list by the time you return.'

Max blinked. My God, she meant it. Maybe he shouldn't marry her at all. Strong, he liked. But a bossy-boots nag was another story.

What she needed, of course, was a night in bed. With him. Those rock-like nipples said something else to the words coming out of her mouth. By the time this week was up, he wouldn't be the only one having cold showers.

But he could be patient, if the rewards were worth it. What better reward could there be than to have Tara back in his arms once more, right where she belonged?

CHAPTER TWELVE

A WEEK was a long time in politics. Or so they said. Probably because of the great changes which could happen in such a relatively short space of time.

When Max looked back over the past seven days he marvelled at the changes which had taken place, mostly within himself.

The tanned man jogging down to the beach at dawn this morning with a surfboard tucked under his arm was not the same man who'd arrogantly thought of his deal with Tara as an endurance test, to be tolerated but not enjoyed. A means to an end. A pain in the neck, as well as in other parts of his body.

Max had not anticipated the delights, or the discoveries he had made during the past week.

Tara had been so right in forbidding all business calls, for starters. He hadn't realised just how much of every day he spent on work and work-related issues. He'd actually suffered withdrawal symptoms at first. But soon, he wasn't giving a thought to whether profits were up or down. Neither did he worry over what new worldwide crisis might happen which would impact on the hotel industry.

No news was definitely good news.

After a few days he'd even revised his earlier decision to just delegate more in future so that he would have more time for Tara and their child. Now he was thinking of downsizing the Royale chain of hotels altogether. Travelling all over the world and spending every day in meetings or having business dinners no longer held such an attraction for him.

Max plunged into the surf, deftly sliding his body face-down onto the board as he hand-paddled out across the waves. The sun had just broken over the horizon, the blue-green sea sparkling under its rays. Once out into deeper water, Max sat up and straddled the board, watching and waiting for just the right wave to ride in.

This was good!

He'd forgotten how much he'd liked surfing. He hadn't done any in years. But when Kate offered him use of the spare surfboards and wetsuits she kept in the garage, he couldn't resist. And, after a few minor disasters, he'd regained his balance, his confidence and his natural athletic skill. Max had been born good at all sports.

Each morning since, he'd spent a few hours in the surf whilst Tara languished in bed. She was still not feeling tippy-top in the mornings. By eleven she would be up and he would return for a shower and a leisurely brunch. Kate was an excellent if old-fashioned cook, paying no mind to the modern dictates of low-fat food. Max might have put on quite a few pounds if he hadn't been using up a few thousand calories each day in the water. Tara was saved by her delicate stomach, keeping to tea and toast.

After brunch, he and Tara would take a beach umbrella and a book, find a nice spot on the side of one of the sand dunes which overlooked the ocean and settle down to read. The first time they'd done this, Max had thought he would have to pretend to enjoy being read to. But Tara was such an expressive reader, and the best-seller she chose to read obviously hadn't been a best-seller for nothing. It was one of those legal thrillers which twisted and turned on every page. The murder trial itself had been riveting. He'd changed his mind on who the killer was several times but finally settled on the wife, and had been tickled pink when he was proved right.

His remark to Tara during one of these early reading sessions that his mother read to his father these days had led to his finally telling her about his reconciliation with his parents. He'd talked to Tara for ages over dinner that night about his parents' marriage and all their misunderstandings. In fact, this past week, he'd talked more about his parents and his growing-up years than he ever had in his life.

Admittedly, there wasn't much else he could do but talk to Tara. She hadn't wavered from her strictly hands-off rule the whole week. Not an easy situation to bear with her going round in an itsy-bitsy bikini most of the time. In the end, he'd ordered that she cover up when she wasn't swimming, mostly for his own frustration's sake but partly because he was sick to death of the ogling of other males on the beach. She'd given him a droll look and totally ignored him.

Max realised at that point that she might never obey any of his orders ever again. The jury was still out on whether he liked that idea, or not.

Still, she'd had some jealousy of her own to contend with. His own ego had been benefiting from some serious stroking with the looks he'd been getting from the local ladies, the mirror telling him that his less hectic and more outdoor lifestyle was suiting him.

He was going to hate having to give it up.

But why would you *have* to? his brain piped up. You're a very wealthy man. And a smart one. Surely you can work something out. If you downsize the hotel chain the way you're going to, the demands on your personal time will be lessened. With all the modern communication technology around, you can keep in touch with the world from anywhere. You don't even have to be in Sydney. You could be up here, in one of those houses right over there…

His gaze scanned the various buildings fronting Wamberal Beach. Some were holiday apartment blocks. Some were large homes. But some were simple and rather small beach houses, built decades ago. Surely one of those owners could be persuaded to sell. He could have it pulled down and build the home of Tara's dream, with a granny flat for Joyce.

No, no, that wouldn't work. Joyce wouldn't like to be that far away from Jen and her children. She was needed to look after the children after school on the days when Tara's sister was at work.

Max hadn't been the only one to talk this past week. Tara had told him things about her family that she hadn't told him before, possibly because he'd never asked. It was no wonder she thought he was only interested in her body.

Actions *were* louder than words.

Max's brain started ticking away. What time was it? Around seven was his best guess. He had twelve hours before he took Tara out to dinner tonight. Twelve hours before he asked her to marry him again.

He had to have more armoury than romantic words and a two-carat diamond. Flashy gifts and verbal promises wouldn't cut it with Tara. Not any more. He needed proof that he meant what he said. When he took her to bed tonight, he wanted more than his ring on her finger. He wanted her to have faith in their marriage. He wanted her trust that he would be a good husband and father.

Max's heart flipped over when he thought of that last part. He was going to become a father. An enormous responsibility. But also, hopefully, a joyful and satisfying experience. But there would be no true joy or satisfaction unless he could be a hands-on father, not a long-distance one, as his own father had been.

No, this was the place to live and bring up his son or daughter. Max resolved to make it happen, come hell or high water. The trouble was, he had to start making it happen in the next twelve hours.

So much to do, yet so little time.

It would be a challenge all right. But Max liked a challenge more than anything else.

Putting his head down, he caught the next wave to shore and started running towards Kate's place.

Tara rose earlier than usual, courtesy of the wonderful discovery that she didn't feel sick that morning. Not even a small swirl of nausea as she made her way from the bed to the bathroom.

It was a good omen, she believed.

The agreed week was over and Max was not planning to sweep her back to Sydney today, as she had feared he might. Yesterday afternoon he'd said he was happy to stay on till Sunday.

Of course, possibly that was because Kate had announced earlier at brunch that she herself was off to Sydney today for a family reunion at her niece's home, and would not be returning till Sunday morning.

Tara had no doubt Max would claim his reward tonight, either in his bed or in hers. No doubt also that once she was in his arms and vulnerable to his will, he was sure to ask her to marry him again. After a week of being with him and not being able to touch him, Tara suspected she would be extra vulnerable tonight. Her forbidding any physical contact this past week had been hard on her as well. Jen had always complained that when she was pregnant, she couldn't stand sex. It seemed with Tara it was just the opposite.

She stepped into the shower and began to lather up her hair with shampoo. But her mind was still on tonight, not her ablutions.

What would she say to Max when he proposed again? What *could* she say? He was the father of her baby, the man she loved. Her answer was probably a foregone conclusion. She knew that. She'd always known that. Her escape up here was just a temporary gesture of defiance.

Yet it had been worth it. She'd regained some control over her life and shown Max she was not a pushover, or weak. And she'd seen a side to Max which had surprised and pleased her. He *was* capable of not living and breathing his work. He was even capable of enjoying life like an ordinary, everyday person.

He loved surfing. And was surprisingly good at it. He was also learning to love books. Soon, he'd be as addicted to reading as she was. She'd also shown him that you didn't have to eat cordon bleu cuisine at five-star restaurants to enjoy eating out. Each evening, she'd insisted they go to one of the local community-based clubs where the meals were quite cheap, often buffet-style for a set price. At one place, they'd had a roast dinner—with a free glass of beer thrown in—for eight dollars each. Max had been amazed, both at the price and the reasonable quality of the food.

But had his pleasure and co-operation this past week been real, or a con?

The truth was Tara still did not totally trust Max to be the kind of husband she wanted. Or the kind of father for their baby. In the past week, her baby had become very real to her. She loved him or her already and refused to subject her precious child to a life full of neglect and insecurity. Money alone did not bring happiness.

If Max couldn't provide the kind of secure family life she wanted for her child, then she just might have to say no to any proposal of marriage. *If* she could find the courage.

It was nine o'clock before Tara made it downstairs, taking time to blow-dry her hair and put some make-up on. She found Kate in her large, cosy kitchen, sitting at her country-style wooden table, having a cup of tea.

'You're up early today,' Kate said on seeing her. 'Feeling better? I'll get you a cuppa.'

'No, don't get up,' Tara returned swiftly. 'I can get it for myself. And yes, I'm feeling much better today. Max still surfing, I presume?'

'Actually, no, he's gone.'

Tara spun round from where she'd already crossed to the kitchen counter. 'Gone? Gone where?'

'To Sydney, he said. On business. But don't worry. He promised he'd be back in plenty of time to take you out for dinner this evening.'

A huge wave of disappointment swamped Tara. 'And there I was,' she muttered, 'thinking he'd been

genuinely enjoying himself surfing every morning.
But I was fooling myself. And he was fooling me.'

'No, I don't think that's the case, Tara. He did go
surfing early, as usual. But he came racing back here
shortly after seven, saying he had some urgent things
he had to do in Sydney before tonight.'

'Such as what?' she snapped.

'He didn't say.'

'No. No, he wouldn't have. That's the old Max I
grew to know and love,' she said sarcastically. 'Some
business brainstorm probably struck out of the blue
and he was off.'

'It might not have been *business* business, Tara, but
personal business. He's probably gone to Sydney to
buy you an engagement ring. How could he ask you
to marry him over dinner tonight without a ring?'

'Now, why didn't I think of that?' Tara said, still
with a bitter edge to her voice. 'I'm sure you're right,
Kate. But trust me, he'll do business business as well
whilst he's there.'

'And is that so very wrong? He is responsible for
running a huge chain of international hotels, Tara. It
could not have been easy for him to drop everything
as you asked for a whole week. I'm sure the main
thing on Max's mind today is tonight. Just before he
left, he asked me to book a table for two at the best
restaurant around. I chose Jardines. Very romantic
place overlooking Terrigal.'

Tara sighed and shook her head at Kate. 'He's won
you over too, hasn't he? Charmed you, as he did my

mother. And now you're doing his bidding, as he expects all women to do. God, but we're both fools.'

'I have never been a fool where men are concerned, my dear,' Kate said with steel in her voice. 'I can always see them for what they are, once I have had the time to observe them properly. I have to confess that my first impression of Max was not too favourable. But then, I had been biased by the fact that you had run away from him. I had been ready to think poorly of him. He didn't help his cause, either, by being a tad arrogant and impatient with me that first day. But I now see your Max for what he really is. Basically, a good man. A decent man. A man willing to do anything to win back the woman he loves. That is a man in a million, my dear. A man to be treasured, not hastily condemned. Wait and see what it is he's up to today before you pass judgement. I think you might be pleasantly surprised.'

Tara decided not to argue with Kate any more. No point. Kate could never know Max as well as she did. Clearly, he'd been on his best behaviour this past week, all with a purpose. Max had a mission, which was to pull the wool over both Kate's and Tara's eyes and get what he wanted. Her, back being his *yes* girl.

Max might not realise it but he'd just made a huge tactical error in going back to Sydney without even speaking to her. By falling back into his old patterns of behaviour, he'd shown her that he hadn't really changed. He was just as selfish and inconsiderate as ever.

Kate stood up and carried her cup and saucer over to load it into the dishwasher. 'I have to get going, love,' she said as she poured in some dishwashing powder then set the machine in motion. 'I'm sure Max will ring you later and explain. You wait and see.'

Tara nodded and smiled, but the moment Kate was gone she marched over to where Kate kept her phone on the wall in the kitchen and took it off the hook. If and when Max did ring, he would not get the satisfaction of a reply. He would be the one who would have to wait and see. Then, when he eventually arrived back, he was in for a big surprise!

CHAPTER THIRTEEN

MAX had been frustrated by his inability to ring Tara all day. The phone company said Kate's phone was off the hook. He tried telling himself this was probably accidental. Kate was an older lady after all. Some older ladies did things like that.

Still, it worried him. And so he hurried. As much as he could. But visiting everyone concerned and selling them on his ideas was not a quick or easy task. It took him most of the day.

Between times, he rang every real-estate agency on the central coast, making enquiries about properties for sale in Wamberal. By four that afternoon, he was back at the penthouse to freshen up and have a quick bite to eat. By four-thirty he was on the road again, heading north towards Wamberal Beach.

The tightness in his stomach became more pronounced the closer he got. Perhaps if Kate had been there with Tara, he might not have felt so agitated. Kate was on his side now. He could see that. But the dear old thing had gone to a family do, leaving Tara alone.

The possibility that Tara had deliberately taken the phone off the hook gnawed away at him. She'd done it once before, hadn't she, when she'd run away? The thought haunted him that she might not be there when he got back.

He should have knocked on her bedroom door this morning and spoken to her personally. But he hadn't wanted to disturb her. Still, he'd left a message for her with Kate, hadn't he?

Hadn't he?

Max tried to recall what he'd actually said.

Not much, he finally realised. Not *enough*.

When would he ever learn? He should have at least written her a personal note.

'Damn and blast,' he muttered, and put his foot down.

But then he remembered what Tara had said about speeding and he slowed down to the limit again.

It was just on six as he turned into Kate's place. There was no gate to open and he followed the gravel driveway round the back of the house, where there were several guest parking bays. The sun was low in the sky and the house looked quiet. Too quiet.

But the back door wasn't locked. Max heaved a huge sigh of relief...till he saw Tara's bag sitting in the front hallway.

A black pit opened up in his stomach. She was leaving.

'Tara?' he called out.

No answer. He checked the downstairs rooms, but she wasn't in any of them. He took the stairs two at a time, his heart thudding behind his ribs. She wasn't in her bedroom, or in the nearby common room, which was a combination television-sitting room with sliding glass doors that led out onto a wide upper deck.

It was there that he found her, standing at the railing, staring out towards the ocean horizon. His heart caught at how beautiful she looked, with her long blonde hair blowing back in the sea breeze and her skin a warm golden colour from their week up here. She was wearing a simple floral sun-dress with tiny straps and very little back. Fawn sandals covered her bare feet.

'Tara,' he said softly.

She turned and his heart caught again. Never had he seen such sadness in her lovely eyes. Such despair.

'I was going to go before you got back,' she said brokenly. 'I wanted to. Oh, how I wanted to! But in the end, I couldn't. I love you too much, Max. I've always loved you too much.'

When her head dropped into her hands and she began to sob, Max just stood there, appalled. Guilt consumed him that he had brought her to this. But then he stepped forward and put his arms around her shaking shoulders, buoyed by the thought that she would feel happier about loving him once she knew what he had done.

She sagged against him, still weeping.

His heart filled to overflowing as he held her close. Maybe she *did* love him too much. But he loved her just as much. Hell, he was willing to change his whole life for her.

'There, there,' he soothed, and began stroking her hair down her back.

She shuddered, then wrenched herself away from him. Her face jerked up to his, tear-stained but defiant.

'Oh, no, Max. You don't get away with things as easily as that. For once, I want you to explain yourself. I want to know exactly what you've been doing today, every single moment. And don't think you can con your way out of things by telling me you went shopping for an engagement ring. That's what Kate thought, the poor deluded woman. And it might even be true. But that would have taken you all of ten minutes. I can see it now. You'd stride into a jewellery shop and tell the fawning female shop assistant to give you the biggest and the best diamond ring they had.'

Max was ruefully amused by her description of his shopping excursion for a ring. It was startlingly accurate. If the situation wasn't so serious, he might even have laughed.

'You're right and you're wrong, Tara. I did do that,' he confessed. 'But not today. I bought a two-carat rock a week ago. It's been up here in my room all week, waiting to be produced on cue tonight. But I took it back to Sydney today and left it there.'

She blinked, then just stared at him.

'I'm not the same man who bought that ring, Tara. During this past week I realised I didn't want to play lord and master with you any more. That is what

Joyce and Jen used to call me, isn't it? For one thing, I want to take you shopping for a ring and let you pick something *you* like. If you'll still have me, that is.'

'That depends, doesn't it?' she said with a proud toss of her head. 'So what *were* you doing all day today?' she demanded to know. 'As if I don't know. You're back to wearing a business suit. That speaks for itself.'

'I'm wearing a business suit because I spent most of the day in serious negotiations. With your family.'

Tara's mouth fell open.

'You would have already known this if you hadn't taken the phone off the hook. I've been trying to ring you all afternoon. Your mother tried to ring you as well. When the number was engaged, I told her Kate was a real chatterbox to stop her from worrying. But I already suspected what you'd done. I promised to get you to ring her once you knew the good news.'

Tara looked perplexed. 'And what good news would that be?'

'Firstly, I've decided to downsize the Royale chain of hotels. The hotels in Europe will be sold as soon as I can get a reasonable price. But I will go through with the purchase of the hotel in Auckland. I'll also keep our three Asian hotels for now. We'd lose too much if we sold those at this point in time. On top of that, it doesn't take as long to fly over to them. Not that I intend doing as much travelling as I once did. I will be delegating more in future. Naturally, I'll keep the Regency Royale in Sydney, and the penthouse. It's always wise to have a Sydney base. And it will make a good place for breaks away.'

'Breaks away from where?' Tara was looking even more perplexed.

'I'm going to buy a house up here for us to live in. *If* you agree to marry me, of course,' he swiftly added, having to remind himself all the time to keep consulting her feelings. This was the most difficult change for him to embrace. He was too used to being the boss, in not having to consult anyone when making decisions.

'It all came to me when I was out surfing this morning,' he charged on. 'What better place to raise a family, I thought, than Wamberal? Of course, I realised straight away that living up here could cause some logistical problems. You'd be a long way from your mother, and your sister. I, too, would be a long way from *my* parents, who I was surprised to find I really want as part of my life again. Poor old things need my help. Hands-on help. I visited them again this morning and realised my mother could not cope alone much longer. There was only one logical solution. They would all have to move up here, lock, stock and barrel.'

'*All* of them? Move up here?'

'Yep. That's what I've been doing today. Putting that plan into action. Not an easy task to accomplish in so short a time, but I managed to at least get it off the ground.'

'You're not joking, are you?'

'Not at all. Would I joke about something like that? You know, I was surprised just how many places there are on the market up here. We have oodles to choose from. We might not even have to do too much renovating. I was suitably impressed, I can tell you. So what do you think? Are you happy with that idea?'

'What? Why, yes, yes, it's a wonderful idea. But Max...' She reached out to touch his arm. 'Are you really sure that this is what you want?' As her eyes searched his, her surprise changed to wariness, and her hand dropped away. 'You're not just doing this to get me to marry you, are you? I won't wake up after the wedding to find you've changed your mind about all this, will I?'

'Come, now, Tara. Would I be foolish enough to do that? No, my darling, this is what I want, too,' he reassured, taking both her hands in his. 'This last week up here with you has taught me so much. You've made me see how much I've been missing with my crazy, jet-setting lifestyle. I don't want to end up like my father. That's something I vowed I would never do. I want to be an integral part of my family's life, not just living on the fringes of it. I want to be a good husband and father. I don't want to just give lip-service to the roles.'

A strange little smile played around her lips. 'Some

lip-service wouldn't go astray at this point in time,' she murmured.

Max stared into her glittering green eyes, the sexual message in her words distracting him from any further verbal persuasion. Instead, he lifted her hands to his mouth, his eyes never leaving hers as he kissed each knuckle in turn.

'Your wish,' he whispered between kisses, 'is my command.'

'No, your wish is *my* command today. Remember?'

'I'm so glad you reminded me.' He placed her arms up around his neck then bent to scoop her up into his arms. 'Your room or mine?'

She smiled. 'Surprise me.'

'No, don't leave me yet,' Tara pleaded, and pulled Max back down into her arms.

They were in the room where Max had slept alone all week, in the bed where she'd wanted to be every single night.

Oh, how she'd missed him; how she'd missed this.

Her arms tightened around him.

'But I'm heavy,' Max protested. 'Are you sure this won't hurt the baby?'

'Of course not. He's only tiny yet.'

Max levered himself up onto his elbows. '*He?* It might be a girl.'

'No. It's a boy.'

He smiled. 'You could be wrong.'

'I could be. But I'm not.'

He shook his head. 'Your mother said you were stubborn. Which reminds me. I haven't called her yet. Don't go away, now.'

Tara moaned in soft protest when he withdrew.

He bent down to kiss her on the lips, then on each breast before straightening. 'Now, don't you dare cover up. I want you to stay exactly as you are.'

She lay there, happily compliant, whilst Max scrambled off the bed.

'Who dropped all these clothes on the floor?' he complained as he swept up his trousers.

'You did,' she told him, ogling him shamelessly as he stood there in the buff, rifling through his pockets.

There was no doubt that the week up here had done him good in more ways than one. He was looking great.

'I put your mum's number in the memory,' he explained as he whisked out his cellphone and pressed a few buttons.

'Joyce? It's Max. Yes, I'm with Tara and she's thrilled to pieces... What? Oh, yes, she said yes... You did say yes to marrying me, darling, didn't you?' he asked as he lay back down beside her on the bed, making her gasp when his free hand slid between her still-parted legs. 'Yes, she can't wait till you're all living up here... Yes, you're so right... Would you like to talk to her, Joyce? Yep, she's right here. Champing at the bit.'

Tara flushed all over as he handed over the phone.

'Mum,' she said somewhat breathlessly. Max was

right. She *was* champing at the bit. But not for conversation with her mother.

'Isn't Max marvellous?' her mother was saying whilst Tara struggled to ignore the sensations Max was evoking. 'He's going to get me a little house close to yours. And he's going to back Dale in a plumbing business. *And* he's going to give them an interest-free loan for a house. He wanted to buy them one outright but Jen and Dale didn't want that. They want to pay their own way.'

Tara did her best to make all the right remarks whilst her mother rattled on. But it was difficult to concentrate on her mother's revelations about Max's generosity whilst the man himself was doing what he did oh, so well.

OK, so Kate had been right. Max was basically a good man. But he could also be downright wicked.

She had to bite her tongue to stop herself from crying out on one occasion. But she was doing some serious squirming. In the end, she couldn't stand it any more. She had to get her mother off the phone.

'Mum, I hate to cut and run but Max made an early reservation for dinner and I haven't even started getting dressed yet.' And wasn't *that* the truth!

'I understand,' Joyce trilled. 'You'll want to make yourself look extra-nice tonight. Ring me tomorrow, would you, and we'll have a nice long talk?'

'Will do, Mum. And tell Jen I'll ring her, too.'

'Oh, yes. Do that. She's very excited. And so are

the kids. They just love the idea of living near a beach.'

'Must go, Mum,' she said through gritted teeth.

She pressed the phone off just as Max's head lifted.

'Don't you mean you must come?' he quipped when she clicked the phone shut and tossed it away.

'You're a sadist,' she threw at him. 'Oh, God, don't stop.'

He grinned down at her. 'This is my night, remember? Don't go telling me what to do and what not to do.'

'Yes, Max,' she said with a sigh.

'Now, first things first. You do agree to marry me, don't you?'

'Yes, Max.'

'And you agree to all my plans.'

'Yes, Max. Except…'

His eyes narrowed on her. 'Except what?'

'Do you think before I have this baby and before you sell all those lovely hotels in Europe, we could go on a trip together and stay in some of them? I have this fantasy about making love in Paris.'

'Are you sure you're well enough to travel?'

'Absolutely. When I woke this morning, there wasn't a trace of morning sickness.'

'In that case, I would love to take you on an overseas trip. We could make it our honeymoon. My fantasies include making love to you in every big city in the world, not just Paris. But first, I think I need to make love to you right here and now.'

Tara sighed when he rolled her onto her side and slid into her from behind, filling her heart as well as her body.

'Oh, Max,' she cried.

He caressed her breasts whilst he kissed her hair, her ear, her shoulder. 'Have I made you truly happy today at long last, my love?'

'Oh, yes.'

'You will tell me in future if and when I'm doing something wrong. I want to make you happy, Tara.'

'I'm very happy,' she choked out. 'Ooh. I really like making love this way. I think it's my favourite.'

'That's good, because we'll be doing it a lot like this in future. I looked up all the websites on pregnancy last Friday night and came across this really interesting one which listed all the safest and most comfortable positions for making love during a pregnancy. This was number one. We can do it like this till well into the last trimester.'

'There are others?' she said, her voice having taken on a faraway sound.

'There's something for every occasion, and every stage of your pregnancy.' His hands dropped down to caress her belly. 'Frankly, I can't wait till this is all big with my baby.'

'You won't find it unattractive?'

'Are you kidding? It's a real turn-on, touching you like this, knowing my child is inside there. And then there's your breasts. They're already larger, you know.'

'Yes. And very sensitive.'

'So I noticed.'

She gasped when he gave the distended tips a gentle tug.

'I... I seem to be more sensitive all round,' she said. 'My body as well as my emotions. I'm going to need a lot of loving, Max.'

'Don't worry. You'll be loved. But slowly, my love. And gently. We don't want to do anything which might put the baby at risk.'

'No, of course not,' she said, still slightly amazed at how much he wanted this child. 'Do you want more children after this, Max?'

'If this pregnancy is anything to go by, I think I'll keep you having babies for quite a few years. I've never seen you look more beautiful or more sexy than you looked today when I saw you out on that veranda.' He didn't add that he'd never seen her look sadder.

Max vowed that he would never let her look that sad again.

'What about names?' he said. 'Have you picked out any names?'

'No. I thought I'd wait and see what he looks like first.'

'Or what *she* looks like.'

'I told you. It's a boy. Only a boy would cause so much trouble.'

'True.'

'Max...you've stopped moving.'

'If I move, I'll be history. I got myself over-excited.'

Tara laughed. 'In that case, we'll just talk for a while till you calm down.'

'Good idea.'

'Max…'

'Mmm?'

'I want to thank you…for all you did today. I can't tell you how much it means to me that you would go to so much trouble to make me happy.'

'My pleasure, princess.'

'Mum sounded ecstatic as well. I'm sure Jen and Dale are, too. You've been very generous. And I think it's really sweet that you're getting along so well with your folks now. I'll have to go and meet them soon.'

'How about tomorrow?'

'Tomorrow would be fine. What time is it now? We're supposed to be going out to dinner tonight, remember?'

'It's only five to seven,' Max said with a quick glance at his watch. 'How long will it take you to get dressed?'

'Not long.'

'In that case, I think we've talked long enough, don't you think?'

'Absolutely.'

Everyone was relocated to Wamberal before the wedding, which took place on Wamberal Beach in August. Tara was an unashamedly pregnant bride, wearing an original gown that Max had bought her in Paris. They'd enjoyed a two-month pre-wedding holiday travelling all around Europe. Their actual honeymoon was spent at home, decorating the nursery in their comparatively modest new house. Max and Tara had decided together that they wanted a simple lifestyle for their family.

Their son was born a week late. A beautiful, placid, happy baby. They named him Stevie.

MILLS & BOON®

Volume 4
on sale from
1st October
2004

Lynne
Graham

International Playboys

An Insatiable
Passion

Available at most branches of WHSmith, Tesco, Martins, Borders,
Eason, Sainsbury's and all good paperback bookshops.

Your opinion is important to us!

Please take a few moments to share your thoughts with us about Mills & Boon® and Silhouette® books. Your comments will ensure that we continue to deliver books you love to read.

> To thank you for your input, everyone who replies will be entered into a prize draw to win a year's supply of their favourite series books*.

1. There are several different series under the Mills & Boon and Silhouette brands. Please tick the box that most accurately represents your reading habit for each series.

Series	Currently Read (have read within last three months)	Used to Read (but do not read currently)	Do Not Read
Mills & Boon			
Modern Romance™	❑	❑	❑
Sensual Romance™	❑	❑	❑
Blaze™	❑	❑	❑
Tender Romance™	❑	❑	❑
Medical Romance™	❑	❑	❑
Historical Romance™	❑	❑	❑
Silhouette			
Special Edition™	❑	❑	❑
Superromance™	❑	❑	❑
Desire™	❑	❑	❑
Sensation™	❑	❑	❑
Intrigue™	❑	❑	❑

2. Where did you buy this book?

From a supermarket ❑   Through our Reader Service™ ❑
From a bookshop ❑   If so please give us your Club Subscription no.
On the Internet ❑
Other _____   _____/_____

3. Please indicate by number which were the 3 most important factors that made you buy this book. (1 = most important).

The picture on the cover ___   I enjoy this series ___
The author ___   The price ___
The title ___   I borrowed/was given this book ___
The description on the back cover ___   Part of a mini-series ___

Other _____

4. How many Mills & Boon and /or Silhouette books do you buy at one time?

I buy ___ books at one time   ❑
I rarely buy a book (less than once a year)   ❑

5. How often do you shop for any Mills & Boon and/or Silhouette books?

One or more times a month ❑   A few times per year ❑
Once every 2-3 months ❑   Never ❑

6. How long have you been reading Mills & Boon® and/or Silhouette®?
_____ years

7. What other types of book do you enjoy reading?

Family sagas eg. Maeve Binchy ❏
Classics eg. Jane Austen ❏
Historical sagas eg. Josephine Cox ❏
Crime/Thrillers eg. John Grisham ❏
Romance eg. Danielle Steel ❏
Science Fiction/Fantasy eg. JRR Tolkien ❏
Contemporary Women's fiction eg. Marian Keyes ❏

8. Do you agree with the following statements about Mills & Boon? Please tick the appropriate boxes.

	Strongly agree	Tend to agree	Neither agree nor disagree	Tend to disagree	Strongly disagree
Mills & Boon offers great value for money.	❏	❏	❏	❏	❏
With Mills & Boon I can always find the right type of story to suit my mood.	❏	❏	❏	❏	❏
I read Mills & Boon books because they offer me an entertaining escape from everyday life.	❏	❏	❏	❏	❏
Mills & Boon stories have improved or stayed the same standard over the time I have been reading them.	❏	❏	❏	❏	❏

9. Which age bracket do you belong to? Your answers will remain confidential.

❏ 16-24   ❏ 25-34   ❏ 35-49   ❏ 50-64   ❏ 65+

THANK YOU for taking the time to tell us what you think! If you would like to be entered into the **FREE prize draw** to win a year's supply of your favourite series books, please enter your name and address below.

Name: _____

Address: _____

_____

Post Code: _____ Tel: _____

Please send your completed questionnaire to the address below:

READER SURVEY, PO Box 676, Richmond, Surrey, TW9 1WU.

FREE!

4 Books
and a surprise gift!

We would like to take this opportunity to thank you for reading this Mills & Boon® book by offering you the chance to take FOUR more specially selected titles from the Modern Romance™ series absolutely FREE! We're also making this offer to introduce you to the benefits of the Reader Service™—

- ★ **FREE home delivery**
- ★ **FREE gifts and competitions**
- ★ **FREE monthly Newsletter**
- ★ **Exclusive Reader Service offers**
- ★ **Books available before they're in the shops**

Accepting these FREE books and gift places you under no obligation to buy, you may cancel at any time, even after receiving your free shipment. Simply complete your details below and return the entire page to the address below. You don't even need a stamp!

YES! Please send me 4 free Modern Romance books and a surprise gift. I understand that unless you hear from me, I will receive 6 superb new titles every month for just £2.69 each, postage and packing free. I am under no obligation to purchase any books and may cancel my subscription at any time. The free books and gift will be mine to keep in any case.

P4ZEF

Ms/Mrs/Miss/Mr ....Initials...................................
BLOCK CAPITALS PLEASE

Surname ....

Address ....

....

....Postcode ....

Send this whole page to:
UK: FREEPOST CN81, Croydon, CR9 3WZ